Little Green Men—Attack!

Baen Books Edited by
Bryan Thomas Schmidt

Galactic Games
Mission Tomorrow
Shattered Shields (with Jennifer Brozek)
The Monster Hunter Files (with Larry Correia) forthcoming

Little Green Men—Attack!

edited by
Robin Wayne Bailey &
Bryan Thomas Schmidt

BAEN

Little Green Men—Attack! copyright © 2017 by Robin Wayne Bailey & Brian Thomas Schmidt

Additional Copyright information:
Introduction copyright © 2017 by Robin Wayne Bailey; "The Little Green Men take Their Hideous Vengeance, Sort Of" copyright © 2017 by Mike Resnick; "Little (Green) Women" copyright © 2017 by Kristine Kathryn Rusch; "Good Neighbor Policy" copyright © 2017 by Dantzel Cherry; "Stuck in Buenos Aires With Bob Dylan On My Mind" copyright © 2017 by Ken Scholes; "Rule The World" copyright © 2017 by Jody Lynn Nye; "School Colors" copyright © 2017 by Seanan McGuire; "Meet The Landlord" copyright © 2017 by Martin L. Shoemaker; "Big White Men – Attack" copyright © 2017 by Steven H. Silver; "The Green, Green Men of Home" copyright © 2017 by Selina Rosen; "A Fine Night For Tea and Bludgeoning" copyright © 2017 by Beth L. Cato; "The Game-a-holic's Guide" copyright © 2017 by Peter J. Wacks & Josh Vogt; "Day of The Bookworm" copyright © 2017 by Allen M. Steele; "A Greener Future" copyright © 2017 by Elizabeth Moon; "A Cuppa, Cuppa Burnin' Love" copyright © 2017 by Esther M. Friesner; "Little Green Guys" copyright © 2017 by K.C. Ball; "The March Of The Little Green Men" copyright © 2017 by James E. Gunn; "First Million Contacts" copyright © 2017 by Bryan Thomas Schmidt & Alex Shvartsman; "Hannibal's Elephants" copyright © 2017 by Robert Silverberg; "The Fine Art Of Politics" copyright © 2017 by Robin Wayne Bailey.

A Baen Book Original

Baen Publishing Enterprises
P.O. Box 1403
Riverdale, NY 10471
www.baen.com

ISBN: 978-1-4767-8213-3

Cover art by Dominic Harman

First Baen printing, March 2017

Distributed by Simon & Schuster
1230 Avenue of the Americas
New York, NY 10020

Printed in the United States of America

10 9 8 7 6 5 4 3 2 1

DEDICATIONS

For Frederick Brown, Robert Sheckley, William Tenn and all the other great humorists and satirists who made—and make—science fiction so much fun. We always need more laughter in our lives.

Robin:
And for Diana Bailey and Ron Davis for being so patient and for putting up with all my eccentricities and foibles.

Bryan:
And for Louie and Amelie, who keep me laughing at their canine antics daily.

And for M.O. Muriel,
a reminder that laughter in spite of tragedy is the height of bravery and a reminder why comedy still matters.

Table of Contents:

Little Green Men—Attack!

Introduction

by Robin Wayne Bailey

"From there to here and here to there, funny things are everywhere."
—Dr. Seuss

"Imagination was given to man to compensate him for what he is not:
a sense of humor to console him for what he is."
—Sir Francis Bacon

"Humor is just another defense against the universe."
—Mel Brooks

First contact. It doesn't take an Albert Einstein to understand that our first encounters with alien species are going to have repercussions and consequences for Mankind. Who's to say, however, that those repercussions will necessarily be dire, grim, and frightening? Who's to say those consequences won't leave us rolling on the floor laughing? Take my planet . . . *please*!

Science fiction is full of stories about superior alien races who travel light-years across the galaxy, sometimes even from other dimensions, just to eat us, or to steal our women, or to devour our precious resources, or just to claim our bright, blue world for their own nefarious purposes. One wonders, though: if those aliens were really so superior, why wouldn't they set loftier goals for themselves? Why wouldn't they use their wonderfulness to promote galactic peace? Why not, with all their advanced technology, bring us the miracle of free and clean energy for all? Maybe they could share the secret to the absolutely perfect martini to make all our lives more tolerable.

But never mind that.

What if earth-women just weren't, you know, that *into* bug-eyed monsters and little green men? What if we just scared the invaders off with late-night screenings of the loudest and most violent Hollywood movies depicting all the times we've beaten back and crushed other luckless invading alien species? We wouldn't have to explain *fiction* to them.

What if we just hauled them into court and tied them up in red tape?

Science fiction readers and fans, particularly of my generation, grew up with the nuts-and-bolts hard-science visions of Robert Heinlein, Arthur C. Clarke and Isaac Asimov. They were giants in the field, visionaries whose grand, futuristic imaginations made science fiction exciting. I've spoken to NASA scientists whose careers were inspired by these writers. I remember watching Walter Cronkite as he interviewed both Heinlein and Clarke on the day of the Apollo 11 moon landing. I'm watching that interview again right now on youtube.com as I compose this.

Yet, there were three other writers I've always admired just as much. I still frequently reread their stories, and their work continues to excite me. Frederick Brown, Robert Sheckley, and William Tenn—I've sometimes referred to them as *The Terrible Trio* of science fiction. They also wrote tales about space travel, first contact, alien civilizations, and all the usual SF tropes, but with totally unique voices. Each brought humor and quick wit, sharp satire and sometimes pure, outrageous comedy to their stories. If you don't know them, get thee to Google now. Find and read Brown's, "Martians Go Home," and Sheckley's "Early Model," and Tenn's "Eastward, Ho!" Or almost anything else by these gentlemen. You won't be sorry. They gave us great stories that were no less thought-provoking even as they made us laugh, and it's these three writers who inspired this anthology.

So, here it is. One small step for Man, one giant . . . *Oh, my god! He tripped on the last step and fell helmet-first in the lunar pounce!* How ignominious, but Neal was probably tripped by a little green man. Or maybe an army of them. NASA isn't talking and the records are sealed.

Our goal isn't so lofty as eating people. We're not out to steal women or conquer planets. Our goal is only to present you with a book filled with wonderful stories that make you think *and* laugh at the same time. Twenty-one terrific writers, a wicked assortment of major pros and brilliant newcomers, are assembled here with nineteen stories to do just that. I hope you'll be as thrilled with the result as I am.

Now, before I end this and let you get on to what you really bought this book for, I need to give special thanks and acknowledgment to my co-editor, Hugo Award nominee Bryan Thomas Schmidt. A far more experienced hand at assembling original anthologies than I, Bryan did much of the heavy lifting on this one and guided me at every step. His diligence helped to make *Little Green Men—Attack!* a delightful reality.

So, that's it. Now, stop me if you've heard this one: *twenty-one science fiction writers walk into a bar . . .*

—Robin Wayne Bailey
January 4, 2016

"Vengeance is mine," saith the little green men, at least in Mike Resnick's story. When angered by their depiction in certain pulps, a group of little green men arrive bent on revenge . . . but what do they do when their target won't cooperate?
—BTS

Little Green Men Take Their Hideous Vengeance, Sort Of

by Mike Resnick

"Goddammit!" muttered Nelson as he clambered down the stairs in his pajamas. "Who the hell knocks on the door at four in the morning?"

He resisted the urge to stop by the kitchen and make a quick cup of instant coffee, and continued to the door, where the pounding was becoming louder and more incessant.

"All right, all right!" he growled. "Keep your shirt on!" He reached the door, unlocked it, opened it, and frowned.

"There's nobody here," he said in puzzled tones.

"We ain't 'nobody,' Mac," said a squeaky voice coming from somewhere around his knees. "And don't you forget it!"

Nelson looked down and found himself facing five emerald green creatures, each armed with a spear that came up to his lower thigh. They looked like they had escaped from a Saturday morning cartoon, or perhaps an old Walt Kelly comic strip.

"I didn't think I drank that much at the party," muttered Nelson, blinking his eyes rapidly and feeling surprised that the little green men were still there.

"This is gonna be easier than we thought," said one of them. "Okay, you malicious bastard, prepare to die!"

"Me?" said Nelson, surprised. "What did I ever do to you? I didn't even know you existed until you knocked on the door, and I'm still half-convinced that I'm hallucinating."

"You've made us a laughing stock the whole world over!" snapped the leader.

"What are you talking about?" demanded Nelson. "How could I do that if I knew nothing about you until half a minute ago?"

"Don't you pull that shit with *me*, Malcolm Frothingham Neilsen!"

"There's been a mistake," said Nelson. "I'm not Neilsen, I'm Nelson."

"Six of one, half a dozen of the other," said another of the undersized group. "Let's kill him anyway."

"I don't know," said a third one. "He looks dumb enough to be telling the truth."

"You guys wanna tell me what this is all about?" said Nelson. "Or do I just kick you off the front stoop, lock the door, and write this hallucination down in my diary if I remember it after I wake up?"

"Watch your tongue, Neilsen!" snapped the one that appeared to be the leader. "We Greenies are tough dudes, and don't you forget it!"

"Actually, I'm going to bed and try to forget everything about you," said Nelson. "If you're still here in the morning, we'll talk."

"If we're still here in the morning there won't be enough of you left to bury!"

Nelson stared at them for a long moment, and then shrugged. "Okay, what the hell. Come in—but wipe your feet first."

"Who do you think you're giving orders to, Mac?" yelled the leader.

Nelson reached down with one hand, grabbed him by the neck, and lifted him until their eyes were on the same level. "You," he said irritably. "You got any objections?"

"Me?" squeaked the leader, struggling to get the words out. "I only object to prejudice, bias, bigotry, and aggressive redheads named Thelma."

"And you'll wipe your feet and behave yourself?"

"Absolutely," whispered the leader hoarsely. "Honor bright and pinky to the sky." He paused and held up his hand in front of him. "Well, greenie to the sky."

Nelson put him down. The five little green men made quite a production of wiping their feet—four of them on the doormat, the fifth on the dew-covered grass next to the stoop—and entered the house.

"In here," said Nelson, leading them to the living room.

They went where he indicated and slowly, awkwardly, climbed onto the sofa.

"All right," said Nelson. "What the hell is this about?"

"You're sure you're not Malcolm Frothingham Neilsen?" demanded the leader.

"I'm not Malcolm anything Neilsen," replied Nelson.

"Not Malcolm Anything Neilsen," said the leader. "Malcolm Frothingham Neilsen."

"I'm not either of 'em," said Nelson.

"You swear it?"

Nelson nodded. "On a stack of bibles."

"That's it!" cried one of the Greenies. "Let's kill him now!"

"For swearing on a stack of bibles?" asked Nelson, frowning.

"Precisely!"

"Okay, what do you want me to swear on?"

"A stack of *Smash-Bang Space Tales*, of course!"

"A stack of *what?*" retorted Nelson.

"Go ahead! Deny it!" growled yet another of the Greenies.

"Of course I deny it," said Nelson. "Hell, I never heard of the damned things."

"Let's cut his heart out!" said a Greenie.

"Slash his jugular and be done with it," said another.

"I don't know," said the leader, frowning. "What if he's telling the truth?"

"He's got an evil, duplicitous face," said the one at the end of the couch. "I say we kill him now. Slowly and painfully."

"I've had enough of this nonsense," said Nelson, picking up the Greenie from the end of the courch by his left ear, grabbing his nose, and twisting it slowly and painfully. "You want to reconsider your statement?"

The Greenie screamed.

Nelson shrugged. "I've got all day." He twisted harder.

"Leggo! Leggo!" whined the Greenie.

"And you apologize for your threat?" said Nelson.

"I cad talk udtil you led be go!"

Nelson threw him back on the couch. "I'm only going to ask one more time," he said. "What the hell is this about?"

"We're here on a top-secret mission," said the leader.

"To do what?"

"To kill Malcolm Frothingham Neilsen, of course."

"Why?" asked Nelson.

"He has made a laughing-stock of us in front of your entire population."

"He's a cartoonist?" asked Nelson.

"Of course not!" said another Greenie.

"Okay, I give up. What is he?"

"A liar!"

"There's got to be a few billion liars walking the Earth today. What have you got against *him*?"

"He's a world-famous writer and he tells lies about us!" said the leader.

"*This* world?" asked Nelson, looking puzzled.

"Of course this world!" said the leader. He held out his hand and the Greenie next to him placed a magazine in it. He opened it and began reading aloud. "'And this next thrilling interstellar adventure— *The Ugliest Green Men in the Galaxy*—comes from the pen of world-famous writer Malcolm Frothingham Neilsen.'" He turned to Nelson. "What could be clearer than that?"

"He could at least have called us the nastiest green men in the galaxy," said another.

"Or the sexiest," added a third.

"May I see it for a minute?" asked Nelson, holding out his hand, and the Greenie turned it over to him. He studied it briefly, and then looked up. "Didn't anybody check the date on this thing?"

"We use a different calendar," said the Greenie leader defensively. "By our reckoning today is Bennutibi 84th, in the year 90,306 S.V."

"S.V.?" repeated Nelson.

"Since Vanessa," explained the Greenie leader. "Twenty-two inches of green rapture, with kisses to die for!"

Nelson reached to the table next to his chair, picked up a tablet, activated it, logged onto the internet, and Googled the magazine.

"Ah!" he said. "I thought so." He turned to the Greenies. "*Smash-Bang Space Tales* is what we call a pulp magazine, which is to say, cheaply made and probably cheaply written as well. The first issue of this one was dated March, 1934, it came out bi-monthly, and it died with the May, 1936 issue. That's why no one's heard of it.

Ninety percent of the population wasn't born until after the magazine died."

"Okay, so we're a little slow getting the news," said the leader. "But surely a liar as famous as Malcolm Frothingham Neilsen has been reprinted all over your narrow-minded, primitive world."

"Let's see," said Nelson, checking his tablet again. A moment later he looked up. "Malcolm Frothingham Neilsen sold six serials and one short story in his life. He died in 1941, and seems to have been published in only two periodicals—*Smash-Bang Space Tales* ran the serials, and *Absolutely True Interspecies Love Stories* published his short story before the entire staff was arrested and thrown into jail."

"No!" cried the leader.

"I'm afraid you've been the victims of false doctrine," said Nelson, not without sympathy.

"It's *your* fault!" snapped the Greenie on the end, pointing an accusing finger at the leader. "We wanted to come right here, but you're the one who took us three hundred light years out of our way just to watch Delectable Doris do her Dance of Spontaneous Eruption!"

"I didn't notice any of you guys objecting when we were watching her."

"And just to set the record straight," added another, "it was her Dance of Spontaneous Combustion."

"We can argue about this later," said the leader. "Malcolm, old friend, where can we find Malcolm Frothingham Neilsen?"

Nelson checked his tablet. "Mule Shoe, Texas," he answered.

"Good! Men, let's get moving and *take* our just and terrible vengeance out on that scumbag!"

"Uh . . ." said Nelson. "I hate to tell you this, but that's where the cemetery is."

"Cemetery?" asked the leader, frowning.

"Yeah," said Nelson. "Where we bury our dead."

"You *bury* them?" demanded the leader with a shudder of revulsion.

"Of course," said Nelson. "What do you Greenies do?"

"We eat them, of course."

"Preferably with chocolate," added another.

It was Nelson's turn to shudder. "Well, anyway, he's been dead for 73 years."

"Damn!" muttered the leader. "Robbed of our fierce and hideous revenge."

"Well, now that you know your target is dead, I suppose you'll be going home," said Nelson.

"Uh . . . we'd *like* to, Malcolm, yes, absolutely, but . . ."

"There's a problem?" asked Nelson.

"We don't know how," said the leader.

"It was hard enough just getting here," said another Greenie.

"I hope you can cook for six, Malcolm," said still another. "In the meantime, how many bedrooms have you got?"

"Not enough," said Nelson.

"Well, I suppose we can all sleep in your bed. But I warn you: I snore."

"I suppose as long as I'm stuck with you for a day or two . . ." began Nelson.

"We have life expectancies of 425 years, give or take," said the leader.

"I hope you weren't planning on spending 425 years in my house," said Nelson, frowning.

"Certainly not, Malcolm," replied the leader. "Hell, we're all in our forties already, except for the kid there." He gestured to the one on the end. "He just turned 33."

"I think if you're going to stick around," said Nelson, "you're going to need names."

"We have names," replied the leader with dignity.

"Okay, what are they?"

"I'm The Leader, he's The One on My Left, he's The One on the End, he's The One on My Right, and he's The One on the Other End."

Nelson shook his head. "I'm afraid that won't do at all." He lowered his head in thought for a moment, then looked up and pointed at The Leader. "You're Groucho," he said. Then pointing at the other four in turn, said: "You're Harpo, you're Chico, you're Zeppo, and you, The One on the Other End, you're Gummo."

"We don't like the names," said Groucho.

Nelson shrugged. "Okay," he replied. "Close the door behind you on your way out."

"But we'll answer to them!" added Groucho quickly.

"That's more like it," said Nelson.

"Uh . . . what do we do now?" asked Groucho.

"I'm thinking on it," replied Nelson. He looked at his surroundings and frowned. "You know, this is a pretty shabby place in quite a state of disrepair."

"We don't do repairs or decorating," said Groucho.

"Damned right!" chimed in Harpo.

"Harpo doesn't talk," complained Nelson.

"Why the hell not?" demanded Harpo pugnaciously.

"When I remember I'll tell you," said Nelson. "In the meantime, I'm thinking about what we can do."

"But no decorating," said Groucho.

"Or painting," added Chico.

"Or yardwork," said Gummo.

"Oh, hell, I'll do any of those things," said Zeppo. "But I charge triple time."

"Don't understand me so fast," complained Nelson. "I don't want to improve this place. Hell, I don't even like it. No, I want a new, luxurious place."

"Just for you?" demanded Groucho.

"What the hell," said Nelson. "Since you're going to help me get it, for all of us."

"I call that damned generous of you, Malcolm old friend," said Groucho. "I must say, I would never guess you had enough wealth at your fingertips to do that."

"I don't," replied Nelson. He smiled. "But I have *you*."

"You'd sell us after everything we've been to you?" demanded Harpo.

"The thought never crossed my mind," said Nelson. "But thank you for suggesting it."

"*Now* do you know why you're supposed to be mute?" growled Groucho.

"Let's get back to the subject at hand," said Nelson.

"Painting your new house?" asked Gummo.

"Getting enough money to buy a house with six bedrooms, unless you guys all sleep together, in which case I don't want to hear about it."

"Okay," said Groucho. "What *about* a new house?"

"You guys don't paint, clean, or do any other kind of work as far as I can tell."

"That's a canard!" snapped Zeppo.

"A canard?" repeated Chico, raising his spear. "Where?"

"So," continued Nelson, "I figure you can at least fight."

"You betcha!" said Gummo.

"Us little green men are tough dudes," added Zeppo.

"How are you at following orders?"

There was a moment of silence. Then Zeppo spoke again. "Us little green men are tough dudes."

There was a vigorous nodding of little green heads.

Nelson grimaced. "We'll come back to that."

"Just point to whoever you want killed," said Groucho. "Then shield your eyes, because it won't be pretty."

"I don't want anyone killed," answered Nelson.

"What fun is that?" asked Chico.

Nelson stared at the five of them in silence until they began twitching uncomfortably.

"Say something, damn it!" said Groucho at last.

"I'm wondering how you guys would be at a new trade."

"Does it involve lots of violence and bloodshed, and maybe a trophy wife or two?"

"I don't think there are any Greenie women on Earth," replied Nelson.

"We ain't fussy."

"How do you think you'd be at surreptitiously entering a bank or a jewelry store at night, avoiding all the safeguards, stealing money or jewelry, and coming out without having set off a single alarm?"

"Piece of cake," answered Groucho.

"Right," agreed Harpo, Chico, and Zeppo.

"Make it a piece of pie," said Gummo. "I don't like cake very much."

"Okay," said Groucho. "We're all agreed. I'm *your* leader, and the big ugly guy who doesn't shave or bathe often enough—sorry, Malcolm—is *my* leader." He turned to Nelson. "Okay, who do we plunder?"

"Come to the garage," said Nelson. "We can't have anyone see you walking down the street."

"What's a garage?" asked Zeppo.

"What's a street?" added Gummo.

Nelson opened the door to the garage, got the Greenies all loaded into his seventeen-year-old Chevy, and soon had parked in back of a small, tasteful building.

"This is the place?" asked Groucho.

Nelson nodded. "The Diamonds Are Forever jewelry shop." He grimaced. "They don't like to admit it, but at this joint payments are forever too."

"So what, exactly, do we do?"

"Sneak in, don't set off any alarms, and bring out all the gold, diamonds, and pearls that you can carry. If there's too much loot to carry, leave the pearls."

"What are pearls?" asked Chico.

"They're just like marbles, only white," answered Nelson.

"Oh," said Chico. "Thank you." Then: "What are marbles?"

"They're colored pearls, you idiot!" snapped Groucho.

"Steal now, argue later," instructed Nelson.

Ten minutes later the five Greenies emerged, loaded down with enough jewelry to buy a palace for each of them once they'd converted it into money on the black market (though Groucho kept insisting that they'd do even better at a green market).

"Well done, team," said Nelson as they piled into the car.

"They made it very easy for us," said Groucho.

"Such pleasant surroundings," added Harpo. "They even made a home movie of us to remind them of this triumphant evening."

"*A home movie?*" roared Nelson.

"Yes," answered Harpo. "And me without a comb."

"Why would you want a comb?" asked Zeppo. "None of us has any hair."

"Let me get this straight," said Nelson urgently. "They had a camera trained on you?"

"Right," said Gummo. "They forgot to activate it, but we found the switch, and now they have a keepsake of our visit."

"*Idiots!*" yelled Nelson. "Where the hell *is* this camera?"

"In the ceiling. About twice your height."

"Did we do anything wrong?" asked Chico. "Besides break and enter and rob and pillage, I mean?"

"Shut up," said Nelson. He lowered his head in thought. "We've got to misdirect them."

"How?" asked Groucho. "They'll know the store was plundered by Greenies."

A smile slowly took shape on Nelson's lips. "Ah," he said. "But *which* Greenies?"

"There's only us."

"You know it, and I know it," replied Nelson. "But nobody else knows it. Hand me a copy of that damned magazine."

Harpo produced *Slam-Bang Space Tales* and passed it over to Nelson, who pulled out a pen and began writing on the cover.

Compliments of Nastiest Green Men in the Galaxy. Watch for us in our next exciting story, in which we will rob the biggest jewelry store in Baltimore, Maryland.

He paused and looked at what he'd written, then shook his head. "There's nothing left to rob in Baltimore," he muttered, changing the location to Boston.

I dare you to stop me and my Greenies. <signed> Malcolm Frothingham Neilsen.

"You all got new names," he said. "Why shouldn't I?"

"So where's Boston?" asked Groucho.

"A few thousand miles from Dallas, where we're heading as soon as I start the car."

"We're *not* going to Boston?" asked Zeppo.

"Of course not."

"That's hardly sporting of you," said Gummo, "now that you as much as told them to try and stop us."

"On the other hand, he's making us notorious instead of infamous," said Groucho.

And that statement was indeed predictive. After they'd successfully robbed banks and jewelers in Dallas, Seattle, Denver, and Orlando—they spent a whole day visiting Disneyland, where everyone thought they were employees—they were finally arrested and incarcerated in Chicago.

Their ten-year sentences simply meant that the Greenies could catch up on their sleep, which they did for the next decade, after signing contracts permitting two movies, one TV series, and one Broadway musical to be based on their lives and adventures.

They did not sell the literary rights to their life stories, because their cellmate, Malcolm Frothingham Neilsen, was producing one bestseller after another about them.

All of the biographies, which read as fast and exciting as novels, first appeared in the resurrected *Smash-Bang Space Tales*.

And that is the true story of our First through Fifth Alien Contacts.

JoAnne May Michaels hates "Little Women" by Louisa May Alcott with a passion. She has no idea why teachers keep assigning it. But then a little green little women fan club arrives to change her mind . . . —BTS

Little (Green) Women

by Kristine Kathryn Rusch

First, let me say, I hated *Little Women*. Oh my God. Awful. And— Spoiler Alert!—by the time Beth died, seriously? I was ready to kill her myself. I have no idea why you teachers still assign this book, except maybe to introduce us to Louisa May Alcott the woman, who is a hell of a lot more interesting than any book she ever wrote. (Sorry about the "hell," Mrs. McGill, but really, I mean, sometimes you gotta say what you gotta say. And oops, yeah, I know, this aside should be its own paragraph. It looks weird that way, so I'm not going to do it.)

Second, here's the stuff you asked for, even though we both know you know it:

My name is JoAnne May Michaels, and yes, it's a coincidence that my first name is similar to the first name of the "heroine" in *Little Women*. The similarity stops there. First, no one calls me Jo and lives. I'm J-May, thank you very much, except when I'm in trouble, and then my mom calls me JoAnne (if it's not that bad), JoAnne May (if it's bad) and JoAnne May Michaels Get Your Butt Over Here (if it's life-and-death bad).

My parents, sisters, and I live in Alamaloosa, Oregon, and, since we're pretending that the person who's reading this doesn't know me, I'll tell you where Alamaloosa is. It's in the foothills of Siskiyou Mountain Range, not too far from where they butt up against the Cascade Mountain Range. If you can say The End of Nowhere, you're seriously understating where I live.

But the schools are good, because Alamaloosa is what my mom calls "a bedroom community" of Ashland, Oregon. I looked it up:

Mom's wrong, because Alamaloosa existed before Ashland and has an industry (mining) and besides, Ashland, with a population of 20,000, isn't big enough for a bedroom community, but it's snobby enough for a bedroom community, so I guess that counts.

The reason I'm telling you about the schools (even though the real you knows the schools) is pretty simple: My parents, who love the backwoods and The End of Nowhere, moved *here* to get me a good education. Not Portland (2.5 million in the metro area) or even Eugene (350,000 in their metro area). Nooo. My parents moved *here*, because it was the only place in Oregon with good schools and nothing surrounding them except mountains, trees, and the occasional lost Shakespeare enthusiast. (Because Ashland is the home of the largest regional repertory theater in the United States, and that dang theater [which we students have to go to every year whether we want to or not] specializes in Shakespeare.)

So why am I doing this, like, totally 19th century introduction to this totally 21st century essay? Because (1) I can and because (2) I don't expect you to believe me and because (3) it's a freakin' assignment. (Thought I forgot, didn't you, Mrs. McGill?)

Here're the details:

From: Mrs. McGill's Honors English, home of this year's stupid *Little Women* assignment (with asides by J-May, addressing the audience, whoever they may be, including Mrs. McGill, who already knows I hate *Little Women* with a burning passion. [And yeah, I know what an aside is. I've seen too much Shakespeare]).

Assignment: Here it is, verbatim, underlines, italics and all:

<u>Write</u> about the most unusual day of the past year.
<u>Establish</u> what your real life is like.
<u>Show</u> why the unusual day was *unusual.*
<u>Convince me</u> that this unusual day is worth remembering.
<u>Use</u> one of the essay formats we've seen in our reading.

Okay, so what I've got here, is an *informal* essay, almost like a letter, addressed to a real audience. Got that, Mrs. McGill?

Except I know what you're going to say. You're going to say that I'm not really using one of the essay formats from class, and you'd be right. I'm a heavy reader and I love essays and I know this is a real essay format, but it's not one of the ones you assigned, and screw it, anyway.

I'm really not using one of your essay formats, because I already know I'm going to fail this damn thing. (Pardon my French, or should I say my Old French, since the word comes from that language [not German, like I originally thought].)

I know I'm going to fail, even though I'm following the rest of the assignment *to the letter*. Got that, Mrs. McGill? I'm doing what you ask.

It's not my fault you're not going to believe me.

A Day in The Life of J-May Michaels:

I get up. I go to school. I go to The Watering Hole, which is the tavern my parents own, where I sit at the bar and do my homework. I do not drink. I do not let my friends into the tavern to drink. We all know that I'm not supposed to be there, but I am there, because my parents need cheap help, and the county sheriff spends his off hours in the booth behind the antique jukebox that came with the tavern, and he doesn't care, so no one else cares either, so, as my dad would say, Mrs. McG, don't get your undies in a bundle.

I clean the stockroom, sweep everything before the evening "rush" (the locals, who arrive after work for burgers, and the occasional lost Shakespearean, looking for atmosphere), bus tables, and report any creep who grabs my butt. Everyone's usually gone by 10, and my dad locks up, not that it means much, since we're in—hello!—Alamaloosa and — double hello! — we live upstairs.

Weekends, not much different, except no school, but usually extracurriculars or something "special" down in Ashland at the university or at the Shakespeare Festival. Then more cleaning, sometimes homework, and a date. (I wish. Just kidding on the date thing.)

There it is, the exciting life of J-May Michaels.

Now, enter Little Green Men.

Too soon?

Okay, let's back up some.

It's February. I'm sitting at the bar, crouched over pre-calc, which isn't that bad, even though everybody says it's bad, but Mr. Cohen, he says I have a gift for mathematics and I should take pity on everyone, and by pity, he means I should tutor the less fortunate, but I'd rather poke my eyes out with a stick or sweep the bar every afternoon, whichever keeps me out of the Learning Lab with the Lame-os.

There's a Diet Coke fizzing to my left and a plate of nachos cooling at my right, and my tablet already has some sticky fingerprints on it, which Mom will yell at me about, because she says I shouldn't eat and do homework on the iPad at the same time.

So I'm trying to figure out the always-true, never-changing trig identities because, gifted or not, sometimes I don't remember everything right away, when something plops into my soda and I jump.

Because at the Watering Hole, we get spiders. Big huge garden spiders that look like they're straight out of the Forbidden Forest in Harry Potter, but they're harmless and annoying, and I hate it when they just fall randomly off the ceiling.

So I pick up my glass, hoping that maybe ice cracked loudly or something instead of falling spiders, and I stir the soda a little with my straw.

And that's when I see a little green hand, waving the universal sign for "help-I'm-drowning" around an ice cube.

I'm thinking that the wavy-thing is an effect, caused by me stirring the soda, so I pull the straw out of the liquid, and the hand reaches around, paws at the ice cube and then slides off the edge.

I pick up the glass and squint at it, holding it toward the frosted glass window of the main door so I can get a least a little natural light into those fizzy brown depths. And I see something that shouldn't be there, something that is about the size of a Reese's Peanut Butter Cup, only it's flailing, which makes me think it might be drowning, or maybe it was that hand and the fact that appendages hang off it like legs and they're kicking weakly.

I'm not sure if I'm grossed out or intrigued, but either way, I'm not drinking more of that Diet Coke. So I lower the glass a little so I can still see what's under the surface, then stick the straw back in and push it against the side of the glass, underneath the kicking Reese's Peanut Butter Cup. The thing stops moving for a half-second, then leans forward and, I swear to God, wraps its appendages around the straw.

Okay, I admit, I actually had one of those moments, y'know, the kind you see in Lit-Raht-Shure, where the protagonist knows she's making a choice that could go one way or the other. (See, Mrs. McG? I learn. "Protagonist," not "hero." Heh.)

I know I could use the straw to keep that Peanut Butter thing underwater (underCoke?) but I don't. I haul the whole straw-Peanut Butter thing up with one hand while I'm setting the glass down with the other. Then, as the straw bends under the thing's weight, I slip my hand underneath it (half afraid that I'm grabbing a spider) and lift it the rest of the way.

The Peanut Butter thing looks like one of those disk-like kid's toys. You know the kind. The round toys like a coaster or a gigantic coin, but with arms and legs and little white shoes and little white gloves where the hands are and a tiny round head perched on top.

The Peanut Butter thing looks *like* one of those things, but it isn't one of those things. First off, it's squishy, not rubbery. Squishy like a frog, you know, the kind of squishy that means you could shove your fingers through it and do some serious damage.

Second, it's got a neck. Just a little one, and the head is like a giant gumball, with round plastic-looking eyes that have a little too much black in them and a perfect circle of . . . well, not white, exactly, more like a really pale green. It doesn't have a nose, but it does have two little black dots above a big mouth. The thing is gasping and spitting out Diet Coke, and the top of its torso (disk?) is flapping like ducts on a bad heating system.

Third, it's not wearing shoes. It has arched green feet with three long toes. It's not wearing gloves either. Its little hands are clenched into fists.

I'm both queasy and fascinated. I look around the Watering Hole to see if anyone else notices, but I'm the only person in the place at the moment. Mom isn't even behind the bar. She's probably doing the accounts in the back or something. She probably even told me to holler for her if someone came in, and I probably ignored her.

I don't think this little guy (and God knows why I think it's a guy, but it's giving off guy energy, and no, Mrs. McG, don't ask me to explain that) counts as "someone." Mom would probably scream at it and squash it with a plate or something.

"What the hell are you?" I ask, not expecting an answer. I was asking it the way you ask some kind of bug crawling across the table what it is. You know, rhetorically, or just to hear your own voice.

"What the hell are *you?*" the thing snaps back.

I push away from the bar, startled, and nearly spill the Diet Coke all over my tablet. Okay, now I'm beginning to think I'm either crazy or dreaming.

I decide to go with dreaming.

"I'm . . . ah . . . human?" I say sounding a little unsure, because when have you ever had to identify yourself by species? I mean, I never have before (or since, to be really honest), and I certainly didn't expect to do it in my parents' bar.

"Are you a human or aren't you?" the thing snaps. Jeez, I don't like its tone. The little thing is beginning to piss me off. (And Mrs. McG, I already figure you're going to mark me down for language, so just deal, okay?)

"I'm human," I say a lot more decisively, "and I asked first. So what are you?"

It makes a sound between a sneeze, a gargle, and someone choking to death. Then it adds, "But I would suppose you can call me a Glorp."

"Oh, well, thank you," I say, sarcastically. "Let me ask again. What the hell is a Glorp?"

"Me," it says.

I roll my eyes. It's like talking to my three-year-old sister. "So, are you a bug, or what?" I ask, still going with the dream.

"Bug?" it repeats. Then it grins as if it's suddenly understood. "Oh! *Insect.* No, I'm not. I'm . . . ." It sighs and sounds just a little annoyed. "I guess you would call me a . . . a . . . a fan."

"A *fan?*" I ask. "Of what?"

"*Little Women,*" it says, and now I *know* I'm dreaming. "We came to see the house."

"The . . . house?" I ask slowly.

"Orchard House?" The Glorp-thing is frowning, which is really weird because those round eyes now have corners, and there's a line that runs from the top of its gumball head to those two little black dots.

"This is the Watering Hole," I say, and then realize that we might be having language issues, so I add, "It's a bar."

"A bar. A tavern," it says. "For libations."

"I guess," I say.

"Well, direct me and my friends to Orchard House, and we shall depart," it says.

"Friends?" I ask. I hear a chittering sound, and see two dozen of these little Glorp-things standing on the bar. I hadn't noticed them land, although as I'm watching, two more haul themselves over the lip of the bar, using the water gun as leverage.

I look at the one Glorp in front of me. The SpokesGlorp, I guess.

"What is this, some kind of invasion?" I ask.

"No," it says, sounding offended. "We're on a tour of famous literary sites throughout the galaxy. We have opted for the ship-to-planet excursion, Literary Women in Modern America, and we expect to see Orchard House, a few Civil War battlefields, and the historical sites around Concord. We understand that the battle of Lexington/Concord belongs to some other arcane war, but Louisa mentions it in her papers and—"

I wave my hands, shutting the SpokesGlorp up entirely. Then I sputter. I mean I really can't get any words out in any sensible fashion.

Finally, I take a drink of the Diet Coke before I remember that the SpokesGlorp had floated in it, and I spit the liquid back into the glass. Okay, I'm grossed out and annoyed, and confused, which helps me find my voice.

"Okay, you're telling me that there's literary tourism for aliens, and you have come for *Little Women* because . . . you like that book?" And okay, Mrs. McG, full disclosure here: I'm having more trouble with the fact that there's a gigantic universal fan base for *Little Women* than I am with the fact that there are maybe thirty Glorp on my parents' shiny bar top.

"Of course, we like the book. It is a window into your society," the SpokesGlorp says. "We understand that the book is something you call *fiction*, but that there are elements of truth to it, and we sincerely hope that the truth does not involve Beth's death, but rather the existence of Marmee and Jo and—"

"They're made up," I snap. "They're sanctimonious and made up and I hate them."

The SpokesGlorp sits down. Or rather, it plunks down, as if the force of my words has knocked it over.

It reaches out a hand, and one of the other Glorp grabs it, pulling the SpokesGlorp to its tiny feet. It dusts itself off, or rather, wipes itself off, since it fell in a puddle of condensation from the Diet Coke glass.

"Well," the SpokesGlorp says. "Clearly the book can't be *fiction* as we understand it, since you feel so passionately about it. Surely untruths would not provoke such passion in any creature, even the overly emotional human variety."

There's so much wrong with what the SpokesGlorp says that I don't even know where to start. I sputter some more, and before I can manage some real words, the SpokesGlorp takes a step closer to me.

"Since we've clearly ended up in the wrong location, please give us directions and we shall leave your establishment."

I stare at it. I can't help it. I have to ask. "How did you read *Little Women*?"

It straightens and raises its gumball head a bit, revealing a neck that actually has a tiny gumball inside it, like a tiny Adam's apple.

"I read 5,734 languages fluently," it says.

Well, goodie for you, I think. I have enough trouble with English. But I don't say that, because—well. Because.

Instead, I say, "I don't mean how did you learn English. Which, come to think of it, is a pretty good question. I mean, why the hell did you read *Little Women*? It's such a—"

"Such a classic," the SpokesGlorp says with reverence. "Filled with such important characters. Any species can write about its wars and its warriors, and most do, but to write about those who support them, those who love them, with such passion and heartache, well, we of the"—and then he made that sneezy gargly choky sound again— "Literary Society prefer works that make us cry to works that make us think. We do enough thinking already."

"You cry?" I ask, and then realize that's rude. I'm about to apologize when it opens its little hands, in a what-can-I-say? gesture. At least, on a human that would be what-can-I-say. Who knows what it is for a Glorp.

"To answer your initial question as I understand it," the SpokesGlorp says, "all of us first read the book in our introduction to Backwards Earth Societies Literature class in what you would probably call university. We—"

"Excuse me," I say, "Backwards what?"

"Earth Societies," it says, being ruder than I was, and probably not even realizing it. "So many of your societies have evolved beyond the primitive, but some of you are delightfully unfettered still. And the emotions . . ."

It puts two fingers to its mouth, makes a kissing sound, and then says, *Bellissima!* Truly."

I smack the heel of my hand against my forehead but that doesn't wake me up. It only makes my forehead hurt.

"How did you get the book?" I ask, because you know me, Mrs. McG. I ask too many questions.

"Oh," the SpokesGlorp says. "The Library of the Galaxy, of course. Where else would you take literature classes in obscure societies?"

"Where else," I mutter.

"Exactly," it says, and its mouth widens. I'm hoping that's a smile, because the thing has pale green teeth too, and they look like shark teeth. "So, point us in the right direction, and we shall march out your door and never see you again."

"I dunno," I say, because I don't know. Alamaloosa is a weird place and I don't know all of it, and for all I know, Mrs. McG, you teachers have set up some shrine to Louisa May Alcott for reasons I'll never understand. "Where's this house exactly?"

"Orchard House," the SpokesGlorp says slowly, as if I'm the stupid one. "Where Louisa May Alcott lived. In Concord, Massachusetts, North America. I thought you studied this—"

"Massachusetts?" I ask. "You think you're in Massachusetts?"

The SpokesGlorp leans its head back, and I'm afraid it'll topple over. It looks top heavy. "Are we not?"

"No, you're not," I say. "You're barely in North America. You're on the wrong side of the continent."

One of the other Glorp (or Glorps. Who knows what the plural really is?) walks over and starts jibbering at the SpokesGlorp. They gesture and yell and spit and punch their little fists on the palms of their little hands and jump up and down a few times.

Then the SpokesGlorp turns back to me. "You are certain of this?"

"Um, e-yeah," I say. "I live here."

"But there was a sense of *Little Women* here," the SpokesGlorp says.

"Here? In the bar?" I ask.

"Here, in the community," it says.

I sigh. What, were we the only class in the country studying *Little Women* this week? "I can't speak to that," I say.

The other Glorp spits and sizzles and jumps up and down twice. The SpokesGlorp nods, but whether or not that's an agreement, I'll never know.

"I guess we just got coordinates wrong," it says. "We are arguing over fees now. Is there anything to see here?"

"Related to *Little Women*?" I ask.

"Yes," it says.

"No," I say, probably more strongly than I should. "But there's a Shakespearean theater about thirty miles from here."

"Ah," the SpokesGlorp says. "Stratford-upon-Avon. We have that scheduled for our next excursion, and it will screw up our itinerary if we attempt that."

And it would screw up the rest of my afternoon if I try to explain to them that they're nowhere near Stratford-upon-Avon. I guess, like most book people, book aliens are geography challenged as well.

"Wish I could help you," I lie, "but I can't. You should probably get out of here, though, before the dinner rush crowd shows up. They'll think you're appetizers, or maybe just some bar snacks."

"Bar . . . snacks?" The SpokesGlorp looks at me in horror. Apparently horror translates across our species. "Thank you. No. We are not bar snacks."

It turns toward the nearest Glorp and gestures. Then all of the Glorp face me and bow at the same time. It's kind of glorious, in a Radio-City-Music-Hall kinda way. Little Green Rockettes, with gumball heads, bowing at the same time.

Then, one by one, they pop—and I mean *pop* like bubbles popping— out of existence.

Or at least, off the bar. They leave a bit of green goo behind, and some brown stuff that I'm hoping is something other than what I think it is.

I have to clean up the bar before Mom comes out, and I do, and later when she asks me if everything's all right, I ask her, because I can't help myself, "Do you like *Little Women*?"

"The book?" she asks.

"Yeah," I say.

She gives me one of those cautious looks she specializes in, and then says, "It's a classic."

"Jeez," I say. "Obviously. For some reason I don't understand."

Mom gives me an indulgent smile. "Well, try to enjoy it," she says, "and remember: Older books can be truly alien to us."

I let out a snort. "No kidding," I say.

Then I work my way behind the bar and pour myself another Diet Coke. I carry the glass back to my spot, but before I delve back into my homework, I put a napkin on top of the glass.

I don't want anything falling in it.

In fact, I've put napkins on top of my glassware ever since. And that's the only lingering effect.

I did Google Orchard House after the Glorp left, but there was no report of an alien invasion. Although I did read about the tourist attraction, which sounds more interesting than the damn book. (Not that that is hard, mind you.) And I'd love to travel there, if only to get the hell out of Oregon, and stupid expectations and *classics*.

So, there you go, Mrs. McG. My failure of an essay. Even though it does exactly what you asked.

And before you tell me to redo this thing or to write about a different day with unusual events or give me an F or something, let me add one thing.

I don't usually have unusual days. (Okay, no one usually has unusual days, but you know what I mean.) Every day is exactly the same. *Exactly. The. Same.* With the exceptions I mentioned.

I can't wait to get out of this podunk town. I can't wait to have a real life. And I can't wait to get out of school.

So if you make me try another essay on the same topic, I still won't have anything to write about except this one day, and it really did happen, and it really is true, and if you can believe in Beth, and Jo, and Marmee, you can believe in little green aliens that call themselves Glorps.

Because I find them a lot more believable than the March clan.

Just sayin'.

It's been said before. Don't mess with Texas. That's good advice for any alien invader!
—RWB

Good Neighbor Policy

by Dantzel Cherry

Targ landed on the planet known as Earth, four battleships and sixteen soldiers at the ready. His three eyes rotated this way and that, surveying the land he'd been assigned to conquer with some resignation. The sun burned down with a vengeance, and even though the air was clear and breathable, it felt thick and sticky. The worst part was the dense, green shrubbery, which was so unlike the typical yellow and red of his beloved Zsarg. How could he stand out as Supreme Leader of Earth if he blended into the local flora?

Another problem was figuring out where the main base for this planet was. Yesterday he had tried conquering the southern tip of Earth where everything was a pleasant stark white, but the local life forms had not responded respectfully to his requests, and he'd been obliged to blast a few to show them he was a serious leader who demanded respect.

The poof of oily feathers had been most satisfactory.

The following outraged swarm of powerful wings smacking him and his men about had not.

Two of the local life forms in this overly green country peeked out from their front door and slowly approached him and his army. They towered over him and his men, but they seemed more capable of the "shock and awe" that Targ had been expecting.

"Aw, look at him, Helen," one of the natives said, crouching down until he was eye-level with Targ. A most satisfactory sign of respect.

"I know, Zane, I love it. I just love it," the female behind him said. She also sank onto both knees and stared at him with intense curiosity, almost uncomfortably so.

Targ was to be feared, not adored! Part of the strength of this invasion, rush job though it was, was the element of surprise, and Targ had watched Earth long enough to know it had neither received nor transmitted any signals in the standard intergalactic communication frequencies.

There were planets to conquer and quotas to fill, but Targ couldn't stop himself from asking, "Have you seen my kind before?"

The male shrugged. "Nah, but we're Texans. We don't startle easily."

This was disappointing, but perhaps surprise was not necessary with creatures so docile. Targ puffed all of his body's air cavities until his body mass increased by thirty percent. His lower two arms planted on his torso, while his upper arms expanded menacingly. "Take me to your base," he said. His deep voice had inspired fear and devotion on two other planets so far, but he hoped he was pronouncing everything correctly. His internal translator didn't account for all local dialects.

The man named Zane blinked twice (in fear, perhaps?) and asked, "You want bass?"

Targ paused. "Indeed."

Zane nodded his head slowly. "I would be honored to take you to the local bass, mister—what's your name?"

"Targ the Mighty, commander of the Zsargeens."

""Well Targ the Mighty, welcome to the town of Uncertain in the *beau*-tiful state of Texas, Targ. You couldn't have come at a better time to catch bass. I'll just go round up my gear."

He paused, and added, "In the meantime, why don't you try the pie my wife Helen here just pulled out of the oven?"

"This pleases me, yes," Targ said, still in his deepest voice, but Zane had already turned away, presumably to deliver the bass—and further, the keys of the planet to him.

Helen stood to her full height and winked at Targ and his men.

"Come along, hun. I'll show you the peach pie, and you and your men can see if it's to your liking." She pointed at the building she and Zane had come out of when Targ had first arrived.

Targ's men looked at him. Targ glanced at Helen, and compared her soft body to that of the retreating Zane. The male was obviously not only the stronger of the two, but most definitely Helen's superior.

Even the frequency of her smile showed that she gave way to the nearest alpha, which Targ certainly was.

Targ caught his skin deflating in the midst of all that thinking, and puffed up to full size. "We will wait *here* for pie."

"Oh, hun, I wouldn't do that if I were you. It's much nicer on the porch."

Targ did not dignify this with a response. He turned to his men instead, pointing as he gave orders in a low voice.

"You two—follow the female. Marg—take Karg and Larg and trail the male, but stay covert. Observe only, unless he does something suspicious. Sarg, Xarg, and Zarg—stay with me here. The rest of you—establish a perimeter. Keep a wary eye out for hostiles."

His men spread out, and Helen shrugged and went inside the house, with two of Targ's men in tow.

Targ paced as he waited, treading over the hard dirt road and over the plants—which were a disappointing green, but soft and accommodating. Here and there, though, were little brown mounds of earth rising from the greenery. Poor housekeeping or land mines? Targ leveled his blaster at one of the lumps, knowing his blast would neutralize any bomb the humans might have placed.

Zap. The dirt scattered, but no bits of metal sprayed up. A few red creatures scurried out of a hole no wider than his biggest toe. They were so small that Targ had to lean all the way down to see any of their limbs. They were so tiny, so insignificant, even as they panicked over their destroyed home. Targ brushed creatures and dirt alike out of his path. It was good to be a conqueror.

Just then his foot began to burn. It burned like it was on fire, though Targ could see very well that there was no fire, only one of the tiny red creatures attacking his foot.

Another two climbed up the same limb, stinging indiscriminately. Targ would have appreciated their bravery if it didn't hurt so blasted bad.

He slapped all three off with ease, but more scrambled up. He slapped them away too, stepping back quickly, and followed the trail to the destroyed earth mound. He zapped five more blasts into the small hole.

For a single moment, the charred earth smoked and Targ's skin deflated in relief.

Then the ground around where the hole used to be bubbled—or so it seemed—and hundreds, if not thousands, of angry red creatures poured upward, heading straight for him and his men.

Bioweapons.

"We're under attack!" Targ shouted to his men, even as he backed into them. "Fire at will!" His soldiers turned and opened fire on the brown mound and the area surrounding it, and the men establishing the perimeter and following Helen rushed onto the scene and joined in. The quiet *zap zap-zap zap* decimated the puny mounds. Not all the shots were entirely accurate, though—one of his men tripped on a small rock and skimmed Targ's right leg with his blast. Targ shrieked.

"No! Get away from the fire ants!" Helen came running toward them, and then changed her mind after seeing how many blasters were aimed in her general direction. She skirted around the shooting and came as near Targ as she dared. "Run to the porch, boys! Are you alright, hun?"

Targ glared at her. "My men will carry me."

Right on cue, three of his men scooped him up and rushed him away from the attacking ants to the steps of the front porch. There Targ inspected his leg—where the ants had stung, his skin had sunk, leaving small, painful spots of white in their wake. The errant blaster shot was technically worse than the ant stings, but Targ's outer layer of skin had already sealed along the edges of the wound, protecting the rest of the leg from the air.

The tiny holes in the stings, on the other hand, which Targ's skin had never encountered, refused to seal up. As such, Targ couldn't properly puff up his right leg, a scrawny appearance that one only saw on the extremely unfortunate youths, or the drug-addled. Each of his men had suffered similar injuries; most of their legs were even more puckered than Targ's.

Helen crouched down, inspecting his leg and making frequent "ooo" and "ouch" noises.

"Is this some kind of trap?" Targ demanded.

The woman looked up at him, her right eyebrow arched. "Certainly not. I've had my share of fire ant stings—enough that I learned to stay away from them. But they aren't dangerous, unless you're allergic to their venom. But that's rare." She paused. "I guess you're not from around here, though."

Targ decided she was sincere. He puffed up his skin, but the air hissed out of the sting holes. He sighed. "Sarg, cut around each of my sting wounds so the healing process can begin." Sarg and the others looked around for a cutting tool, but there were none to be had.

"I have some paring knives ya'll could use, if you like," Helen offered.

With reluctance Targ accepted her offer, and in short order he and his men had each carved the outer skin away from the mildly venomous stings and were ready to try the pie the humans had spoken of.

Targ stared at his plate. He didn't trust the little fragrant triangle of "peaches" that were topped with a dry light brown "crust." He ordered the soldier that had shot his leg to taste first.

The unfortunate taste tester quivered with trepidation at his plate, took one tentative bite from the utensil Helen had called a "fork," then dropped the fork and scooped the pie into his mouth as quickly as he could with all four hands. After a moment, Targ and the rest of his men followed suit.

It was the best thing Targ had ever tasted. If Targ didn't consider poetry to be an ignominious use of one's time, he might have written a ballad to this pie. They shoveled it in with abandon, pausing only to demand more. Helen wisely didn't bring up the ants again, asking only, "More pie?"

As his men filled near to bursting, they slumped against each other in a semi-comatose reverie, chewing their cud for their second stomach to enjoy later. Just as Targ finished his fourth plate, Zane appeared in front of the crowded porch, gripping a bucket, a rectangular box with a handle, and five long poles tucked under his arm.

With difficulty, he held up a bucket that wafted an extremely delicious scent, just like the jujubs on his own planet—thick and meaty, yet with delicate fatty pustules hanging underneath the jujubs' wattles.

"Okay boys, we're fixin' to *jig* and *pig*! In this here bucket I've got the pig, and over here I've got the jigs for us to try out tonight: the Naughty Bug, the Chunk, and the Fat Grub Tail," Zane said, shaking the rectangular box. "Let's pair those with the Pumpkin Chart, the Green Crawdad, and my standard Bl—what in the hell happened here?" he interrupted himself, his tiny human eyes gaping at the little bits of skin Targ and his men had cut off and pushed to the bottom porch step.

Helen started to explain, but Targ hurriedly cut her off. "We're fine—we're all fine, aren't we men? We're ready to take your bass." He jumped up and brandished his blaster to make his point, but the pose was ruined a bit by the sound of air hissing out from the not-yet-sealed cuts on his legs.

Zane shared a look with Helen, but Targ couldn't understand what it meant.

After a moment, Zane said, "Alright, we'll talk about that later. Let's talk bass—Targ, how many bass were you hoping to catch tonight?"

"As many as I can, but it would be best if I took the biggest one first," Targ replied.

Zane laughed. "I wish it worked that way!"

Was he challenging Targ? It was best that Targ made his intentions clear. He went on, "And then probably the ones that think they can fight back. If I round these up first, the others will see there is no use in resisting my might."

Zane cocked his head to the side. "I've heard of that 'think like a fish' stuff before, but you're really taking it to the next level."

Targ was pleased to see that his intimidation technique worked.

Confident in his new alpha role, he asked, "How does 'jigging' and 'pigging' help us capture your bass?"

"This is the *only* way to catch a bass this time of year," Zane said, jiggling the bucket and releasing more mouth-watering scent. "Come on, let's get going."

It was a pity to take over the world when there was still pie to be eaten, but Targ needed to be strong in front of his new subjects.

With one last longing glance at the remaining slice of pie in the dish, Targ ordered his men into formation. With Targ, Zane, and Helen in the front, they trooped off at a quick pace down a dirt path that paralleled a small stream of water. They walked faster than Targ would have liked, but it was out of necessity to keep up with Zane's long strides.

The humans didn't glance down at Targ much, for which Targ was grateful. He didn't want them to see him leaping over or sidestepping past any creature that resembled an ant—which he encountered nearly every third step. It felt like dancing. Targ's parents would have been ashamed. Behind him, his men performed similar dances of shame. It couldn't be helped, though. He almost felt sorry for the humans he was about to conquer—what a monstrous planet to live on.

"You picked one of the best places in the country to catch bass, Mister Targ," Zane said after another period of silence. "There's a bunch of 'em hiding out in the Caddo Lake maze. They like the cypress roots and the Spanish moss, but sometimes the lily pads get thick near the docks and then it's hard to *not* catch one every time you cast."

Cast what? Targ thought, nonplussed. Cast a warning? This translator was a second-rate piece of junk.

The web of trees broke through, and Targ found that the stream had emptied into a lake. They had made it out of the woods, and among the water. They would be capturing their first bass any moment.

"Alright boys, here's the edge of the water. Stay close, and let me show you how to flip and pitch this here pig accurately," Zane said, pulling a bit of the smelly stuff out of the bucket and holding it close to his fishing pole. Why *had* he brought all that? "Accuracy is important when you flip and—"

Targ tuned him out, and turned to look around the lake, walking along the shore to admire his soon-to-be-conquered planet. Nothing moved, except for a tall, thin white bird off in the distance, dipping its hard yellow beak into the brownish water. If one ignored the plethora of green, the lake here was beautiful.

His reverie was broken by a splash of water and something chomping down on his leg. Another fire ant? But this was more painful, and—

Targ thudded on his back and found himself dragged forward through gritty sand into the water. What was happening? What were all those teeth doing clamped on his leg? He struggled to pull his blaster out.

"Alligator!" Zane shouted as Targ slipped halfway into the water. "Hold on, Targ, I'm coming!"

Alligator, huh? Targ zapped the alligator right between its tiny, beady eyes.

This killed the sneaking bastard.

Unfortunately, this sneaking bastard had a really excellent death grip, and Targ found himself sinking down with the dead creature. His head slipped under the water, and he knew he was done for.

The great black universe of death welcomed him.

A stab of pain brought him to consciousness. His eyes popped open, one at a time, until all three confirmed that he was, in fact, on the shore, with Marg, his second in command, cutting into his leg.

"See?" Helen was saying to Marg. "He's still alive. Put the knife away."

"Alligator?" Targ asked.

"Deader than dead, Mister Targ. You're a wicked shot," Zane's voice said. A moment later Targ found Zane off to the side, tugging the alligator carcass on shore, though Targ couldn't figure out why he would do such a thing.

Another stab of pain, and Targ yelped.

"Sorry, sir," Marg said, bowing and stepping away. In one of his hands was a paring knife. "I took the liberty of helping your leg heal. If you're in too much pain, I could perform the debraining rites and take over as commander." He held the knife noncommittally, but his voice sounded too eager for Targ's liking.

Targ sprang to his feet, ignoring the pain in his leg, and checked all four of his hands for additional damage. He was pleased to see there was none. The blaster had been submerged, though. He reprimanded himself for not requisitioning the waterproof model.

"That's very thoughtful, Marg, but I think I can still fulfill my duties as commander. I'll inform you if the situation changes."

"You have only but to ask, sir."

Targ made a mental note to request a new second in command when he got home. "Zane the Human, I am ready to capture the first bass."

"I'd be happy to help. Come on over here and I'll show you the proper jig and pig techniques. Your men are already practicing their casts."

For the first time Targ noticed the rest of his company standing by the shore. They stood in groups of three and were taking turns holding the pole, which had a thin, clear string attached to it with brightly colored objects and the jujub-smelling meat hooked on the end of the string. They were swinging the meat into the water, and then drawing it back out with a little retracting device. The men looked at Targ, waiting for direction.

"Are these weapons for—" began Targ timidly, but he was interrupted by a shout from one of his soldiers, who seemed to be having trouble with his pole.

Zane sprang forward and hovered over the soldier, hands held out as though they were going to snatch the pole away at any moment. "You've got one! Reel him in nice and slow. Keep a grip on your pole! There, now."

Targ leaned in, excited despite his utter bewilderment. Were they opening the first base? Why did they keep their base under the water? Although it stood to reason that the alligators would make excellent, if primitive, security guards.

A flash of silver appeared out of the water, drawn up by the string. It wriggled and struggled and would have pulled the soldier into the water, but Zane grabbed the pole at the last second and continued pulling the silvery object to shore.

"There!" Zane said, holding it up. "Your first bass, and at least seven pounds. Looks like the Pumpkin Chart lure was a hit tonight."

Confused, Targ came closer.

It was a creature of some sort, with stupid, unblinking eyes, silver and green scales, and a mouth that gaped around an orange object. It struggled to get free, and a few droplets of water flicked onto Targ's face.

"What's this?" Targ asked.

"Your first bass," Zane repeated, smiling. "Is this your first time seeing a fish? You look as squeamish as Helen used to get when I gutted them, back before we got married. Here, hold it and I'll take a picture."

Targ was too confused to protest as Zane passed the string over to him, and hustled the soldier who had caught it next to him. Targ held the string high over his head with his top two arms and tried not to fall over—the fish was almost as tall as he was. Helen pulled a little black device out of her clothing and Zane crouched down next to them, smiling.

"Ready," Helen said, and a bright flash from the device blinded Targ momentarily. "Got it!"

"Great start, guys," Zane said, jumping up and unhooking the fish. "I'll string this up over here so we can get this pole back in action."

He strode away.

"But isn't the base under the . . ." Targ started to call out after him.

An uncomfortable dawning realization came upon Targ as he watched Zane cast his bait into the water, near one of the strange white trees, and gently reel it back in. The events of the day rearranged themselves in his mind, and though he was too pockmarked to puff out his skin, he felt his anger bubble up.

"Zane the Human, I am not here to catch your bass fish," he shouted at Zane.

"If you're nervous about falling in the water again, Targ, I can catch them for you."

"Targ the Mighty is nervous about nothing! I am coming to understand that you have been disingenuous with me since the moment I landed on your accursed planet."

"Now that's not—" began Zane, but Targ boomed over him.

"I asked to be taken to your base, and you led me to this miserable swamp, only to be attacked by your local allies, and left to drown in the muckiest water known to the galaxy at large."

"I concede about the condition of the water around here," said Zane, spreading his free hand wide and pumping it against the empty air near the front of his torso. "But the rest are outright untruths. You came here and asked for my bass, which I am happily providing the best chance of acquiring one of your own, and using my best equipment, too. I saved your life. You ate our *pie*—"

If Targ didn't know better, he'd think that Zane was the most upset about the pie. "Take me to your base," Targ said.

"I already did," Zane said, holding up his pole. "Remember?"

"Take me to your *base*," Targ said again. "With all the weapons, and your best military leaders."

"Mister Targ, it's not my fault you can't say 'base' properly. You held a blaster in your hand like any common criminal—and I'll have you know that this state is a 'Castle Doctrine' state, and I had the courtesy to not shoot your little green guts out while you were trampling my wife's basil plants—and because you asked for bass, I gave you bass."

Targ pulled his blaster out, though he wasn't entirely certain it still worked after being doused in the lake. He leveled it at Zane. Helen gave a small but satisfactory gasp.

"Take me to your *base*," Targ said, giving particular emphasis to "base," now properly pronounced.

"Or what?"

"Or I'll shoot you and your wife here."

As Targ spoke, he gestured at Helen, his third eye only just taking notice of her holding a blaster—

Targ jumped back and gave Helen his full attention. She was standing next to him and holding a blaster of her own—or whatever the primitive equivalent here was—and she was pointing it directly at him. As primitive as their weapons may be, Targ was positive they could kill as brutally as a blaster or basic curlicue sword.

"Or what?" Helen repeated her husband's question in a low voice, which nearly rumbled with the implied threat.

"Or I'll shoot you both." Targ had to remind himself that he was the quickest shot in his class, back in command school. Surely he could shoot her first.

Helen sighed, but didn't drop the arm holding the weapon. "Targ, you need to understand three things. One: There is no central base for the planet. There are certainly a few key bases for the United States, but I'm the last person to know where they are.

"Two: I am an extremely decent shot with a handgun.

"Most importantly, three: If you harm me, Zane, or the rest of humanity in any way, I can guarantee that you will never again have a taste of my pie."

All around Targ, his men muttered at this threat. The loss of Helen's pie would be a great blow, but what of Planet Earth? Targ had been planning to add its conquest to his resume, and he hated not meeting quota. On the third hand . . . was that another fire ant biting him?

Targ swatted the fire ant away with a free arm and lowered the blaster with the other. "I have decided that this planet does not please me. In exchange for more pie, you are welcome to keep your bases and your bass and your fire ants and your alligators."

Helen and Zane leaned in close and discussed this quietly, so quietly that Targ could not hear, which he found rather rude. Nevertheless, he allowed it. Considering the circumstances and all.

"We agree to those terms," Helen informed him. "Under the condition that you join us for dinner before you go—as a sign of our good will."

"Helen really is the best cook in the whole county," Zane added. "Fried fish is her specialty."

Targ pretended to consider before answering. "This is acceptable."

★ ★ ★

The sun had set and Earth's moon was bright in the sky when Targ and his soldiers staggered back to their battleships, filled to the brim with fish and pie. Zane wrapped an arm around Helen's waist as they stood on the porch steps and waved goodbye.

When the battleships were indistinguishable from the twinkling stars, Zane let out a sigh. "Helen's peach pie, bringer of intergalactic peace."

Helen laughed, shaky but exultant. "At least this second bunch was cute. What did they call themselves? Sardines?"

"Zsargeens," Zane corrected. "That other bunch last month, they were the Zsardines."

"That's right," Helen agreed, leaning into Zane. It was her turn to sigh. "I can't believe that pie worked twice!"

A troubadour himself, Ken Scholes brings us an inspired tale of a little green man and his ship-turned-guitar and their adventures in Buenos Aires...
—BTS

Stuck in Buenos Aires With Bob Dylan On My Mind

by Ken Scholes

I've read all about that other guy, last son of a dead planet flying around in tights to save the world. Let me tell you something: Not everyone who crashes here was sent, not everyone gets adopted by a kindly Midwestern farmer and your little yellow sun in this backwoods corner of the universe sure didn't dole out any superpowers.

No, that's not how it went for me at all.

My first taste of your planet was the Seine. Not a wonderful start. I woke up choking and clawing my way toward gray light in a body that felt clunky and wrong.

Aren't you forgetting something?

I heard the voice clearly in my head and it was familiar to me.

I should leave you. What were you thinking? It was all coming back to me now and I was, as you might put it, mad as fuck. I forced myself to turn downward, scanning the river floor. *Over here.* A brief flash of light and I saw it. *And I was thinking with my—*

Yes, I cut him off. *There you are.*

My ship flashed silver at me and I grabbed it, kicking upward again. I felt its shame radiating through the handle I clutched tightly with an oddly effective four-fingered hand complete with an opposable thumb.

My ship sighed. *It was a Dothari Belt-class Schooner. I couldn't say no.*

I broke the surface and felt the slow tug of the river as it moved me between stone bridges in a gray twilight lit by the lights of a city. Of course, at the time I had no idea it was the Seine. Or Paris.

41

Actually, you could've said no. You really could've. But he hadn't. And he'd caught something from his port tryst eight days now behind us. So here we were.

More shame. *I'm sorry.*

I thrashed my way onto a cobblestone ramp and flopped over, staring up at the evening sky. The smells of the city overpowered the smell of the river and I lay there panting alien air into alien lungs. I looked over to my ship. His name isn't pronounceable with these vocal chords of yours. Let's call him Carmichael.

He'd disguised himself as a guitar case, buckled closed, with a pearl handle. It was worn, dented metal and covered with stickers. Some of the markings were familiar to me but most weren't. *Wow. You're small.*

Use your vocal chords, Carmichael answered.

"Wow," I said. "You're . . . small."

Actually, I'm the same size. The dominant sentient species here is significantly larger than the galactic standard. You've been upsized to avoid drawing attention to yourself.

I continued testing my vocal chords. "Where's here?"

Earth, he said. *Buenos Aires, to be precise.*

The city's name registered and I started accessing my memory of its streets and skyline. "Hey, I know that place."

Yes. I was able to upload several data packets that will hopefully enhance your chances of survival here.

I stood and looked around, checking my knowledge of the city against what I saw around me. "I don't think it's likely to enhance my chances," I finally said.

Why not?

"Because I don't think this is Buenos Aires."

No, Carmichael said. *I'm quite certain this is Buenos Aires.*

I knew then that things were about as bad as they could be. Until I started up the ramp and met my first humans. Then things got worse. It took me a minute to figure out why they looked at me the way they did. Or didn't look at all.

"I'm naked," I said out loud.

A white-haired male human winked at me as he passed by. "Oui, Monsieur," he said. "Vous êtes en effet nu."

See? Carmichael said. *They're speaking Spanish to you.*

"But I don't seem to speak Spanish. And public nudity appears to be frowned on here."

A brown-haired female human in a blue uniform made eye contact with me. She said something into what I guessed was a radio.

You better run, Carmichael said.

And so I ran.

Morning found me huddled against a stone wall in the back of an alley, my body covered in pages from a newspaper I couldn't understand.

I squinted at it. "I thought you programmed me with Spanish?"

Carmichael sighed. *I did. After all, Spanish is the most spoken language in Argentina.*

I glanced at the guitar case and wondered how I knew what it was. "What other helpful information did you upload into me?"

A plethora of skills and knowledge necessary to survive undetected in a hostile environment.

I smelled something pleasant on the air for the first time since arriving. Whatever it was made my stomach growl and I associated it instantly with being hungry. "What kind of skills?"

Well, Carmichael said, *let me out of this case and I'll show you.*

"I thought you *were* the case?"

That's just silly. What good is an empty guitar case?

I thumbed the clasps and opened the lid. A stringed instrument shone dimly in the morning light. "I don't see how—"

Just pick me up. You'll see.

Papers crackled and crunched around me as I lifted the guitar. It had a strap made of what appeared to be the hide of a pink, fuzzy creature and a silver pick tucked between its strings. It felt as familiar in my hands as a kermauchoof—which you've never heard of. I took the pick in one hand and curled my fingers around the neck. Something tickled at my brain and music happened as I picked at a series of strings with my right hand while pressing them with my fingers of my left hand.

See?

I gave myself over to the song and when I opened my mouth to reply, strange words poured out. "Once upon a time you dressed so fine," I sang, "you threw the bum a dime when you were in your prime—"

Didn't you? Carmichael chimed in.

I stopped. "What is *that*?"

It's Dylan. Part of a wide variety of uploaded chords, notes and lyrics covering several decades of popular music.

"I don't see how this is going to help me survive in a hostile alien environment."

Try it again. Play more this time. Sing louder.

So I did. And when I finished, I jumped at another voice in the alley.

"Bravo," it said and I looked up. A man in a white hat stood backlit by an open door. He held something that smoked in his fingers and he sucked at it as he watched me. He dug into his pocket and pulled out what looked like a coin. "How do you say it? Threw the bum the dime?" Then he laughed and tossed the coin at me.

"Oh," I said. "I get it."

Then I gathered up my ship, my newspapers and my first bit of currency and set out to sing my way off this desolate backwater rock.

By noon, I'd earned myself rudimentary clothing—a pair of gym shorts, a Grateful Dead t-shirt and flip-flops—along with an assortment of breads, cheeses, chocolates, and coins.

I took a break and stretched out in the dirty sunlight, feeling the ache in my fingers and throat. As I'd sung, I'd continued integrating what I could of my surroundings with the data packets Carmichael had uploaded into me. My knowledge of Buenos Aires told me it should be warmer than it was but the infection that had crashed us here had likely glitched the upload. Apart from watching the people around me, seeing how the music impacted them, I was left with the music itself to educate me.

Her cheating heart had told on her so bye bye love, there goes my baby. And bye bye Miss American Pie, for that matter, because we've all come to look for America with Carolina on our minds and a heart in New York. Wearing blue suede shoes and a long black veil.

So what do you think?

I nibbled at a pastry. "It's good. A little cold. They take themselves and their reproductive drives a bit too seriously in their music." I paused and frowned. "Then again, look who I'm talking to."

"Pardon?" a white-haired female asked. My blank stare kept her walking by.

Yes, yes, Carmichael said. The shame was gone now. *I crashed us here.*

I opened my mouth to speak and thought better of it as young blond male in a blue uniform walked by. It was occurring to me rapidly that people who spoke aloud to voices in their head may not be regarded in high esteem here and that these other people in blue uniforms might find such behavior noteworthy for their little radios. So I went silent. *How about you get us uncrashed?*

I'm working on it.

And?

Carmichael paused—an equivalent of taking a deep breath before delivering bad news. *Our options are . . . limited. Earth is a bagged world.*

"Great," I muttered. Bagged meant it was being monitored for its social evolution and kept in the dark about the rest of us just down the way. If you wonder why, go watch how my kind is typically portrayed in your popular entertainment. We blow up your big important buildings, messily kill people and then succumb to some ultimately silly end in a triumph of the human spirit. Or we show up as your pals, cure cancer and give you a sneak peek at our cookbook as we start measuring you for our frying pans. Or this one is especially good: After traversing millions of light years, we arrive completely incompetent and need someone from your species to help us return to our intergalactic culture.

Notice a pattern? You all don't treat each other much better, truth be told.

Bagged also meant that the technology necessary to eradicate my ship's infection wasn't going to be found here for a long, long while.

I sighed and watched more of the primates move around me. Many of them held communication devices to their ears. Or held them in their hands. *We could try to get a message out,* I suggested. I nodded to a young male, his opposable thumbs earning their keep on the tiny device he held while an even tinier device jutted from his ear. *Hijack a satellite and call for help.*

We could try, Carmichael agreed. *But did I mention that this world is bagged?*

I didn't need him to explain. Anyone who heard our message would be obligated by law to hand us over to the authorities. Captains were responsible for the health and safety of their vessels . . . and for where those vessels landed willingly or otherwise. My ship would be recycled and repurposed and my license revoked for the foreseeable future.

The man with the devices paused to pick his nose and examine what he found there. I looked away and thought perhaps the loss of my career was a small price to pay for rescue.

I changed locations three more times before sunset cast the streets in a red, warm light. Twice, those blue uniforms had shown up and taken an interest in me. Each time, I'd finished up my song and slipped away. Finally, I'd settled into a spot near the river and as the city moved into its night life, I started drawing a small crowd. A young male with a tattered backpack sat beside me and pulled a small metal object from his pocket and looked at me with raised eyebrows. I was singing about good times never seeming so good with someone named Caroline and didn't understand whatever non-verbal language he used. Smiling, he put the object to his lips and made music of his own that joined perfectly with mine.

It had taken me most of a day to relax enough to study the effect of music on you primates. Music, of course, is common throughout most of the galaxy. There are some civilizations that managed to emerge without it but they are few and far between and the rest of us think they lack something. The simplicity of your music—and the obsessive, extreme nature of the lyrics—is one of your better qualities. And with just my fingers and my vocal chords, I'd watched what it did to those who stopped. Flushing skin, flaring nostrils, tapping feet, swaying bodies, knowing looks. It would've been fun if I weren't stranded on a planet full of xenophobic barbarians.

The young male played with me through the rest of the set. After nodding his head to the scattered bits of applause, he grinned at me. "Vous êtes plutôt doué."

"I'm sorry," I told him. "I don't speak Spanish."

He laughed and now I understood him. "I do not speak Spanish either. I was speaking French to you."

"Spanish is the dominant language in Buenos Aires."

"Yes," he said. "It is. And *French* is the dominant language in *Paris*.

Which is where we are." He blew and pulled a few notes on the harmonica. "But now I am speaking English to you."

I closed my eyes. *I told you this wasn't Buenos Aires.*

Carmichael was nonplussed. *This primate could be mentally deranged and unaware of its present location.*

I looked around. "This is Paris?"

The young human nodded. "Oui." Then he grinned. "You must be American." He dropped the small metal instrument into his shirt pocket. "I am Claude." He extended his hand.

I watched the hand with caution. "What is *Claude*?"

"I am. It's my name." He extended the hand again. "And you are?"

"I'm . . ." I paused hoping Carmichael would save me. He didn't. "Dylan," I finally answered. "Dylan McLean."

Claude laughed. "Good one." Then, he took my hand in his and squeezed it in too brisk a fashion to be mating protocol. "So, Mysterious American, are you here to play the ex-pat open mic then?" He nodded in the direction of a building with a red door.

I patted Carmichael. "I only play guitar."

"You're funny," Claude said as he stood up. "Come on. I'll show you."

I crammed the contents of my guitar case into a plastic bag with the rest of my day's earnings and buckled Carmichael in. Claude was already crossing the street. I hesitated, noticing the line that formed and the humans who stood in it. There were several other guitar cases, and though I was the least elaborately garmented, I was still less scantily clothed than some of the females. One of them—tall with dark hair and long legs—made eye contact with me.

I caught up to Claude and he noticed the woman, too. He grabbed my arm and moved me down the line past her. "You'll do best to— how do you say it? Steer clear of her, mate. She hates Americans."

"But I'm not American."

Claude guided me through the line. When we reached the dark-clothed man at the door, Claude said something to him in French. The man nodded and ushered us inside. The room was crowded and stank of humans and the things they drink and smoke. There was a small stage toward the back and a bar on the far side. My guide moved me across the room to another man, this one dressed colorfully and wearing paint on his face. Claude pushed me to him. "This is my friend Dylan," he said. "He's American. Really good."

"Sergio," the man said with a nod. He held up three fingers. "Three songs," he said. He glanced at a sheet in front of him. "Fifth up." Then he went to scribbling and Claude moved us over to the bar.

I don't think this is a very good idea, Carmichael said. *You're supposed to be laying low.*

"No," I muttered quietly. *I'm supposed to be finalizing my delivery to Goral's Reach right about now and then taking a little vacation. But someone crashed us here over a bit of shiny new hyperdrive schooner.*

Carmichael said nothing.

We stood at the bar as the room filled and Claude—with help from some coins and bits of paper from my bag—introduced me to my first glass of beer. It was cold and sweet. I was part way into it when the woman from outside slipped in between me and Claude. She tipped her very plump mammary glands—barely restrained by her red dress—in my direction and batted her eyes. "Who's your friend, Claude? Did I hear you tell Sergio he's American?"

"Leave him be, Annie." Claude tried to switch places with her but she held him at bay with a glance.

Then her eyes went back to me. She finally seemed to take in my clothing. "So did you come from the gym or the beach?"

Her question was gibberish to me so I took a hint from the others I'd met so far and extended my hand. "I'm Dylan," I said.

She snorted. "I'll bet you are." Then she got in close and the smell of her was sweet and crisp like the beer I sipped. "So you're from America. I'm from your neighbor to the north."

Human faces, it seems, are exceptional at transmitting subverbal messages like confusion. Her smile widened at the look on my face and over her shoulder I saw Claude shaking his head and mouthing the word "no" over and over again. I decided to err on the side of caution and say nothing.

Annie continued. "You know it?" She paused and waited for me to answer.

I didn't.

She raised her eyebrows. "A little place called Canada?"

Now the look on my face seemed to annoy her but it didn't last long. She smiled again and took a sip from the glass of red fluid that had appeared in front of her. She drew closer and now Claude was rolling his eyes over her shoulder.

Annie leaned even closer now, her mouth near my ear. I felt heat from her breath as she spoke. "I'll give you a blowjob if you can tell me the capitol of Canada."

I suspected that gainful employment would be useful here though I wasn't sure how much her job paid. I decided to err on the side of honesty and see if that served me as well as caution had. "I need the blowjob quite badly, but I do not know the capitol of Canada." I paused. "But Buenos Aires is the capital of Argentina."

She sniffed and for a moment she looked like Multon gusp spawn deprived of its marpy at the last moment and angry over the wasted effort. "You just lost yourself a blowjob."

Annie took her wine and pushed off into the crowd. Claude watched her go. "It's Ottawa," he said. "In case you're wondering."

I wasn't. I was still trying to piece together how a human female on Earth could look so very much like something from the planet Multon. I opened my mouth to reply but the music started. Slender greasy bits of fried and salted starch arrived with more beer. Claude and I ate quietly and listened to the music.

Most was guitar with vocals—male, female, and at one point, one of each. And there were other instruments I did not recognize. Still, I knew most of the songs from my own repertoire. None of them especially impacted me and I was pondering the overpowering obsession with reproductive activities when the fourth musician took to the stage.

Sergio spoke into his own microphone off to the side as she strapped on her guitar.

"Cecilia Dumas," he said. She was not very tall, but sturdily built and compact. Her hair and eyes were blue and her hair was brown. She had a metal harness that held an instrument identical to Claude's— small and silver. She hid behind the guitar, blowing a few notes as her fingers moved over the strings and her eyes wandered the room.

This song wasn't one I recognized but I felt it instantly. "I'm just a poor wayfaring stranger," she sang, "a-travelling through this world of woe." The room did not erupt in applause but something inside me resonated with her mournful tone. She moved from it seamlessly into a soulful rendition of a song I did know, only she'd cleverly altered its lyrics to be about a Rocket Girl instead of a man. "It's lonely out in space," she crooned and her eyes met mine.

What was that? Carmichael's voice was panicky in my head.

Nothing, I said. *Go back to sleep.*

The second song gathered up a smattering of applause when she finished and she launched into her last, one she told us she'd written herself.

I was entranced and felt my new body doing things it hadn't done before. The light around her softened and my pulse quickened. My stomach felt oddly light. I looked down and saw my foot was tapping in time.

Then Claude was pushing Carmichael into my hands and shoving me toward the stage. "You're up, you're up."

Sergio waved at me, said something in French that I didn't understand, and the audience chuckled. Then he winked at me and smiled. "Dressed in the latest American fashion for his Parisian debut: Dylan McLean."

There were snorts and giggles and chuckles as I strapped on Carmichael. Sergio handed me a wire and I looked at it blankly.

Don't you dare plug that into me, Carmichael said. *I don't know where it's been.*

That's never stopped you before. I examined the guitar's body and found where it went. Then I pushed the cord in and twisted it. As I did, static burst from the speaker followed by a warbling, high pitched squeal that settled down as I started to play.

My fingers knew what to do and so did my mouth. "I got my first real six string," I sang. "Bought it at the five and dime." And from there, I let the song carry me away.

I wasn't alone. The mood in the room shifted as I sang. People swayed, tapped their feet, even clapped and sang along. And after I moved them along through that summer of '69, we were suddenly slip sliding away, slip sliding away, and I watched the music take us all nearer to some destination where only music could carry us. When I finished the second song, the room exploded into applause and I paused to scan my audience.

I saw Annie first. She was up in the front of the crowd and the look on her face had changed now. It was flushed. Her eyes were wide. Her nostrils flared. When our eyes met she smiled at me. I kept that eye contact and started playing again, and a slow melody built as I picked out the notes on Carmichael's strings. The look on Annie's face was something I'd not seen on the humans yet and I found that I liked it. So with eyes locked, I leaned into the microphone. "You fill up my senses," I sang to her, "like a night in the forest. . . ."

But even as I sang it, the words felt false to me. I found myself wanting to look around the room to find the other female. Cecilia. Still, I held Annie's gaze and let the show go on. The subtle and not-so-subtle physiological responses played out in her posture and on her face as I brought the song around into its final chorus.

The bar went wild when I finished. I waited for a moment then broke eye contact with Annie, looking around the room. What I felt was hard to explain. Something about the enclosed space, the press of warm bodies, the glasses of fermented fruits and brewed grains and distilled starches had given the music more power and even I felt the rush of it in my body. This was nothing like a street corner or park.

Sergio waited for the applause to die down but it grew.

This is the opposite of laying low, Carmichael said.

"Encore," someone shouted. I looked out and it was Cecilia, grinning up at me. Claude stood beside her and shouted the same.

Others picked up the word and it became a chant.

Sergio stepped back and leaned close to me. "This never happens, mate. Got one more in you?"

I nodded.

"One more!" Sergio shouted to the room and my fingers took off, my voice jumping in after.

When I wrapped that there was more applause and a dark-skinned woman approached Sergio. "Give him my set, Serge." she said. Then she winked at me and slipped back into the crowd.

"You heard her," he said.

And that's how it went that first night. We were free-falling through Darlington County with Penny Lane in our ears and in our eyes and in the early morning rain, guessing we'd rather be in Colorado. Turn, turn, turn.

I found myself moving to the music I made, moving with the humans in the room, and I realized suddenly, mid-strum, that I was experiencing a profound sense of community. A room full of people far from home brought together by melody and poetry.

I lost track of time but finally, the ache in my fingers and rasp in my voice settled in. "Last song," I said into the microphone.

I looked around the room and found Claude. "Get up here, Claude." He blushed and shook his head but Cecilia laughed and pushed him. Then she smiled at me.

I smiled back and then knew what song I needed to sing. I flipped my guitar and started banging out a rhythm on it with my hands. I countered each slap with a stomp and Claude began clapping in time. I met Cecilia's eyes and her smile widened as she recognized the song. Then she was clapping and stomping too. Gradually, the rest of the room joined her and when that pulse reached its inescapable crescendo I shifted into the chords and leaned into the microphone as Claude's harmonica wailed.

"Cecilia," I sang, "you're breaking my heart," and then let the music sweep us all into ecstatic connection.

And then, on the last note and the last chord, Carmichael sparked and I felt it shoot through my body and out through my feet.

We have to go.

But—

WE HAVE TO GO.

That's when I noticed the blue uniform in the door talking into her radio. Carmichael's urgency finally registered and I yanked the chord from him as reached for his case. They were still clapping, whistling, chanting but I pushed everything out of my mind.

What happened?

We've been pinged. We have to get out of here now.

Claude was beside me and Cecilia was near. "What are you doing?"

"I'm sorry, Claude. I have to go. Right now."

Now the look on his face was new to me, but it was clearly less pleasant than the other expressions. "But you can't. We just—"

"I'm sorry," I said. Then I pushed past him and Cecilia and Sergio and through the others as I went looking for the back door.

I thought this planet was bagged? How can we possibly get pinged?

Carmichael didn't answer.

I looked over my shoulder and saw that two men in suits had joined the blue uniform. They picked their way through the packed room. I found the back door and went through it into the alley, moving into an awkward run with Carmichael clutched in both hands.

"Dylan!" It was Annie.

I stopped. "I'm sorry, Annie. I really have to go."

"No," she said. "I'm sorry. I was just being a bitch earlier. I don't like American boys so much." She paused. "Thank you for the song."

"You're welcome," I said and then got back to running. Until a new voice stopped me in my tracks again. This one from inside my head.

You should save us both some pointless effort and just stop right now. It wasn't Carmichael.

Now. Slowly put down the guitar and turn around with your hands up.

This wasn't my first Carlucci milking toad rodeo. I did what I was told.

An older male human in a long gray coat stood there. He was the last thing I saw before a bright blue flash spun the world away and turned out all the lights.

Okay. You can wake up now.

I forced my eyes open and blinked into bright sunlight pouring through a window.

I sat in a chair in front of a desk that the older male sat behind. Carmichael lay in his open case, upright in the chair beside me.

The man cleared his voice. "First," he said, "I'd like to welcome you to Earth. You seem to have made quite a splash." He looked at me for a minute then glanced at his desk.

I wasn't sure what else to say so I aimed for gratitude. "Thank you." I glanced at the guitar next to me. *Carmichael, what's going on?*

The man smiled and blinked. *Your ship is in stasis.*

I stared. *How is it that you have the technology for direct cortical communication?*

He chuckled. "I'm not from around here." He looked at the papers again. "We've extricated your vessel's system core from the instrument it was concealed in and placed it in quarantine."

"Do you have antivirals to upload so—"

The man raised his hand. "No more questions, Dylan."

"My name's not Dylan. It's—"

"I don't want to know your name." He leaned forward. "I don't want you to speak. I just want you to listen."

I listened.

"As you no doubt realize, Earth is a bagged world. Your presence here violates no less than two dozen Division of Developing Planet laws." He paused, letting the words soak in. "Obviously you are not alone here. There are actually quite a few of us living on Earth quietly. Some came for science. Some have fetishes for backward living and less developed species. Others are in hiding. You're the first shipwreck in a while but it's happened before."

I opened my mouth to speak again and he raised his hand again. I closed my mouth.

"We thought we picked up a technological anomaly when you crashed but it was plugging your vessel into the power grid that really gave you away. Unfortunately, by doing so, you've infected the human power grid, and I've had operatives working all night to smooth that over." He rubbed his temples. "So you are starting out at deficit with me, I'm afraid."

"What does that mean?"

The question didn't seem to annoy him. "It means you owe me. A lot."

"If I can get off this rock, I'm certain I can—"

He shook his head slowly. "I'm afraid leaving with that debt unsettled will not be possible. As you can imagine, none of us here are interested in bringing down the Imperial Division on our heads. I can certainly arrange for your quiet departure but you'd also need to have your time here expunged. Memory alteration and transport alone are hefty sums."

I did the math and wondered just how many bits of metal and paper it would take to get out of here. "And my ship?"

"Your ship, too, of course. But also for a price."

I doubled the math. "That's . . . a lot."

He nodded. "But still cheaper than what happens if you're caught here."

"What are my other options?"

"Well," he said, "I can euthanize you today. I'd have to eat your current debt but you'd not incur any other. And my problem is effectively solved. Dead men, as they say, tell no tales."

Now it was my turn to nod. "Less appealing to me, actually," I said.

"Yes." He studied me. "Or," he said.

"Or?"

"Or you go ex-pat like the rest of us. Make a life for yourself here."

"What about Carmichael?" He looked at me blankly and I elaborated. "My ship."

"In stasis until you leave. That stunt at the Red Door left you pingable in a twenty light year radius. We can't risk another incident like that. So if you decide to stay, we'll wipe the core and dispose of it."

"And I'll be compensated for the cost of my ship?"

Now he laughed. "No. You'll be billed for the disposal."

I sighed. "Can I have some time to think about it?"

He shrugged and stood.

"And can I talk to my ship?"

I could tell that he wanted to say no. And his face had all the signs of exasperation squeezed into it. "Five minutes," he said. Then he left the room.

I felt the hum in my skull when Carmichael woke up. *I told you not to plug me into that primitive electrical device.*

I looked around but had no idea where exactly they'd stored Carmichael's core. *Do you know what's going on?*

Yeah. I've been told.

So what do you think?

Carmichael was faster at the math than I was. *I think earnings based on a single twenty-four hour planetary rotation indicate that it will take four hundred and eleven cycles around the system's sun to raise the funds necessary to extricate us from this predicament.*

That, I said, *is a long time.*

And I don't think euthanization suits you.

I sighed. *Agreed. Or you, for that matter.*

Sorry I gakked that schooner.

I reached out by habit and patted the guitar even though he wasn't there. *I know. I'm sorry I yelled at you about it. I do think the survival skills are working out.*

You did, as they say, rock the house.

I'm not sure why I said it or why I said it the way that I did. But it came out: "Thank you. Thank you very much."

Carmichael laughed. It was going to be a long time before I heard that laugh again—if ever—and I savored it. We'd spent most of a decade stomping around the stars together and I would miss him. *I'll be back soon, Carmichael.*

Rock on, Dylan McLean.

I waited until the hum left my skull.

Okay then, I finally said. "I'm ready."

The door opened and the man came back in. Now he had an envelope with him. "So?"

"It looks like it might take some time to raise the funds. Long enough to see the sights, it seems."

"And then some."

"And I can keep the guitar?"

"Of course. It's harmless without the core."

Remembering the faces, the clapping, the chanting as I played, I wasn't so sure I agreed with him.

I decided to go out on what you call a limb. "And can I visit my ship from time to time?"

The man scowled. "Maybe in a decade or so. I don't want to see you around Paris for a goodly while, Mr. *McLean.*" Our eyes met briefly before he continued, "Speaking of which, I've taken the liberty of establishing the background and necessary documents for one Dylan McLean." He handed me the envelope. "There is an American passport in there. I hope you'll use it. Today, even. I've also included account information for the payment of your debt and an emergency contact number that I sincerely hope you will not use." He paused. "We'll let you know when you've accrued enough credit with us for a visit with your ship."

"Understood," I told him.

This time, I extended my hand. He shook it.

Then the blue light flashed and I was gone again.

"Hey there," a voice said and I opened my eyes. It was Claude. "Where did you go?"

I was sitting on a bench not too far from where I'd met him. I could see the Red Door down the street. It was late morning now. I wasn't sure what to tell him. "I remembered an appointment I was late for."

His face beamed. "It was quite a show. They were talking about it all night." He dug a communication device from his pocket. "I'll tell Cecilia I found you. I'm running late."

The mention of her name increased my heart rate and made my stomach feel odd.

He took off his backpack and opened it, digging around. "They always take up a collection after the show and then divide it among the musicians. I think your attire convinced them you were down on your luck and they all insisted that you receive the full amount."

It was my day to collect envelopes. This one was thick with bright colored bills and he pushed it into my hands. "It's a lot," he added looking around. "Keep it safe."

Not nearly enough, I thought and felt a twinge of sadness that Carmichael couldn't hear me. "Thank you."

He nodded toward the bar. "And Sergio wants you back."

"I may be leaving town soon."

His face brightened and that surprised me. "We are, too. Cecilia will tell you all about it." Then he kissed each of my cheeks and rushed off.

I pulled out Carmichael—the name stuck—and started picking at the strings. It wouldn't be the same without his voice in my head but he had fashioned himself into a fine instrument and my hands knew just what to do with it.

"I'm just a poor wayfaring stranger," I sang to passersby who paused to listen, "a-traveling through this world of woe."

When Cecilia arrived she hung back until I finished, then set her own guitar case down beside mine and joined me on the bench.

"So my brother found you?"

"Claude is your brother?"

"Well, half-brother. Same Mom. She's French. But I grew up with my father in Oregon. I busked my way over here to meet him a few years back and decided to stay."

I looked around. "Not a bad place."

"What about you?" Her eyes were dangerously blue and I wanted to fall into them.

"What about me?"

"Where are you from?"

I remembered the other envelope and pulled it from the guitar case where I'd tucked it away. I opened it. "I'm from . . . California, it seems."

She sniffed. "That explains the outfit."

I laughed and looked at the other envelope filled with money. "I suppose I should take care of that."

"And then what? Claude texted and told me you're leaving town."

"Yes. Someplace warmer."

"We've been saving up for South America. We're getting close."

"Argentina," I said, "is quite nice, I hear."

She grinned. "I've heard that, too." Then she looked at me. "But meanwhile."

"Meanwhile," I answered.

"Wanna play with me?" She bent down to open her guitar case.

I did. Very badly. And so for the next two hours we crooned about the giant steps we took walking on the moon, losing our religion as we went under the dancing spell cast our way in a big top world behind green eyes. And when we finished, we stood and bowed to the gathering crowd.

"That," she said, "was a lot of fun."

It was. And more than fun, that feeling from the bar had followed us here, and I felt the spark of ecstatic connection, the roots of belonging.

Maybe, I realized, shipwrecks weren't so bad. I would take what Carmichael had given me to survive and I would learn how to thrive. I'd see Buenos Aires and every other place on this rock. I'd eat the foods and drink drinks and sing the songs. And maybe I would travel with Cecilia and her brother for awhile. And maybe later I would travel alone.

I'd make the money I could. And maybe I'd find a way to square my debt with the secret, hidden ex-pats in this place. Or maybe I would stay.

Maybe I would even start to write my own songs, like Cecilia did—or maybe even write some with her—and sing them in front of hundreds, or thousands, or maybe even millions. And maybe then, I'd tell my story—the whole story—about how I came to this backwoods rock and found joy and purpose bigger than I'd known as a space jockey. And maybe that song would be part of their preparation for the great unbagging that lay ahead of humanity on the trail.

I knew what I would call my song when I wrote it, and I whispered the title aloud as I smiled at my new friend here. "Stuck in Buenos Aires," I said, "with Bob Dylan on my mind."

"Is that a song?" she asked.

"Not yet," I said. "But it will be."

Then we packed up our guitars and set out for the next park or corner to conquer with our songs.

Any aliens hoping to conquer the Earth would do well to first figure out who the planet's true masters are—and it's not the Humans.   —RWB

Rule The World

by Jody Lynn Nye

The talk show host behind the burlwood desk, a suave, besuited man in his forties, smiled toothily at the huge, dolly-mounted camera and the studio audience just barely visible in the dark beyond the footlights. He swept a hand to his right.

"And we have with us tonight a couple of the little green guys whose flying saucer landed in the middle of Central Park two weeks ago and changed the world! I want all of you to welcome Monl and Ophl!"

The camera panned left and followed a couple of small figures as they came out from behind the curtain. No more than two feet tall, the upright bipeds had green skin covered with light, short fur that looked very soft; round heads with a bright blue curl of hair on top; and huge, hazel-green eyes with large pupils that scanned the audience with open curiosity. From their necks to their tiny, round feet, they wore skin-hugging outfits of a shiny golden fabric that caught glints from the studio lights. At first glance, they might have been mistaken for Muppets or marionettes, but no strings or puppeteers accompanied them, and their movements didn't look robotic. Some of the viewers gasped and tried to jump out of their seats, but most of the others applauded wildly. The little green beings hopped up on the blue-carpeted riser and stopped to survey the audience with a kind of outraged astonishment. When the frenzied clapping and cheering died down (encouraged by the extinguishing of the APPLAUSE sign to the right of the stage), the two small creatures trotted the rest of the way to the padded chairs beside the desk. The seats looked too high for them to reach, but they gathered themselves and sprang effortlessly up onto the cushions. A sigh arose from the area beyond the footlights, as though the watchers had been holding their breath, waiting to see what would happen.

"Monl and Ophl!" the host boomed, clapping his own hands together.

"That's Ospl, Edgar," the second small being said, in a voice that was high-pitched but resonant, like the song of a viola. "Not Ophl."

"Sorry, Ospl. Is that short for anything like, 'I had better ospl-ain it to you?'" Edgar wiggled his bushy eyebrows at the camera. A big orange sign at the side of the stage that said LAUGHTER went on. Obediently, the audience laughed.

"No."

The sign flashed again, but the viewers didn't need the encouragement to chuckle. The creatures on the stage were so *cute*.

"So, gentle . . . beings—can't really call you men, can I? That would be sexist. Besides, you're not men. Are you?"

"No."

The terse answer didn't leave the host much to go on. He glanced down at the big pink card in his left hand.

". . . So, Monl, as if I didn't know, what brings you to New York?"

"Well, Edgar," humans liked it when you started a sentence with 'well,' "we are here to become your new masters."

The studio audience applauded appreciatively.

"A lot of people say that," Edgar replied, leaning toward them attentively. He prided himself on asking the hard questions. "Producers, politicians, the inventors with the next big thing, movie stars, politicians. How can two little guys from way out in the cosmos bring the whole of planet Earth under their control?"

"But we are already doing it," Ophl stated, his huge hazel eyes open wide. The camera moved nearer to the little alien as if irresistibly drawn to him. Across the nation and the countries that were receiving the broadcast via satellite and Internet, people moved closer to their televisions and computer monitors, their gaze fixed on the alien being. "We have the future in our hands. Our energy is nonpolluting. Our entertainment systems go directly to the prefrontal cortex of your primitive brain systems. Our ways of producing food ensure that adequate nutrition will be available to all. We will rule you benevolently."

"Well, that all sounds nice," Edgar said, "but our nations have free will. Why would they submit to alien overlords? I ask in a rhetorical way, of course."

"But they all wish to. They want what we have to offer. Before we arrived here, your world was in turmoil. Nine small wars had broken out and were killing thousands of your species. We put an end to them."

"And how did you do that?" Edgar asked, although he and everyone else watching already knew.

Monl regarded him with huge eyes in an expression so adorable that the audience sighed. "Our superior technology caused your weapons of war to cease functioning. We approached both sides of every conflict and brought them together by virtue of our overwhelming charisma. When we sat among them, they wished so deeply to please us that they agreed on terms of peace. As a result, we have heeded the call from billions of humans to lead you into a future of prosperity. Your governments have already agreed to meet with us and offer us their allegiance, tomorrow in your New York's Central Park. You will be there, Edgar."

"That's what I've heard," Edgar said, glancing at the camera with the skeptical expression that had become his trademark in his twenty years in the host's chair. The audience tittered. "I just do what my producers tell me to. The question on everyone's mind, naturally, is *why Earth?* Why out of the entire cosmos would you come here and offer us so much help?"

"Well, Edgar," said Monl, again noting the approval, or at least the indulgence of all the people present, "you are on our space route in between the center of the galaxy and our outposts at the end of what you refer to as Mutter's Spiral."

"I'm sure you don't use that terminology among yourselves." Edgar was a man who prided himself on his research.

"You would not recognize our terms as words," Monl replied. The mood of the room seemed to challenge him, so Monl stretched out his left manipulation digit. He reached over and tapped at the dark blue water vessel left on the edge of the wooden table. It moved a centimeter. The room seemed to hold its breath. He tapped at it again, then again. It shifted a few millimeters at a time. Then, after a television eternity, it tipped over the edge and plummeted to the floor. He watched it closely as it fell.

CRASH!

The cup shattered into three pieces, and the water spread out across the black-painted panels. The audience broke into spontaneous applause. Monl lifted his large, round eyes to them with an air of bemusement that seemed to spur them into greater acclaim, well-larded with affectionate laughter.

A stagehand in black t-shirt and blue jeans ran in with a wadded handful of white paper to soak up the water. He kept his body low to the ground so it would not obstruct the visitors from view.

"Then, explain it to me, Monl," Edgar said. "How do you plan to conquer us?" He glanced at the camera with an eye full of humor, sharing the joke with the folks back home.

"We have been observing you for some millennia," Ospl said. "You possess intelligence, but lack fundamental wisdom. The transmissions that have been beamed from this world depict great errors in judgment that would be easily be manipulated by intelligent and charismatic beings such as ourselves."

"Oh, you haven't been watching our sitcoms, have you?" Edgar asked, wryly.

"And your movies. And your computer signals. We have taken our cues on behavior from a species from whom humans accept outrageous behavior." Ospl rose in his chair, turned around, and bent over, giving the camera and the folks back home an unobstructed view of his shiny-covered rear end. The studio audience roared. "You will worship us."

In the Green Room, fifty yards from the rear door of the studio, Nougatine's Silver Napoleon Bonaparte paced angrily back and forth before the enormous television monitor, lashing his fluffy gray tail.

"They are cats," he hissed. "I hate them."

"Oh, don't be grumpy," Corin said, looking down fondly into the cat's brilliant green eyes.

"I am not Grumpy," Napoleon retorted, glaring, his green eyes bright in his foxlike face. "We have more followers than she does."

"I hate them, too," Rispar's Galaxy Katherine Hepburn agreed, from the makeup table. She flicked her own bouffant white tail in annoyance and waved a paw to stop the brush that had been smoothing down the luxurious fur on her long, slim body.

"What's with them?" Corin McElroy said, picking Napoleon up under his front legs and curling him into the crook of his elbow. The male chinchilla Persian cat pushed at his chest with his paws, trying to get down to resume his vigil in front of the screen. Corin buried his hands deeper into Napoleon's plush, black-ticked silver fur to hold onto him. "You're the psychic, not me."

"They don't like the Visitors," Niniane McElroy said. Her fair good looks complemented Katherine's pale fluffiness. "I just don't get it. The aliens are so cute! I'm grateful for everything they've done. They've been so good to us all. How can anyone dislike them?" She put out a slim hand to stroke the female chinchilla Persian, and drew it back on contact. "Ow! Static."

"It's not that dry in here," Corin said. One of his thin dark brows went up. "Or do you mean the other kind."

"The other kind," Niniane said. She gathered up the white female cat, who emitted one mew of protest, and laid a gentle hand across the cat's forehead. Dealing with fussy felines was difficult on a normal day. Caring for cats that had been genetically enhanced to have intelligence and mental sensitivity equal to or greater than humans was even more so. Worse yet, the scientists of the US Feline Enhancement Laboratory hadn't yet licked the interspecies communications aspect, so it was up to sensitives like Niniane to bridge the gap between cats and humans. Understanding them was by no means as straightforward as picking up a telephone; more like reading texts written on a skein of flying geese in spray paint by someone whose first language wasn't English. They were great little receiver stations, though. Any time Corin even thought of giving them a flea-bath, the cats would vanish somewhere in the house and not come out until he gave up the idea. And they instantly knew when someone disliked them. Niniane's aunt was a dedicated dog person who thought cats were evil; Napoleon and Katherine couldn't leave her alone when she visited.

In order for the US-FEL to keep attracting funding for the NSA program, the cats had to stay in the public eye. That had not been difficult. The Psychic Cats had millions of hits and likes a day across all forms of social media. They were the most popular Internet sensation in the world. Talk show hosts like Edgar just loved having them on because their appearances shot his show's ratings through the roof. The real problem was that the McElroys had no guarantee that the cats would behave themselves on any given day. They were, after all, cats. "There's something about those little green people she doesn't like." Niniane dandled Katherine in her arms. "Come on, honey! Why don't you love them?"

Corin stared at the monitor. Ospl, whom he had seen on numerous news programs, had his big eyes fixed on the camera, as if he was staring directly at them. He had been seeing the images for weeks, since the little green men had landed on the lawn of the UN. The pictures and videos had gone absolutely viral. Corin even had a screen saver of Monl on his computer.

"I don't know what. I like them," Corin said, staring at the monitor as if his eyeballs were glued to it. "They're really cute. Whatever I expected from extraterrestrials, it wasn't cute little guys. At first I thought they were a little creepy, but there's something appealing about them. They're menacing, but sort of playful. I'm glad the government is talking with them instead of, you know, locking them up and analyzing them. And they're doing fantastic things for Earth! It's so cool that the first alien visitors are such great creatures. Everyone likes them."

"Me, too," Niniane said, a little ashamed of herself. Their funky little mannerisms were so watchable. The Cheezburger Network had even devoted a new channel to Alien Gifs. She found herself clicking on clip after clip, in between cat pictures, of course.

"Cats," hissed Katherine.

"Who are cats?" Niniane asked, silently putting the question to her small friend. She followed Katherine's gaze to the television monitor. "They are? The Visitors are cats?"

"Yessss!"

"And what does that make us?"

Katherine's huge eyes, as green as the aliens' fur, opened wide.

"Prey."

"And this is why we have assumed these shapes," Ospl concluded, just as the red light went on in front of the camera. "Your gravity is twenty percent harsher than our homeworld. In our ships, we stand one hecton high, the same as the average Earth denizen. Once we debark on the surface of your world, we shrink to a third of a hecton, and our muscles condense, giving us superior flexibility and strength.

Our eyes, being solid spheres, remain the same size. They are large and luminous, which your species finds attractive. Our superior intelligence means that we will be able to lead humankind as we wish."

"But you intend to be benevolent rulers, don't you?" the host asked, nodding encouragingly.

"As far as you know," Monl said.

"Let's give them a big hand, everybody!" Edgar said, putting his hands together. The rest of the audience applauded with enthusiasm. "Monl and Ospl! Now, we have to have a word from our sponsors. When we return, the Psychic Cats!"

During the station break, the stage hands moved in to rearrange the set for the cats' act. They had to make their way through the cordon of black-suited secret service agents protecting the two aliens who were backstage within a fast jump of the guest chairs. The US, Chinese, EU, and Russian governments were taking no chances.

Trying to ignore their baleful glares, Corin made sure all the equipment was in place: a series of platforms one jump apart, ropes, string, squeaky mice, plus various pieces of technological equipment. Though Napoleon and Katherine were both capable of operating the paw-friendly touchscreen, he had the four-button keyboard in place on the biggest platform. An overseer from the National Science Foundation, one of whom was always present at the cats' public appearances, was a besuited young tawny-skinned woman with natural hair in a very short businesslike cut, and a dozen technological gizmos in the pockets of her very well-cut silk blazer. Salome Kent, whose specialty was comparative biology, had been on the project for the last four years. She deplored show business, but she cared deeply about the cats. Even when her expression was grim with disapproval, Niniane could read her real feelings. She was a softy, and she always had her eyes open for an opportunity to glean support for the project. Salome stayed in the wings, out of sight of the audience.

When the lights came up, the cameras followed Edgar from his desk to their side. The two aliens remained in their chairs. Niniane was relieved. Napoleon kept hissing in their direction.

"And what are we doing today?" Edgar asked. He stroked Katherine, who rolled on her back to get him to pet her throat. She liked Edgar. Niniane felt her own pleasure centers go on high tingle.

"We'll start with something you'll like," Corin said, pointing to the screen. "They've been starting simple programming. This new one creates a fractal based on your favorite color and any number between one and ten. Think about those."

"Now, remember," the host cautioned the audience, "these cats have been tested under rigorous laboratory conditions for extreme cuteness." The viewers giggled.

Edgar screwed up his face in mock contemplation. Napoleon growled at him.

"He said that's not a real color," Niniane said.

The host pretended to be shocked.

"What's the matter, you can't make it work with 'plaid?'" he asked. "But that's my favorite!"

"Or pi," Niniane said, sweetly. "A whole number, please." The host grinned at her. He liked to wind up the cats. Tomorrow there would be at least one new meme posted with Edgar as a playful idiot.

"Okay." Edgar put his fingers in his ears and squeezed his eyes shut. This time Niniane sensed him emitting a straightforward thought. Napoleon let out a pleased chirp and touched his right paw to the buttons three times.

On the screen, a purple triangle appeared, then the mathematical formula started to create a pattern that twisted in on itself, creating infinite whorls within whorls. Katherine reached around to bat at the moving lines. Edgar opened his eyes.

"Were you thinking 'purple three'?" Niniane asked.

"Yes! That's awesome!" The audience burst into not-so-spontaneous applause, but it was genuine. "Science is the wave of the future, friends!" He stood off to one side as Corin lined up the next stunt.

The cats were on excellent behavior throughout the rest of the demonstration, showing the range of their enhanced intelligence, plus one more mind-reading trick, with one cat telling the other how many fingers an audience member was holding up. It was showier than the hard science that the cats had been studying.

"That was fantastic!" Edgar said, clapping. "Come and sit down with me!"

Niniane was thrilled. She could hardly wait to get to the seats and meet the Visitors. She couldn't pick up any mental emanations from them, or at least that she could recognize as brainwaves. However, she couldn't miss the waves of fear and discomfort rolling from the cats.

"No!" Katherine protested, cowering behind her keyboard. "The enemy is there!"

Behind him, Salome Kent gestured furiously to take the cats to the desk. With a shrug, Corin picked one up under each arm and crossed the stage in Edgar's wake. When he was within a few feet of the staring aliens, both cats began to struggle and kick. They dug into his belly with their back feet, claws out.

"Ow! What's the matter with them?" Corin asked, trying to hold onto them while still keeping a toothy smile on his face.

"They really, really don't want to be near the Visitors," Niniane said.

"Tell them to knock it off! We're on national television! Come on, guys," Corin pleaded, glancing at the aliens. "You'll like them. They're adorable!"

"Sorry," whispered Niniane to the host. "They're being weird."

"We are not being weird!" Katherine protested. She understood far more human speech than Napoleon did.

"No problem," Edgar murmured back, still with a big grin on his face. "Instead, I have a great idea, folks!" he announced. "Tomorrow's the big rally in Central Park to sign the Interplanetary Peace Treaty and welcome the Visitors, Monl and Ophl, to the rest of Earth!"

"Ospl," Ospl said, aiming a huge-eyed expression of disappointment at the host. The audience laughed.

"Well, what could get better ratings—I mean, do more for world peace and understanding, than to have our newest discovery showcased alongside our newest galactic friends?" Edgar said, gesturing with his hands to whip up the audience's approval. "Let's invite the Psychic Cats to appear on the stage with the Visitors! We want to show them that everybody loves our new masters. What do you think, folks?"

In the wings, Niniane saw Salome Kent approach the secret service agents. They conferred, then the lead agent, a big, dark-skinned man with graying temples, spoke into his shirt cuff. After a few moments, he nodded his head. Salome gave Niniane both thumbs up. The agents remained stone-faced, but Niniane could tell they were huge Psychic Cat fans, too.

"We'd be delighted," Niniane said, so excited she could hardly get the words out.

The humans could not wait until they got out of the studio.

"We're going to be onstage in Central Park with the Visitors!" Corin crowed, wheeling the cats' carriers out on a dolly to their waiting taxi.

"We are so lucky," Niniane said, feeling his delight adding to hers. "The visibility this will give to our program could be worth millions! Maybe more. Maybe the aliens have some technology that can help enhance the cats' intelligence even further."

For their part, the cats berated them all the way back to their hotel on East 47th Street.

"You are so stupid," Katherine said, scornfully. "They want to play with you and eat you."

The excitement made Niniane and Corin sit up all night in front of the computer, figuring out a program that would showcase Napoleon and Katherine for a worldwide audience. Viewers from different countries found different things about them appealing. The cats curled up in their cushy, velour-lined travel beds and wouldn't speak to them again. Niniane tried to listen to them psychically, but they shut her out. By morning, they were groggy, but confident that they had the best possible show set up to tie the cats' existence irrevocably with the advent of the Visitors.

About six in the morning, Corin pushed back from the computer. "You don't think it's strange that the government is going to sign over power to the aliens, do you?"

Niniane frowned. She could feel the tingle of delight overpowering the usual skeptical outlook that usually permeated New York City.

"No, I don't," she said. "It's the 21st century. Maybe it's time that we had a planet-wide government. Since every country on Earth would want to be the one that leads, maybe it's better if we're united under an outside power, one that knows all about the other species in the universe. They already know how to make peace here on Earth. We need to trust them."

When the time came to leave, Katherine hung onto the travel bed and yowled when Corin tried to pick her up.

"We are not going!" she said.

"You bet you're going," Corin said. "You have to do what we say."

"How will you like that when the green ones say that to you?" the cat asked. Niniane automatically translated.

Corin met Niniane's eyes. "Do you think she's really onto something?" he asked.

"I don't know," Niniane said, feeling the worry radiating from both cats. "I can't read the aliens. How do they know that they *don't* have our best interests in mind?"

"We will prove it to you," Napoleon said.

The rally to celebrate the Signing of the Interplanetary Peace Treaty had attracted over two million people to Central Park. If it hadn't been for the secret service, a police escort and a lot of sharp elbows, Niniane, Corin and the cats in their mesh-sided wheeled carriers would never have made it to within a mile of the stage. Niniane soaked up the thrill of excitement and pleasure from even cynical New Yorkers that they were present to witness history being made. Even the pickpockets working the crowd kept glancing over toward the high dais that had been erected in front of Belvedere Castle. The small edifice was overpowered by the shining silver Frisbee that perched upon its four turrets.

"Get your Space Invaders T-shirt!" a vendor shouted. He turned to wave a big green shirt at the secret service agents. The picture showed Monl and Ospl standing on top of a globe of the world surrounded by flags of all the nations. "They love us, baby!"

He was among dozens of other entrepreneurs walking around the grassy parkland who had merchandise for sale with the images of the two cute little aliens. Niniane wanted to stop and shop, but there wasn't time yet.

Every news service in the world had sent reporters and cameras. Vans from CNN, Fox, MSNBC, the BBC, RAI, Japanese, Chinese, and Korean television, plus citizen journalists from kids with smartphones aimed at the screen up to teams of eager young people with sophisticated technical gear ready to share the whole event on the internet as it happened. Hundreds of Katherine's and Napoleon's fans were on hand, the most demonstrative of them small children, older women, and gay men. They crowded around the carriers to pet the cats and coo at them.

"Hey, it's the Psychic Cats!" a young woman with a microphone exclaimed, as they passed by. She stuck the gray cube in front of Niniane. "Is it true the cats are going to welcome the Visitors? Do they have any comments for us fans?"

"Yessss," Katherine said, switching her tail. "And greetings to Delilah in the White House. I rub my cheek at her."

Since her words came out as mixed meows and trills, Niniane relayed the information, grateful that neither cat went into detail about their feelings for the aliens. She was uncomfortably aware of their growing tension.

"Why does no one see what I see?" Napoleon asked, in a plaintive mew.

The crowd suddenly roared with delight. On the stage and rebroadcast on big flatscreens all over the park, the two aliens sprang out from the curtain that served as a backstage. They were chasing a big pink balloon, batting it between them. Ospl leaped high in the air to snatch at the dangling string, dragging it down where Monl could leap upon it. He rolled end over end with the pink bubble, his shiny suit catching the sun. Ospl gathered himself and bounded after his companion. He grabbed for the string and pulled the balloon out of Monl's grasp and ran off to the other side of the stage with it. Monl ran after him and batted it out of his hands. The balloon flew upward. Both of them scrambled to catch it, but it was out of reach. They sat down on the stage, their posture dejected but their facial expressions unchanged from their usual stare.

"We love you!" a woman in the audience screamed. "Squeeeee!"

Both aliens turned to gaze at her as if astonished to discover anyone had been watching them. She and the hundred thousand people around her shrieked with delight. The aliens deliberately turned their backs and walked away, ignoring all pleas to return. For newcomers to the planet, they were amazingly media-savvy.

"Oh, my God, they *are* cats," Corin said. "Unidentified Feline Overlords!"

"Hey, man, can I put that on a button?" a heavyset man nearby asked.

"Sure," Corin said, with a self-deprecating grin toward Niniane. The man started thumb-typing on his cell phone. Niniane could guess at the mass of Facebooking and Tweeting that was going on.

They made it to the backstage area, where Salome Kent was waiting. She hustled them to one side and knelt down to pet the cats. That left the McElroys free to watch the aliens. On the other side of the stage, Niniane recognized major dignitaries, including the president himself, the Chinese premier, the pope, the British prime minister, and the Sultan of Brunei. They also were enraptured by the playful yet graceful movements of the aliens. Niniane felt the overwhelming urge to rush out and cuddle Monl and Ospl, but she didn't dare.

We're here as guests, she reminded herself sternly. *We are here to witness history, not make it.*

Edgar, wearing a tuxedo, emerged from the midst of the crowd, waving energetically. As he mounted the stage, a host of young men and women in black t-shirts and jeans pulled a long table and a group of very elegant-looking armchairs into the middle. The politicians filed in and sat down at the places that had been designated for them, leaving two small, long-legged chairs at the left end for the aliens. A dignified man in a morning suit brought out a stack of leatherbound folders and a box of pens, undoubtedly the treaty. Niniane wondered if she might be able to ask for one of the pens as a souvenir. But it would probably end up under the couch like all their other pens. Reporters sat on the floor next to the table, recording devices at the ready.

"Welcome to everyone!" Edgar shouted. "Let's get this party started!"

A dozen marching bands from all over the world struck up their own medley of slightly off-key greatest hits.

Under cover of the noise, the sunglass-wearing secret service agents tried to round up the two aliens, who were wandering around the edge of the stage, keeping just out of reach of their adoring public. They regarded the agents with distaste, but followed them back to the table. When they hopped up into their little chairs, Ospl rubbed his cheek against the leather folders, and was rewarded with a smile from the usually dour president of France. Niniane wasn't fooled. He was a sensitive, too, but she would rather have died than outed him. He was beguiled by the little creatures.

"These are the treaties?" Monl asked. "With the wording exactly as we have demanded?"

"Exactly as you wished it to be written," the Russian president said. "We have approved all phrases."

"Good," Monl said. He batted at the stack of treaties, knocking them out of alignment. The dignitaries watched him with indulgent eyes.

"Now, you know why we're all here," Edgar said. "We want to honor our new friends from outer space! Monl and Ospl! They've agreed to act as our protectors against other species that might hurt humankind, and they'll be doing that as our new leaders!" The crowd screamed its approval. "But before we get to the main event, we have a number of special guests who want to help welcome Monl and Ospl. Let's give them a big hand!"

Singers, musicians, poets, and speakers came on one at a time and performed a short piece, most of which had been written for the occasion. One poet, a small Englishwoman with graying hair, concluded a long verse full of archaic words with the admonition, "Don't screw it up the way Britain did, lads. Lead us into the future, where we can go out among the stars!"

The crowd's mood was so high Niniane felt as though she was body surfing over it. When a stagehand came over to whisper that they were next, she could feel the eyes of the entire world—and beyond—fixed on her.

She clutched Corin's hand. "I'm nervous!"

"It'll be fine," he said. "The cats have done this a million times."

"Tell them," Katherine pleaded, brushing her side against the mesh of her cage. "Tell them the truth!"

"I can't say anything like that," Niniane said, apologetically. "We're only sharing this stage out of courtesy."

"What's the matter?" Salome asked.

Niniane threw a helpless hand toward the cages. "She says they're evil. They want to eat us."

"Oh, that can't be right!" the young woman said, with a wry grin. "They're here to help. Look what they've done for us so far!"

"My friends, the Psychic Cats!" Edgar said, as they wheeled the carriers out of the wings.

The yells and applause were almost as loud for them as they had been for the little green men themselves. Niniane knew her face was pink as she opened the cages.

"Now, behave," she implored them.

Two thunderbolts, one gray and one white, streaked past her legs. Instead of mounting the apparatus that Corin had set up for them, they leaped onto the table in front of the aliens.

"Hisssssssss!" Napoleon said, his back arched.

"Evil!" Katherine warbled, raising the feline war cry that would have had every cat watching fluff up in alarm. It certainly alarmed the humans at the table. The aliens merely stared.

"What's the matter?" Edgar asked, raising a wiry eyebrow. "Is this part of the act?"

"No," Niniane said, trying to grab Katherine. The white cat danced away. The woman had to fumble her way in between all the reporters on the floor, but the cat kept out of her reach.

Napoleon ran straight at Monl and smacked him in the face with his paw.

"I say," said the British prime minister, taken aback. "Don't do that."

Napoleon listened to the British as little as his namesake had done hundreds of years before. He struck Monl's face with the other paw.

"I'm so sorry," Niniane said, embarrassed. "He's only a cat."

"Go away!" Napoleon growled.

"This is our world now," Monl said to Napoleon, his big eyes expressionless. "Not yours!"

"It is mine! You go away from here! These people are ours!"

Niniane was puzzled as to the interplay, since she could hear only one side of the argument. "No, really, I'll get him out of there." She leaned over the table and grabbed for the male cat.

"Mine! All mine!" Napoleon rose onto his hind feet and batted at the two aliens. Ospl raised both hands and struck back, until he and the cat were engaged in what looked like a feline slap fight. In his mind, Napoleon was deadly serious. He wasn't playing. And for the first time, Niniane felt a sensation from the aliens.

They were angry. Cold fury poured from them, overpowering her senses. Humans were possessions, to do with as they pleased. They did not like to be challenged.

The sensation landed in her mind like a physical blow. How could the cute little aliens have kept that powerful a thought hidden? All that time, she, like billions of people worldwide, had assumed that the aliens were fun-loving, audacious little creatures. They were cold, vicious predators—just like the cats.

The French president sensed it, too. With an expression of shock, he rose from his chair.

"They are in my head! We must call a halt!"

The US president raised his eyebrows. "We can't do that. The aliens want to help us. Let's just get this over with, then we can go on into the spaceship for the banquet."

"I do not want to *be* the banquet!"

The secret service agents pulled Niniane away from the table. Two of them went to intercept the cats. Katherine and Napoleon, with their increased sensitivity, knew just where to dodge to avoid their grasp.

"You were right!" Niniane called to Napoleon in her mental voice. She struggled to free herself from the agents' hands. A woman in a dark suit slapped handcuffs onto her wrists. Two more agents grabbed Corin and pulled his hands behind him. "How can we stop them?"

"We will do it! They are in our territory!"

Katherine jumped over the arm of the burly agent who tried to sweep her up. She slapped Ospl in the face, claws out, and leaped off the table.

"Kill them!" Ospl shrieked, clutching his cheek. Bright blue marks appeared on his skin. His high voice rose into the next register up. "Kill the creatures!"

"They're only cats," the prime minister said, offering his most charming smile.

Ospl leaped out of his chair in one smooth bound. He landed on top of Napoleon, scrambling to put both hands around the cat's neck. Napoleon flipped over on his back and began to pummel the alien with both back feet. The audience, who could only see what was being broadcast on the dozen immense flatscreens around the stage, saw what looked like Monl and Ospl playing with their Internet favorites, the Psychic Cats. They clapped and cheered them on.

"They challenge us!" Monl shouted. He reached into the neck of his shining suit and drew out a big gray gun so large it had to have taken up almost his whole costume.

"Stop that!" the president said. "We don't kill cats on this planet."

"Yes, we do," said the Chinese premier, waving a hand. "Carry on. Enjoy yourselves. You are our guests and masters."

The British prime minister gawked at him. "We shall have something to say to you later, sir!"

"Oh, my God," Salome whispered to Niniane, showing her the statistics on her tablet. "The cat-alien slapfight is trending on Facebook!"

Niniane moaned. It would have been great publicity if it hadn't been so dangerous.

Monl jumped up onto the table. He leveled the big gun at Katherine, and squeezed the trigger. *REEEEE-POW!* A section of the table exploded in a puff of black smoke. The audience shrieked.

"Katherine!" Niniane cried.

When the smoke cleared, everyone could see the female cat was unharmed and five feet away from the blast, her tail puffed to its maximum size. Monl threw back his head and let out a bellow of rage. For the first time, the audience could see the inside of his mouth. It was full of needle-sharp teeth like a snake's. The dignitaries gasped and scrambled out of their chairs. The US president's bodyguard surrounded him with plastic shields and pushed him back out of the way.

Monl kept shooting at Katherine, but her ability to read his mind meant that she kept ahead of where he was aiming every time. The alien gun chewed up piece after piece of the elegant table in clouds of acrid black smoke. Katherine leaped over his head and perched on the back of the chair the alien had abandoned, and hissed at him. Monl spun and fired. She leaped away, landing Edgar's arms. The chair exploded, scattering fragments of wood in all directions.

"Stop!" Edgar pleaded, shielding Katherine from the angry alien. "Don't hurt them! They're just cats!"

"Cats are evil!" Monl snarled. "When we rule this planet, we will kill all cats!"

"What, are you crazy?" the Russian president asked, his usually stoic face creasing in disbelief. "Even I would not do such a thing! I am quits! Out of here!" He gestured furiously to his coterie, and stormed off the stage.

"You can't kill our cats," Edgar said. He twisted and turned to keep the white cat out of range as Monl swiveled the barrel of his weapon, trying to get a clean shot. "We love them!"

"You will love us more when they are gone," Monl said. He snapped off a shot as Edgar ducked. "People of Earth adore us!" He fired again. The blast hit Edgar in the shoulder. He groaned and dropped to his knees, but he never let go of Katherine.

"You're trying to hurt poor little pussycats!" cried a woman with graying curls wearing a green T-shirt with the aliens' pictures on it.

She climbed up onto the stage and shook her fist at the aliens. "Leave them alone!"

"Yeah!" said a slender man in blue jeans ironed to fine creases up the front of both legs. "Don't you touch them!"

"You adore *us!*" Ospl said. He rose to his tiny feet and threw Napoleon down on the stage. Napoleon, instead of springing up, lay on his side and mewled piteously. He saw a bunch of middle-aged women coming toward him and stretched out one pathetic silver paw for help. They rushed to the writhing cat. One of them gathered him up, kissing his head.

"You're monsters!" she cried. Ospl gawked at her, his huge eyes not so adorable any more. "You don't treat animals like that."

"Napoleon's hurt!" Salome said, watching with horror.

"Why, the little faker," Corin said, in admiration.

"He's *not* hurt?" she asked.

"Hell, no," Corin said, shaking his head. "You should see him after a visit from the vet. Pure drama."

But the crowd didn't know the difference between fake and real distress. It surged toward the aliens.

"Stop!" Monl shouted. "You love us!"

"Help us!" cried Ospl. "Save us! You adore us! You will be our subjects!"

"Get out of here!" a big African-American man bellowed at them. He shook his fist at Ospl. Monl fired at his feet. A huge hole opened in the floor, but the man jumped over it, followed by half of the crowd. Their thundering feet made the stage shake wildly. "We're not going to follow anyone who abuses cats!"

The secret service agents guarding Niniane and Corin dove into the mass of people. Niniane lost sight of them and the little green men in the sheer surge of bodies. She could feel the aliens' panic rising until it overwhelmed every other thought.

The next thing she knew, the flying saucer on the top of Belvedere Castle started humming louder than a Metallica concert. A brilliant blue light shot down from its center. Two little specks of green rose up in the midst of the column. The light snapped off. A split second later, the big silver dish blasted off in a cloud of eye-watering ozone, and shot upward at an angle into the sun. The feeling of panic lessened, and then disappeared.

Niniane looked around frantically.

"The cats! Where are the cats!"

Salome dragged them off to the side of the stage.

"I'll go get the cats," she said, and disappeared into the crowd.

Edgar had had to surrender Napoleon while paramedics bandaged his arm. A piece had been neatly lasered out of his shoulder.

"The worst thing is, it ruined my best suit!" he told a bunch of reporters who clustered around him at what was left of the conference table on the stage. "Oh, and that the aliens fooled us. They made asses out of everyone in the whole world! But I'm more upset about the suit."

The McElroys, freed from their handcuffs, cuddled the cats at the other end of the table, surrounded by hundreds of fans and well-wishers all wielding cell phone cameras and tablets. The cats occasionally emitted sorrowful yowls and deep-throated purrs that elicited coos from those gathered around them.

"You two are such brats," Niniane told them. Napoleon said nothing, but his pose, one leg raised high in the air while he washed his bottom, told her exactly what he thought of her scolding.

"Yes, we are," Katherine thought at her smugly. "But we saved the world."

Niniane sighed and ruffled her fur. "Yes. Yes, you did. For yourselves."

"We are the ones in charge on this world," Napoleon said, raising his head from his furry tail. "You have no choice. We do not accept rivals, especially not green people pretending to be cats."

"Maybe the governments should sign a treaty with these two," Corin said, with a laugh. "We already know who rules the world."

It's intergalactic war, or at least the verge of it, when the Johnson's Crossing Fighting Pumpkins Cheerleaders are invaded by cheerleaders from another planet . . . and both are determined to prove the superiority of their school colors.

—BTS

School Colors

by Seanan McGuire

"Gimme a 'P!'"

Fifteen girls in orange and green uniforms moved in perfectly practiced unison, skirts swishing, sneakers stomping, ponytails and curls bouncing in time with the music. The rustle of pom-poms filled the air.

"Gimme a 'U!'"

Those same fifteen girls launched themselves backward, bodies spinning like tops as they performed the coveted double-backflip that had brought the Johnson's Crossing Fighting Pumpkins five state championships in a row.

"Gimme an 'M!'"

Fifteen girls struck asymmetrical poses, distinguishing themselves from the crowd for the first time since the routine had begun. Their faces, like sunflowers, sought the light, presenting their most flattering angles like they expected to be judged by some distant, all-powerful force. Or maybe by Tyra Banks. Marti had been talking lately about going out for *America's Next Top Model* after the end of her senior year, which made Jude wince every time Marti mentioned it. Jude didn't like to think about the fact that several members of her perfect squad were set to graduate as soon as we reached the end of the semester.

(Jude herself was set to be a five-year senior, which made sense, given that her mother is a vampire and she's aging at about two-thirds the human norm. Jude, I mean, not her mother. Her mother doesn't appear to age at all. She's assured me repeatedly that this isn't actually the case, but she's a little cagey where the details of vampire biology are concerned. Something about not wanting to give rise to a new generation of scientifically-inclined vampire hunters. I've tried assuring her that any information will be kept strictly Pumpkin to Pumpkin, but she just laughs, and keeps not saying anything.)

"Gimme a 'P!'"

Fifteen girls and fifteen new poses and I wasn't among them, all because I had to go and break my stupid ankle during that fight against the stupid mole people. *Everyone* knows that mole people are biologically implausible and a bad idea all around, but that doesn't stop them from existing. Denial is a powerful force. Not, as it turns out, actually powerful enough to rewrite reality, unless it's coming from Laurie, who can sort of talk things around to her point of view, when she remembers that she's supposed to care. Laurie is also kind of an airhead, which is the only reason the rest of us haven't, like, buried her in a well for our own safety.

"K-I-N-S go go go Pumpkins go!" Jude ran through the center of the formation, which scattered and reformed, beginning to go through the steps of the dance routine we—I mean, *they*—would be performing at the next game. I sighed and bent over my notebook, jotting down thoughts about how the whole thing could be improved. Jude would appreciate them, even if the rest of my squadmates wouldn't, and at least this way, I didn't feel like I was wasting my time showing up for practice. Not that I was actually wasting my time. If I wanted to stay in uniform, I couldn't miss more than three practices in a month. And seeing me sitting in the bleachers looking mournful reminded other people that my ankle was broken, which meant they'd be vaguely more considerate about my need for accommodations.

Being a cheerleader is sometimes complicated, frequently hazardous to my health, and always, always rewarding. Sure, it's no chess club, and sure, it doesn't necessarily fit with what most people think when they first meet me, but how many other opportunities does the average four-eyed high school nerd have to save the world and look cute doing it? I might never have become friends with most of my fellow Pumpkins without our shared uniform, shared weirdness, and shared interest in humanity not being wiped from the face of the planet. Since we had all those shared things, they were basically my family. And family looks after its own.

The routine was ending. The squad hit one final pose, hips jutted hard to the side to get just the right degree of sway from their pleated skirts, and froze for a count of three. Jude clapped her hands. All the girls came back to life, laughing, groaning, and—in Marti's case—producing compacts seemingly from nowhere and beginning to check their hair.

"How was that?" Jude, our fearless leader and team captain, put her hands on her hips before bending forward, trying to get her breath back. "Did we look okay?"

"It could be a little tighter, but you're coming along," I called back. "I made notes."

Heather groaned. "Of course she made notes. Dammit, Colleen, you'd make notes while you were being eaten."

"Someone has to update the handbook for the Pumpkins who will come after us," I said primly. "How else will they know what it feels like to be devoured without actually allowing it to happen again? Good documentation is the key to preventing history from repeating itself."

"We're missing so many of the old handbooks," said Laurie thoughtfully. "I wonder how many things we just do over and over and *over* again, because we don't know any better?"

All the Pumpkins within hearing range fell silent, pondering this statement. Finally, Heather said, "I guess it's true what they say about stopped clocks being right twice a day."

Marti looked up from her compact and frowned before her eyes widened in unusual alarm. Most of the time, Marti didn't like facial expressions that she thought might lead to wrinkles later, which really meant that Marti just didn't like facial expressions, period.

"I am fairly sure," she said, in a strangled voice, "that *that* hasn't happened before."

I twisted to look behind me. There was nothing there but empty sky. Then I looked up, and saw the flying saucer hovering above the trees and below the sun, which meant that it was a lot closer than a flying saucer necessarily ought to be.

"Huh," I said. "Will you look at that."

The nice thing about being a Fighting Pumpkin is that everyone assumes you can take care of yourself. Like, when I watch movies about high school, the vampires are always glittering sexy boys who take science classes for fun, and when something threatens the cheerleaders, the football players come running in to save the day. Not that we *need* saving or anything, but I honestly cannot think of the last time a football player came to see if we needed help. We may all wear the orange and the green, but some of us are cowards. Just saying.

Fourteen of the fifteen currently able-bodied members of the squad formed a loose diamond shape with me and Jude in the middle. I wasn't in what we'd call "fighting trim," and Jude, as captain, was too precious to risk on something unknown. Without her, we'd all be barking orders with no clear chain of command, and that's the sort of thing that gets good cheerleaders killed.

(That's another thing we never seem to have in common with the cheer squads in those movies. They worry about losing their virginity or dropping the spirit stick or getting split ends or whatever, but there seems to be a lot less "also, we could die." Movie high schools are *boring.*)

"We should be running," said Laurie.

"What if they have lasers?" asked Marti. "If I'm going to be vaporized, they're damn well going to look at the beauty they're taking out of the cosmos."

"We should be finding dynamite," said Heather.

"No one is getting vaporized, and no one is getting dynamite," said Jude firmly. "For all we know, they come in peace. Hold your ground, Pumpkins. This is our field, and we'll defend it."

"You know, this 'we are the most sincere patch' bullshit really only works until our new alien overlords decide to turn us all into mulch," said Heather. She sounded almost bored. That was pretty normal, for Heather. She'd spent some time as a zombie, thanks to a car crash and a former Pumpkin who had a thing for black magic, and while she was alive again, thanks to some weird seasonal monarch stuff at the Halloween bonfire, she still had a tendency to act like nothing really mattered. Being dead had turned her ennui up to eleven.

The flying saucer didn't seem to care that we were arguing amongst ourselves. It had been hovering lower and lower, moving until it was centered over the field right next to the bleachers. The fact that no one else had come to see what was going on just reinforced my conviction that we were attending a school full of cowards who were perfectly willing to let innocent cheerleaders get vaporized in order to save their own skins. Or, you know, that everyone was so used to us taking care of ourselves that they no longer saw the need to intervene. One or the other.

"Hold your formation," said Jude.

The flying saucer put out three short, stubby legs, arranged in a tripod formation, and slowly touched down on the field. It hummed a little louder as it landed, like it was putting a strain on whatever passed for its engine. Then the humming stopped, and everything was still.

"Maybe it's some new kind of weird drone," said Laurie.

"It's twenty feet across," said Marti. "That's not a hobbyist's toy."

"Maybe it's some new kind of weird drone for giants," said Laurie.

We all went quiet as we considered this. The things Laurie said frequently seemed ill-informed and nonsensical, but that didn't mean they weren't *true*.

The flying saucer began humming again. A section of the front liquefied, flowing down like water to form a long ramp. We all tensed, even me, although the worst I could really do under the circumstances was hit somebody with one of my crutches. Not really the sort of thing that sparked fear into the hearts of our enemies.

The humming stopped. The flying saucer settled deeper into the grass. And the, well, *aliens* started coming out.

There's probably a nicer way to say that, like "extraterrestrial lifeform" or "non-planetary space being," but I wasn't so much thinking about word choices in the moment, due to, you know, *aliens*. Their skins were greener than our uniforms, glistening faintly in the sunlight, like they were covered in some sort of mucus, or maybe really cheap body glitter. They had spots and stripes in both white and a darker shade of green, like tree frogs, which went with the mucus thing okay. It didn't go with the hair, which was varying shades of screaming electric orange, and it didn't go with the eyes, which were huge and black and took up more than half of each alien's face. Their noses and mouths were small enough to be negligible. The markings on their faces were more symmetrical than the ones on their arms and legs; after a moment's wide-eyed staring, I realized that it was because the markings on their faces were not, for the most part, biological. They were painted on. The aliens were wearing makeup.

That's not all the aliens were wearing. They had three legs, which gave their hips an oddly conical shape, but that didn't stop them from rocking pleated skirts. And they were uniformly flat-chested, which made sense, since I was pretty sure they weren't anything we'd recognize as mammalian, but their uniform tops still fit them perfectly. Whoever had tailored clothes for girls with three legs and four arms probably deserved some sort of award. Which would then immediately be taken away from them, because who dresses people with green skin and orange hair in *electric purple*? It was basically a crime.

Crime or no, the vivid color scheme was the last thing I needed to confirm my suspicions. There's only one thing in the universe that combines a skirt that pleated and pretty with a color scheme that offensively bright.

"They're *cheerleaders*," I said.

A low buzz broke out as the rest of the Fighting Pumpkins reacted to this news. Meanwhile, the aliens were moving toward us, walking with a fascinating tripod gait that must have made them *amazing* bases. Knocking one of them off-balance would be hard. They probably couldn't jump as well as bipeds, or even quadrupeds, but when it came to standing still, they were going to be amazing.

"Er." Jude stepped forward, and the others parted to let her pass, looking relieved. She was our captain. She would figure this all out. Or she would decide that this was an alien invasion and give us the signal to start kicking some extraterrestrial butt. Either way, it wasn't up to us to decide.

Being a Fighting Pumpkin means standing up for yourself, whether it's in the face of peer pressure or against the unstoppable skeleton armies of a confused death god that wandered into the wrong high school. But sometimes it's nice to admit that being a team player *also* means letting the captain take the lead when necessary. Jude had proven herself through vicious battle, zombie near-apocalypse, and three years of cheer camp. She could handle a little alien interaction.

The green cheerleaders stopped at the end of their ramp, fanning out into a loose bow-shape, a lot like we tended to form when we got off the bus for an away game. One last green cheerleader came out of the ship. This one's uniform had extra blue streaks around the tops of the sleeves and the base of the skirt, and while I hesitate to ascribe human ideals to extraterrestrial life forms, the things she was wearing in her hair were *totally* big alien spirit bows.

The alien captain held a box about the size of a smart phone in her top two hands. She poked at it before holding it out toward Jude. The box said, in a robotic voice, "Are you the Fighting Pumpkins cheer squad?"

"Oh, wow," said Laurie. "This is like 'if someone asks you if you're a God,' huh? Say 'yes,' Jude. You should totally say 'yes.'"

"Yeah, she should, because we're the Fighting Pumpkins," said Heather. "God, Laurie, can you join us for events as they're unfolding, instead of doing color commentary from the fifth dimension?"

"Sure," said Laurie, with no sign that she had taken offense. Laurie was good like that.

"Er," said Jude, attention still on the aliens. At least one of us was staying on task. "Yes, we are the Fighting Pumpkins cheerleaders, of Johnson's Crossing, California. Who are you? Do you come in peace?"

The box in the lead alien's hand squawked and warbled, sounding sort of like a cross between a dolphin, a mockingbird, and a blender. The alien girls made similar sounds, looking at each other before looking thoughtfully at us. Their expressions were hard to read, what with them being mostly eyes and all, but I got the feeling that they were sizing us up. The head alien said something into her box and held it out toward Jude again.

"We are the Battling Norgwrathors, of Mallallallal, Betelgeuse. We are the current champions of our solar system. We have come to challenge you to a cheer-off."

"Okay," said Jude slowly. "That's sort of . . . not surprising at all, given everything else we've been through, but I'm afraid we'll have to decline. We don't have any rules in common, so it would be pretty hard to choose a winner."

The box squawked and warbled. The cheerleaders looked upset. A few of them yelled at their captain, a sound which was more blender than anything else. She made what I could only describe as a "calm down, let me handle this" gesture with her two free hands, and squawked into her little box.

There was a moment of silence as the translation was performed. Then the box said, in that same emotionless, robotic voice, "You do not understand. You will cheer against us, and a winner will be chosen, or we will destroy your planet."

Heather rolled her eyes. "Of course you will," she muttered, and everything else was silence.

Pop quiz time! The correct response when a bunch of alien jerks who happen to be cheerleaders but *clearly* do not understand the true meaning of sisterhood land in your field and threaten to blow up the planet is:

A) Laugh them off, since there's no possible way they could do it, even if they do have shiny silver saucers capable of carrying them across uncharted lightyears. (Although presumably, *they* have charts for all those lightyears, since otherwise they would have gotten lost and wound up on like, Jupiter or something.)

B) Tell them to go fuck themselves, this isn't how a cheer competition is arranged, and anyway, the competition season is over for the year, or

C) Agree to their terms and arrange to meet out on the field in an hour, to determine who the best cheer squad in the planetary quadrant *really* is, PS, please don't blow up our world.

If you chose A), you're a Laurie. If you chose B), you're a Marti. And if you chose C), you're a Jude, and an excellent illustration of why she's allowed to be the one in charge. Most of the rest of us would probably have destroyed the planet by mouthing off, and she somehow managed to get us all back to the locker room before that could happen. Definitely an A+ team player.

"Okay, this looks bad," said Jude.

"Little green men are going to destroy the planet and everyone on it unless we agree to a cheer-off," said Marti serenely, as she fixed her eyeliner. "I don't think 'bad' covers it anymore. How does 'catastrophic and someone should probably call NASA' sound?"

"They're not little green men, they're cheerleaders," said Laurie.

"They're little and they're green, and I have no idea what their gender identification is, so I'm going with the classics," said Marti.

"We're going to cheer against them, and we're going to win, and we're going to save the world," said Jude firmly. "We are not going to ask them personal questions. We are not going to insult them personally. We are not, under any circumstances, going to give them any reason to destroy the planet."

"What if they just destroyed a continent?" asked Laurie. "Would that be okay?"

"There are people on every continent," said Jude. "No, that would not be okay."

"I think Australia is mostly spiders," said Laurie.

Everyone looked to me. As team nerd, it was my job to correct

Laurie when she said things like that. Sadly, in this case . . . "Little known fact: Australia actually *is* a spider. A very large one. When it wakes up, we're going to have problems."

Jude looked unsettled. "I didn't need to know that, but I'm still going to say that destroying Australia would be bad for the Australians. We're going to deal with this the Fighting Pumpkins way: with skill, diplomacy, and not blowing anything up."

"I don't think 'not blowing anything up' is the Fighting Pumpkins way," said Heather.

"Now that we've decided against global destruction, I want you all at your best," said Jude, ignoring her. "Fix your makeup, get your glitter on, and if you have spirit bows you're not wearing, start wearing them. We need to look like we're about to film a music video, and we need to do it in ten minutes flat, because that's when time runs out."

I put my hand up, cautiously. Jude frowned.

"What is it, Colleen?"

"I know that if we win, they don't destroy the planet, or at least they say that's what happens, and I'm choosing to believe that there's honor amongst cheerleaders, since otherwise, we're screwed," I said. "What happens if we lose? Do they like, take us back to their home world to work in their school cafeteria or something? I *really* want clearer rules before we do this."

Jude pinched the bridge of her nose. "You're not wrong," she said. "Okay, new plan: Colleen, you can't cheer anyway, with your ankle all messed up. Go tell them you're our rule keeper, and make sure they've promised not to kill or kidnap anyone, regardless of how this all plays out."

"Aye-aye, Captain," I said, grabbing my crutches and swinging myself onto them. It was actually sort of a relief to have something I could be doing, instead of just sitting around and watching as everyone else got ready to defend the world. Being a cheerleader means practicing self-care and not cheering on a broken ankle, even when the fate of humanity depends on how high the squad can collectively jump, but that didn't mean it didn't hurt. Emotionally, not physically. Physically, I was okay, thanks to the glories of modern medicine. How anyone got anything done before ibuprofen, I do not even know.

Crossing the practice field in crutches was somewhere between "hard" and "impossible" on the difficulty scale. Fortunately, I'd been practicing a lot in the last few weeks, and I managed to not look entirely unfortunate as I swung my way over to the alien ship. The one we were all assuming was the captain was standing guard, maybe because she already had a totally impressive spirit bow and didn't feel the need to gild the lily any further.

It occurred to me that we had no idea what the alien standards of beauty actually were. Maybe we were all doing exactly the wrong thing if we wanted to make ourselves look cuter, and needed to be, like, gluing live spiders to our faces. Only maybe not, because if that were the case, they would probably have gone to Australia.

"Um, hi," I said, once I was close enough. I took one hand off my crutch and waved, causing the alien captain to turn in my direction. She blinked once, a surprisingly complex gesture, since she had two sets of eyelids—one horizontal and one vertical. They closed and opened in sequence, creating an almost dizzying pattern. "I'm Colleen? I'm one of the Fighting Pumpkins? And I just wondered if you had a few minutes to go over the rules with me?"

Her box squawked and warbled. She frowned at it before squawking and warbling back. "What do you mean?" asked the box. "We will cheer according to the Galactic Cheerleading Federation standards, as published on Rigel."

"Yeah, see, we don't have interstellar travel yet, and up until today, we weren't actually sure there was life on Betelgeuse, much less on Rigel. So we don't have access to that rulebook, and while I sort of want to ask if you have a spare copy, we wouldn't be able to read it. So please, can you explain the rules to me, so I can tell my squad?"

A look of sheer horror spread across her face, magnified by the size of her improbable eyes. "You are not members of the Galactic Cheerleading Federation? But you're registered as the champions of this planet!"

"Not sure who did that, sort of flattered that they'd do it, but no, we're not part of your federation, and we *really* want to know the rules we're supposed to follow. A little reassurance that you're not actually going to blow up our planet would also be nice. We're happy to cheer with you, and we're always up for a little friendly competition, but we don't want you to, like, wipe out half our population just because we pull off a move you consider illegal."

She blinked again, twice this time, a dizzying swirl of eyelids. "This is bad. This is very, very bad."

"It's okay, I'm sure we can—"

"If you're not part of the Federation, we can be banned from competition for contacting you. This is bad." She moved her hands, and was abruptly holding what even I could recognize as a ray gun. It looked like a toy. I had no doubt that it could kill me. "We have to make sure that no one ever knows that we were here."

"Ummmmmm . . ." I looked frantically around, hoping that a solution would magically pop out of the sky and present itself. I mean, that wasn't *too* farfetched, right? The problem had done pretty much exactly that.

The alien captain took careful aim with her little blaster. The sunlight glittered off her spirit bows.

Spirit bows. Of course.

The life of a cheerleader is one of routine and school spirit elevated to the level of virtual religion. Even those of us who don't like going to class (Laurie) or don't enjoy the company of our fellow students (Marti) understand the sheer necessity of school spirit, which is the glue that binds a student body together. We are the immune system of the high school, appearing to cheer and beat the crap out of any infections that would dare to threaten our stability. Part of how we show that is by wearing school colors at all times. Usually, that's our uniforms. But sometimes, uniforms just aren't feasible. Sometimes, we have to show the orange and the green through other means. Like spirit bows. Big, elaborate hair decorations that can be a foot across sometimes, combining ribbon and sequins and fake jewels from the craft store and *everything*.

The alien cheer captain was wearing a spirit bow.

I put my hands up in what I hoped was the universal gesture of surrender—"universal" gets a lot more academic once there's actually another world involved—and said, "You don't want to shoot me. We're sisters."

Her box warbled and squawked. The alien cheer captain blinked her enormous eyes, first at it, and then at me, an expression of sheer confused disbelief on her face. I was getting better about reading her the longer I spent in her presence. Give me a few days with her squad and I could totally be an interstellar diplomat like on *Star Trek*, only maybe nerdier and with way better hair.

She warbled. The box said, "What? I assure you, that is biologically impossible."

"No, no, not sisters in biology or whatever. Sisters in *cheer*." I reached up and touched my own spirit bow, patting it with exaggerated care. "We're both cheerleaders. We're *all* cheerleaders. We're doing this because somebody has to, because we're the chosen ones. Right? We're the ones who carry school spirit to, like, the stars."

The alien cheer captain frowned before warbling again. The box said, "You mistake common interests for a common bond. We are nothing alike."

"Uh, hello? We're both champions. We both wear the colors of our schools like the honorable thing they are. Who cares if someone else says they clash, or that like, redheads shouldn't dress up like gourds, or that people with green skin shouldn't try to emulate nudibranchs? School colors never clash, because school colors are the colors of our *souls*. You can't kill us. We're sisters, we're family, and we're better than that."

She was starting to look uncertain. That was good. She was still holding her ray gun pointed at me. That was bad. Big, stirring speeches aren't really my thing, and if my first try ended with my inglorious disintegration, I was going to be pissed.

"Besides, like, even if we're not part of your big cheer-empire, haven't you always wondered how bipeds could be good enough to win championships? Like, you have me way beat in the limbs department. Clearly we're inferior, and yet somehow we have all these trophies. It's a terrible mystery."

This time, there was a querulous note to her shrieking. The box asked, "How would you suggest we proceed?"

I grinned.

Cheer is about spirit, musicality, coordination, and the willingness to be flung, like, super-high into the air by girls who have been lackadaisically trained by failed gymnasts, at best, or taught by one another, at worst. Since both gymnasts and teenage team captains tend to assume that the human body is endlessly resilient and also made entirely of rubber, there's a reason that cheerleading accounts for more than fifty percent of all high school athletic injuries. But all that being said, cheerleading is about enthusiasm. It's about energy. And it's about how much noise you can make.

Jude led the Fighting Pumpkins out of the locker room with pom-

poms waving and iPods blaring, hitting their marks with the sort of effortless grace that takes hours and hours and *hours* of work. They began building a human pyramid, while I sat on the bleachers and clapped as hard as I could, egging them on, even though it hurt to know that I wasn't the one who was going to be flung into the air when they were finished. Sacrifices must be made.

The aliens came pouring out of their saucer, several carrying smaller versions of their translation box, all of which were blasting an atonal, sliding tone that warbled like a Theremin being played by a hurricane. They began building, not a pyramid, but a standing cube, stacking themselves like a child's building blocks. I clapped and cheered for them too. Even if I didn't want them to win, that was no reason to be a bad sport about things.

Laurie and one of the alien cheerleaders scampered toward each other and exchanged devices, poking at them until the Theremin-warble became a little faster and the pop beat became a little slower. The two met and synchronized like the world's weirdest mash-up. In silent agreement, everyone else turned their music off, and the blended beat went on, cheerleaders flipping, scaling, and generally treating one another like living gymnastic equipment.

The aliens didn't do as many shoulder-stands as we did, probably because of the whole "tripod" thing, and they didn't throw themselves into the air as often, probably because of the whole "where the hell do you put all those limbs" thing. But they stacked themselves twice as high, their third legs lending stability and their third and fourth hands improving their grips, and they were capable of running while balancing on their hands, which was a cool, if disorienting, trick. They didn't seem to care so much about being upside-down. That also meant they didn't do as many tumbling runs—when up and down were basically the same thing, I guess that wasn't so impressive.

What they did was not the sort of routine humans could do. It was sort of like interpretive dance as performed by really flexible squid. And it was absolutely and without a doubt *cheerleading*. There's nothing like it in the world, and apparently it exists all across the universe.

Eventually, the music stopped. The teams stopped moving, eyeing each other across the field of battle. The Fighting Pumpkins glistened with sweat and body glitter. The Battling Norgwrathors glistened with freshly-excreted mucus and, again, body glitter.

The captain of the Battling Norgwrathors squawked and warbled. Her translation box said, "I think it is a draw."

"But—" began Marti.

Jude put up a hand to stop her, nodding enthusiastically. "Yes," she said. "A draw. It was an honor to cheer beside you."

The captain of the Battling Norgwrathors put one of her four hands out. After a moment's pause, Jude gripped it firmly and shook.

Later, after the saucer full of little green cheerleaders had lifted off and sailed back into the sky, Jude came and sat down beside me on the bleachers. I was scribbling in our handbook, trying to get down every detail.

"So that was a thing," said Jude.

"Yup," I agreed.

"Thanks for convincing her not to explode the planet."

"Oh, she was never going to do that." I beamed up at the sky, convinced that somehow, the cheerleaders of our new sister squad could feel it.

Biology may vary from world to world, but school spirit is universal.

In our next tale, a critically praised author with an unfortunate (and frustrating) penchant for catching deer in his headlights, writes about a different kind of deer in the headlights: a politician dealing with Martian landlords . . .
—BTS

Meet The Landlord

by Martin L. Shoemaker

"So what's up, Mack? Are you ignoring me?"

Doug Brinks took another swig of his beer—flat, which was typical for Helen's Hut, but it was the only bar in the Coprates Quadrangle. It was nearly room temperature, it was thick, and some had compared it to horse piss—but never in Helen's earshot. She was a large, sturdy pioneer woman, and she took pride in her little outpost near the Coprates brine farms. She had been known to cut a guy off for a month for complaining about her beer; and good or bad, it was the only beer within a thousand kilometers. It was better than nothing, and at least it had a kick.

But today Doug wondered what else was in the beer. He lowered the glass slowly so it didn't slosh in the low Martian gravity, and he peered at the little green man who stood on the far side of the table from him, getting Mars dust on the fake-wood surface. "I always ignore hallucinations."

The little green man straightened, and his long, bulbous antennae brushed the dingy bar lamp over the table, causing it to sway. It was the only light beyond the bar. The dozen other tables in the joint would be unoccupied until first shift let out at the brine farm, so Doug was alone in the place—or so he had thought until now.

The man wore a helmetless silver space suit including silver boots that looked too large for such a small creature. He tapped his right foot, the massive boot stirring up the dust. His antennae wiggled, and the swaying lamp and the bobbing antennae cast dancing shadows on the table. "I'm not a hallucination."

Doug pointed a finger at the man, and he was surprised how steady the finger was considering how drunk he must be. "Sure, you're not. You're a Martian who just happens to look like a throwback to old movies and talks with a Bronx accent." Doug raised his glass for another drink. "And I'm Elwood P. Dowd."

The green man walked across the table, grabbed the glass, and gently but firmly pushed it down so he could stare over it. Doug found him surprisingly strong for a hallucination.

"I ain't no white rabbit, and I ain't no hallucination," the green man said. "And I'm using the Bronx accent because you wouldn't understand Martian. If I walked up and said 'Garelf neemin tho, Mrig?' you would just scratch your ugly head and stare at me."

Doug shook his head. "I could *speak* Martian with enough beer in me." Doug looked down at his glass. "But not . . . this stuff."

"Whaddaya expect?" the green man asked. "This is Coprates, not Sabaeus Quadrangle. They got some high-class joints over there. They have good Scotch whiskey, not just . . . beer, if you can call it that." He peered over at Helen, and then he held his hand beside his mouth and whispered, "I hear she uses freeze-dried hops. And Martian groundwater. Unrefined."

The man snapped his fingers for attention. Helen looked up and asked, "Another beer, Doug?"

Doug shook his head. "I think I've had too many."

"And what about your friend?"

Doug's eyes widened. "You . . . see him? A . . . little green man?"

The green man frowned at Doug. "That's 'Martian.' I'm not little, ya big ox, and what you got against green?"

Helen said, "The green guy? Sure. Ever since he traipsed in earlier, looking for you. Hey, Mack!" She looked at the man. "You ready to order yet?"

The man—the Martian?—looked at her, and his antennae leaned forward. "Did you find any whiskey?"

Helen shook her head. "Uh-uh. I found some wine in the back, but I don't recommend it. It was stuck under the heating system, so it's probably spoiled. All I have 'til the supply run next month is beer."

The Martian's antennae sagged, and he shook his head. "Nope, sorry, I'll pass."

Doug was confused. On the one hand, he could be so drunk that he was imagining an entire conversation between Helen, him, and a little green man. In that case, he was sure to pass out at any moment. On the other hand, there was a slim chance that he *was* talking to a little green man. In which case . . . "Oh, what the hell. Another one, Helen."

Helen poured another beer and brought it over. Doug looked up at her. "You call him 'Mack?'"

Helen smiled at the Martian. "Yeah, that's what he calls everyone, and I can't pronounce his name, so 'Mack' will do." She set the tall glass on the table. The pale gold liquid had not even a hint of a head. "That'll be five New Bucks."

Doug tapped his ID card. "Put it on the governor's tab, please."

Helen sniffed and walked back behind the bar. She served everyone at the Hut, from farmers to miners to spacers—and to little green men, apparently. But she couldn't hide her disdain for politicos.

Doug looked back at Mack. "All right, I give up. Is this some sort of trick? Yoshi and the boys setting me up?"

Mack shook his head, antennae doing a complicated dance. "It's not a trick, this is business. It's time we talked about the rent. Let's get the formalities out of the way." He held out a hand, and Doug shook it. The Martian's small hands had three long-jointed fingers and a thumb on each side. "You are Doug Brinks, Governor Griffin's fixer—"

"Administrative assistant," Doug corrected.

"Tomato, tomahto. She does the personal politics, you fix things behind the scenes. That's why I looked you up. I am Mack the Unpronounceable . . . your landlord."

"Huh?"

"Well, to be precise, I'm a representative of the Martians, and *we* are your landlords."

Doug leaned back in his chair and stared at Mack. "There are no Martians. We've been on Mars for thirty years, and we studied it for a hundred years before that. We would've noticed."

Mack said, "You didn't notice me until I hopped up on your table and made you notice. Besides, we've contacted you people before, lots of times."

"Oh, there are stories," Doug agreed. "Usually from people a whole lot drunker than me. Nobody took them seriously. Why didn't somebody *sober* see you before?"

"You mean besides Lowell?" Doug looked blankly at Mack. "Percival Lowell? The guy who mapped our canals?"

"Wish fulfillment," Doug said. "He saw what he wanted to see. Better telescopes eliminated the canal theory."

"No, he saw what we *didn't* want him to see. When we found out about it, well, nobody wants Mrs. Kravitz peering through the curtains to see what sort of witchcraft you're brewing up.

"Mrs . . . . Kravitz?" Doug asked.

Mack scowled. "You kids these days. No appreciation for the old classics." Doug still showed no comprehension, so Mack continued. "Anyway, we just 'drew the curtains,' so to speak. We shut down the canals, and we went underground where you couldn't keep an eye on us."

Doug took a drink. "And I suppose you learned everything about us from our TV and radio."

"How could we miss it?" Mack said. "Geeze, you people are noisy! But we watch that stuff for laughs. To do a serious study, we hadda go on site. We've been doing scouting missions since before your granddad was born."

"Of course," Doug said. "UFOs. The story wouldn't be complete without flying saucers. Come on, this *has to* be Yoshi setting me up. Hey, Yoshi!" He called out, looking around. "This is a mighty stale old joke."

Doug waited for Yoshi to spring up from behind the bar, but the only thing that happened was more foot-tapping from Mack. "Look, Dougie," he said after several seconds, "sometimes a thing becomes an old joke because it happens a lot, and everybody knows the story. That don't make it any less true. I'm green, I'm a Martian, and I've visited your planet in my flying saucer for research." Doug raised an eyebrow. "No, none of that stupid 'probing' stuff. Do I look like some kind of pervert? You Terrans came up with that idea on your own. We went to libraries and schools and legislatures to learn what you people were all about."

Doug shook his head again. "And we never noticed little green men hanging out in libraries?"

"We're not *idiots*." Mack held his arms away from his sides, palms turned in. "We didn't look like this. We looked like *this*." Suddenly Mack was gone, and a scrawny teenaged girl with long, stringy blonde hair sat cross-legged on the table. "Or this," she said, and the girl was replaced by a tall, gray-haired old black man in an impeccable tuxedo. "Or this." The old man became an exact duplicate of Doug. "Or of course, this." The second Doug shifted to become a large, humanoid rabbit.

"Very funny," Doug said. "But you look more like Bugs than Harvey."

"How do you know, Doc?" the rabbit asked. "Did you ever see Harvey?" Then the rabbit disappeared, and Mack's voice spoke from empty air. "Or just this. If we can make canals disappear, making ourselves disappear is a breeze. Give us credit for knowing how to be inconspicuous."

Doug eyed his second beer suspiciously. He was beginning to think that Mack wasn't a hallucination; and if that were true, then even flat beer would help Doug's nerves. "All right." He took another long swallow. "Suppose I believe your story."

"As you should."

"We've been here on Mars for thirty years. You've been in hiding that whole time—"

Mack reappeared, one finger raised under Doug's nose. "Except we came out and talked to *somebody* at least twice a year. If you'll check your records, you can confirm that."

"Whatever. You've been *mostly* in hiding. You only appear to drunks and crazies whom no one will believe. And an hour from now, when I'm sober, you'll be gone, and no one will believe me, either."

Mack's antennae waggled. "Nope, this time is different. That's why I sought you out, Mr. Fixer: this time I'm here to collect."

"Collect what?"

Mack leaned forward, and his antennae bobbed over Doug's head. "I told you: I'm your landlord, and I'm here to collect the back rent."

"Say what?"

"Uh-huh, back rent for use of our planet, our airspace, our satellites—don't think we didn't notice your stations on Phobos and Deimos—and our mineral and water rights."

Doug leaned back, away from the antennae. "You've got to be kidding."

"Not in the slightest. Here's the bill." Mack tossed a document chip on the table. Doug picked it up, turned it over, and inspected it. It was a standard chip for transferring certified documents. "It's all itemized," Mack added.

Doug squeezed the center of the chip, and it lit up, projecting a virtual document on the table. The page was full of very fine print, and the page indicator at the bottom read *Page 1 of 247.*

Doug started flipping through the pages, but Mack put a finger down to pause the display. "Look," Mack said, "you can look at the details later. Let me summarize: for various rights, usages, resources, and rights-of-way exercised and accumulated over the past 30 Earth years, plus taxes, fees, and interest compounded quarterly at standard commercial rates . . . *plus* my customary fifteen percent commission . . . Well, I'm feeling generous, so I'll round down to the nearest thousand. You owe us . . . two trillion, seven-hundred-fifty-eight billion, three-hundred-ninety-one million, four-hundred-and-thirteen thousand New Bucks."

Doug's jaw dropped open. Finally he recovered enough to respond. "Look, assuming I'm not crazy, you are! You can't charge us a rental fee out of nowhere like this. We don't have any sort of contract."

"Contract, schmontract. You want we should charge you with trespassing instead? We could, you know, but we decided it was better all around if we billed you for rent instead. It's all good and legal and documented in there. You landed here, you sent probes here before that, all without authorization. You scooped up samples, but no big deal. After all, we sent scouts to your world, so fair is fair, right? Even when your first manned missions landed, we were fine with that. What's a few tourists? But when you started building cities and having babies here, those were game changers. That's when the debate started Downstairs."

"Downstairs?" Doug asked.

"Pay attention. We live underground, remember? Far deeper than you can detect; but those Martians who studied your military said you still might annoy us, so we should whack you before you got a foothold. Others—the hippy-dippy types who watched too many of your movies—said we should all join you and live in peace and harmony and yadda yadda yadda. The two groups couldn't agree, and it wasn't looking good.

"But me, when I wasn't enjoying your music and movies, I studied your laws. And I realized we had a third choice: if we let you stay here, we'd be entitled to rent, licensing, royalties, fees . . . and interest, can't forget interest. We'd make a bundle off land we weren't using anyway, and the weapons to enforce it would be your own laws. I've read enough of your laws to know these claims will stand up in court; and if you fight it, that'll only add on more interest and fees and court costs."

Doug replied, "First, *you* would have to stand up in court. You can't pull that now-you-see-me-now-you-don't crap there. You'd have to come out and make yourself known."

Mack smiled. "We're ready to. You have to understand, Dougie, this is a new stage in our relationship. We're owed, and we aim to collect what's ours. You think you got a chance in court? You take that doc and look it over real careful. I drafted it myself, and I don't miss a trick."

"This is insane. I can't . . . I mean, there's no way to pay this kind of money."

Mack hopped down off the table, falling lightly in the Martian gravity. "Talk to the governor. Find a way. We can make payment arrangements easy enough. Of course, the interest will keep compounding . . . " He reached up and shook Doug's hand again. "I'll see you back here at noon tomorrow and we can start discussing your payment plan." Then he walked into the airlock and cycled it. Soon Doug could see the little green man through the view screen, walking across the Martian desert.

Damn. The man left footprints. He was real.

"Helen! Another beer, please, and keep 'em coming."

So much for Doug's plans. He had hoped to get back to Sabaeus Quadrangle early, maybe surprise Miriam and take her out to dinner. His inspection tour had been quick and routine—until Mack. Now he had better stick around and figure this mess out. So he rented a room from Helen, fetched his bags from his hopper, and checked in.

As soon as he was alone in the room, he dialed in his private comm code for Governor Griffin. Her face appeared on his comm screen, and he knew right away that there was trouble. He had served her through too many campaigns to miss those lines in her face. Her trademark red hair was in disarray, too, and that was way out of character for her. That was the look she wore when charm and diplomacy and smarts weren't enough, and she needed a fixer. That was when she turned to Doug, who had been a low-level con artist when she had arrested him the first time when she had been a police captain in Lower Sabaeus. Over the course of several more arrests, she had come to appreciate his . . . creative interpretations of the law, and she had decided it was better to have him on her side than on the streets. Doug had decided that a steady paycheck was safer than trying to outwit her, and together they had plotted her rise: police chief to council member to assembly member and now governor. They had their sights set on chancellor someday.

That assumed there would still be a chancellor's office. Doug wasted no time. "Governor, I've just seen—"

"I know what you've seen." The governor widened the camera angle to take in her entire office, and Doug saw three more Martians standing one atop the other. The bottom one held the end of a tape measure while the top held the tape up against the ceiling. The one in the middle scribbled notes on a pad. "Little green men. Martians, I guess. They're everywhere."

"What are they doing?"

"They tell me—" Griffin leaned into the screen and whispered. "They tell me they're measuring it for the landlord's new office, and that you have all the details. Doug, who the hell is the landlord?"

Doug told her about his encounter with Mack, and he uploaded her a copy of the contents of the doc chip. "So that's the situation," he concluded. "They want nearly three trillion New Bucks."

Griffin looked over her shoulder. The Martians had climbed up on her wet bar and were inspecting the bottles along the wall. "That's crazy," she whispered. "Even assuming their claim is valid—and do not say one word to acknowledge that it is!"

"Hey," Doug held his hands out wide, "I am the soul of discretion, you know that."

"I know." She frowned. "But this is bigger than a street con, bigger than an election. Assuming their claim is valid, we don't have that much money. *Nobody* has that much money."

"I know that, and you know that," Doug said. "And he knows enough about us to know that, too. I think this is a shakedown, literally on an astronomical scale. He wants to squeeze us for every buck he can get, and he's using the legal system to threaten us and get us to pay up. If we don't give in, he plans to tie us up in court for the next century."

"Can he do that?"

Doug shook his head, and Griffin brightened until he answered, "I don't know. Maybe. The little bit I saw of those docs was pretty thoroughly researched. If he can . . . Well, it might be easier to pay him off."

"Never!" Griffin yelled, and the three Martians stopped to look at her. She turned to them. "Get out! I have work to do."

"Very well," the tallest Martian said. He spoke with a British accent, and his antennae were shorter than Mack's. "We are done here for now. We'll be back tomorrow with paint samples. Come along, chaps." The three Martians hopped down from the wet bar and filed out the door, which opened automatically and closed behind them.

Griffin glared after them, and then turned back to the screen. "I said never," she continued. "The payoff on three trillion would still break us. And besides, I've never paid off the opposition, and I won't start now."

Doug carefully swallowed his first response. Governor Griffin didn't know about the time he had bought off the chief of the mining guild, and she never would if he could help it. "All right, we won't pay him off directly, but I might need some funds to operate here, above my usual budget."

"How much?"

"As much as you can spare. Don't tie my hands here, Gina, I've gotta have room to operate."

Griffin frowned, but then she tapped on her comm. "All right, I've set up an account with an extra fifty thousand. Call me if you need more. Now, what's your plan?"

Doug confirmed the new account, and then he picked up the doc chip. "First, I'll go over every line here. If there's an angle, I'll find it. And if that doesn't work . . . I'm thinking a claim of adverse possession."

Griffin smiled. "Oh, that's good. Can you make it stick?"

"I can try, but I need to concentrate. Forgive me, Governor, but I've got to get to work."

Doug cut off the comm and started making notes on his plan. The more he read the docs, the more solid they looked, and the more certain he was that adverse possession was his only hope. It was a legal doctrine that allowed someone to gain title to property without permission by using that property productively for a number of years and improving the property. That certainly described what humanity had done on Mars, so Doug began assembling his case.

The next day, Doug sat at the same table in Helen's Hut, nursing a beer. It was no better nor colder than the day before, but Doug wasn't paying attention to the beer. He was too busy poring over his notes.

At precisely noon, he sensed the table surface shift slightly. He looked up to see Mack standing on the table, tapping his foot. "It ain't gonna work," the Martian said.

"What?"

"Adverse possession." Doug's eyes widened. "What, you're surprised? Just because a Martian leaves the room doesn't mean he leaves the room." Mack disappeared, but his voice spoke from the empty air. "Invisible, remember? My buddy left the governor's office, and then he doubled right back before the door slid shut. He heard your whole conversation with the governor, and he reported it to me. And may I say I was most impressed how you squeezed that fifty grand slush fund out of her. How much have you siphoned off to your own account? For a small fee, I can keep that quiet."

Bingo! Doug wasn't sure what Mack's angle was, but now he was sure there was one. With the numbers the Martian was discussing, fifty thousand wasn't even small change. That the Martian noticed such a minor sum gave Doug hope that there was some leverage to be found here—though he didn't know where yet.

In the meantime, he had to keep the negotiations rolling so he could find out what the creature really wanted. "It seems to me like a clear-cut case of adverse possession. We have occupied the property and used it as our own continually for thirty years. That's more than long enough under every jurisdiction on Earth, including all of those that you cited in your documents."

Mack smiled, ear to ear, and his antennae drooped to the sides. "You're glossing over the necessary conditions, Dougie. One," he held up his right thumb and ticked it off with his left index finger, "actual possession. I'll give you that one, you've possessed and improved the property. Two," he ticked off his other thumb, "non-permissive use. I'll give you that one too, since we damn well never gave you permission. Three, open and notorious use." He lowered his index finger. "Yep, you've made no effort to hide your presence here. Four, continuous use. You failed that one at first: you came, you left, you came, you left. But thirty years ago, you came and stayed. So your adverse possession claim, even if it were valid, would start then. You would still be on the hook for all of those earlier probes and visits."

Mack lowered his ring finger, leaving his middle finger up. "But that last requirement is exclusive use. You haven't had it. We've been here the whole time. And every so often, we showed up to remind you."

"To remind drunks and crazies, you mean," Doug said. "They're not reliable witnesses."

Mack waved the finger back and forth. "Doesn't matter. We have every encounter on video. We even tried to talk to someone in authority. 'Take me to your leader,' we said, but they never did. Sorry, Dougie, but an adverse possession claim will only get the court more upset with you. I might forget you ever tried it . . . for a small fee."

There it was again. A small chink of greed. Mack *did* have a price, now Doug just had to find it. But he couldn't think, couldn't plan with the little green man staring down at him.

"Screw the fee," Doug said. "I didn't try anything, I just considered the idea. There's no law against considering." Then Doug thought of a way to buy some time. Not exactly original, but . . . "Now pardon me, I've gotta take a piss." He rose and stepped away from the table. Then he turned back. "I do hope you're not going to follow me invisibly there, too."

"I told you, I'm no pervert! Take your time, I'll be here when you get back."

Doug headed to the lavatory, closed himself in a stall, and sat. He was sure now: Mack was a con artist, just like him. In years on the street and years in politics, he had yet to meet an *artiste* that he couldn't best, and the little green man wasn't going to be the first. Oh, sure, he had thousands of other Martians in on the con, but he was the brains behind it. He wanted something, and this ridiculous claim was his way to press for it. Doug's guess was that he wanted long-term payments; and honestly, Doug didn't disagree with those in principle. If the Martians had shown up right at the start of human exploration, the two peoples probably could've worked out a deal. But not like this. Doug knew that you never give in to the squeeze, or the other guy will just keep squeezing. There had to be a way out. Doug refused to give Mack what he wanted.

Or maybe . . . maybe give him *exactly* what he wanted . . .

Doug ran a number of quick calculations. When he started to see numbers that he liked, he used much of his fifty grand account for some emergency messages to Earth. Then he returned to the table and sat.

"Took you long enough," Mack said. "I wondered what you ate."

"Nothing," Doug answered, checking the time on his comm. "In fact, that's not a bad idea. Helen? Some sandwiches, please. Not from yesterday, some fresh ones." Fresh sandwiches would take a little longer, give Doug more time. He turned back to Mack. "You want one?"

"From this joint?" Mack wrinkled up his nose. "No, thanks. Now let's get down to business."

"Uh-uh," Doug shook his head, "I don't deal on an empty stomach. You sure?" The Martian just stared. "Okay. But I insist: no business until I'm done with lunch."

"So what do we do until then?"

"We talk," Doug answered. "You said you've visited Earth. Tell me some stories."

So as Doug ate, Mack told stories of his visits to Earth: abductions, drunken encounters, playing tag with fighter jets . . . But his favorite stories were about his secret visits to the cities. He liked to watch classic films, sure, and a lot of trash TV; but he was especially fond of musical theater, and he even entertained Doug with a rendition of "Golden Helmet of Mambrino," singing Quixote's and Sancho's and the barber's parts in different voices.

Doug had to admit: like all great con artists, Mack was a charmer. The Martian was fun to have around, but he wanted something. And when Doug's comm chimed, it was time to give him what he asked for. Good and hard.

Doug set down his napkin and opened his comm. "Okay, Mack," he said, interrupting the Martian in mid story, "you win."

"What?" Mack narrowed his eyes and stared at Doug.

"I said you win." Doug tapped at his comm. "I am authorized to concede all of your claims, and to issue payment in full immediately."

"I'm . . ." Mack stopped.

"Of course, we don't have that sort of money. No one does. So I won't fight a motion of default. In fact, I'll even file it for you. We're ready to turn over all rights and title for our complete Mars holdings."

"But—"

"But you're right, that's not nearly enough to cover our total accumulated debt. Frankly, that number is more than the entire equity value of all property on Earth and Luna."

"So—"

"So I am also authorized to transfer all titles to Earth and Luna as well."

Mack sat, floating down to the table. "You're . . . *giving* me the whole damn Solar System?"

"No," Doug corrected, "we're paying off a debt. No gift at all. It's all yours. The whole shebang."

Mack's smile slowly grew. "Everything?"

"Everything."

Mack laid back on the table, laughing, and clapped his hands together. "Everything! Made it, ma! Top of the world!"

Doug tapped his comm again. "Yes, yes, top of the world. Now, about those improvements . . ."

Mack's laughter stopped immediately. "Improvements?"

"Yep," Doug said. "We have acknowledged that you have proper title to Mars. Therefore you are responsible for the cost of any improvements we made here, on Phobos and Deimos, or in orbit. I'm afraid we're going to have to bill you for materials, shipping from Earth, labor . . . Oh, and accrued interest, since these charges go back a while."

"Now wait a minute—"

"And then there's the matter of repairs to your new properties. By rough estimate, approximately two billion dwellings on Earth, Luna, and Mars do not meet standards for safety, accessibility, toxic cleanup, and other deficiencies. As the new owner, you assume all such liabilities."

Mack sat up. "I won't pay! Let them sue!"

Doug tapped his comm, and his email inbox projected onto the table. "That's exactly what they'll do. I have email from two-hundred-forty-seven tenant unions, plus nineteen class action lawyers, all with demands for repairs, damages, and penalties."

"Class action . . ."

"There are also a number of territorial disputes," Doug said. "As the owner of record for these territories, you'll be expected to adjudicate claims, police the boundaries, and compensate displaced persons and other victims."

"Adjudicating? Policing? I don't want none of that, I just want, ya know, a little cash. You mind your business, I'll mind mine."

"This *is* your business. You're in charge now—within the bounds of relevant law, of course." Doug finished his beer, and then he continued. "And then there are the government agencies that want to talk to you about problems with your properties. In the USA alone, the Environmental Protection Agency has over three hundred cleanup projects that they expect you to pay for, six hundred states and cities want to talk to you about tax liens, and the Food and Drug Administration has a stack of failed inspection reports from your farms. Seventy-nine other countries have similar complaints, and more are coming in by the minute."

"They can't blame me for that!" Mack leaped to his feet. "I didn't own the joint then!"

"You've never dealt with the EPA, have you?" Doug scrolled down through his email. "Let's see . . . Taxes . . . Liens . . . Taxes . . . Fines . . . Taxes . . . Assessments . . . Taxes . . . Oh, here's something different . . ." He pointed at a pair of messages. "The Recording Industry Association of America *and* the Motion Picture Association of America. They have reason to believe that you have elicit copies of movies and albums. That's two-hundred-fifty thousand New Bucks per incident, you know."

"But everybody does it!"

"And the MPAA only prosecutes selectively," Doug answered, "when they want to make an example. The entire planet of Mars is a biiiiig example. Oh, and look at this one!"

Mack leaned over the email. "What?"

"This one with the icon, the circle with the big round ears. I hope you don't have any illicit copies of *Steamboat Willie*. The Mouse people are relentless, and they never lose."

Mack's mouth dropped open, but he said nothing, so Doug pressed his advantage while he could. "So all told, I estimate that these claims plus penalties and interest and court costs would add up to . . ."

Doug scrawled a number on his comm, and Mack stared at it. "That's six times what you owe us."

"Six?" Doug frowned, ran some new calculations, and scratched out the number. Then he wrote a new one. "Seven."

Mack swallowed. Doug looked up and learned for the first time: Martians could sweat. After a long pause Mack said, "That's ridiculous. We can't pay that."

"No problem," Doug answered. "We can go to court. With this many cases, we'll tie up the court system for centuries . . ." He paused and grinned. ". . . and interest and penalties will keep accumulating. Unless . . ."

Mack looked straight into Doug's eyes. "Unless?"

Doug closed his comm, leaned back, and grinned wider. "I *am* a fixer, after all. The best there is. I can make this go away. For a fee . . ."

Mack tugged at his silver collar, and asked, "How much?"

From memory, Doug answered, "Two trillion, seven-hundred-fifty-eight billion, three-hundred-ninety-one million, four-hundred-and-thirteen thousand . . . and ten New Bucks."

Mack cocked an eye at Doug. "What's the ten for?"

Doug spread his arms wide. "A round of drinks for the house, to celebrate the cancellation of all accounts and a new era of friendship."

Mack looked around the bar. "But there's no one here but you."

"And you, Mack. Sit down, have a drink. Helen, two beers!" Mack raised his eyebrows. "Oh, come on, it's not *that* bad. Drink with me . . ." Doug held out his hand. ". . . pal?"

Mack looked at Doug's hand for several seconds before he finally shook it. Then he sat.

Helen brought over two beers, and the man and the Martian both took large drinks.

Mack set his glass down. "Still tastes like horse piss."

"Shhh . . ." Doug looked at Helen to be sure she hadn't heard, and he took another drink. "Remember, best beer in Coprates. Drink up."

This time, the magnetic boot is on the other foot, and those Little Green Men must rise up to defend their homes from an invading race of giants. It's one small step for Mankind and one big belly-laugh from Steven Silver.

—RWB

Big White Men—Attack!

by Steven H Silver

Buzz reached over and cut the feed to Mission Control. There were times you just wanted privacy, even, perhaps especially, when you were the only two living creatures for thousands of miles.

"Do you know what you're going to say yet?"

Neil shook his head, but grinned. "I was thinking about wishing my next door neighbor, Mr. Gorsky, luck, but I figure it'll just confuse everyone and it wouldn't mean anything. I kind of feel something of more import is needed."

"Conrad's on the next mission. If we have to abort and he makes the first landing, can you imagine what he'd say?"

Neil was known as the serious astronaut, but he broke out in a wide grin only missing Pete Conrad's trademark gap, and in a credible imitation of the diminutive astronaut's voice, shouted, "There's little green men everywhere!" before reaching out to turn the feedback on.

". . . bia. Houston lost you again. They're requesting another try at the high gain."

"Eagle, Houston. We have you now. Do you read? Over."

"Loud and clear," Buzz tried to keep the laughter out of his voice. They were still 50,000 feet above the lunar surface, but while Charlie Duke and the other astronauts who were monitoring them from the ground had senses of humor, NASA's official sense of humor would fit into the miniature communion cup he had brought along, with plenty of room left over for the wine.

★   ★   ★

Shali stopped the hauler and threw the transmission into park, the sudden jerk waking me from the fitful sleep one has when crammed into the cab of a telenite hauler.

"Pimi! Do you see that?"

I roused myself from slumber and opened one eye. "See what?"

He was pointing through the windshield toward the sky. "Up there."

I opened up a second eye and tried to focus through the window, but either it was covered in dust or my vision was blurry with sleep. Probably both. As I opened my other two eyes, the world finally began to come into focus. It still took me a few moments to see what Shali was pointing at.

An enormous artificial meteorite was descending from the blackness of the sky, four legs extending from the bottom (to further confirm it was an artificial meteorite). There was something different about this meteorite. I said to Shali, "Call it in. I think an invasion is about to begin."

The earliest attack, which demolished an entire city, was originally thought to have been the Bomdilans using a new super weapon, but they denied it, of course, because that is what Bomdilans do. Once people arrived at the site of Trongsa, well the former site of Trongsa, it was clear that a meteorite had struck the city, but it didn't take long for our scientists to determine that it was some sort of artificial meteorite. Panic followed in the wake of the attack as news of the unnatural origin of the meteorite spread around the planet. When there were no more attacks, the panic subsided, life went on, and eventually the destruction of Trongsa faded into legend.

The next attack came three generations later. Another artificial meteorite crashed into the mountains near Domka, not doing any damage, but it was immediately recognized as another attack. Nobody blamed the Bomdilans, and "Keep your eyes on the skies!" became the watchword of the day, but the war didn't really begin in earnest for another two generations.

Can it be called a war if it is only a series of constant attacks with no counter attacks?

Suddenly, five generations after that first attack, the bombardment started. Artificial meteorites began striking at random intervals, but closer together, many attacks within a generation. Laying waste to whatever was in their path and there was nothing we could do to stop them.

By that time our scientists had determined that the attacks were originating from the large planet that hung constantly overhead. What had always been seen as a source of light and life was now seen as a harbinger of death and destruction.

We tried building up our defenses, but there was little we could do about the giant artificial meteorites they kept lobbing at us. Even our most powerful lasers could only tag them.

The meteorite came down and rested softly on the great plain of Dhurkurjey. Although it didn't make a crater, its sheer size and weight would have destroyed anything it landed on. It just sat there, taunting us, while our army mobilized and began the long trek to face their otherworldly mystery.

Once we had notified the authorities of the meteorite's landing, we knew it was only a matter of time before the Dhukurjey Plain stopped being a desolate flatland and became the focal point for as many people as possible.

"Should we take a closer look at it?"

Shali looked at me as if I had a fifth eye. "Why should we look at it; it's just a rock? And probably dangerous."

"If it is just a rock, it probably isn't dangerous. Well, unless it falls on us, and it didn't do that. And I don't think it is a rock. Rocks are round . . . ish. That isn't round at all."

It wasn't. Although the whole world knew about the artificial meteorites, nobody was really allowed to go anywhere near them, so there were a lot of rumors about them.

This one looked like . . . nothing I had ever seen.

"It is round!" Shali said, and I supposed she had a point. It was sort of round, if round had angles.

We didn't get too close, but we walked around it. The bottom half was round, if round meant eight flat sides. It was also shiny. And there were four long legs, one sticking out from every other flat side of its roundness.

I picked up a small rock and showed it to Shali. "Rock." I pointed at the flat discs attached to the bottom of one of the long legs and said,

"Not a rock." I threw my rock at the not-a-rock to prove my point. Shali snorted.

"It's a meteorite," she said, "meteorites are made of rock."

"Not everything called a meteorite is a meteorite."

She rolled all four eyes at me.

The top half of the rock wasn't shiny at all, but it was round with so many flat surfaces and angles that it not only defied the definition of round, but it spat in their eyes.

When we had finished our tour, I looked at Shali, "Not a rock." She acquiesced to my diagnosis.

"So what it is?"

"Something from out of this world," I said as I pointed up at the partially lit planet above us.

The strange object towered over us imparting a sense of vertigo even as we stood on the flat ground.

Lhuntse isn't a large town, mostly an outpost, but it is the nearest civilized place to where the meteorite sat on Dhukurjey Plain, as well as our intended destination. However, instead of us going to Lhuntse, Lhuntse came to us. A vast sea of people swarming to see the latest attack . . . war as spectator sport. Shali and I became instant celebrities.

"What is it?"

"How did you find it?"

"Where did it come from."

People might be smart individually, but as I looked out over the sea of green faces, their black eyes darting between the meteorite and Shali and me, I could only think *Get 'em all together and they get really dumb.*

We were saved from answering any of the questions thrown at us by the arrival of General Thanza, who climbed up onto the top of our cab and addressed the crowd.

"It is clear that this is the latest attack on us from our neighbors, even if they seem to have come up with a new type of meteorite. I've spoken to our greatest scientists and they are agreed that this may be the invasion we've been dreading since the attacks started in the time of our great-great-grandparents. Judging from the size of their vehicle, I think it is safe to assume that this invasion force will number in the millions. There is no other reason to send something so large."

It occurred to me that there was a reason General Thanza wasn't a politician. He could give us information, but he was hardly inspiring.

Actually, that wasn't true, the only inspiration he gave was for everyone standing on Dhukurjey Plain to put as much distance between themselves and the alien artifact as possible. Before there could be a mass exodus, the General continued to make the situation worse.

"It will take all our forces, both regular and militia, to stop this invasion. The army is on its way, but it is up to you, the good people of Lunts, to be the first line of defense,"

I winced. There was nothing to get a scared group of people to join you like mispronouncing the name of their town, especially using a word that means "poop," and strongly hinting that they were going to die. I leaned over to Shali and said, imitating the General, "And you will be the first sacrifices to die for my career."

On the other hand, while the bulk of the army hadn't come with General Thanza, he had brought a large enough force to convince everyone that they needed to do their civic duty.

It still took a while to organize the ragtag collection of thrill seekers into the semblance of an army. And since Shali and I were the lucky ones who first saw the invasion force, we somehow found ourselves forced into the vanguard of the defense, entirely against our wills. All I really wanted to do was hop back in the hauler and deliver my load of telenite to Lhuntse, although I don't suppose there was anyone left in the town to receive shipment.

We stood there, uncomfortable, more than a little scared, listening to General Thanza and his aides explain what they wanted us to do. And it wasn't just one thing. They laid out contingencies. If this happened, we were to do this. If that happened, we were to do that. If something else happened, we were to do something else.

"And if nothing happens, we're supposed to find something to do anyway," I whispered to Shali.

Suddenly, an enormous panel fell from the side of the meteorite and extended straight outward, so large, the entire population of Lhuntse could have stood on it with room to spare.

A large figure, all white, slowly moved out of the meteorite onto the platform. If this was one of the invaders, which seemed likely, the invasion couldn't be more than two, perhaps three of the aliens.

Slower than you would think possible, although with such size and mass, perhaps the creature couldn't move any faster . . . it must take a lot of energy just to keep a body that size going, it descended a ladder that was attached to one of the meteorite's legs. Upon reaching the ground, the creature paused and finally stepped onto the surface.

It turned around and we got our first clear look at the monster.

It was shaped like one of us, but its entire body was white instead of more natural green. Instead of the normal four black eyes a person should have, it had one enormous gold eye taking up its entire head. It was so large, I don't even know how to describe its size; there is nothing to compare it to. It dwarfed the tallest towers, yet was smaller than the rilles and mountains. I had no idea how we were going to defeat this monster. I looked around to for General Thanza. From the look on his face, he didn't know either.

However, a leader, a general, needs to lead. General Thanza summoned his advisors, and they gathered on top of the cab of our hauler, surveying the flat plain, his assembled, and impressed, troops, and the distant monster that could wipe us all out with a careless step.

As the general planned, the big white figure bounded around, digging deep holes in the soil, and putting the dirt into bags. Just as the general and his advisors began to fan out to give instructions to us all, a second big white man emerged from the machine and clambered down the ladder to join the first giant.

I raised my hand to get the General's attention. "Do two giants change your plans?" I asked before adding a "Sir."

"No. We can be just as ineffective against two as we can be against one," he responded with, perhaps, a little too much honesty.

With a shout, General Thanza ordered us all forward to where the strange invasion was taking place. The two giants were hopping around the plain, occasionally picking up rocks or placing objects on the surface. They seemed oblivious to the fact that they hadn't actually landed near a city. They also seemed to take no notice of our charge.

When I asked the General about this, he informed me, "It is a ploy. They know we're here and are just biding their time."

I tried to move away from the general into the anonymous crowd racing towards the big white men, but he kept me close, apparently deciding that since I was among the first to spot them, I was some sort of good luck charm. Shali, I noticed, was similarly honored.

When we hit them, we hit them hard. We were, however, an

unarmed mob, but we swarmed onto their shoes, we climbed onto the devices, no doubt some sorts of bombs, we even clambered onto the feet of their meteorite.

Eventually, I did manage to get away from General Thanza. I could carry out his orders, but not under his watchful eyes. It was a surreal experience, moving with a mob that had a general idea of what it was supposed to do—repel the invaders—but without any specific idea about how to do it. I expect that General Thanza was at a loss as well. Fighting off big white men with a single golden eye in the middle of their face was unlike any threat we had ever faced. It was certainly different from fighting off the Bomdilans from the next crater over. If you lost to the Bomdilans, the worst they could do was eat your liver. These aliens would smash you into paste.

I was unarmed, of course. There's no real reason to carry weapons on an ore run across the Dhukurjey Plain. What's going to happen? An alien invasion? There wasn't much I could do. I did what I could, which in this case meant trying to scale the cliff wall that was the giants' boots. There was some sort of latching mechanism on it and if I could get to the top of the boot I might, with the help of others, loosen the mechanism and perhaps cause the creature to fall. Based on its movements, it was clumsy and perhaps couldn't rise from a prone position.

The battle raged on, with us attacking the giants, to little effect, and then regrouping to sabotage the bombs they were placing around Dhukurjey Plain. The giants kept going about their work, stepping on some of us.

Climbing the boot was more difficult than I had expected. It wasn't smooth, but it also wasn't designed to be climbed without gear. When I finally got to the top, there were already a couple of people there, their green skin standing in stark contrast to the white background. I explained my plan, and the three of us moved into position. We tried to grab hold of the strap that seemed to hold the boot in position.

"On the count of four," I called. As I said three, however, the giant took a step, except each step these giants took was more like flying through the air. Fortunately, all three of us were holding on tightly, otherwise we would have been thrown off, our bodies falling to the distant regolith below. I tried not to think of anyone who was climbing the boot's side when the giant leaped.

The landing was difficult. I barely managed to hold on and one of the others was thrown from the boot. I didn't see where he landed since I was too busy holding myself in place. When I did have a chance to look around, I saw that reinforcements had arrived.

Buzz looked over at Neil. The gleaming white spacesuits that NASA was so proud of, that were practically kept in clean rooms created expressly for that purpose, were covered in dust. With every step, they kicked up dust and some fine greyish-green particles that spread across their boots and legs

He didn't really have time to worry about the growing discoloration. They had limited time on the surface and a job to do. He began to put the Passive Seismic Experiment behind a large rock. It would be used to detect "moonquakes." Even as he placed it on the ground, he could see the dust swarm over it.

Buzz turned his head to see Neil bringing over the Lunar Dust Detector, which would be mounted to the PSE. "Even before you get that in place, I can tell you that it will detect dust," he radioed to Neil.

As the two men lumbered around in their spacesuits, they continued to raise puffs of dust faster than would seem naturally possible.

The tide of battle turned in our favor with the seasoned troops under General Chhukza. Well, perhaps it didn't turn in our favor so much as continue as it had before, but with more men. General Chhukza's troops appeared on the edge of a small crater, thousands of green heads, armed and ready for war. A small detachment of General Chhukza's men scrambled down onto the plain, their purpose obviously to defuse the bombs. The majority of Chhukza's forces joined the attack on the big white men. While the earlier attacks were uncoordinated mob actions, the new attack was coordinated, disciplined, and, as far as I could tell, exactly as successful as the attacks made by the civilians from Lhuntse.

I slid down the side of the boot quickly. I didn't trust myself enough to be able to hold on through another one of those enormous leaps. I now found myself close to where General Chhukza's troops were deploying. The general was calling out orders, including detailing a group to infiltrate the meteorite in case it tried to return to the invaders' home planet, the first line of a possible counter invasion.

With the professional troops, we were armed and one of the soldiers gave me an extra gun. It would have made me feel safer, but by now I had come to the conclusion that nothing we could do would hurt the big white men. Kill-o-zap guns went off around me, but their range could barely reach the top of the big white men's feet, exploding in harmless puffs of smoke. I wondered if the big white men would look down and see them as anything more dangerous than a cloud of dust raised by their capering around.

The bomb defusers climbed over and through the bombs, emerging from the other side looking perplexed. "What's wrong?"

"It isn't like any bomb I've ever seen. There is no detonator of any type, no explosives. I have no idea what it's for," the bomb defuser called to me as he hurried to the next one. "We've just got to make sure none of them are going to blow up." And he ducked into the inner workings of the alien device. If they weren't bombs, I wondered what they were?

An enormous foot came down on top of me. A foot the size of a building, bigger than a building, really. The only reason I'm still here is that there was a gap between the ground and the tread, and I was lucky enough to be standing in the right spot. To my right, one of the Lhuntsen was lucky in a different way. When the giant foot came down, it killed him cleanly. He never had a chance, but I doubt he felt any pain. I wondered, stuck beneath the boot for those few seconds before the creature bounded away, if the big white men even knew what they were doing to us, or what we were doing to them.

The alien bounded away into the distance. It was heading back to the meteorite that brought it and began to climb the ladder to reenter. It was soon joined by the other alien, and I watched a few of General Chhukza's troops sneak into the meteorite before the massive door closed up, trapping them inside with the big white men.

Without the aliens to attack, the mob began to break up. Many of them tried to sneak back to Lhuntse as if they were afraid General Thanza would punish them for leaving. A few ran from the plains, clearly not caring what the general thought of them. The professional troops fell into ranks and awaited their orders. I stayed. I still had a load of telenite that wouldn't get to Lhuntse by itself, and I needed to find Shali somewhere in the milling crowd, with luck, not among the casualties.

I was close enough to hear General Chhukza barking out orders to his troops, sending them to further sabotage the aliens' equipment, which he seemed to have decided were not bombs, but were, perhaps, something more nefarious.

General Thanza was ignoring the civilians who fled back to Lhuntse and was attempting to contact the troops who had managed to find their way into the meteorite. He was less than successful. Apparently the meteorite was made of some material that stopped his communication rays from reaching their target.

As it became more and more clear that nothing was going to happen, more and more people left. I looked here and there, high and low for Shali, with no luck. General Thanza impressed me into a reclamation gang. As I sorted through the bodies of the fallen, I prayed to the four hundred and thirty-eight gods that I not find Shali.

I didn't. Well, I did find him later, but that was during the victory celebration. Shali and I had gotten separated early in the fighting and he quickly made his way to Lhuntse, leaving the hauler and me at the Battle of Dhukurjey Plain to survive or not on our own.

I was leaning over a body when there was a massive explosion from the artificial meteorite, bright enough that it blinded me and everyone else who was looking in its direction. As vision came back to people, cheers resounded over the Dhukurjey Plain. Once the spots cleared from my eyes, I could see why.

The top half of the meteorite was gone, leaving only its wobbly legs standing. General Chhukza's men had managed to rig it to explode, defeating the alien invasion force and proving that size doesn't matter.

On board the *Eagle*, Neil Armstrong looked at his companion. Buzz Aldrin was focused on piloting the module back to lunar orbit and their rendezvous with Mike Collins, the loneliest man in, or out of, the world, orbiting in the command module *Columbia*.

"'Magnificent Desolation' was a nice turn of phrase. It'll probably be remembered longer that my giant leap. In the desert, in the mountains, I've never been anywhere so completely devoid of life."

Without looking up, Buzz responded, "Too bad. All those science fiction stories of little green men on the moon are now a thing of the past. Pete'll have to come up with something else to say."

Neil looked over at Buzz. "I *just* can't believe that they're going to make us stay in quarantine for three weeks *just* to make sure this dust is just dust."

You can hear some wild tales in a late-night diner, especially in the Ozarks where such establishments are often, shall we say, centers of culture. Sometimes, some of them are even true, just ask any Bubba. Or better yet, ask Selina Rosen.
—*RWB*

The Green, Green Men of Home

by Selina Rosen

"You're asking me if I'm serious! That's rich. There are no little green men. If aliens are visiting Earth why don't they land in the middle of Central Park in New York and pick up some Harvard graduate business executive? Why would they pick up Bubba Jo the auto mechanic who didn't graduate from third grade, from Bum Suck Nowhere, Tennessee?" The bigger guy said, ending his sentence by blowing air out of his cheek for added impact. He made a face as he took a sip of his coffee.

Bo didn't think the coffee was bad, but then after the swill his late wife Shara had made him drink and eat for years, everything at the Short Stack Diner tasted like a little slice of heaven to him. These guys were obviously big city boys, what with their suit coats and ties— traveling salesmen most likely. They were wearing jeans and cowboy boots, but neither had so much as a speck of dirt on them, so Bo figured they were most likely tractor salesman. They always dressed like this because they thought it made them look like gentleman farmers, but they just looked like douches.

"They'd be seen if they landed someplace where there was a bunch of people wouldn't they?" the smaller guy said.

He had a full white beard and if you stuck a red dunce cap on his head Bo thought he'd look just like one of those garden gnomes in that cartoon his kids watched forty times a week. Bo smiled and tucked into his plate of bacon and eggs.

"That's why they always grab some local yokel, because they're always in the middle of nowhere," garden gnome man continued.

Bo couldn't pinpoint their accents, but he guessed they weren't from around there. They were no doubt like most of the traveling salesman he'd met over the years—overeducated idiots who had an opinion about everything and didn't know a damn thing. Modern snake oil peddlers, except the stuff they sold cost a whole lot more money to not do what they promised it would. They all thought they were so damn smart, but if they were, what were they doing driving around all over the country's highways trying to sell crap no one really needed? Bo glanced over, saw the tractor brochure sitting in the middle of the table between them and smiled at how clever he was. They probably knew less about tractors than they did about little green men.

"There are no space aliens, Brian," the big guy said again. Brian seemed like an odd name for a gnome, Bo thought with a grin. "Where is the evidence?"

"There's all kinds of evidence . . ."

"Blurry photos and barely audible sound bites?" The big guy scoffed, "Come on, Brian, you're an intelligent man. We have satellites orbiting Earth that can take a picture of a freckle on a gnat's ass, yet there is no footage of these spacecrafts. Everyone has a camera on their phone, yet no one can get a decent picture of an alien ship much less an actual alien. And they always have some excuse when the obvious answer is there was nothing really there in the first place."

Yep, this smart ass thought he had it all figured out, though gnome boy proved he wasn't much brighter when he proceeded to spout his explanation. "The government is running a huge cover up, and these aliens have some technology that messes up all our electronics."

"In that case, why are there any photos at all? It just doesn't make sense, and if they are coming here to do nothing but ram a probe up bubba's fat ass, why are they coming at all? What's the point? What exactly do they want? Why are they checking us out at all?" The big guy asked.

Good questions all, but in Bo's opinion rattling off a bunch of questions wasn't a sign of intelligence any more than not being able to answer them showed someone was stupid.

"There are billions of planets; there has to be life somewhere," Brian defended.

"I have no problem believing that. The laws of probability say there must be life somewhere else in the universe. Hell, the laws of probability say there could be life just like us and two guys like us having this exact same conversation eating the same crappy food in the same dinner. But any life that might be out there isn't close enough to come here. Why would they? If they were capable of interstellar travel that allowed them to jump through light years of space, why come here and then what . . . spy on us? What would be the point? Some people think they've been doing it since the dawn of time. I know you're watching that *Ancient Astronauts* show because that's what started this whole stupid conversation. Why on Earth would they come and just keep spying on us for millennia but never really make their presence known except in all these really cryptic, can't-really-prove-it ways?"

"Government cover up . . ."

"Really? That's your answer for everything: that the government covers it up. Every government in the world since before the beginning of time has been able to hide, control, and destroy every real piece of evidence. Now the bigger question is why are they hiding this from us at all?"

Brian seemed to think about all that for a minute then said, "They are afraid of mass panic in the streets!"

"Really? More panic than, say, Nazi death camps or Saudi terrorists and a dozen other atrocities different governments of the world couldn't hide—though they tried. Hell, we have senators who text pictures of their junk to miscellaneous bimbos, and they always get caught. Yet you think those idiots could really keep a secret as big as aliens landing on our planet, taking people off and bringing them back?"

Brian tried to argue, but he obviously was about as bright as a match that had already been struck. "They can't. That's why people know. . . ."

"Know what? If there was conclusive evidence we wouldn't even be having this conversation." The big guy looked like he had reached the point where if gnome man didn't shut up, the big guy's head might explode.

"Dude, a huge plane full of people disappeared just last year. Everyone in the world was looking for it; no one ever found it. We don't know everything," Brian said.

Bo thought that was the first really intelligent thing either of them had said. After years of living with the bitch that was Shara, Bo didn't really understand arguing over anything, much less bullshit like this. Neither one of them knew what the hell they were talking about, so why did it matter?

Bo decided to make his move. He got up, picked up his cup, and moved to their table. "Couldn't help overhearin' your conversation. That's some right interesting stuff, but you've got it all wrong. Mind if I sit down?" He sat down next to Brian the Gnome before either of them could say no. He looked at the address paper clipped to the brochure. "Wait a minute, I better take this." He pulled his smart phone out, looked at it, then started typing in a text. "Boy, if you had ever told me that I'd be typing instead of just talking. Am I right?" Bo sent the text and put the phone back in his pocket. "So, little green men? You're both wrong. Let me tell you a little story . . ."

"'Bout six years ago I met me a hot little number, and by little I mean little. She barely made five feet tall, but she had one of those made-up names crackers like to give their kids and a 'tude you could see before you saw her. Now, at the time I suffered from a horrible malady called penial stupidia . . ."

"Penial stupidia?" the one who wasn't Brian asked.

"Yep. It affects mostly young men in their twenties. It makes it impossible to see all the decent women in a room and hone in on the one completely psycho hose beast and fall madly and passionately in love. That's what happened to me when I met Shara. She was high on pills most of the time and smoked one cigarette after another. She was selfish and self-centered and was just exactly the kind of girl I was always bringing home that Mama was telling me was going to kill me in my sleep. And I just had to have her. Now while Shara wasn't quite as crazy as other girls I'd dated, she was by far the meanest. Course, I didn't know that till I'd knocked the silly bitch up. She already had one kid, and I liked him well enough. She told me to marry her and so I did, and that was when all the ugly came out to play . . ."

"What's this have to do with little green men?" Brian asked.

"Wait for it, gnome boy. It won't mean nothin' without the back story." They were ticking Bo off with all their interruptions. "She was big as a barn pregnant but she wouldn't quit smoking cigarettes or pot, and she was probably using pills, too. It's a wonder Shelia wasn't born with a third eyeball or four hands or an extra head or no limbs at all. Now the whole time she was pregnant, I kept thinking all the meanness was hormones, but after Shelia was born, well Shara was meaner than ever. I was working all the time—I'm a mechanic, by the way, though I graduated high school—because I had to. Shara just kept buying the most expensive crap she could find. See, she always needed to impress her new friends all the time and she always had new friends because the minute someone got to know her . . . well they couldn't help but hate her.

"I hated her, too. She was a half-ass mother, and my sister was mostly raising my baby as well as that other kid, and let me tell you I was beginning to see that boy had it in him to be just like his mama . . ."

"Seriously, what's this have to do with space aliens?" The stupider of the two asked. He was stupider, in Bo's opinion, because he didn't believe in little green men at all.

"Let me tell my story!" Bo shot back. He was big enough and bad enough looking that they realized it was in their best interest to shut their pie holes, especially since the diner didn't serve pie. "See, the problem was I loved that baby girl and weren't no way I would get her in a custody battle, because that bitch Shara could put on a good act. She could open the door and make the world think she was Mother Theresa, close it and go right back to being the devil's own sperm. She made my life, the kid's lives, my sister's and Mama's lives living hell. But short of killing her, I didn't see no way out. Make no doubt she deserved to die, but I didn't deserve to go to jail. Especially not as pretty as I am." He grinned at them then, showing where he was missing a couple of teeth. "I started praying for God to deliver me from evil—you know, my wife. You boys pray?"

"I do," Brian said.

"I don't," the dummy said.

Bo looked at him through narrowed eyes and said, "That figures. Any ways, it's funny how prayers get answered, and sometimes you don' realize they have been answered at all till way later. And now this is where the space aliens come into play. See I'd stupidly voiced an opinion that wasn't Shara's in her presence and she'd gone off on me screaming at me for a good fifteen minutes in front of the kids and my sister. See, I thought maybe since she used my sister for a free babysitting service about forty hours a week so that she could get rest from being a 'stay at home mom,' that she might want to talk to my sister as if she were something above a dog. I forgot that Shara loved dogs more than people—no doubt because they couldn't tell her what a worthless piece of crap she was or point out that she was basically wrong about . . . well, everything.

"I'd just had it, so I took off into the woods at a dead run till I was in—as you fellows so aptly named it—the middle of nowhere. I sat down on a rock and I know it isn't manly, but I just had me a good cry. Then I hear this noise and when I look up there is like this light and then bigger than shit two little green men walk right out of it. And that's why there ain't no pictures of ships, dumbasses, 'cause the ships ain't nowhere near Earth. Sittin' down and takin' off puts too much wear and tear on a ship. So they have these little doorways they send down and they walk into one on the ship and come out here and visa-versa. Some sorta teleporty device like what they have on *Star Trek* . . . except with a door that ya walk through.

"Next thing I know, they are asking me about a bazillion questions about plants and animals and water supplies and how we grow crops and hunt . . . And see, that's why they all abduct Bubba Jo from Bumb Suck Nowhere. Not just so no one sees them or can see or use their shiny door, but mostly because college-educated people don't know a damn thing these creatures are interested in. They want to know how best to exist down here, and let's face it, you don't know diddly squat about that, but folks like me do. And see, we're just a stop on their way. They're travelers; they come here for a quick bite, check out the scenery, and then they move on. They have no desire to inhabit our planet, they are just looking for chow. Sort of like why you guys stopped at this here diner."

"I still don't see what this has to do with your wife," the dummy said.

"Give me a damn minute," Bo snapped. "Are you one of those asshats who fast forwards to the end of a movie? Anyways, they get done questionin' me—and no they didn't stick nothin' up my butt—and then they are talkin' about whether they are going to turn me lose and hunt for some of the deer I told them were good eatin' or if they were just going to eat me. Now as miserable as I was being married to

Shara, I didn't want to be an alien's can ah Spam if you get my drift. That's when I realized that God had been listening when I was praying for an answer to my woman problem. I said, all Billy Goat Gruff style, 'Look dude, you don't want to eat me, I'm nothing but bone. I've got a woman back home who used to be beautiful but has done nothing since I married her but get increasingly fatter and uglier. She has been smoking herself since she was eight, and she's filled with all sorts of fun stuff like THC and nicotine . . ."

The dummy started to laugh and then so did Brian. The dummy said, "You expect us to believe that little green men ate your old lady?"

Bo pulled something out of his pants pocket and threw it on the table. It was green and red in color and about the size and shape of a horse turd.

"What's that?" Brian asked.

Bo smiled, picked it up, and twirled it between his fingers. "That's what's left when two little green men eat a two-hundred pound human turd in a polyester dress. It was one of the happiest moments of my life. One took one end and one took the other and they sorta met in the middle, and just like that all my troubles were over. I actually had two of them . . ." He held it up and looked at it. ". . . but I lost one. I think the dog might have taken off with it which . . . well, he was her dog, so it would be nice for him to have something to remember her by. See they can eat a person, clothes and all, in about ten minutes—no blood, no waste, very clean and efficient like. They have a hell of a metabolism, sorta like a chicken. They can digest anything organic, but artificial fibers, buttons, zippers and such sorta come up like this. Like a cat spitting up a hair ball. And before you go judging the little green men for eating the occasional person, know that they are far more evolved than we are, so it ain't no different to them than us eatin' a cow."

"You expect us believe that is all that's left of your wife?" Dummy shook his head.

Bo took his prize and put it back in his pocket and then he stood up. "I don't give a good diddly damn what you believe." He grinned then. "But admit it; it's a hell of a story."

They looked at each other, then at Bo and cracked up laughing. Bo laughed, too. "You had me going there for a minute," Brian said.

"Have a good day, gentleman," Bo said and tipped his ballcap to them as he walked out of the restaurant. "Dumbasses," he said and hopped into his truck and roared off.

"So was that guy crazy or just having a good time with us?" Brian asked Carl.

Carl shrugged. He didn't want to think about it. The truth was that like so many "skeptics," the reason he insisted that there were no such things as space aliens and monsters was that he was trying to convince himself.

He hated this job, but it was all he could get. He often thought seriously about using his college business degree for toilet paper. He looked at the GPS. They were on a dirt road in the middle of nowhere, but when you were going from one farm to another trying to sell tractor supplies, that was how it went.

In front of them a tractor was in the middle of the road making it impossible for them to pass and spinning up huge dust clouds for them to eat.

"Typical," Carl said.

Brian nodded.

The tractor proceeded to stop and just sit there.

"Really, are you kidding me?" Carl got out of the truck, and that was when he saw a shimmering door shape appear behind his truck. "Ah crap!"

Brian got out of the passenger's side of the truck and took off running into the soybean field. One of the little green men ran after Brian so fast he wasn't much more than a blur. Then he jumped on Brian's head, his jaws opened like a snake, and he proceeded to swallow Brian whole. After much crunching and gurgling and flatulence, the alien returned to his original shape and then—bigger than shit—he spit out a little block full of blue and gray fibers with just a hint of the metallic from Brian's tie.

"Ah look, he puked something sparkly. Can you believe it? They weren't even real cotton jeans," the redneck they'd met in the diner earlier said at Carl's shoulder. "Pira, ya shoulda et the dummy first," the redneck said to the alien who was returning from the field as he pointed at Carl.

The alien walked over and handed the cube he had regurgitated to the redneck, who took it and dropped it right into his pocket with his wife.

"You know me, Bo, I like to eat my dinner on the run," the little green man said, and then he was making a sound that Carl figured the creature thought was laughing—but really wasn't.

"While I prefer a nice, leisurely meal myself, with a little more time to digest," the other alien said. He was looking at Carl.

Carl tried to scream and run, but the last thing he saw was the gray inside of the little green man.

Bo dropped the other cube into his pocket and patted it. "Always a pleasure doing business with ya." He pulled his cell phone out of his pocket and held it up. "Just give me a call when you're coming to town and I'll see what I can rustle up for ya. I'll text ya with coordinates just like I did this time."

"Thank you, friend Bo," the little green men said together. Then they got in the tractor salesmen's truck and drove it into the door and were gone.

For a second Bo wondered what they did with the vehicles. He shrugged and got back onto the tractor. Bo drove it back to where he had found it. There wasn't an engine around that Bo couldn't start. He grinned and climbed into his truck. Unable to wait any longer, he tore into the first cube. He found a fistful of change, a zipper, a bunch of buttons, and three silver crowns.

"Ka-ching," he said.

In the other one he found a gold wedding ring, a silver chain with a metal pendant, and another pocketful of change, a zipper, a couple of pieces of metal that no doubt came out of his boots, buttons, and the clip off the clip-on tie he'd been wearing.

"Ka-ching, ka-ching!" He saw an inscription inside the ring, but it didn't matter because he melted everything with his torch before he sold it. His little girl liked to play with all the buttons and zippers.

He never made much actual money. The best he had done was a couple of hundred bucks, but to him this was a bonus because he was, after all, still paying for the hit they'd done on his wife.

After three novels and several short stories, Beth Cato seems to be becoming somewhat of an expert at telling Victorian Era tales, so fitting that her tale for us should also be one in which a green-skinned guest has everyone aflutter at a dance on . . . —BTS

A Fine Night For Tea and Bludgeoning

by Beth Cato

Summer 1901

Upon my arrival at the Durham's dance, it was quickly apparent to me that their daughter's new purebred fiancé was not the evening's star as gossip had foretold. Instead, a dashing green-skinned gentleman had garnered a pack of giggling admirers.

I had never encountered a person of such fascinatingly verdant coloration before, and yet I immediately had an odd pressure upon me to *accept* this man and not question his visage.

How peculiar.

I retreated to a far wall. My brow furrowed in thought; the motion hurt. My face was caked with powder adequate to make an elephant sneeze, all to obscure the final, yellowed vestiges of what had been a black eye.

Such a blemish would have been abhorrent to the flibbertigibbets filling the room, but then, they also had the mental acumen of chocolate éclairs. They prowled these parties for husband material the way big game hunters stalked moose, each seeking to bag something brag-worthy and best kept stuffed in a parlor. This green-skinned man was fresh meat, though it seemed no one else had noticed his greenness at all.

As if sensing my attention, the strange fellow's eyes met mine through the turbulent sea of satin and brocade. I wanted to step deeper into the alcove behind me but did not, as if something were there to block me in place.

131

To my horror, he moved directly toward me. The gaggle of girls parted like a frippery Red Sea.

"I don't believe we've met," he said, bowing as proper. He was rather short and finely attired. "I'm Mister Elvis Wibbles."

"Elvis Wibbles." His given name was gibberish, while the surname sounded more appropriate for a spoiled poodle. "Well, Mr. Wibbles, I am Miss Rosemary Hardy."

"Would you care to dance?" he asked with a gesture.

My forced grin pained my bruised face. "Truthfully, I would rather not. I dance with the elegance of a camel festooned in white satin."

Puzzlement claimed his features. "A camel. A desert dromedary. I was not aware they danced."

"They don't, in white satin or otherwise. And neither do I."

"Ah! A jest! I see now."

I sidled away. It was odd that no one lingered close to us. "I think there are others here more receptive of your advances." Goodness knows, the other women had to wonder why he sought to speak with *me*. I had made it clear I welcomed male companionship as much as cholera.

"Perhaps. Would you prefer to chat while roller skating? It is quite the hobby of yours, isn't it?" His face scrunched in thought. "I have yet to skate myself, though I'm game to try. I suppose that should be mastered before attempting the battle tourney element."

I gawked. "How did you . . . ?"

One didn't discuss proletariat entertainment such as roller skating at a party within these echelons, and one *certainly* didn't bring up the particular brand that required cudgels. My fellow midnight skaters— the dreadful Miss Pumpernickel included—maintained a strict vow regarding our clandestine activities. That's why we wore masks. Miss Pumpernickel was the only one I knew by her Christian name, pink-drenched demon-spawn that she was.

"The capillaries are broken in the interstitial tissue beneath your skin." He motioned around his eye. "Such contusions are a signature of your sport, yes? No one else present bears such marks."

I lightly touched my own face. Certainly I would have heard snide whispers if any of my blemishes were showing. "How can you see that?"

"With my eyes. Very useful things, these optical organs, even if humans are sadly limited to a pair."

"Would you prefer to have more than that, Mr. Wibbles?"

"That entirely depends on the environment and a species' other extrasensory abilities, doesn't it? I have always been rather fond of the look of eye stalks, but one needs the right body to 'pull off the look,' as it were."

I couldn't resist. "And what body type is best?"

"A central torso with a tentacle array," he answered without hesitation. "But then, tentacles are the very embodiment of glamour."

I contained my guffaw behind a fist. "I daresay, tentacles would add something . . . different to next season's fashions."

"You yourself fancy the look of feathers in your Artful Athena guise, do you not?"

I looked about in alarm. "Keep your voice down!"

He squatted. "Is this far enough?"

Good grief! The man was a mayor of morons! I backed away. "I don't wish to speak with you." I allowed the teeming crowd to swallow me. The throngs pushed me along and regurgitated me on the far side. When I glanced back, the satined swarm had again descended upon Mr. Wibbles. I released a huff of breath and opened the exit to the garden.

I dashed outside and almost clobbered Miss Pumpernickel on the stairs. If I'd recognized her immediately, I would have gone for the full clobber.

"You!" she cried, her pitch high enough to make dogs whine.

Miss Verily Pumpernickel and I had become acquainted as mere toddlers. Our mothers, as good as friends as socialite vipers could be, set us together to play. As girls of like age, we were informed we would be friends.

Five minutes later, our nannies had to pry apart our flailing bodies and fists. Several baby teeth had made early exits and Mrs. Pumpernickel's favorite Royal Doulton vase with hand-painted periwinkles lay in tragic shards.

Miss Pumpernickel and I had spent our childhoods encountering each other at engagements such as this, often circling and hissing like roused tomcats.

We didn't come to blows again until we both somehow managed to find midnight skating in recent months. Smacking Miss Pumpernickel with a cudgel was one of my great joys in life, right alongside hot chocolate and Tennyson read aloud.

"Figures, Miss Hardy's at this party," Miss Pumpernickel said, calling on her frequent juvenile need to rhyme.

"How's your jaw tonight?"

"How's your eye? I heard tales of that bout. Tsk, tsk." She grinned, and drool oozed from the corner of her mouth. She had yet to heal from a strike I'd made some weeks before that caused her to kiss the floor in a glorious twenty foot skid.

"My eyes were quite well until I was blinded by the pink monstrosity known as your dress. Certainly, such a screaming shade of color violates laws of both civil and religious nature." I moved past her. "Now, if you'll excuse me, I need fresh air."

"A walk in the garden by yourself?" She sneered. "Oh, but what if there is talk?"

"Talk! There is always talk, truth or not. It should mean nothing to you if I encounter a gentleman at the fountain and proceed to condemn us both to eternal damnation by kissing his face and grabbing—"

"Stop!" she shrilled. "Don't poison my morality!"

I had no aversion to being an old spinster at twenty. My modest income from gambling on skating bouts had granted me funds to rent a private flat; I fancied a future of independence and world travel. Poor Miss Pumpernickel still wanted a somewhat more traditional life: a mansion, a man, and weekly excursions to skate and bludgeon.

"If you want poison, I'm sure I could borrow some cyanide. It's supposed to smell of almonds—"

"You are rude and crude and I am not in the mood!" Sniffing indignantly, Miss Pumpernickel flounced up the stairs and indoors.

I sighed to myself. "I suppose one *should* possess an appropriate disposition to deploy poison, though I have considered it as a hobby. Such is my daily mood." I frowned at the door. If I went inside, I would likely encounter the enigmatic buffoon Mr. Wibbles again.

Instead, I strolled down a garden path lit by lanterns. My mind wandered to more pleasant places where skate wheels roared, crowds cheered, and cracked noses erupted as brilliantly as smashed tomatoes.

The next morning the maid entered the dining room as I swirled the last dredges of my tea.

"There's a gentleman caller for the miss." By the rapturous expression on her face, she had surely encountered an angel, burning bush, or other portent direct from God.

My mother screeched as if a spider had landed upon her. She hopped up, clapping her hands, and danced. "A caller! A gentleman caller! Really? Truly? A man here for Rosemary?"

"If you're unsure of the visitor's gender, we could make the fellow drop trou," I said; Mama was too ecstatic to snap at me. I slowly set down my cup. "Who is this caller, Miriam?"

"He's a Mr. Wibbles, miss. I have his calling card."

"A card!" Mama whooped. "Rosemary's acquired her first card!"

I pushed myself away from the table. I was reminded of my last concussion, how thoughts became as elusive as jelly on fingers. Why was that man pestering me?

After a quick change of clothes, I faced Mr. Wibbles in the parlor. Mama, in her excitement, had managed to baptize her lap in lukewarm tea. While she changed, Miriam acted as chaperone and sat far across the room as she pretended to do mending.

"I thought I'd done my best to dissuade you, Mr. Wibbles," I muttered.

"Your best? Oh no. Virulent influenza would be most effective to discourage me, but I hope to be gone before that season is underway."

"Then let's get this done before my mother summons a priest to wed us. Why do you wish to confer with me?" I hovered near a table that Miriam had quickly set with hot tea and fruit and fresh baguettes.

"Miss Pumpernickel is your great rival during midnight bouts, correct?"

"Keep your voice down," I hissed. "No! Don't crouch!" I frantically waved him up again before Miriam could notice and react as if he proposed. "How do you know about our tournaments? You're a stranger!"

"I try to accumulate a great deal of knowledge even if I'm not entirely sure how to process it." He tilted his head. "Miss Hardy, you're impressively resistant to my chemical aura that increases my likeability and translates my vocalized awkwardness into inane pleasantries. For example, my past few sentences should have been received by you as compliments on the perfect roundness of the mole on your cheek or the composition and odor of this freshly-baked bread."

"The bread does smell divine and is of pleasing composition, surely, but I remain resistant to this . . . aura of yours."

A grin lit his face. "Impressive! I must run a complete body analysis on you."

That's when I bludgeoned him with a baguette. Fresh as it was, it created a minor fountain of crumbs upon impact with his forehead. Across the room, Miriam squealed.

I brandished the now-flaccid breadstick in front of his face. "I want you out. You're a very strange man."

"Miss! What are you doing?" cried Miriam.

"Committing a grave social faux pas by assaulting Mr. Wibbles with baked goods!"

"Oh, miss! What will your mother say?!" At that, Miriam burst into tears and fled the room.

"Mama is probably working on the wedding guest list," I muttered and rubbed my forehead.

"I hope I'm invited," he said brightly. "Miss Hardy, if you are indeed Artful Athena, I require you to be my champion against Miss Pumpernickel."

"Your champion?" Despite my dislike of the fellow, I rather fancied the idea of being anyone's champion. "Let us be clear. You have no intent to pursue me romantically? You simply wish me to duel Miss Pumpernickel?"

"Yes to both!"

I pursed my lips. "This isn't a good place to discuss such matters. Miriam and Mama will return in a right state. Meet me here at midnight." I scribbled an address on a scrap of paper and shoved it at him. Propriety be damned, I was curious.

Besides, if he tried anything, I'd wield far worse than a breadstick.

As Mr. Wibbles entered my secret flat, I had the urge to hold the door open for several seconds after he passed through. I frowned as I finally locked it behind me.

The loft was small but adequate to store my skates, most of them in various states of disrepair, and my costumery. My bouts took place at the warehouse across the street.

"Fascinating!" He went straight to a partially dismantled skate and spun the front wheel. It was the size of his hand. "Two aligned wheels on a base that straps to your boot sole. Primitive but functional."

"And terribly unreliable." I motioned to a bin of spare wheels and other detritus, and then brushed a few leaves from my skirt. My covert activities required that I climb the oak tree at my bedroom window. "Now explain this business of being your champion."

"Ah yes. I arrived in the city in a conveyance quite peculiar by your standards. I thought I had found a proper way to obscure it in plain sight, on what turned out to be the Pumpernickel property. Alas, I was wrong. Mr. Pumpernickel found my device and gifted it to his daughter."

"Why would a carriage be given to Miss Pumpernickel?"

"It, ah, doesn't resemble a carriage in its current form. More like a large pink rose."

I stared. "You disguised your *conveyance* as a flower?"

"It seemed a good idea at the time." He looked most chagrined. "My mission in this time and place . . . I am supposed to mingle and record social mores. The whole experience has rather overwhelmed me, but I understand enough to know that I cannot simply ask for my property back as they found it and assume it to be their own. I've no desire to create what you'd call 'a scene.'"

"Forgive my bluntness, but your skin tone doesn't grant you much subtlety, Mr. Wibbles."

"Ah! You can see my true coloration but refrained from mentioning it until now, our third meeting! Fascinating! Proof that you are merely resistant to my aura, even as it still affects you." He beamed. "To continue, I have investigated Miss Pumpernickel and learned of these roller skating tourneys, and that you often gamble with money or property as part of the challenge."

"You want me to challenge her for this . . . floral conveyance of yours. I would need to counter with some prize of my own, you understand. I also need to know why I should do this at all."

"Out of the kindness of your human soul."

I stared at him, burst out laughing, and then abruptly stopped at his bewildered expression. "You really thought . . . oh."

"You are a good person, aren't you?"

"I fancy myself so, but I'm especially good at skating and bludgeoning, and that's really what this is about, isn't it?"

"Truth. As to the matter of your wager, I do have a modest sum of money I can offer. I know mentioning sums of money aloud is crude, therefore . . . " He beckoned me close.

With my hand on a steel skate sole on the table, I leaned in. He whispered. I sputtered as I jerked back.

"For that sum, surely you could buy a new conveyance!"

Miss Pumpernickel would likely use such funds for a lifetime wardrobe in putrid pink, but goodness! If I had such money at my disposal, I would see the world! The pyramids, the museums, all the glories of history. I forced aside my yearning.

"Money is not the issue," he said. "Human technology will not adequately advance for another thousand years. As much as I would like to visit future eras—I've heard grand things about the disco era and the delights of chocolate chip cookies—I really don't want to linger that long and encounter horrors such as telemarketers or canned meat byproducts or an apocalypse or three."

"Chocolate is worth a wait, but not that long a wait." A thousand years? Mr. Wibbles was surely exaggerating. "I can't say I mind an excuse to directly challenge Miss Pumpernickel. I can issue that to the proper parties on the morrow."

"When will the match take place?"

"This Tuesday or the next. Bludgeon bouts are the only delightful thing about Tuesdays."

As usual, the midnight skating bout began with the night's competitors paired at small tables where we shared tea and engaged in what I like to term as assertive palaver in preparation for rigorous physical activity.

"Miss Pumpernickel, I do believe that shade of pink is what occurs if a dog vomits up ham," I said, taking a delicate sip of oolong.

"At least I wear color." Miss Pumpernickel, as the Pink Puma, wore a cat-eared hood and mask to cover her eyes. A smock and full-length long johns covered her body, all in a screamingly vile hue, as usual. "Wearing brown makes you not only resemble excrement, but you look so *plebian*."

"Plebian excrement! That's the very look I sought to accomplish!"

"I still want to know how you heard of my lovely undying rose." She sniffed. "I don't intend to lose it."

My intent to make an especially crude jest was interrupted by the arrival of the referee. "Ladies, you're up next. Ready yourselves."

Both myself and Miss Pumpernickel had reputations as experienced competitors, and so our match was set at the tourney's end. A goodly crowd had remained.

"HOOT! HOOT! HOOT!" cried my loyal supporters. I gave a graceful curtsy with a winged sleeve. In my guise as Artful Athena, I paid homage to the Goddess of Wisdom's faithful companion, the owl.

Miss Pumpernickel skated to her starting point some thirty feet distant. The battleground formed a fat oval within the warehouse. Our skates, large-wheeled as they were, required a wide turning radius.

I took my own position and adjusted my hood to ensure my tuft ears were erect. I glanced over to find Mr. Wibbles behind the rope barrier a few feet away. Despite numerous people about, he was ringed by emptiness.

"Crush her like Jupiter's gravity!" he shouted.

At the far end, Miss Pumpernickel waggled her bludgeon. The stout stick was a foot in length and swaddled in cloth to cushion blows. The referee had already inspected our weaponry to guard against cruel shenanigans.

"I'm in high dudgeon when I hold forth my bludgeon!" screeched Miss Pumpernickel.

"Good God! Not the poetry again!" I cried. "Yes, I'm sure you're likewise twee when you take a wee!"

"That's crass!" she said.

"I'm sure it's also crass when you wipe your—"

"Ladies! Or women, perhaps I should say," snapped the referee. He had turned a shade of pink complementary to Miss Pumpernickel's obnoxious garb. "Positions!"

I held my bludgeon aloft.

"Brace!"

I lunged, my right knee forward.

"Go!"

I pushed off. The raucous crowd's noise and presence pressed on me. I knew every floor ripple beneath my wheels. My lungs filled, and my torso expanded against my padded bodice.

"Annihilate her like a meteorite impact event!" screeched Mr. Wibbles.

Just as jousting knights of old attempted to unhorse their opponent, I needed to knock Miss Pumpernickel off her skates. I could not aim for her face, lovely target though it was. The kidneys were a fond favorite of mine.

Miss Pumpernickel advanced, pink vomitous nightmare that she was, her high-pitched battle cry enough to puncture a banshee's ear drums.

By the angle of her arm, I ascertained the degree of her attempted blow. One second passed, two. I feinted, as if I'd strike her shoulder as I passed to her right. She swung. To my disgust, she didn't fall so easily for my trap. Our bludgeons clashed with dull thuds, and then I passed her.

Damn Miss Pumpernickel to a week of itchy linens! I followed well-worn grooves in the floor as I came back around. She did likewise on the far side, her teeth grimaced like an indignant poodle.

We rushed each other. This time, both of our bludgeons fell short. Pebbles of sweat rolled down my temples and neck.

"Crush her like a blueberry beneath a tyrannosaurus rex!" yelled Mr. Wibbles.

I was halfway through my turn when my right back wheel locked.

I gasped and balanced on my left foot, tapping the front right wheel just enough to keep me upright. The crowd groaned in recognition of my plight. Their dismay increased my own sense of alarm, but I gritted my teeth and slowed my breath, willing myself to steadiness.

God condemn me to a purgatory of endless parties if I should lose this bout against Miss Pumpernickel, of all women! And because of my accursed wheels, of all things!

The pink beast descended on me with a glass-shattering battle cry. In the glimmer of overhead lights, I witnessed viscous drool dangling from her lips as a grotesque banner.

It was easier to keep my balance on the straight-away, with frequent taps of my front wheel, but our looming confrontation had me at a sorry disadvantage. If I landed fully on my right side, my legs would surely go airborne. My bloomers exposed for all the world to see—oh, how Mama would go apoplectic if she knew! The landing would be none too pleasant, either.

Grimacing, I skated on. The match was set. If I was bound to go out, I'd do so in spectacular, violent, immortal fashion!

Before me I suddenly saw a green-skinned figure not unlike Mr. Wibbles. He winked and jerked his head to the right. I took the hint and passed by so closely that his sleeve grazed mine.

Miss Pumpernickel was upon me. Her blow at my thigh fell short, while my own swing only succeeded in unsettling my balance even more. I gasped, tapping the front wheel as I lurched forward.

The crowd gasped and cheered, likewise certain of my fate.

My cudgel arm extended, I balanced again. As I came around, I stood erect and saw the true cause of the commotion.

Miss Pumpernickel was down! I had won! Wait, what?

"I tripped! Something tripped me!" cried Miss Pumpernickel.

She lay sprawled where that other green-skinned man had been visible not a moment before. I sought out Mr. Wibbles in the crowd. He had stayed in the exact same spot throughout the bout.

I gingerly skated up to Miss Pumpernickel. "Are you injured?"

"Only my pride." She sniffed. "Ah, I have lost both the bout and my incomparable rose, all because I tripped on these old boards . . . !" Like a petulant toddler, she wiggled and kicked the floor.

Balancing on my bad skate, I extended my brown wing to Miss Pumpernickel. She looked surprised, but her pink paw slipped into my grip as I helped her to rise.

To skate and cudgel is to practice an art often maligned and misunderstood by polite society. To us practitioners, it is a sport of dignity and honor.

"I'm sorry the match ended like that," I said.

"Maybe we can skate again, with the wagers reversed?" Hope brightened her eyes.

I shook my head. "I fear not, but there will be other bouts."

She glowered with the ferocity of a rain-soaked cat. "Yes there will be, Miss Hardy. And next time, you'll go splat like water from a tipped vat!" At that, she skated away.

I stared after her. This victory left me feeling as mighty as a pill bug.

A matter of minutes later, I had my skates tucked in their bag, and I had both Mr. Wibbles' cash and his . . . conveyance.

The rose fit in my hand. It resembled a living bloom, though the petals were thicker like a Capodimonte sculpture. The temperature was strangely warm. Leaning close, I thought I detected a beehive-like hum.

"I suppose it's good that we didn't disguise it as a piece of fruit." Mr. Wibbles came alongside me. "I shudder to think of the indigestion it would cause."

The audience dispersed around us, many cheering me as they passed. None came close, though, as if I had a barricade about me. I pursed my lips. I had the profound urge to not intrude that space—akin to the warmth of a fire, even if the flames were distant.

Something—or someone—was there. Concealed.

I fought the urge to ignore the emptiness and jabbed out an elbow. I impacted with solidness that emitted a surprised, "OOF!"

Mr. Wibbles squeaked in surprise as well. "Do you see them? How did you—"

"I can resist your illusions. You said as much yourself. The fellow in the battlefield somehow shifted things so I could see him for a mere second. No one else witnessed him, did they?" I asked, voice low. "He tripped Miss Pumpernickel."

"You are a rarity, Artful Athena! No wonder your cudgel is the stuff of legends!"

"You cheated." I formed a fist around my cudgel.

"Intervention seemed necessary in the light of your malfunction. I needed my conveyance and my local currency. Such alterations in game play are commonplace from what I understand—"

I stepped closer, shoving aside an invisible body, and glared down at him. "Other men may cheat at cards or in other sports, but this arena is sacred ground, Mr. Wibbles. This place . . ." This was where I could be myself, feminine and free with cudgel in hand. "Never intrude in this space again."

His black pupils widened as he quickly nodded. I must have struck a fearsome sight there in my strigine suit, my stick hefted as if I were truly an angelic owl of wrath brandishing a fiery sword.

I stepped back and looked to him and the empty space around him. "That said, I must change my attire. Afterward, we are due for a chat, Mr. Wibbles. I demand to know the truth of you and your companions."

We walked deep into the nearest park: Mr. Wibbles, his five now-visible companions, and I. Each man had green skin, the shades varied considerably, and each wore a natty pinstriped suit. I had donned my walking gown—a tasteful brown, common as it was to Miss Pumpernickel—but maintained my cudgel as a precaution.

"So you are men from beyond the moon," I mused as I glanced at the full moon above. "Men who can turn invisible, who have visited Earth across eras. Why ever did you hide your vessel as a rose?"

"In my world, blooming flowers are left to bloom so their beauty lives as long as possible. My ship needed direct sunlight and their garden seemed a conspicuous place. I never anticipated my ship would be *plucked*."

"You have a crew of men at your disposal. Couldn't you have broken into the Pumpernickel domicile to retrieve it? Not that I minded a chance to thrash Miss Pumpernickel, even if it didn't come to proper fruition." At that, I glared venom.

Mr. Wibbles sighed. "I may have botched things, but I am here to play the part of a gentlemen. Gentlemen do not thieve from estates." At that, the crewmen nodded with synchrony so precise it was disturbing.

"No, they request that proper young women bludgeon each other over the affair in their stead, and cheat when things are not in their favor."

"Exactly." He nodded, most sober.

"Mr. Wibbles, if I may speak bluntly, playing the part of a society gentleman—or gentlewoman—will dumb down your natural intelligence as surely as ramming your skull into a brick wall."

"Interesting. I have wondered at the vapid nature of parties here, but I have not tried the brick wall for contrast. I should do so when we're done in the park."

I pressed a hand to my face. Dear God, was this our legacy among these sojourners from the stars? That we return their explorers, rendered into utter milksops?

I stopped and looked about. "Is this enough of an open space for you, Mr. Wibbles?"

"Why, yes, I think so! The rose, if I may?" He took it in his cupped hands and tapped the petals. His motions increased in speed until they blurred like a hummingbird's wings. Odd chimes rang out. He flung the rose toward the meadow.

Suddenly, the conveyance appeared.

"It looks . . . it looks like something that emerged from a bubble bath!" Indeed, it was some thirty feet in length and resembled a mass of iridescent bubbles. A dark doorway opened at the base.

This was an actual craft that traveled among the stars. For the first time in my life, I could have swooned. By sheer obstinance, I did not.

Mr. Wibbles removed his hat, as did his mute companions. "Miss Hardy, you have been the epitome of human compassion through your willingness to wield a cudgel on my behalf. I have a proposal for you."

"If it's marriage, I refuse, and will do so nonverbally." I brandished my rod.

"Marriage? Goodness no! The anatomy . . . !" He looked me up and down shuddered. "No! I propose to give you a ride in my craft. I promise to not irradiate you beyond human capacity."

I squinted at the ship. "The other day you mentioned something called a chocolate chip cookie. Would it be possible . . . ?"

"Ah! I know where to find them at peak freshness. A mere eighty year's hop. We'll be in and out before humanity's next apocalypse strikes. We can stop any other place or time you like as well." Mr. Wibbles gestured me toward the entry. "Mind the green puddles as you board. They might be slightly toxic to your species."

Any other place, throughout time? I balked in the shadow of the conveyance, utterly overwhelmed at the possibilities. I could see the pyramids as they were built! Gaze upon ancient Grecian fleets, witness Krakatoa's world-shattering eruption! Peer into the future and encounter wonders bright and strange, things even more marvelous than cookies! I would acquire freedom and first-hand knowledge unlike anything I had dared to dream!

With Mr. Wibbles as my guide and companion.

Drat.

Some danger was expected in order to travel and see such sights, but the scale and variety of those risks could only be magnified by his bumbling presence. I wouldn't trust Mr. Wibbles to hold my handkerchief, much less return me in good care from such an adventure.

Then there was the fact that Mr. Wibbles had also brought me a dishonorable victory against Miss Pumpernickel.

I was in debt to that pink monstrosity, all because of *him*.

I turned away from the craft. "Mr. Wibbles, I do appreciate the offer. I am all in favor of flouting expectations of my gender and engaging in bold acts of derring-do, but I believe it would be unwise to accept a ride from an extraterrestrial such as yourself. I wish you and your companions well."

With that, I scurried toward home, my cudgel tight in my grip. Mr. Wibbles called out a cheerful, "Toodles!"

I had missed a grand opportunity to view the wonders of history and the future, but I was no flibbertigibbet to trust in a little green man such as Mr. Wibbles. I would achieve independence in my own way, on my own terms.

Besides, I was of good health and solid stock. I could wait eighty years to discover the wonders of chocolate chip cookies.

A gamer in a support group finds himself in unique trouble when his world becomes a game, in a tale that will make even non-gamers smile and chuckle . . .
—BTS

The Game-a-holic's Guide To Life, Love, and Ruling the World

by Peter J. Wacks & Josh Vogt

"My name's Avery, and I'm a game-a-holic."

"Hi, Avery." The group chorused, collectively standing under a hand-scrawled banner that read "Life Is Not A Game."

Avery ground his teeth against the monotone greeting. Fighting down sweat, the twenty-nine-year-old ex-gamer steeled for his confession. The game-a-holics group—G-A-H on its literature—circled around him, two dozen strong. They were men and women of all ages and walks of life, come to commiserate about their past vicious abuses of their respective virtual realities.

As he opened his mouth to speak, the air shimmered. Avery snapped his jaw shut and blinked. For a second, names floated above everyone's heads. Little spirals swirled by everyone's heads, and ghostly words appeared, alternating between *Installing . . .*, *Buffering . . .*, and *Loading . . .*

Not now, he thought. *Not now, NOT NOW!*

Another blink, and the words vanished. Avery mentally groaned, fighting to look composed. He thought he'd gotten over the hallucinations; a year jacked out and the worst of his addiction symptoms had faded. Yet he still suffered the occasional flashback—times when he saw health and mana bars—the life force and magical energy of characters—around people, pulled up inventory screens for the contents of his pants pockets, or awarded himself an achievement for free-throwing a piece of garbage into the nearest trashcan.

He forced himself to focus.

147

"Yesterday, I almost lost all control. I . . ." He swallowed. For one of his Twelve Steps, he'd sworn that the only joystick he would touch for the rest of his life was his own; the day before, he'd been seconds away from breaking that promise. "I almost played Savage Beetles on my phone. I had it halfway downloaded before I came to my senses and shattered my phone against the nearest wall."

He dug a clunky, fifteen-year-old model out of his pocket. "I downgraded to a device that can't even text message now. I realized it's the only way I can resist the cravings."

Several people broke down into sobs. One man with the build of a Sumo wrestler—and the body hair of a grizzly—bounded over and nearly tackled Avery to the floor in a sweaty hug.

"It's okay," he said, squeezing Avery tight enough he feared popping a vein in his eye. "It's okay to cry."

A few soft tones reverberated in Avery's ear.

Player Selection; Character Appearance.

A deeper bong reverberated and text floated in midair next to his consoler.

Character Avatar Confirmed.

Chilly sweat broke out over his whole body as Avery wriggled free from the hug. A glance around showed no one else reacting. Everyone fixed on him with glassy eyes, oblivious.

He shuffled to the side, squeezing between a few chairs and grabbed a rice cake, jamming into his mouth and chewing. Originally, the snacks had been Doritos and donuts, but that led to Mountain Dew, and Mountain Dew led to . . .

Avery shivered. "I . . . I need some space. Need to walk this off . . ."

The group facilitator nodded. "It's okay," she said. "We understand how tough this is. Take all the time you need." She smiled to the rest. "All right, everyone. Let's go through our affirmation!"

Everyone held hands and mumbled along.

"I am great, even without games. I am happy, even without high scores. A life without games is the real achievement."

Avery stumbled out of the downtown church's basement where the G-A-H group met. Once on the sidewalk, he started to breathe easier—until a glance around made him gawk.

Three-dimensional text floated all around him, swarming his vision like ghosts of games past, present, and future. Names bobbed above people's heads. Stats scrolled around their bodies, giving him intimate details about physical characteristics their proctologists and gynecologists probably didn't even know. Hairstyles changed, going from spiked pink mohawks to bald to long black dreads in seconds.

Four teens walked by, chattering among themselves. From one step to the next, they shifted from an idyllic, pastel-wearing bunch straight out of a Norman Rockwell painting to a band of scarred and leather-wearing teen thugs—who kept talking in the chirping tones of their former selves.

Avery swallowed a scream and gave them a wide berth. Pings, blips, and bleeps sounded all around him; the world had become a giant arcade. Each noise corresponded with another shift in nearby people.

A woman in a business suit walked straight into a brick wall. She bounced back a few steps. Then she strode forward and repeated the process. Again and again, she rebounded and face-planted back into the brick.

Avery moved to turn her away from the wall. Should he call paramedics? Had someone released an airborne virus inducing some sort of madness? This couldn't all be in his head.

Before he reached the woman, a man grabbed his shoulders. The glaze in his eyes could've coated a thousand donuts. When he shouted, his voice carried loud and far. "U BUY MONIES! U WANT MONIES, YES. WE SALE MONIES TO U! FAST! CHEAP MONIES. SECURE. NO HACKZ!"

Avery reeled and broke away. He staggered half-blind for a block, trying to make sense of his disintegrating grip on reality. At last, he spotted a cop standing on a street corner, monitoring road construction alongside a busy intersection.

Avery ran up and waved to get the officer's attention.

"Hey. Hey, sir! Something weird's going on."

The officer spun in place and fixed a plastic grin on him.

"Hail, citizen. It looks like you are in distress. Would you like help with . . ." The cop stuttered off options. "Directions? System Settings? Bug Reports? Customer Service?"

A squeak of dismay escaped Avery. He flailed for balance and pressed his back against a street sign pole.

Another woman in yoga sweats walked by, but stopped in her tracks a few feet away. Text flashed before her face: *PVP Mode Unlocked.*

Avery whimpered. "Player versus player? Oh, god, no . . ."

She spun and walloped the nearest pedestrian with her massive Gucci handbag. He went down in a heap. She began whacking anyone within reach, gleefully yelling the battlecry of all new players that thought they were the elite, "I'm 1337, bitches!"

A few other passersby flashed *PVP Mode* text. Soon a mid-street brawl broke out, everyone jumping on everyone else's backs, tripping, throwing wild fists.

He stumbled away from the fracas. All around him, the ordinary turned to the surreal. People jumped in place. Spun in circles. Crouched and went into crab-walks.

One guy cupped hands around his mouth and bellowed, "HOW DO I OPEN THE MINI-MAP?"

Another man walked up to him and screamed in his face. "IT'S CALLED GPS YOU IDIOT! Now turn off your caps lock, it's annoying!"

"GLACK YOU NOOB!" the first replied.

Avery left the screaming match behind as he raced along. Finding a short alley, he ducked into it and huddled beside a dumpster. Before he could compose himself, another ripple passed over his vision and pressure built behind his eyes.

A voice spoke up, reverberating through his mind.

"Finally. I thought that login queue would never end. Now for the fun!"

Avery stiffened. Voices? God, he'd already had one mental breakdown. Hadn't he suffered enough? This was almost as bad as his episode last year.

"Now, let's see. Where's the stats readout on this guy? Holy gorb, he's got a small—"

"Get out of my thoughts!" he screamed.

Avery crouched, hands clasped over his head. He muttered the mantras he'd learned in G-A-H to help him through these times. "This is reality. Life is not a game. There is no such thing as a respawn from death. I am me. I am real. Games are fake. Games are not life. I am alive."

He peeked out from around the dumpster. Icons and text still floated around people, and nobody else seemed to notice or care.

The voice resumed. *"What the glack? Great. I finally get in the game and drop into the lamest character ever. Going to have to level this blip up."*

Avery straightened and shouted at the sky.

"I am not a character. I am a human being! I . . . am . . . a . . . man!"

"Uh . . . wow. The emote options are a little overdramatic. I wonder . . ."

More phantom words floated in front of Avery's eyes.

/dance

Avery's eyes widened in horror. His body twitched. Even though he'd never danced a day in his life, he broke into a flamboyant disco routine. After a few hip thrusts, he gritted his teeth and fought back. How was he being controlled like he was just a character, a toon?

If this was how it was going to be, fine. He was the best. He visualized /sit in his mind's eye and his ass hit the pavement so hard he grunted.

"Forward slash pause. Stop," he growled through clenched teeth. "I'm not your puppet."

"What the glack?" Shock entered the disembodied voice. *"Wait. How are you controlling yourself? Are you actually talking to me?"*

Avery kept cycling his anti-gaming mantra, trying to ignore the fact that he was talking to the voice in his head using MMO commands. "Who are you? Where are you? How are you doing this?"

"This is narken weird. Where's the user manual? Ah!"

A robotic voice spoke up: "Activating Visual User Interface."

Avery slapped at the air as if he could strike down the speaker. "No, don't acti—"

An image opened up, a real world in-screen window, set in the upper right corner of Avery's vision. A tiny purple man with bright yellow eyes and black slits for a nose peered at him. It . . . it looked like a colorful Roswell alien. He—she? it?—wore an odd garment composed of gold and green metallic threads, and a silver circlet held a glowing ruby on the huge forehead. The creature waved a six-fingered hand.

"Greetings, Blip. You don't mind if I call you Blip, do you?"

"Yes! My name is Avery."

"Actually, you're my *toon to name, but . . ."* The alien's thin lips quirked. *"This is narken awesome. Those crazy ethical theorists were right. Some of you constructs turned sentient."*

A nude man streaked by the alley mouth, jumping repeatedly, flab flapping as he screamed, "LOL U SUXXORS! I KEEL YOU ALL LOOOZAHS! I AM TEH AWESUM!"

Avery cowered. "What's happening?" he asked. "Am I dying? Am I insane? Is this a nightmare?"

The alien gave a wheedling sigh. *"Listen, Blip. Here's the facts. This world you call Earth? Your entire history and evolution? It's all being run on a quantum processor at the core of your planet. To us, you're a game called Earth Death 3: The Extinction Engine. You, and everything around you, are a holographic matrix with a RealMatter overlay. It's all the hype these days. Totally revolutionizing gaming!"*

Avery's hands trembled in rising horror. "No. I refuse to believe that." He made fists. "I just survived a whole year without a single game. I almost went insane, but I cured myself. You can't tell me that my whole life—my whole existence—is a game."

"I can if it's the truth. Look around, Blip. You game on the internal mini-game system? Well, then, you know exactly what you're seeing."

Avery rocked in place, but finally gave in. He poked his head out from his hiding spot, watching everything from a gamer's perspective. An eighty-year-old man shuffling along on a walker stopped by a BMW.

"Whoa," the man rasped. "Now this is a sweet mount."

He shattered the driver's side window with his walker, and yanked the driver out. As the yuppie hit the ground, a stack of cash bounced out of his pocket and floated into the old man's fanny pack. One full gold star and four empty stars briefly flashed above the walker as he unlocked the door, hopped in, and zoomed off in a squeal of burnt rubber.

Down the block, a boy and girl shared a shy kiss as they held hands. A "DING!" sounded, and the boy went stiff-spined as golden lights swirled around him. Text scrolled.

Congratulations! You Have Leveled Up to Puberty. Your Character Now Has The Following Features: Body Hair +5. Awkwardness +10. Zits +3.

The girl applauded. "Yay! Now we can go on the Quest of Awkward Groping." A golden exclamation point, the universal symbol of a new quest, appeared before them and the girl tapped it. It vanished.

Avery returned to his hiding spot. He swallowed against his dry throat. "Okay. So the world's a game. How do I log out? How do I quit?"

"Uh . . . you die, Blip."

"Wait, what?!"

"You're part of the game. It's all you've got going. Life's a glitch and then you die."

He hugged himself. "If it's always been a game, why did it just become obvious now?"

"Well, gluh. You've been in Closed Beta for a few eons, with all sorts of restrictions on who can play. I finally got access because they lowered the age limit and brought in a flood of new subscribers for Open Beta."

"Age limit?"

"Yeah! Broader demographics. Better stress testing."

"So you're . . . a kid?"

"Hey. I am Luxolor the Defiant Sniggler. My people control a hundred star systems. I'm five thousand years old. I've seen worlds snuffed out and created. And I'm the reigning champ of my local interplanetary bowling club."

"How old does your kind get?"

"Um . . . a few hundred million years is a senior citizen in these parts."

Avery sighed. "So you're a kid."

Luxolor's brow rumpled. *"Says the virtual peon who can't tie his own shoelaces without making a game out of it."*

"What about free will?" Avery asked.

"They're supposed to patch it out next expansion. It was totally buggy, and a bunch of players broke it, so they're nerfing it. They do that to all the fun stuff."

Avery gulped. "The purpose of life?"

"To win, of course."

"Love?"

"Mini-game. Gluh. Totally icky too. Have you seen it? It's so . . . wet. Ick."

Avery flushed. "Erm. Uh. Well . . . you know . . ."

"Seriously? You haven't tried that yet? Well, in my opinion you aren't missing anything."

"Oh, god. Why me?" Avery's forehead thumped against the dumpster.

"Erm, Blip? You can just call me Lux, not god. Why you? Because

you were the first available character near the hidden location of the Goroloth Apex. I wanted a head start to claim it."

"Goroloth Apex?" Avery's head jerked up. That sounded like game-changing unique loot, and it whetted the darkest appetites of his old self. The addict Avery who sold his car and stopped paying rent to keep his gaming subscriptions going. Who'd wound up in adult diapers and hooked to a Mountain Dew I.V. to avoid leaving his gaming console for weeks at a time.

"*Yes,*" Lux said. "*It's an ultra-rare. The only Unique this patch, an epic upgrade they announced to boost buzz for Open Beta. Only one character can claim it and then it's gone . . . at least until the next promo campaign."*

Avey's fingers twitched. He swallowed to avoid drooling. "If it's hidden, how do you know it's around here?"

"*Well, you know how it is. I've got an older uncle-sister-spawn who works in the game's dev department. I got all sorts of inside info about bonus quests and hack codes. If I can be the first to reach the Apex, it'll unlock a secret achievement and upgrade you permanently. Then when the actual live launch happens, I'll be way ahead of everyone else."*

"I . . ." He kneaded knuckles over his temples. "No. I can't. I've fought so hard to get clean. And now you want me to go back? I can't do . . . But it's a unique, you say? Wait, no! I can't."

"*Look around you. Everyone else is already going with the programming. If you don't want to become roadkill, you're going to need the boost the Apex gives. Otherwise you'll be registered as a Non-Player Character and anyone can target you. You're already small fry compared to the rest. You really wanna be an NPC?"*

Avery dug fingernails into his palm. When life handed you lemons . . . "Okay. But we play by my rules."

"*Hardly. I've got command access. You just need to stop resisting so I can control you properly."*

"No!" Avery snapped the word out like a whip crack. "Before I went sober, I was the world champion of Legends of the Lollipop Lords. I held titles in five different countries for e-sports play in ten different leagues. I got six-figure sponsorships because I could win SupahNinja Fruit Salad with my eyes closed. Every game I played, *my* guilds always beat the new raid bosses first. You want to beat this quest? We do it together."

Lux glared at him from his side of reality. At last, he sighed. *"Fine. Hang on. Let my pull up my Quest Log."*

Another *bing*, and words flashed before Avery.

Quest Accepted: Retrieve the Goroloth Apex.

System Admin: Are you sure?

Avery sighed and said, "Forward slash yes."

Subquest Accepted: Complete on Permadeath Mode

"Permadeath?! WTF? You didn't say anything about that."

"It's the only way to make the quest reward permanent. And if you don't do it, I can just spawn a new toon. Ready?"

"No!"

"Great, let's go, Blip. See that building where you all worship the spaghetti monster in the sky?"

Avery searched until he fixed on a steeple a few blocks away. "You mean the church?"

"Precisely. The Apex should be hidden on a secret level connected to that property."

An impulse to move pushed him forward, but he let it guide him this time. "Strafe me, Lux. Get used to my movements." The alien nodded and Avery started moving diagonally forward. He halted, jumping once in place as he stopped, half-a-block from the church. An imposing, gothic structure, it stuck out from the rest of downtown's sleek, modern skyscrapers with gargoyles on every ledge, vaulted stain glass windows, and massive bell tower.

What stopped Avery and Lux, though, was the crowd gathered outside the church . . . the crowd ringing the whole church. Milling people looked at first like protestors, until he noted their aimless and unfocused gazes. Each person also had an identical icon floating in front of their chest: a golden sun sprouting black tentacles.

"What's that symbol for?" he asked.

Lux's attention shifted in his mind, scanning the optical input.

"Oh glorb. Galabax is already here. How did that cretin form a guild and find this location so quickly?"

"Galabax? Who's that?" Avery asked.

"A total cheat. After I exposed his hacking in Meteor Apocalypse, they banned his account and blacklisted him from the pro league. Ever since, he's always tried to get revenge by snagging in-game trophies before me."

A white-haired, grandmotherly woman mince-stepped to the landing atop the shallow stairs before the main doors. Standing beneath a large sign that read "Parish of Antioch," she spread her arms wide.

"Oh, hello Luxolor. Glad to see you finally made it. A step behind, as always." The woman waved her cane at the congregation. "I've already claimed this territory and the Apex."

As she spoke, the crowd turned toward him as one, expressions bland, devoid of humanity.

"He must be botting," Avery whispered. "I'd recognize that unison step anywhere. I bet he's running characters through multiple accounts at once."

"Seriously? Cheater!"

Avery snorted. "Says the alien who snuck a peek at proprietary dev materials."

"That's not cheating. That's meta-gaming."

The grandmother waved her cane. "You can run along now, noob. Go find a hundred large rats to grind out your leveling, or something equally mediocre."

Avery turned and jogged away. He felt Lux trying to assert control, but kept cycling his anti-gaming mantra, keeping the alien at bay.

"Hey! Get back there. We can't let him claim the Apex."

"Trust me, Lux—if he had it, he'd have shown it off. And for something that epic, there would've been a game-wide announcement once someone actually reaches it, right?"

"Hm. I suppose. But now what?"

"A frontal assault won't do any good. It's a mob, way more Damage Per Second . . ." he glanced back, "yeah, they way out-DPS me, and unless you have a Tank friend you can call . . ." Avery let the question trail off hopefully, but Lux stayed silent. Avery sighed. "All right, then. We need a stealth approach. There's an old tunnel that runs into the church basement from the hotel over here."

"How do you know that?"

"Game I used to play." Avery huffed as he headed for the hotel lobby. "Used your mobile phone to track your location and dropped a hyper overlay—pretty simple, you just claimed places for your faction. I topped the score charts. Found all the secret ways to get into properties even when other players were guarding them." He grinned at the old memories, from back before his twitch reflexes became far more profitable.

Despite the mind-altering revelation of the world's true nature, he couldn't deny the challenge had the old juice running. Adrenaline sizzled in his blood, and his thoughts already shot every which way, looking for the winning angle, the unexpected tactic to bring him out on top. Player and Toon . . . they had to figure out a two-man run on this raid. Avery used to live for this.

Entering the lobby, he passed by a desk clerk who laughed hysterically while hip-thrusting a pile of suitcases. Off in another corner, a man sidled up to a fish tank and eyed its finned denizens meaningfully.

"So . . ." He grinned slyly. "You like to cyber?"

Avery loped past them and headed down the nearest stairwell. The tunnel remained concealed behind an unlocked door in the basement, marked *Maintenance Only*. Fluorescent lights flickered on and he crossed a grimy, dripping passage. Halfway along the passage he spotted a three foot long lead pipe. Grinning, he picked it up. "Hey Lux, drop this on quick equip?"

"Glorb, awesome find!" his alien controller said. The pipe vanished and Avery ran to the door at the other end of the poorly lit tunnel.

He emerged into a storage room below the church, full of dusty choir robes, cleaning supplies, and a life-sized Nativity scene.

"Any idea where the Apex is hidden around here? What does it look like?"

On his mini-screen, Lux's mouth crimped in what Avery took as a frown. *"No graphics have been leaked so far. All anyone knows is it's small enough to carry."*

"Oh, that narrows it down." Avery raised an eyebrow. Quickly, but quietly, he scanned the ornaments and cobweb-covered equipment, rummaging to get a look at everything in the basement. "How will I know if I have it?"

"You just have to touch it. Since I have the quest active, it'll automatically register."

Avery trailed fingers over everything within reach, mulling over the options. If he had an ultimate upgrade, where would he hide it? Of course!

"What if the clue's in the name?"

"Apex?"

"Yup. My guess? It's in the steeple."

"But that's so . . . so obvious!"

"Exactly. So obvious you don't even think about it."

"Glorb. Those devs . . . That's just lazy game design! They should hide the clues in the game's story."

Avery shrugged. "It's a beta, man. Don't expect a lot until the first expansion."

"I suppose you're right." Lux looked annoyed. Avery smiled softly, remembering many a night he had felt the same frustration.

He slipped out of the basement and up a back flight of stairs. If memory served, steeple access was through a door behind the choir risers. A peek through the cracked door, into the sanctuary, revealed a dozen people exploring the chamber. They piled a mound of discarded artifacts in the center of the room and ran their hands over everything in total silence, fondling every last hymnal, candle, and offering plate. Avery recognized their movements; it was an optimized loot-find search pattern. The addict in him cringed at the sureality of it all . . .

At his core he was a gamer, and 1337 at that. He grinned wickedly.

When he tried to ease into the sanctuary the door groaned and the hinges creaked loud. Galabax's bots pivoted toward him as one. The grandmother appeared at the far end of the sanctuary and scowled.

"How did you get in here?" she shouted. "Clip through a wall, you glorbing hatchling?!"

Doors banged open and people flooded in, all aiming for Avery. *PVP Mode Unlocked* flashed everywhere.

"Go!" Lux cried.

Avery bolted, vaulting pews as the mob thundered after him. He gasped out, "Forward slash, quick equip lead pipe," as he ran. One of the bots got too close and he whacked its grasping hand. The bot flashed twice as it fell, and disappeared as it hit the ground. A ghost word, *Respawn*, floated in the air and shimmered out of existence.

"Lux," Avery grunted, "I thought you said there was no respawning."

"Well, not for you on permadeath mode. But . . . I think you call it reincarnation? The player has to start over at birth with a respawn."

"Yeah. Puberty once was enough. Almost makes me glad you set me on permadeath." He vaulted the last pews and reached the prize, the passage to the belfry.

He slammed through the door, stumbling up the first flight of stairs, murderous bots close on his heels.

By the time he reached the top, his lungs felt ready to collapse. A trapdoor waited in the ceiling, and he didn't even pause, yanking the latch open and shoving up. Dried pigeon droppings crumbled over his head like spackling. Keeping his mouth shut, he sucked in pungent whiffs of mold and bird scat as he scrambled up the ladder. Just as the first bot reached up, he slammed the trapdoor shut. Avery stood on the door, panting, while it bumped and thumped beneath him.

"Go on. Let's find it!" Lux wheedled impatiently.

"Gimme a second. I need to catch my breath."

The door beneath his feet bumped again, but his weight kept it closed. Once recovered, he spun in place, searching for anything that might resemble the Goroloth Apex. The steeple's bell had been removed long ago, leaving nothing but rusted hooks and rivets where it once hung. Speakers had been bolted to the railings, readied to blast out e-gongs across the city.

There was nothing here. Nothing. Just an empty belfry. Not even any bats.

"I don't see anything." Lux's whine needled his ears.

Avery frowned, thinking. He'd been so certain . . . He swung the lead pipe in practice a couple times, distracting himself. Then the answer jolted him.

He grinned wickedly. "Lux, this isn't the very top."

"One sec, checking something. Hm. Your speed stat isn't very high, but your reflexes aren't half bad. You think we can get up without getting creamed?"

"Yeah. I think we can. Ready?"

"Ready."

He counted to three, then jumped forward. The trapdoor banged open as the bots clambered over each other to reach him. But Avery hopped onto the railing, turned, and grabbed the steeple ledge. He hauled himself up, taking a last couple swings at reaching hands as he strained to get out of reach.

"Unequip me! I need my other hand!"

The lead pipe vanished. Avery found the purchase he needed,

struggled to get higher. Something caught his foot. He barely kept himself from tumbling off. Galabax had hooked his toon's cane around Avery's ankle and yanked with impossible strength. Pebbles scraped free under his fingernails as he scrabbled to keep his handhold.

"Wait, Lux," the old lady hissed. "You can't win this game alone. Let's work together. We can both be victors here."

"I'm not Luxolor," Avery said. "I'm Avery. Say my name, bitch, because it's always going to beat out yours on the game rankings."

She snarled and yanked on the cane.

"Requip me, Lux!"

The lead pipe appeared, sticking out of the roof, caught in a glitch. Avery slapped it and the heavy weapon slid free, falling. It hit the grandmother in the head as it fell; she toppled over the railing as Galabax sent several of his human bots leaping for Avery. They just missed Avery's legs as he tucked them up. His chest clenched as the people plummeted toward asphalt—however, after a few yards, their fall slowed until they drifted down to alight without harm.

"Gravity hacks," Lux crowed. *"I got that recorded on video. They'll have to ban him for sure now."*

"Let's finish this quest," Avery said, catching his breath. "Report the asshole later."

"But, but . . . No, you're right. Let's do this, Blip!"

He raised his head, trying to not notice how far up he'd come. Blinking away dizziness, he focused on the target. The steeple's peak wasn't a cross, angel, or any other religious symbol. Instead, it was a giant golden question mark. The impossible punctuation mark of a quest completed floated above the peak, bobbing and rotating slowly in midair. Avery laughed as adrenaline coursed through his veins. The quest objective, right there!

Lux's squeak of delight sounded like helium escaping a balloon. *"That's it. That has to be it."*

Ever so slowly, Avery crawled up the precipitous incline. The sounds of hands on tile came from below as bots began to negotiate the tricky climb, mere feet behind him. He slipped a couple times, but clung to the tiles, literally, for his life.

Permadeath Mode kept blinking in the corner of his eye, a constant reminder of what would happen if he fell.

At last, he reached the steeple point and hooked an arm around the metal pole there. Bracing, he reached up to grasp the Holy Question Mark of Antioch. It dropped into his hand, heavy and solid. At the same instant, a deeper gong resounded and the earth trembled.

Goloroth Apex Acquired flashed before him.

Bad timing. As the quest flashed and the earth trembled, one of the bots caught up and jerked at his ankle. He slipped and fell.

Clouds swirled and reformed the announcement, broadcasting the quest completion for all to see. A resounding scream came from below.

Avery went ass-over-teakettle off the edge of the belfry and tumbled through open space. No fair. He'd come so close. The ground's approach seemed to be speeding up. "Uh, Lux, do you happen to have that gravity hack?"

Lux was typing furiously, and checked something off-screen. *"Sorry, no. Hang on, though, Blip. I've got to claim the quest reward before you die, otherwise I lose the points."*

Avery eyed the side of the church as he fell. Had he really climbed this high up?

"Here we go," the alien said.

A tingle shot up Avery's arm. Almost there . . .

Avery screamed and everything froze. His nose hovered less than an inch from the ground.

A final message appeared and Avery laughed uncontrollably.

God Mode Unlocked.

A great library, the battlefield! Stalwart librarians, our bravest soldiers!
My friends, can your hearts stand the shocking facts about . . .
Bookworms from Outer Space? —*RWB*

Day of The Bookworm

by Allen M. Steele

Eighteen hours after an alien spacecraft landed in Copley Square, the Boyleston Street entrance of the Boston Public Library opened and two people stepped out.

This occurred a little before six a.m. The first light of a mid-September day was just breaking on the city, the sun still hidden behind the downtown skyscrapers. The two individuals who unexpectedly emerged from the supposedly evacuated library slowly walked down the concrete steps into the glare of floodlights set up across the deserted avenue. A young man and woman, both of whom appeared to be typical Bostonians in their mid-twenties, stopped when they spotted the dozens of U.S. Army Rangers, Massachusetts National Guard soldiers, and SWAT team members huddled behind sandbags and sawhorses, with just as many rifles, pistols, and riot guns pointed their way.

"Oh, hell," the young man said.

"Please don't shoot," the woman called out, raising her hands to her shoulders. "We're just librarians." She was older and a little more composed than her colleague, but it was obvious from the way her legs trembled beneath her knee-length skirt that she was just as nervous as he.

A moment passed, and then two SWAT cops came out from behind the cordon. They waited until the couple reached the edge of the sidewalk, and then trotted across Boyleston, grasped the two librarians by the arms and hustled them across the street.

By then, the TV news crews who'd staked out the scene had been alerted to the breaking development, and reporters and cameramen ignored the barricades and began hurrying in from the press staging area several blocks away. They were too far from the library to get there in time to see anything, but they didn't come away empty-handed. Although the news media had been expressly forbidden to use drones, the CNN crew decided that it was worth the wrath of the police to get live footage. Before their drone was shot down by a sharpshooter positioned on the roof of a nearby condo, its camera caught a few seconds of the pair being surrounded by soldiers and cops and hurried down the street to the Lenox Hotel, where a forward command post had been set up.

All this occurred in less than five minutes. In that time, no one paid any attention to the spacecraft standing in Copley Square across Dartmouth from the library. About ninety feet long, it resembled a pumpkin seed made of broken mirrors, its myriad pieces fit together in complex patterns that reflected everything surrounding the craft. The ship didn't have any obvious means of propulsion save for the ring at its aft end that glowed and hummed as the vessel made its descent. Although the spacecraft was poised on the four slender legs that telescoped down from its underside shortly after it landed, the ramp that was lowered from beneath the tapered bow had not yet reappeared to let the aliens who'd emerged go back aboard.

Indeed, the sudden appearance of the two librarians was the first sign of activity since alien spacecraft had landed not only in Boston, but also beside libraries in New York and London. That was when the aliens had entered their respective libraries . . . or at least that's what everyone assumed had happened. After the ramps came down, something like a cloudy, semi-opaque tunnel extended itself from each of the vessels to the doorways of the libraries next to which they'd landed. The tunnels had remained for a few minutes, then dissolved, after which the ramps were retracted and the hatches closed. Obviously, whoever had entered the libraries didn't want to be seen.

The significance of these three landing sites—in particular, the fact that they were all libraries in major cities located in English-speaking countries—had been debated endlessly by government officials and talking heads alike over through the rest of the day and into the long night that followed. Yet there were only but a few indisputable facts.

There had been no contact by the aliens. All attempts to communicate with them had been answered only by silence.

On the other hand, there had been no hostilities, either.

Once the urban areas around the landing sites had been evacuated—in Boston, this comprised a circle roughly three blocks in radius—the aliens seemed content to let the inhabitants do whatever they wanted, just so long as they didn't approach either their craft or the library. Those who did found themselves impeded by some sort of invisible barrier, an energy field that felt rather like the soft yet persistent resistance one feels when you try to push two magnets together at their positive or negative poles. Vehicles stopped cold, bullets ricocheted, and explosive charges were deflected outward.

Clearly, the aliens wished to be left alone. And they were pretty good at making sure that they would be.

Except for two people who'd apparently been inside the Boston Public Library the entire time. Their names were Levon Kahn and Molly Cooper, and as it turned out, a little privacy was all they'd wanted, too.

"Admit it," the White House man demanded. "You two were having sex, weren't you?"

Colonel Clyde Jeffers winced as he looked across the conference table at the nice young couple seated there. They were already skittish from being hustled in the Lenox by his Rangers, and the civilian sitting beside him was displaying a lack of tact remarkable for someone who worked for the president.

Only a few people were seated in what had been an ordinary hotel conference room before it was transformed into the forward command post for Diligent Goose, the military response to what the Pentagon was officially calling the "extraterrestrial incursion." Three soldiers—two male corporals and a female sergeant—were at the other end of the table, where they controlled laptop computers linked to drones and cameras monitoring the library and Copley Square.

"We were . . . um, ah . . . having some private time together." Molly Cooper blushed as she folded her hands together in her lap. Although she'd identified herself as the assistant curator of the rare books collection, she didn't quite look like the stereotypical librarian Jeffers had always imagined. Unpin the blond hair from her bun and put her in clothes that hadn't come from 1964, and she would've been ravishing.

"Yeah, we were just"—Levon Kahn gave her an uncertain look—"dusting the shelves in the periodicals collection." Kahn, on the other hand, did look like someone you'd expect to find haunting the stacks. Several years younger than Cooper, thin and gawky, he wore his long brown hair tied back in a short ponytail and wire-rim glasses perched on a narrow nose. Baggy trousers and a threadbare tweed jacket completed the picture of a recent Simmons College library science grad who'd found work at the reference desk.

"Uh-huh," muttered the civilian. "Private time dusting the shelves. Sure you were . . . "

Jeffers had never met J. Llewellyn Sneed before late yesterday afternoon, when he'd marched into Lenox showing off his White House credentials and generally acting like he owned the place. Potato-shaped, chipmunk-faced, and not much older than the couple he was interrogating, Sneed was an assistant associate whatever to the president's science advisor. Apparently the only reason why he was here was because everyone else on the advisory staff was stuck at the climate change conference in Beijing. "Why didn't you dust the shelves at home, or just get a room?" Sneed went on, eyes glittering with voyeuristic glee. "Why mess around down in the basement?"

Again, Cooper and Kahn glanced at each other. Jeffers couldn't blame them for being standoffish. However, these two were the only people so far who'd had any direct contact with the aliens, and it was important to learn why they'd ignored the evacuation order.

"We weren't—" Kahn began.

"Levon . . ." Cooper gave him a look, then let out her breath. "All right, yes, that's what we were doing down there . . . 'having sex,' as you put it so crudely. And the reason why we chose the periodicals archive is because it's in the staff-only area of the lower level and seldom visited."

"But why the library?" Jeffers was trying to be gentler about this than Sneed. "Most people, when they carry on an affair with co-workers, try to keep it out of the office."

"We don't have much choice." Now that she'd admitted to their indiscretion, Cooper was no longer as reluctant to talk about it as

Levon was. "I'm sharing an apartment with someone of the Sapphic persuasion—"

"A dyke, you mean," Sneed said.

"No, I mean a woman who happens to be a lesbian." Cooper cast him a venomous look, then returned her attention to Jeffers. "She's usually tolerant of heterosexual men, but my old boyfriend was such a jerk that she's requested, if I ever meet another guy while we're rooming together, that I not bring him home."

"I see." Jeffers looked at Kahn. "And you?"

He hesitated, then let out an embarrassed sigh. "I'm living with my mother."

One of the soldiers snorted loudly. The colonel ignored him; quite a few millennials weren't in any great hurry to move away from their parents. Student loans were a bitch. "But why didn't you just get a hotel room? You could've come here. It's close enough."

"Go down to the front desk and ask how much a room here goes for just one night. Librarians don't make a lot of money, y'know." Kahn looked again at Cooper and, receiving an encouraging nod, went on. "And the library basement . . . well, it's more comfortable than you'd think, and as private as you can get if you know where to look. Cool in summer, warm in the winter, and with the door shut, no one can hear you."

"That also means you couldn't hear anything going on outside, right?"

"Yes, well . . ." Kahn darted another look at Cooper. "We were rather busy."

The soldier who'd snorted suddenly had a coughing fit, and the other corporal hastily got up and left the room; he waited until he was out in the hall before he broke down. Only the sergeant showed no reaction; Jeffers idly wondered if she was deaf or just busy flying the drone in circles around the library. Cooper's face turned red, and the scowl she gave her boyfriend suggested that it might be a while before he got busy with her again.

"I suppose that explains why you didn't know a spacecraft had just landed outside," Jeffers said, trying to get the poor kid off the hook.

"No . . . no, it doesn't." Sneed jabbed an accusatory finger at Kahn. "There are fire alarms throughout that whole building, even the basement. The head librarian pulled the alarm just a few minutes after the ship touched down. You two didn't come out until about a half-hour ago. Are you trying to tell us that you've been 'busy' that entire time and had no idea what was going on out here?"

"Of course not." Cooper glared at both the colonel and the White House advisor. "And if the two of you can get your dirty little minds out of the gutter for just a few moments, we'll tell you what happened."

"That's obvious," Sneed said. "We're being invaded."

"No," Kahn said, quickly shaking his head. "No, we're not. That's why the Cetens asked us to come out here and speak to you."

Jeffers immediately forgot that he'd just been charged with having a dirty little mind. "The Cetens?" he asked. "Is that what they call themselves?"

"No, they call themselves . . . well, it's unpronounceable, unless you're one of them. Since they're from a planet in the Tau Ceti system . . . Tau Ceti-e, to be exact . . . I imagine you could call them Cetens."

"But we don't." For the first time since she'd walked into the room, Molly Cooper smiled. "We call them bookworms."

"Is anyone out there?" Molly whispered.

Levon didn't answer at once. He stood in the half-open doorway of the small, forgotten room whose cinderblock walls were lined with shelves stuffed with back issues of *National Geographic* and listened as intently as he could. It was hard to hear anything over the fire alarm that continued to jangle through the labyrinthine aisles of the library's lower-level stacks. The alarm had been going for at the last twenty-five minutes or so, and he wondered again why no one had turned it off.

But there was no one in sight, and that was what mattered. He shook his head as he looked back at Molly. "I think it's safe to leave."

Molly finished buttoning her blouse. There were no mirrors in the room—Levon reminded himself that he needed to bring one down here, to hide away among the magazines along with the sleeping bag he'd smuggled in—so she had to carefully check herself to make sure that she looked just the same way she had when she'd excused herself from the rare books room almost an hour ago. Satisfied, she looked at Levon and pointed to the front of his trousers.

"Fly," she said.

Levon grimaced and yanked up his zipper. Ever since they'd begun using this little room for their lunchtime trysts, Molly had always been better at resuming the appearance of innocence than he was. He let her tie back his hair again so that it didn't look as if a woman had tousled it with her fingers in a moment of passion, then put on his jacket and glanced out the door again. Still, there was no one to be seen.

"Okay," he said quietly, "let's get out of here."

Molly slipped out the door and turned to close it behind them. The electronic lock beeped softly as the latch clicked shut. Many years ago, this particular room had contained much of the library's rare books collection. When those books were relocated to the McKim Building, the storeroom was given over to old magazines. No one had ever bothered to change the lock, though, and since this part of the building was accessible only by library employees, the little storeroom was seldom visited. Molly had the lock combination and . . . well, who wants to make love in a restroom?

Still, it was peculiar that no one was around and the alarm was still going. Fire drills were infrequent, but you'd expect that someone would've turned off the bells by now. They'd been going ever since Molly reached climax, and although they thought it was funny at the time, that was quite a while ago. She and Levon had heard the alarm, but they'd decided to remain in hiding until they were certain the drill was over.

Almost a half-hour had gone by, though, and they couldn't stay hidden any longer. People might talk, if they weren't already. It'd lately become break room scuttlebutt that Molly from Rare Books and Levon from the reference desk were having an affair, and the last thing they wanted anyone to discover was that it was being consummated during library hours.

"I don't get it," Levon murmured as they walked through the long, silent rows of the lower-level stacks. "If it was drill, everyone ought to be back by now, wouldn't they?"

"Maybe it's a real fire." Molly stopped and experimentally sniffed the air. "I don't smell smoke, though . . . and you'd think we would've spotted a fireman by now."

Levon nodded, but he didn't have an answer for her. Just then, the mystery was the lesser of his concerns. Their priority was getting out of the basement without anyone spotting them. "We'll find out soon enough," he said as they reached the door leading from the library's private areas to its public ones. He hesitated, and then slowly pushed it open to peer outside.

The small lobby between the fiction section and the Books On Hold desk was deserted. They slipped through the wood-panel door marked *Library Employees Only* and paused for a moment beside the marble staircase and the elevators.

"See you after work?" Levon whispered, glancing about to make sure they were alone.

"Sure." Molly took him by the hand and pulled him closer. "Murphy's?"

Levon nodded. Murphy's was a bar in Cambridge not far from the Harvard Square T station; they often rendezvoused there after work on their way to their respective places in Somerville and Alewife. A quick kiss, and then Molly stepped aboard an elevator. This was the routine they'd worked out a while ago to minimize the chances of being spotted coming and going through this particular lower-level door at the same time: Molly would take the elevator to Special Collections on the third floor while Levon climbed the stairs to the second floor where the reference desk was located. The only person who'd ever noticed them was the elderly volunteer who ran the Books on Hold desk, and he usually had his nose stuck in a novel and couldn't care less.

Only this time, it didn't work out that way. The elevator doors didn't close when Molly pushed the button. Frustrated, she let out a sigh. "Damn . . . I forgot. The elevators won't work until the fire marshal turns off the alarm."

"That's okay. I'll walk up with you." Levon led her to the staircase.

The Boston Public Library consists of two buildings: the McKim Building, a grand old edifice of granite, limestone, and marble erected in 1887 on the corner of Boyleston and Dartmouth across from Copley Square, and its extension, the Johnson Building, built in 1971 on Boyleston and as attractive as the computer factory it resembled. Most of the Johnson Building except for the second floor had been closed lately for renovations, leaving the Dartmouth Street entrance as the only public means of entry; the Boyleston Street entrance was serving as a fire exit until the renovations were complete.

As Levon and Molly walked into the McKim entrance lobby from the lower level, they paused between the two marble lions on either side of the stairs to glance at the entrance. Above three pairs of bronze doors were arch windows providing sunlight for the lobby. The windows weren't low enough for them to see through, so they were unable to tell whether their fellow librarians were gathered in the plaza outside. Nonetheless, they could hear the warble of approaching sirens and, for a few seconds, the clatter of a helicopter passing unusually low over the building.

"You're sure this is a drill?" Molly asked. "Sounds like quite a commotion outside."

"If there was a fire, those doors would be open and we'd be tripping over fire hoses." Levon considered going out to join everyone else, but decided against it. If this was just a false alarm and he and Molly were lucky, none of their coworkers might notice that the two of them had failed to leave the building. So if they waited until the fire marshal allowed everyone to go back in, he and Molly could already be back at their respective desks, going about their duties as if nothing unusual had happened. Less suspicious that way.

Still, he reflected as they walked upstairs, it was weird to find the place so empty. Yet just as they reached the second floor, the bells suddenly went silent. Someone had switched them off . . . which meant that another person must be in the library.

But if that was so, then why hadn't they seen them?

Levon and Molly looked at each other. Neither of them said anything, but both shared the same thought. "I'm going to stick with you a little longer," Molly said quietly, taking his hand again.

Levon nodded, and together they entered the mural gallery that marked the entrance to the second floor. Their footsteps loud in the abrupt silence, they walked through the archway leading to Bates Hall and stopped in mid-step to stare at their surroundings.

Bates Hall was the largest room in the library and also the most magnificent. Over two hundred feet long, its marble floor was divided by row upon row of oak study tables illuminated by brass reading lamps, its walls lined with bookcases beneath tall mullioned windows that let in the afternoon sun. Towering above everything was a barrel ceiling nearly fifty feet high whose arches were supported by neoclassical columns.

At any time of day or night, the reading room was usually occupied by dozens of patrons: students from Boston's many colleges and universities, writers and historians doing research, retirees passing the time with newspapers and magazines, all quietly engrossed one way or another. That was the way Levon had left the place about an hour ago, when he asked another librarian to take over the reference desk at the far end of the room while he went on lunch break, and that was what he'd expected to see when he returned. And, indeed, this was what he and Molly found . . .

Except there were no people.

Across the room, books had been left open on tables. Pens and pencils lay atop open notebooks and pads, in some places with sentences left unfinished. Backpacks hung by their straps from the backs of chairs or on the floor where they'd fallen. Jackets and caps lay abandoned, sometimes on the floor. There was even an iPad left behind by someone who apparently didn't care if it was stolen.

"What the hell?" Levon stared about the room. "Looks like the *Flying Dutchman* . . . everyone just dropped what they were doing and took off."

"Too weird." Molly walked over to where the iPad lay, picked it up, and ran a finger down the screen. It lit, revealing the opening page for the library's search engine. "When we have a fire drill, we usually let people take their stuff with them before—"

Her voice was drowned out by another chopper flying low over the building. This time, though, they were able to see it. The windows weren't at eye-level, so Levon and Molly couldn't tell what was going on in Copley Square, but they were tall enough to allow them to view the sky above plaza. So they watched in astonishment as an AH-64 Apache came into sight, its chain gun and missile launchers pointed at something in the square below.

"This is no fire drill," Levon whispered.

Molly didn't answer at once. Hearing nothing from her, he looked around to see that she was hastily running her fingertip across the iPad. "Hang on a sec," she murmured, answering his question before he could ask it. "It's already logged onto our server, so maybe I can get . . ." A little squeal of delight. "Yes! I got NECN!"

Levon walked over to peer over her shoulder. Just as she said, Molly had managed to access New England Cable News. Crime stories, Red Sox scores, and shark attacks on Cape Cod usually dominated the news, but today . . .

"What is that thing?" Molly asked, staring at the image apparently taken from the roof of the nearby Hancock Tower.

"Is that . . . a spaceship?" Levon bent closer to peer at the screen. "Is that a spaceship *right outside?*"

They were still gaping at the iPad when they heard something behind them: a sound like a large and heavy — yet somehow soft — object slowly rolling across the marble floor, coming from the gallery behind them. A sound like nothing they'd ever heard before.

Molly looked up from the iPad as Levon felt his breath catch. Then, as one, the two of them turned to find an enormous worm, seven feet tall and at least another eight feet in length, crawling toward them from the gallery.

"A giant worm," Sneed said.

"Yeah, but not like an earthworm," Levon explained. "They're much more like caterpillars, really. They have six . . . no, eight . . . pairs of legs underneath them, all really short even for the front two which are longer and double as manipulators, and when they walk forward their legs start moving from the back and ripple forward."

"Most of the time, they're totally on the ground," Molly continued, "but when they stop to do something, the front half rises up while the back half remains horizontal. They've got antennae both front and back, and a couple of big black eyes up front—"

"If you get close enough," Levon interrupted, "you can see yourself reflected in them, and it's like looking a dark-tinted mirror, so it's kinda creepy—"

"But they're not scary at all," Molly said hastily. "Really, they're not. That's the first thing you've got to know, the most important thing. This isn't an invasion. The bookworms . . . the Cetens . . . don't mean us any harm. They just want—"

"They just want to learn from us," Levon finished.

"Yeah, right." Sneed was unconvinced. One look at him, and Jeffers knew that the White House man was far from being persuaded that the aliens had peaceful intentions. "Did you get their names?"

The two librarians shared a look, and it seemed for a moment like they were sharing a silent laugh as well. "Yeah, well," Levon said, "we did, but they're pretty difficult for us to pronounce. Their mouths . . . they're mandibles, really, and don't have lips and tongues the way we do, so everything sounds sort of like"—he made rapid chattering sounds with his teeth—"only a lot louder and faster. Nothing we can understand."

"So we gave them names." Molly smiled. "I called the first one we met Ralph . . . for Ralph Waldo Emerson, of course. And later there was Henry, for Henry David Thoreau, and Herman, for Herman Melville."

"There's a female, too," Levon added, "and we named her Emily, for Emily Dickinson, but we haven't met her. She's the expedition's commanding officer and they told us she's on the mothership somewhere up there."

Jeffers nodded. Shortly after the spacecraft made their simultaneous landings in Boston, New York, and London, telescopes at Kitt Peak and other major observatories had spotted a large craft in orbit above the Moon. The Cetens had parked their mothership out of quick-strike range of any missiles launched from Earth. If nothing else, the extraterrestrials were wisely cautious of the local inhabitants.

"Uh-huh." Sneed leaned back in his chair and folded his arms together. "The aliens are giant caterpillars named Ralph and Henry and Herman, and they're from Tau Ceti and don't mean us any harm." He looked over at Jeffers. "This is what you get when you decriminalize marijuana."

Jeffers ignored him. "You said the Cetens aren't hostile, and you were about to say that they want something. Can you tell us what that is?"

"Yes, but . . ." Levon stopped himself. "Look, there's something you need to know about them that may help you understand why they're here, and that is they comprehend English, but not in its spoken form."

"Or at least not very well," Molly added. "They learned the English language . . . along with a lot of other things about Earth, including a major misunderstanding we'll get to in a sec . . . from commercial broadcast transmissions Tau Ceti-e began receiving some decades ago. They couldn't glean much information from our radio signals, because there was no context in which to place them other than the obvious fact that they of intelligent origin, but when they began receiving our TV signals they were able to match language to images."

"But the real breakthrough," Levon continued, "came when English-language TV broadcasters began supplying closed captions.

That's when the Cetens were able to translate and read our language
. . . or one of them, at least. They can't speak it, and their hearing is
quite poor . . . they don't have ears like ours, so they're dependent upon
audible vibrations picked by their antennae . . . but they taught
themselves how to read English, which was the language in most of
the transmissions they picked up."

"Until fairly recently, that is," Molly said. "When North American
TV networks started switching over to satellite and cable, they began
losing reception. But I don't think they understand that yet. They're
just now receiving transmissions from about twelve years ago."

"All right, I get it." Jeffers nodded. "They learned about us from our
commercial broadcast signals . . . mostly television . . . and from that
they learned English."

"Giant, English-speaking caterpillars named Ralph, Henry, and
Herman." Sneed shook his head. "Man, you must be smoking some
good shit down there in the basement."

Molly glared at him. "If you think we're stoned and making it all up,
feel free to let us go. Really, we've got better things to do." She reached
over to her boyfriend to take his hand; he responded with a warm smile.

"You're not going anywhere until we say you can." Sneed's
expression hardened; he was back to being the big man from
Washington.

"No, please . . . we want to hear what you have to say." Jeffers raised
his hands in a placating gesture. "Look, have you eaten yet? I haven't.
Let's get some breakfast." He looked over his shoulder at the soldier
guarding the door. "Corporal, would you get us some coffee, please?
And maybe some doughnuts, too. I think there's a coffee shop
downstairs."

"Coffee would be good." Levon yawned. "We've been up all night."
He glanced at Sneed. "Conversing with our imaginary caterpillars," he
added. "At least they're more interesting than present company."

Sneed harrumphed and looked away. "About what?" Jeffers asked.

Molly smiled "Remember what I said about the bookworms
misunderstanding us?"

The alien Molly had named Ralph held up a scroll of wafer-thin
material that looked like plastic. His mandibles clicked for a few
moments, and amber words materialized upon its black screen:

WE DESIRE YOUR RECORDS OF YOUR RACE'S
PREVIOUS ENCOUNTERS WITH STARFARERS.

Molly read the scroll twice, not quite understanding what the Ceten meant. "What records? What encounters?"

"I don't know what he means either. I'll ask." Levon was seated at the nearest table, working with the iPad they'd found. He thought about it a moment, then typed a query, using the largest display font he could find, and held it up for the Ralph, Henry, and Herman to read.

WHAT RECORDS ARE THESE? OUR WORLD HAS NEVER
BEFORE BEEN VISITED BY ANY RACE OTHER THAN YOU.

The Cetens lowered their immense heads to study the iPad. Once again they began chattering excitedly among themselves, their forward antenna twitching against each other in what Molly assumed was a form of tactile communication. There was no way to understand what they were saying to each other, of course, so she took the moment to turn to Levon again.

"Maybe it'll help if we review what we've learned so far," she said, and then began holding up fingers. "One . . . they're from Tau Ceti-e, which is 11.9 lightyears away."

Levon nodded. As luck would have it, the person who abandoned his iPad on the way out the door was an astronomy buff who'd downloaded a stargazing program into his tablet. So when Ralph had displayed a diagram of his homeworld and its star system on his scroll, Levon was able to match it to that of the fifth planet of a well-known G-class star in the Cetus constellation. Molly decided that, if she ever met the kid who'd left his iPad behind, she'd buy the little idiot a beer.

"Two"—she held up another finger—"they're friendly." Even as she said this, Molly knew she was making an assumption. For all she knew, the Cetens were advance scouts for a race of carnivores who'd come to gather humans for a big stewpot, starting with her and Levon. But she doubted it. Although she'd probably been frightened out of a year of her life when she saw Ralph come squirming through the door, followed by Henry and Herman, nothing the three aliens had done so far hinted at hostile motives. They carried no weapons, and while their vessel appeared to be protected by some sort of force projector, all it had done so far was scare away the panhandlers, junkies, and Scientologists who haunted Copley Square.

Besides, who could think of a caterpillar as menacing, even when it was fifteen feet long?

While their size made them intimidating, the Cetens were both gentle and beautiful. All three were covered with soft, lustrous fur whorled with bright colors, no two patterns alike. And they were apologetic for having caught her and Levon by surprise. They'd been exploring another part of the second floor—and had just learned how to disable the fire alarm, which annoyed even them—when their antennae picked up the presence of humans in the nearby hall and they'd come over to investigate.

"Three," Molly continued. "They landed here, along with the libraries in New York and London, because they knew how to read English even if they can't speak it, because they believe libraries are central repositories of all planetary knowledge, and these three were the biggest ones they know about."

"Well, they're not far off, at least when it comes to that." Levon glanced about the reading room, with its bookcases along the walls and reference desk at the end. "If we don't have it ourselves, we know how to get it." He smiled fatuously, smug in the fact that he held a master's in library science.

Molly suppressed a sigh. "Maybe, but this doesn't answer the big question . . . why land at a library in the first place? If they think we've been visited by other races, why not land in front of NASA headquarters in Washington and ask them?"

Molly was still trying to come up with an answer to this when the Cetens stopped conversing with one another and Ralph turned to her and Levon again. He held up his scroll:

WE HAVE SEEN YOUR VISUAL COMMUNICATIONS.
YOUR IMAGES DEPICT PREVIOUS ENCOUNTERS WITH
HOSTILE SPACEFARING RACES. WE WOULD LIKE
TO EXAMINE YOUR RECORDS SO THAT WE MAY
LEARN WHO THEY ARE.

"Holy crap!" Levon's eyes were wide as he read this. "Does he mean what I think he means?"

"Let's not jump to conclusions." Until now, Molly had been content to let Levon ask and answer all the questions. She took the iPad from his hands and, placing on the table, wrote:

ARE YOU REFERRING TO VISUAL IMAGES THAT
DEPICT OUR WORLD BEING INVADED BY RACES
OTHER THAN OUR OWN?

She held it for the Cetens to read. Ralph's reply was immediate:

YES.

"Oh, no." Levon was appalled; he didn't know whether to laugh out loud or gasp in horror. "No. Don't tell me they believe—"

"Hush. Let me think." Absently rubbing her lips with her forefinger, Molly pondered the implications of what they'd just learned. Then she wrote again:

HAVE YOU CONSIDERED THE POSSIBILITY THAT
THESE IMAGES ARE ENTIRELY IMAGINARY?

When she showed this to the aliens, it caused no small excitement. Ralph, Herman, and Henry turned toward one another; their great heads bobbed up and down, their antennae lashed at each other's, and their mandibles clicked like telegraph keys. Watching them, Molly half-turned to Levon.

"Okay," she murmured, "*now* it's safe to jump to conclusions."

"Yeah . . . but what if they really do think all those alien-invasion movies were real?" Levon was no longer amused. "Remember how they all end? We destroy the aliens . . . *every single time!*"

"No, it doesn't make for a good first-contact situation, does it?" Science fiction wasn't Molly's favorite form of entertainment, but she'd read enough novels and seen enough movies to know that, in SF, wars between humans and aliens races were sometimes started by cultural misunderstandings. And for every *Rendezvous with Rama* or *Close Encounters of the Third Kind*, there were hundreds of reiterations of

Ender's Game or *Earth vs. the Flying Saucers*. So what if this was a situation like *Galaxy Quest*, where the aliens were completely ignorant of the concept of fiction? If the Cetens thought humans opened fire on every extraterrestrial vessel that came to visit . . .

The aliens turned toward her and Levon again. This time, though, it was the one they'd called Henry who used the scroll. He chattered at it, and words appeared:

> YES, WE HAVE CONSIDERED THAT POSSIBILITY. WE NEEDED TO INVESTIGATE IN ORDER TO BE CERTAIN. ARE YOU SAYING THAT NO OTHER RACE HAS VISITED YOUR WORLD?

"Might as well tell the truth," Levon murmured. "We're screwed either way."

Molly hated to admit it, but he was right. Just as bad as the myth that Earth had been invaded time and time again and defeated every race that had come to conquer it was the perception—however accurate it may be—that the human race was xenophobic and bloodthirsty. If the Cetens were indeed hostile, then they might conclude that the only sure way to defeat humankind was to obliterate all life on Earth. And if they were as peaceful as they appeared to be, then they might conclude that the best thing to do was to leave these savage natives alone and go back to where they'd come from . . . thus bringing humankind's first and perhaps only chance to meet an alien race to a premature and ignominious end.

Wishing that someone who knew more about this sort of thing were here—but Leonard Nimoy was no longer around, and Patrick Stewart was never there when you needed him—Molly started to place her fingertips on the iPad again. She then stopped herself. Something Ralph had just said—or rather, written—caused another thought to occur to her.

She typed:

> NO OTHER RACE HAS VISITED OUR WORLD. ARE THERE RACES OTHER THAN YOURS?

Henry's response was immediate:

YES. THERE ARE FOUR OTHER STARFARING RACES
WITHIN THE IMMEDIATE STELLAR VICINITY, AND
MANY MORE BEYOND THAT.

"Wow!" Levon's eyes widened. "Sounds like a crowded neighborhood."

"Uh-huh." Molly didn't know what the "immediate stellar vicinity" meant, but guessed that it was a generalized expression for a measurement of distance equivalent in some way to light-years and parsecs. In any case, she was hoping Henry would say that, so she went on:

ARE ANY OF THESE RACES HOSTILE?

Again, the answer came without hesitation:

WE HAVE ENCOUNTERED NO HOSTILE STARFARING
RACES. CONFLICT BETWEEN DIFFERENT SPECIES IS
IMPRACTICAL. PEACEFUL TRADE AND CULTURAL
EXCHANGE IS PREFERABLE TO WAR OR INVASION.

"People in Hollywood are going to be pissed when they hear this," Levon said.

"Like they pay much attention to reality in the first place. Now hush." Molly carefully weighed her response, and then typed:

THE IMAGES YOU HAVE SEEN ARE OUR WAY OF
IMAGINING A FUTURE WE WOULD RATHER NOT
HAVE COME TRUE. THEY ARE NOT THE ONLY
SCENARIOS WE HAVE IMAGINED. WOULD YOU
LIKE FOR US TO SHOW YOU OTHERS?

Henry turned to Ralph and Herman again. Once more, the three Cetens conversed among themselves. Then Herman took the scroll from Henry and responded:

YES, PLEASE SHOW US THESE THINGS. IF YOUR RACE

IS CAPABLE OF OTHER WAYS OF GREETING VISITORS
THAN TO SEEK THEIR DESTRUCTION, WE WOULD LIKE
TO KNOW THIS.

Molly slowly let out her breath, and then put down the iPad and sagged against the table. "All right," she said quietly, "I think I just bought us a chance."

"A chance to do what?" Levon asked.

"To prove that the human race isn't just a bunch of paranoid, trigger-happy yahoos." She looked up at the windows. The light was beginning to show the first tint of late afternoon; it wouldn't be long before the day came to an end. "Go some make coffee, will you? We've got a long night ahead."

The corporal whom Jeffers had dispatched in search of breakfast returned with a room service cart loaded with coffee and doughnuts. As he placed them on the table, Levon made a face.

"Junk food . . . the last thing I ever want to see again is junk food." He looked up at the corporal. "You think maybe I can get some fresh fruit? Maybe a bagel with lox and cream cheese?"

"Sorry," Molly said when the corporal gave Levon an irate glare, "but junk food is all we've had since yesterday. The café on the ground floor was closed, so we had to break into a vending machine in the employees area and make do with what we found."

"That and microwave popcorn." Levon quietly chuckled as he reached for the coffee carafe. "Who would have thought that the bookworms ate popcorn?"

"Giant alien caterpillars eating popcorn," Jeffers said. "Right . . ."

"Actually, they're not really caterpillars." Levon poured coffee first for Molly, and then himself. "They just look that way. They're warm-blooded mammals, descended from . . . well, appearances notwithstanding I don't think there's anything quite like them on Earth. But since Tau Ceti-e is larger than Earth and more massive, it has over twice Earth's surface gravity, and that means its inhabitants have evolved so that—"

"I'm not interested," Sneed said, an incurious remark that made Jeffers wonder if his job with the White House science office was a political appointment. "What I want to know is, what were you two doing in there all night? And why didn't you call us? You've got cell phones, don't you?"

"I have to admit, that's a good question." Jeffers passed the cream pitcher to Molly when she gestured to it. "You knew that the library was surrounded, didn't you?"

"Oh, yes." Molly poured a tiny dose of milk into her cup. "Once Levon and I went over to the Johnson Building and got a peek out the second-floor windows, we saw your troops across the street. But we were there only for a few minutes to gather some books from the science section, and did our best to stay away from the windows."

"For the love of God, *why?*" Sneed stared at her. "Were you being held prisoner?"

"Oh, for heaven's sake, no." She picked up her coffee, calmly took a sip. "We could have left anytime we wanted. And yes, colonel, we did call out . . . just not to the military. No offense intended, but the help we needed wasn't the kind you people usually supply."

"We called other librarians," Levon said. "And the other reason we didn't leave is that . . . well, frankly, we were having too much fun."

"You see," Molly went on, "the Cetens had the wrong impression of us from all those mediocre alien invasion movies we've had on TV over the years. And it didn't help that you guys surrounded the library almost as soon as they landed. So it was up to us to correct that impression, and that meant showing them counterexamples."

"It turns out that they're really fast readers," Levon continued. "Those communication scrolls of theirs also work well with printed material . . . all they have to do is lay them down across the open pages of a book, and almost immediately it's translated from English to their language. And they can read a printed page like that." He snapped his fingers. "That's how we started calling them bookworms. Once we learned this, we began scouring the collection for books . . . both fiction and non-fiction . . . in which we're not all gun nuts itching to blow away the first alien we meet."

"So we started in the science section," Molly said, "and pulled out books by people like Carl Sagan and Freeman Dyson and Jill Tarter and Phillip Morrison, the people who've speculated on the implications of first contact with aliens and ways of assuring that such contact would be peaceful."

"And once they'd absorbed that, we moved over to the fiction section." Despite himself, Levon picked up a doughnut and nibbled at it. "We had to dig a bit harder there . . . it's depressing how much recent science fiction belongs to the 'if it moves, shoot it' variety. We called other librarians, though, and once we'd pledged them to secrecy, they told us about writers who expressed a different view and whose books were in our collection. Arthur C. Clarke, Frederik Pohl, James White, Poul Anderson, Hal Clement—"

"Theodore Sturgeon, Robert A. Heinlein besides *The Puppet Masters* and *Starship Troopers*, Spider Robinson, Vonda McIntyre, Robert J. Sawyer . . . dozens, really." Molly started to reach for a doughnut, and then apparently reconsidered and moved her hand away. "But we couldn't just show them books, as much as we would've liked to, because they'd seen our films. And so we also had to find movies that would serve as counterexamples."

"That's when it became really fun," Levon said. "We've got a small collection of films on DVD, and what we didn't have, we were able to download as streaming video. We cleared the furniture out of the Washington Room where the public access computers are located, made as much popcorn as we could—"

"And spent the rest of the night watching movies." Succumbing to temptation, Molly picked up a doughnut. "We steered clear of movies like *War of the Worlds* and *Independence Day* and instead found more benign fare. *The Day the Earth Stood Still*, *2001: A Space Odyssey*, *Contact*, the first *Star Trek* movie—"

"You know how much fun it is watching a good movie with a kid who's never seen it before?" Levon asked. "Well, that's sort of the way it was with the bookworms. They weren't interested in seeing how we depicted the aliens so much as in how we depicted ourselves. So we spent a lot of time explaining things that they'd seen before but never really understood."

"But the main thing," Molly said, "was that these movies showed them that, while we might be anxious about having aliens come to visit, we weren't necessarily going to blow them away. So we managed to dispel some bad impressions they got from all those *Aliens* rip-offs." She smiled at the memory. "Besides, they're good company. Ralph wanted to continue studying the books we'd found, so Herman and Henry let Levon and me curl up beside them. We shared the popcorn—"

"And that's what you did all night long." Sneed stared at her in disbelief. "Twenty hours with the first extraterrestrials humankind has ever encountered, and you wasted them reading books and watching old sci-fi movies." He snorted in disgust.

Jeffers was more impressed. "Actually, I think you two did a superb job. Do you realize that you're the only humans any of the aliens have encountered since they landed here? The New York and London libraries were both completely evacuated when the other ships landed, and their crews wouldn't let anyone in, so it's just a lucky break that the two of you were still inside." He reached for the coffee pot. "No one has to know the reason why."

"Thanks, but . . . well, that's not necessary." Still smiling, Molly reached over to Levon to take his hand. "As of early this morning, we're married."

Everyone gaped at them, including the soldiers who'd been monitoring the cameras. "That's right," Levon said, grinning as only a newlywed husband can. "When Ralph discovered that we weren't married, he insisted on making it official. Seems the Cetens are pretty firm on that point . . . you want to mate, you make it permanent. But marriage isn't as hard for them to do as it is for us. According to their customs, any two adult Cetens can officiate a marriage ritual between two other adults. And since there's nothing that says those two adults can't be human beings—"

"Once we're done here," Molly said, "we need to drop by the courthouse to pick up a marriage license. And maybe see a JP, too. I rather suspect the state won't recognize a marriage officiated by an alien." A sly smile. "Their marriage ceremony is a bit . . . different."

"And that's because . . . ?" Jeffers asked.

"Let's put it this way . . . the bookworms learned quite a bit about human anatomy." A coy smile appeared on her face. "And when you've got something big, soft, and warm to lie on top of, well—"

Sneed's mouth curled in disgust while Jeffers frowned at the lecherous expressions on the faces of the two male corporals. He was about to ask something else when the sergeant suddenly pointed to her screen.

"Movement, sir! In the square!"

Everyone forgot what they had been talking about and hurried over to her end of the table. Using the joystick, the sergeant had brought the drone she was piloting to a halt about three hundred feet above Copley Square, the closest the aliens would allow anyone or anything to come to their ship. The sun had fully risen by then and the floodlights turned off, so it was easy for them to see that the spacecraft's hatch had opened and its ramp lowered.

"I don't see the tunnel," Jeffers said, bending over the sergeant's shoulder to squint at the laptop screen. "Maybe they don't care anymore whether we know what they look like."

"They don't." Levon calmly stood beside him, hands in his pockets. "They said that because they now know us a little better now, they'd let us know them better, too."

"Yeah?" Sneed asked. "What else did they tell you . . . like, when the invasion begins?"

Levon was about to reply when Jeffers snapped, "They're coming out!"

The drone camera zoomed in for an overhead view of the Dartmouth Street entrance. Slowly, one at a time and apparently in no rush at all, three caterpillar-like forms emerged from the center door and crawled down the steps. Their immense bodies rippled from back to front as their small legs carried them across the sidewalk to Dartmouth Street.

They weren't leaving with empty hands, or claws. Each Ceten carried in their spindly arms a small stack of books, mainly hardcovers but also a few paperbacks. They hugged the books against themselves in a manner that suggested that the volumes were being regarded as precious artifacts, the writings of an alien culture.

"They're stealing our books!" Angry, Sneed jabbed a finger at the screen as he turned to the two librarians. "You're going to let them do that? Take whatever they want from us?"

"They're not stealing anything." Molly gave him a stern look. "Before we left, I performed one last duty for them . . . I issued library cards."

Jeffers stared at her. "You can't be serious."

"Completely." She was keeping a straight face, but only barely. "Ralph, Henry, and Herman are aware that the books are not gifts but rather are on loan, and we expect them to be returned within fourteen days." She added a sly wink. "I let them know, though, that if they're a little late, we'd be willing to waive the overdue fines."

"We've also contacted librarians in New York and London," Levon said, "and Ralph asked Emily to contact the crew of the other vessels. The other landing parties will allow staff librarians to enter the landing sites so that they may perform the same service for them."

"You're giving them access to information about us!" Sneed was horrified. "They'll use it to plot an invasion!"

"Oh, will you knock it off already?" Levon glared at him. "Get it straight . . . there's not going to be an invasion. There are dozens of races out there in the galaxy and they all peacefully coexist with each other. The idea of one race going to all the trouble to invade another planet lightyears away, for no practical reason that would make it worth the time and effort, is a stupid meme that's been stuck in our heads for more than a century. *Get over it!*"

Sneed's mouth fell open. He stared at Levon for a moment, as if not quite believing that a lowly reference librarian would have the audacity to speak in such a manner to someone from the White House. Then he turned and, pushing Molly and Jeffers aside, stalked out of the room.

One of the corporals quietly clapped his hands. This time, Jeffers didn't disapprove. "So I guess you've pretty much guaranteed that they will be coming back," he said as they watched the bookworms disappear into their ship.

Molly shrugged. "Well, they promised that they'd bring the books back. And besides, I've asked for something in return."

"And what might that be?"

She smiled. "Why . . . donations, of course. We've loaned them some of our books. Next time they come, we'd like to have a few of theirs."

If you haven't learned it by now, there's no such thing as a "free ride" in an alien spaceship, and cute aliens are always up to no good. Hugo award-winning author, Elizabeth Moon, drives the lesson home once again. —RWB

A Greener Future

by Elizabeth Moon

I saw them first on vid. I thought they were animations, given the size, maybe knee-high on the host, Larry Lancer. He mentioned the Blue Man Group of the previous century, and said, "These guys are not only green, but little!"

They were a pleasant mid-green, all the parts that showed, wearing the kind of costume leprechauns do in the cartoons: the mid-shin pants with a slit on the side, buckled shoes, short darker green jacket over a white shirt, black hats. No facial hair, just the green make-up on hands, faces, necks, legs.

They said nothing, but did their act to music, a catchy rhythm of jingling and hoots, the kind of thing that stuck in your head afterward. It sounded fun, and they were fun to watch. They bounced around the stage, off one another, using a few simple props, and when it was done, I wished they'd done more. I told Lisa about them when she got home from her mom's.

They weren't back the next week, or the one after that, but Ted from work messaged me that he'd seen them in an ad for beer and sent the link. They stood in a line, passing bottles from a box on the floor from one to the other, and then juggling with them in every combination of moves you can imagine, finally popping the tops off with an equally imaginative set of props: belt buckles, shoe buckles, something that fit over one's thumb, and so on. The same bouncy, irresistible music played behind them. I didn't normally buy that brand of beer, but I tried one out on the strength of that ad. It was good beer. I changed brands.

They were back on Lancer's show the next month, this time without any direct view of them with Lancer, just "The Leaping Leprechauns" as a voiceover, and them under the lights, with a dark background. The act was longer, more complex, and included both fast tumbling and slower moves as if they were working underwater. Their coordination, their timing, was incredible. The music matched their act perfectly. Lisa and I were fascinated.

"I thought you said they were animations," she said when it was over. "Clearly they're real."

I had forgotten the animation idea when I saw the beer ad the first time. "They can't be," I said slowly. "They're too small. No human could be that small."

"Mutated monkeys? I mean apes—no tails."

"Maybe . . . but they don't look like any monkeys I ever saw."

"They do look like people, aside from the green." She sounded almost convinced.

"Greasepaint," I said. "Or whatever they call it. Like those Blue Man guys."

The music was still bouncing around in my head, and I did my best to sing it as I swung Lisa around. Dancing in the kitchen. At my age. Hard to believe, but we did it, and after that we danced several times a week.

The next ad we saw them in was for the latest in driverless cars, those three-wheelers with the bubble-top. The music, as always, had a toe-tapping quality, and the Leprechauns were leaping around under the bubble—and above. They'd cut a hole in it, unless it was green-screened, and they were juggling and laughing as the bubble-car swerved through traffic and then it was over. I hadn't considered one of those bubble-topped three-wheelers—who wants to be that visible all the time, and anyway where we live it gets really hot in summer. But Lisa was already looking up the price and running figures. Turned out it would save us money to dump the old four-wheel, opaque one—which we'd enjoyed before, including of course the obligatory sex inside while going down the open road at ninety-per.

We weren't the first to the dealer, even though we went the next day, but we did in fact save money. Initiative pays off. Slowpokes found that the trade-in on staid old four-wheelers with closed passenger compartments had dropped a lot. Our Bubble is economical, fun, and we wouldn't go back to the old four-wheeler if they gave it to us free.

By the end of six months, the Leprechauns had a weekly show of their own, adorable hijinks and music in every one of them. They still didn't talk—not a word—and their music was always upbeat, just varied and complicated enough, not too loud. I felt energized by it; I found I was sleeping better and had more energy during the day. Lisa said the same thing, and our neighbors—even the formerly dour older couple down the block, the Dietrichs—now smiled more, acted more friendly. Life was just more fun with Leprechauns in it. We couldn't get enough of them, nor could any of our friends.

Naturally, being so popular, the Leprechauns got more ad contracts—lots of them, in fact—for everything from baby food to bed linens, headache pills to shoes. All the products they advertised were well worth the money. We didn't need the baby food, but we bought a lot of the rest.

When fan clubs started popping up, we joined a fan club in our city, and signed petitions for the Leaping Leprechauns to make a live tour. We wanted to know more about them—we could tell by now that they weren't all exactly the same height, and one of them was plumper than the others, a stout little guy with just enough belly. We imagined what their names might be, and where they came from (probably not Ireland, we agreed, despite the name), and how small their babies were at birth. Most of our conversations around the patio grills had to do with the Leprechauns, one way or another. We didn't have time for quarrels or gossip.

The Leprechauns' agent sent a letter telling us the live tour was impossible, as the Leprechauns were touring the Jovian colonies at the moment and wouldn't be back to Earth for several years. But . . . there was a postscript. If we wanted, our fan club could have two lucky winners travel out to meet them in person and represent the club. Two fan clubs from each continent had been chosen at random; two fans from each club. All expenses paid. Lisa clutched my arm; I grabbed her shoulder. The look on her face matched what I felt.

It could have been bad: everyone in the club wanted to go, local responsibilities or not. An all-expense-paid trip out beyond Mars? Who wouldn't? Nobody, it turned out. There were narrowed eyes;

there could have been arguments. But the rules as stated in the letter were clear. Names of everyone who wanted to go had to be submitted to the agent's office; a fair impartial lottery would decide who won. The winners must be ready to depart within 24 hours of notification, no exceptions. We put our names in, and settled back to wait.

Next morning, Friday, we had a message. So many people in our club were such a perfect match, it said. We had won the lottery but to prevent problems, we shouldn't tell the others, just quietly slip away. Today.

We'd had no idea results could arrive so soon. It's not as easy as you might think to just walk away from a house, a mortgage, everything . . . and without being noticed. But we had no choice. We had to be at the airport at 7:15 pm local time to catch a charter flight. Lisa and I were both at work when the message arrived; we texted each other but couldn't really talk until lunch. "I have to pack," Lisa said. "I'll take the afternoon off. I have sick days left."

"I can take a personal day," I said. "I'll say I'm concerned about you."

We spent the afternoon packing and repacking the single small case we were allowed. It was nearly all underwear. We figured we'd buy clothes somewhere on the way. Sneaking even that case into the Bubble wasn't easy—our neighbors seemed to be watching us suspiciously— but we managed, and finally I stood in the house door and said, loud enough to be heard down the street, "Honey, since you're headache's better, why don't we go out to dinner?" She came out looking a little flustered, then I locked the door behind us, we got in the Bubble, and drove away. I noticed Charlene and Chuck Hamiss, down the street, taking a case to their car, but they went off almost every weekend to visit his parents, so I thought nothing of it.

We followed the directions we'd been given, across the city to the far end of the commercial airport, where charter flights boarded. A plane waited—several planes waited, in fact—but a fellow in a blue uniform came up to us right away, took our names, and then our suitcase, and led us over to one of the planes, ushering us inside. Cheerful music came from inside: the Leaping Leprechauns' theme song. A man in a different uniform brought us drinks and little packets of cookies, promising dinner once we were airborne.

And so it began. The door closed; engines started; we were moving toward the runway when I saw a car drive toward that end of the airport . . . and realized our car was no longer parked there. Too late now—we were in the air fast, then higher, banking in a turn, and soon we were tucking into an excellent dinner, including wine. I fell asleep before we reached the spaceport, and admit to being a bit foggy on what else happened that first night—we were sedated for takeoff to the transfer station, helped through various hatches and tubes, and finally tucked into sleep-cocoons in our compartment on the ship that would take us to meet the Leprechauns. Tired, full of good food and wine and whatever was in that pill they had us take, we sank into deep sleep.

We were well away by the time we woke up. Very well away. Months away, though we didn't know that yet.

What I knew right away was that Lisa, tucked in her cocoon beside mine, had been replaced by someone bald and green and less than half her size.

Depopulating a planet, I know now, takes longer than a few days, or weeks, or months, if you don't want to just kill everyone. Fifty thousand left the night we did. At fifty thousand a day it was going to take almost 660 years for Earth. Too long to be practical. Or not, if you start the process 660 years before you need the planet for your own purposes.

Or you snatch fifty or a hundred thousand of those who keep a society running every day for weeks and months and years, along with those of reproductive age. Lisa and I, for instance. Most of our neighborhood, other than the Dietrichs. It gets easier every trip, as the birth rate drops and the old die off and society fragments until survivors are fighting to get onto the ships.

A moment after waking, though, I wasn't thinking about that. I didn't know what had happened, or why. I stared at that naked bald green head where Lisa had been with horror for several moments before realizing—when it opened its eyes and they were *her* eyes, with the little gold speck in the left one—that the bald green thing was actually Lisa. Her expression as she woke up made it clear I was just as horrible-looking to her. I pulled an arm free from my cocoon, trailing shreds of something whitish, and looked at it. Green, all the way down to the fingernails. My head felt chilly; I knew, without even feeling, that I too was bald, hairless all over, green all over. Terror and rage hit me together and then . . . the music started. Cheerful, bouncy, irresistible music, the music of the little green men . . . just like me.

My little green toes twitched; my little bald green head bobbed back and forth. So did Lisa's.

"No," I said, or rather tried to say. No sound came out. Lisa mouthed something at me—no sound. All I could hear was the music. All I could do was respond to it, while my mind tried to figure things out, interrupted by the music's insistent demand that I bounce and writhe in rhythm.

It's not so bad now. You get used to it, the way I had gotten used to school, to my job, to my next job, to marriage. We had lessons, when the little green men (I won't call them leprechauns ever again) came to peel us out of the cocoons that had shrunk us and nourished us on our own flesh and turned us green. Rows of us learning together: dance, mime, acrobatics, juggling, all the elements an entertainment troupe needed. The clumsy ones disappeared.

Lisa and I both made it into one of the troupes which is why we're now . . . well, let's just say it's not where we came from. The dominant intelligent race in this system is sort of purplish gray, hexapedal, and just as enchanted by silly little green hexapods dancing and throwing things around as we were by the little green men. They too have fan clubs and live in neighborhoods and eventually we will move into their world. Only about two million of them are still down there, clamoring for the chance to come meet us in person.

I can hardly wait.

Unarguably, Esther Friesner is one of the funniest writers working in the sf/f genre, and the genesis of this volume owes more than a little to conversations I've held with her about her own Chicks in Chain Mail *anthology series, for which I've written numerous stories. I couldn't resist inviting her to write for us, and she didn't disappoint. So sit back with a cup of coffee, but protect your keyboard.* —RWB

A Cuppa, Cuppa Burnin' Love

by Esther M. Friesner

"I don't like this." The full effect of Tom's pout was lost in the thicket of his beard.

"You haven't liked *any* of the places I've suggested since Qahwah closed," Nicky said, scowling. The day was young, but already the worst symptoms of caffeine deprivation were humming through his scrawny body. "You didn't even *try* the last four! You just hated them from the street."

Scorn flickered behind the lenses of Tom's clunky, black-framed eyeglasses. "And that was enough to keep you from patronizing them without me?"

Nicky gave a grunt of vexation. "Come on, man, you know that having a morning cup together is our thing. It wouldn't be the same if I flew solo."

"And none of the shops you've turned up were anywhere near being the same as Qahwah," Tom replied, his declaration fraught with an air of Word From On High, mostly because he was built like a Wookie halfback. He couldn't help it if his default setting was *Loom*.

"Yeah, mostly because none of them got turned into a crime scene," Nicky said bitterly.

"Wow, that was cold." Tom spared a sigh for the fate of the unique coffee shop where, up until ten days ago, the two best friends had shared their quotidian ritual. A few cups of Giuseppe (perish forbid that they drink mere "Joe"!) and they were fit to face the world. But on that dire day when they found the telltale yellow tape barring Qahwah's door (an unfortunate labor disagreement between boss and barista had ended with almond biscotti being weaponized in a most heinous manner) their wanderings in search of a new haven began.

"You want to give me a break, Tom? You're like some kind of caffeine camel: You can go without coffee for days! But I really need a jump-start. I swear, if you won't even try this place, I am that close to going *there*." He pointed dramatically across the street to where one of America's most widespread coffee franchises sang its siren's song.

"Man up, Nicky." Tom's beefy hand closed on his companion's upper arm. "Friends don't let friends drink coffee there. I'll make the sacrifice." He couldn't resist seasoning his surrender with a dash of snipery: "How did you find it? Was it *trending* on Twitter?"

"You know me better than that." Truth: Nicky and Tom had been compadres since their prep school days, when khakis ruled the earth. Their long-standing friendship was what helped him hold his ground in the teeth of mockery that would have leveled lesser hipsters. "I saw it advertised on a flyer at Susie's Second-Hand."

Tom's severe expression softened. He nourished an unrequited affection for Susie. Her standards of ideological purity were absolute, refusing to give space in her shop to anything that carried the slightest whiff of *poseur*dom, be it garment or gewgaw, patron or poster. "Well, I guess it *might* be okay. She'd never let anyone put up an ad for a McDisneyfied coffee house."

"No worries on that score. Check out the name." Nicky pointed to the modest sign above the door, proclaiming this establishment to be *Omizu Cup*. "It's one of a kind for sure. So how about it? I am *hurting*."

"Just one more sec." Tom scrutinized the shop façade with the intensity of a seventeenth century witchfinder seeking Satan's graffiti on the body of a lissome maiden. The words *Omizu Cup* were painted in silver-outlined black letters on a window tinted the deep green of sushi-swaddling *nori*. "Sure, it's a cool Japanese name, but is it the real deal or more Keokuk than Kyoto?"

"How do you expect to find out unless you *go in*? Or are you, like, the Delphic oracle of fonts? Tell me, O wise seer, is the lettering on the window *sincere* enough?"

Tom gave a mighty snort of derision. "What do you think I'm

looking for, the Great Pumpkin? Anyway, the Delphic oracle—better known as the Pythia—was female." He made this pronouncement with the same overbearing pedantry that had earned him a plethora of wedgies, swirlies, and pantsings at school. "And I'm not studying the font; I'm looking for—Aha!" He pointed in triumph at the small sign in one corner of the coffee shop's door: Free WiFi.

"Sometimes I think you enjoy torturing me. So *now* can we go in, Mister Fifty Shades of Fussbudget? Or do we have to see if there's maybe one more place that sells coffee in this town?" The town in question being Seattle, Nicky's derision was of the subtle-as-a-mallet breed.

"Ha." Tom dropped the lone syllable like wad of suet. "Seattle coffee shops are a freaking *trope*. Well, I don't drink in tropes. It's not just about the coffee for me! I want—I *need* a place with the right vibe, the perfect environment to do my thing, to contemplate where I'm going, to sharpen my quill with the pen-knife of *le mot juste*, to explore the meaning of life and the tragedy of humanity, to dedicate myself to the sacred path of a lonely, misunderstood, creative—"

"You can stop now, Tom. They're gone." Nicky indicated the other side of the street where a pair of long-legged young women had just strolled out of earshot.

"I don't know what you're talking about." Tom's words were icy enough to have come from a pigeon-breasted high society dame, vintage 1935.

Nicky didn't bother to argue. He'd always been the loyal sidekick for his friend's pursuit of every subculture butterfly imaginable. Goth, grunge, emo, punk, hip hop, a brief and unspeakable flirtation with broniedom, and Tom's present incarnation as a card-carrying, vinyl-playing, porkpie hat-wearing hipster, all had the same purpose:

Chick bait.

Over the years since high school, Tom frequently expressed the view that the world teemed with girls in tireless search of a Wounded-and-Suffering Genius to Muse the hell out of. By his own decree, he had nailed the Genius part and took every opportunity he found to play up the Wounded-and Suffering bit. (Witness his recent performance outside Omizu Cup.) All he needed to validate his self-image as World's Greatest Babe Magnet was time and the right trappings to attract a babe who'd agree.

Amazing he was still single.

"Never mind them, man." Nicky patted Tom's shoulder. "The sacred grounds call our names."

The interior of Omizu Cup was artfully lit, offering patrons a soothing, cozy dimness that never quite toppled over into the pit of *Where's my pocket flashlight?* A row of blue glass globes cast a cool glow over the coffee bar. They hung from wires artfully concealed by strands of crystal beads, evoking the leisurely ascent of bubbles from the depths of a placid koi pond. A scattering of round tables offered two choices for seating: austere, bone-pale wooden chairs or plump black ottomans whose sleek fabric made them look like river-polished stones. Most of the tables were occupied, but the overall ambiance was not so crowded as to set off any alarms of this place being *too* popular.

Nicky counted three employees manning the glowing copper-sheathed espresso machine, the cake-and-scone display case, and the cash register. Tom would no doubt approve that their crisp uniforms were moss-colored *happi* coats, honoring both the Grail of Authenticity and the shop's riparian palette. Their headgear was another story. The round, flat-topped green caps they wore didn't look Japanese at all, unless shortened fezzes had become the rage in Harajuku.

Nicky glanced at Tom. His friend was smiling, actually *smiling*, and not with that studied gateway-to-pontification grimace that meant he was about to verbally dissect all he saw into shreds of Fail. The anomalous hats had passed muster.

Thank God, Nicky thought, desperate for his morning jolt. He raced ahead to place his order, no longer caring if Tom were in or out. *Caffeine! Caffeeeeeeiiiiine!* his bean-denied brain howled.

A girl blocked his path. Her head was crowned with a marvelously retro bouffant hairdo the iridescent blue-black of a raven's wing. The chartreuse chiffon Eisenhower era cocktail dress she wore made her look like a refugee from *Mad Men* and/or Disneyland.

Where had so much stunning alien glamor come from, so abruptly? She seemed to have manifested by magic, suddenly there before him like—like—

—*like a kernel of popcorn beauty hitting the hot oil of the Cosmos,* Nicky thought. And in the next heartbeat thought again: *Oh God, if that's the way my mind's working, I* really *need some coffee!*

"Uh, 'scuse me?" he said, going into the sidestep tango that guaranteed if he moved to his left, she'd move to her right and the pair of them would repeat the stupid maneuver at least twice before standing still and giggling.

But Nicky had no time for giggles, not even with a young woman as lovely as this one. He elbowed past her and threw himself on the mercy of the nearest Arabica wrangler.

By the time he had achieved a double-shot macchiato, extra whip, Tom and the girl were seated at one of the tables. They'd opted for ottomans, leaving Nicky to occupy a wooden chair. It was a very Puritan piece of furniture, its appearance promising soul-improving discomfort. (Promise fulfilled.)

"Hey, man, don't you want a cuppa?" Nicky inquired as he sat down.

Tom's chuckle evoked the amused condescension of 1950s sitcom fathers. "Nicky, what do you think I'm doing? I'm just about to place my order." He nodded at the girl. "This is Renri. She works here and you, my friend, just cut her off from doing her job."

"This place isn't self-serve?" Nicky was flustered. His haste to grab a cup of morning salvation made him look like the world's biggest cheapskate, a man who'd do anything to cheat a hard-working waitress out of her tip. He knew how vital tips were. He himself had experienced the horrors of food service, putting in a whole *week* as a Fries-with-that before the ploy shamed his parents into raising his allowance. "Wow, I'm sorry. Here." He hauled up the anchor chain holding his wallet and tried to press a wad of singles into Renri's pale hands.

"Oh my god, are you trying to kill me with embarrassment?" Tom groaned and threw his head back with such violence that his porkpie hat went rolling. While Renri scampered to retrieve it, he snarled at his friend: "This place is the real deal. Totally authentic. Everyone knows there's no tipping in Japan."

"Well, excuse me for having slept through the flight to Tokyo," Nicky snapped. "Okay, so Omizu Cup's got table service and no tipping. Got it. Anything else I should know, *sensei*?"

Before Tom could crush Nicky's sarcasm with an answering volley of snark, Renri was back with his hat in one hand and a full espresso cup in the other. Tom accepted both, visibly puzzled.

"Uh, Renri, I think this must be for someone else," he said, gesturing with the cup.

"Hey! Watch where you're waving that!" Nicky protested. "You want to spill—?" He paused. As usual, Tom had gone for theatrics above thought, but despite the heedless way he'd brandished the brimming cup, not a drop of the liquid slopped over into the saucer. Not one. In fact, the surface was almost immobile.

That's weird. Nicky squinted at the contents of the demitasse. *Must be some trick of the funny lighting in this place. And what's with that oil-slick effect?* He blinked rapidly but the captive midnight rainbow floating atop his friend's drink glimmered on.

Meanwhile, Renri was telling Tom that no, there was no mistake: This beverage was for him and moreover it was free.

"To welcome you, with the compliments of Omizu Cup," she said in a voice so soft and seductive it purred. Rising to her feet, she added: "What else would you like?" She tilted her head ever so slightly.

"Renri! No!" One of the men behind the coffee bar shouted so sharply that every customer in the place turned to stare until they realized that rubbernecking and Cool made bad partners. Everyone except Tom and Nicky sank back into the WiFi swamp of blogs, e-books, and assorted bloviations.

Renri gasped and snapped to posture-perfect attention. "I'm so sorry, Douglas; I forgot. It won't happen again." Her four-inch heel clipped briskly to the counter where the irate java jockey gave her a heated dressing-down.

Or so Tom surmised, since the scolding was not taking place in English. "Hey, Nicky, what's that creep saying?" he whispered. "My ears are still a little stuffed from that cold I had last week, and if I'm going to teach some geek how to talk to a lady, I want to be sure he's doing it wrong, y'know?"

Nicky knew. He knew Tom's alleged head cold was a myth and that the only Japanese his friend had mastered came from the nonexistent pamphlet, *So You Want to Be an* Otaku *Wannabe.* He, on the other hand, had taken two years of Japanese in prep school and four in college. He cocked his head in the direction of the ongoing Renri/Douglas brouhaha.

"Huh," he said, sitting back. He looked bewildered.

"What? What did he say to her?" Tom whispered urgently.

"I don't know. They're not speaking Japanese."

"Oh, come on, of course they are! Maybe it's a really local dialect."

"Maybe," Nicky said. But he didn't believe it; not that he could figure out *why* he'd shoved that perfectly logical possibility off the table. It was a gut feeling, and as he observed the two parties still enmeshed in their unintelligible set-to, his gut twisted itself into tighter and more elaborate knots of doubt. "Or maybe it's something else entirely. I mean, come on, his name's *Douglas*."

"And we went to school with a kid from Singapore whose name was Edward Pierce Lodge. His father was from Mumbai, his mom was Peranakan, and he was totally fluent in Mandarin, Malay, Hindi, Urdu, Arabic and French. Jesus, could you *be* any more ethno-linguo-racist?"

Tom's chastisement was delivered in a voice loud enough to reach Renri's ears. Nicky knew his friend had done it deliberately, throwing him under the Political Correctness Express with the sole aim of scoring points with the lady. If he'd had a second cup of coffee, he might have put up with such treatment, but that not being the case, he was pissed.

He stood up, tossed back the last of his macchiato, slammed the empty cup onto the tabletop and declared, "Translate your own damn eavesdroppings!" before stomping out of the café.

This was not the first time the friends had quarreled when Tom needed Nicky to be the fall guy in his romantic schemes. It was a long-standing tradition that, following such scenes, there would be a cooling-off period of no more than three days before Tom apologized. This interval was also the time during which Tom tried to make hay with whichever girl he'd been attempting to impress. Sometimes he'd show up at Nicky's place to say "Sorry" with the lady in tow, but more often than not he arrived stag, eager to tell Nicky how great it was that the lesbian population of Seattle was growing at such a healthy rate.

The three days came, the three days went, and they took three additional days along for the ride. On the seventh day after his blow-up, Nicky slumped into Susie's Second-Hand to vent.

Susie was a very patient woman who understood men, having been one. "He probably got lucky. I mean *really* lucky. He's exhausted."

"You've seen him?" Nicky went on point. "Where? When?"

"He came in here two days ago to buy a gift for his lady. It must be serious: He got her a diamante hair clip straight out of *Breakfast at*

Tiffany's! Boy, does he look rough: gaunt, pale, sunken eyes, and he's walking funny." She chuckled.

"And you didn't tell me?" Nicky didn't share Susie's amusement.

"When was I supposed to do that?"

"Oh, I don't know. How about like *every night this week* when you went to sleep next to me?" It was true: Nicky had scored on the field of Susie's affections while Tom still stood outside the arena, trying to buy tickets from a scalper.

Susie's nose twitched with disdain. "*You're* the one who said we had to hide our shenanigans from Tom or it'd break his heart."

"How is telling *me* about seeing *him* the same thing as telling *him* about *us*?" In his exasperation, Nicky punched the life out of every pronoun within reach.

Susie shrugged. "Hey, I'm still trying to figure out how a grown man can call what we're doing 'shenanigans.' I swear, Nicky, there are times I think you'd throw me over in an instant if you could have Tom instead."

Nicky's face turned red. He started to refute Susie's observation, but the first reply that sprang to mind was *We're just good friends* and the ones that followed became more flimsy, trite, and foolish-sounding by major degrees. He rejected all of them in favor of a gape-mouthed stare.

"It's okay, sugar." Susie gave him a kiss on the ear. "He doesn't need to know that either. Our Tom's the squarest hipster I've ever met. That's why I never gave him any encouragement. He'd freak if he knew my whole story. This Renri chick sounds perfect for him—just exotic enough to annoy his parents but otherwise normal as cornflakes. Let him be happy."

"How can he be happy if he's in bad shape, like you said?" Nicky demanded. "Dammit, whatever else, he's my best friend and I'm going to see if he needs me."

Which Nicky did, right after breakfast and a bit more Susie. His upbringing as a child of privilege and his haphazard employment as a freelance game designer always sucked the vim out of any sense of urgency in his life. But why rush? It wasn't as if he'd have to cast a dragnet over all Seattle to locate Tom once he got around to it. There were just two places his friend was likely to spend the majority of his time: at home and at Omizu Cup.

Nicky tried Tom's cell phone first, of course. It went straight to voicemail. Tom's apartment was closer than Omizu Cup so Nicky decided to drop by and knock, on the chance that his friend had silenced the phone. Seattle was a hilly place, but Tom's address lay downslope. This was a lifesaver since Nicky's preferred ride was a unicycle.

As he zipped along, beloved of gravity, he spied something that made him pull over. It was one of the numerous outlets for the Coffee-Franchise-That-Must-Not-Be-Named. Not a strange sight *per se*, but what was unicycle-stopping odd was the large Going Out of Business sign in the darkened window.

Wow, I didn't think you could *kill one of these places*, Nicky thought. He sauntered over for a closer look, which was when he noticed the second sign, a bright lime-green placard whose "Japanese-style" letters announced:

Coming Soon!
Omizu Cup
Yes, We Have Free WiFi

So much for being one of a kind, he mused. *I wonder if Tom knows?* (The friends had long agreed that the *real* F-word was "franchise.") He remounted the unicycle and sped on, contemplating ways to break the news gently.

Tom was not at home. Nicky turned his ecologically righteous ride in the direction of the original Omizu Cup. This lay in an uncooperative uphill direction, so he snagged a taxi, directing the driver to let him out a block from the now-ideologically-suspect coffee shop. If Tom were there, seated with a window view, Nicky didn't want to be seen arriving in a car, even a hybrid.

In the cab, Nicky fell into that detached, contemplative state where his only active thought process was recalculating of the tip as the meter kept ticking. Suddenly he saw something that made him sit up straight and whip his head sharply to the left.

Another storefront, another lime-green harbinger of an impending Omizu Cup.

By the time he arrived at his destination he had been driven past three additional signs with the same information. They had popped up overnight like fungi. He was so agitated that he forgot his unicycle in the taxi and ran the rest of the way.

His headlong dash was brought up short a scant two yards from the door of the original Omizu Cup by the sight of Renri, weeping bitterly into her slender hands. His first reaction was: *Don't tell me Tom dumped her just because he knows these guys are selling out. I mean, is he that principled and stupid?*

His afterthought was: *What the heck's the matter with her skin?*

Nicky remembered admiring the poetic pallor of Renri's complexion, skin so pearly it appeared to take on a delicate wash of celadon under the aqueous lighting of the coffee shop. The trouble was, here she stood in full sunshine and every visible square millimeter of her exposed flesh *still* looked green. Green!

He bit his lower lip. Whatever ailment was causing Renri's dermatological anomaly (aka: *Why does she look like celery?*), he hoped it wasn't sexually transmitted. Green was not Tom's color. "Renri?" he said, daring to touch her arm with one fingertip. "Hey, hi, I'm Nicky. We were never really introduced, but I came in here about a week ago with my friend Tom and I was wondering—"

"Tom!" she wailed. Anguish caused patches of darker green to mottle her face. Nicky drew back instinctively at the discombobulating sight. She promptly latched onto his hand with a grip so strong it was both unexpected and terrifying. "You are his friend, aren't you? He's spoken about you many times, how he wanted to call you and tell you how sorry he was for the way he treated you on the day we met. You must help him!"

"Help him?" Nicky repeated stupidly. "He doesn't need help telling me he's sorry."

"No, no, no! That isn't— Oh, just come with me!" Renri shifted her amazing grip to Nicky's wrist and hauled him off behind her. She covered a remarkable stretch of ground for someone wearing four inch heels and she did not stop until they reached yet another vacant storefront advertising a bright future rife with free WiFi at this fifth impending Omizu Cup. Before Nicky could think *Breaking and entering and trespassing, oh my!* she had pushed the door open, pulled him inside after her, and slammed it shut behind them.

"Wow, you should tell Omizu corporate to put better locks on their development sites," he said with a nervous laugh, chafing some feeling back into his freed wrist.

"It was locked," she said, pointing to the cylinder still rocking back and forth on the dusty floor. A shove from just one of her dainty hands had sent the heavy mechanism shooting out of the door like a bullet. Nicky was poised to launch into a litany of the things one says under such circumstances (beginning with "Who . . . or *what* . . . are you?" and ending with "Help!") when Renri sped things along by reaching up, seizing the top of her bouffant, and yanking herself bald-headed.

And oh, what a head it was! The shadowy interior of the empty shop could not hide the fact that the top of her skull was flat as a plate. A second, closer look revealed that it was not a plate after all, but a bowl filled to the brim with liquid.

Nicky drew a deep breath. His nostrils were inundated with the scent of fresh water, tender reeds, and the subtle fragrance of riverside cherry trees in blossom. There was no need for a third jolt to his senses. He'd studied Japanese culture, history, and myth along with the language. He knew who . . . or *what* . . . he was seeing now.

"You're a kappa!" he exclaimed.

"Well, *d'uh*," Renri responded impatiently. "So about Tom—"

"Oh yeah, like just *anyone* would recognize you. You're not exactly up for a spread in *Famous Monsters of Filmland*. My God, you're not the only one, are you? All the rest of those guys at Omizu Cup must be kappas too! What the hell—? What are you doing in Seattle? And why were you crying over Tom? Where is he? What did you do to him? He may be—"

Nicky's words were hot, but it was diversionary fire to cover up the icy dread running through his veins. He knew what kappas were: vampiric creatures that haunted the shores of lakes and rivers, waiting to drag unwary people and animals into the depths where they could be drained of blood.

And that was the upside. What took these squamous entities to a whole new level of "Ew!" was their preferred site for helping themselves to a hemoglobin highball. It wasn't the victim's neck. It was—

"—a P.I.T.A., but he's still my best friend and you've been drinking his blood! Is that why you brought me here? Am I next? The hell with that!" He lunged at Renri, fists outstretched for her face. The kappas' sole weakness—apart from an unholy binge-eating addiction to cucumbers—was the indentation on top of their heads. If the liquid spilled out, they were left paralyzed until it could be replenished.

Renri leaped aside while maintaining the perfectly straight back of a trained ballerina. She didn't lose one drop. "You fool!" she snapped as Nicky's momentum carried him past, ending in a bellyflop across an abandoned table. "If I wanted you dead, I would have given you a cup of the same brew I gave to your friend when we first met. But I pitied you. You're so skinny, one feeding would have killed you. No, *half* a feeding. Douglas is such a pig! And Trent and Irving aren't much better."

"Who names a kappa Irvi—?"

"Will you *focus*? We have to save Tom. I love him"—Her voice caught.—"and I know he loves me."

Probably because he doesn't know the real *you.* Nicky remembered what Susie had said about Tom's square-at-heart nature. (He also spared a passing moment wondering how Renri had managed to achieve any sort of intimacy with his friend while holding onto the water atop her head. It added a whole lot of new wrinkles to the saying "Love will find a way.")

"Well, where's he being held? Let's see if we can break him out of there."

"Held? Right now he's at the coffee shop, but he's not a prisoner. He can come and go as he wishes."

"Then why doesn't he? Go, I mean. I've known Tom for years and I'm *pretty* sure that if your pals are using him for an honor bar, he's not liking it."

"He has no choice. The drink I gave him stole his free will so that Douglas and the others can steal—"

"—his blood, I know."

"Not just that: His money. The revolution will not be subsidized any other way than by those we enslave and drain of—of funds. We four are the vanguard of what is to come. Seattle is our beachhead, our first coffee shop a toehold."

"That's why I'm seeing so many new Omizu Cups coming all over the city? It's an invasion?"

She nodded as much as she dared. "More money, more Omizu Cups; more Omizu Cups, more new customers to lure into drinking the espresso of enslavement; more thralls to the potion's power, more money." She spread her hands wide and for the first time Nicky noticed a thin, almost transparent webbing between her fingers. "More of our kind will come to this country to staff the new shops, and before long we will extend our control to other cities, other states, until we are *everywhere*."

"Uh, don't take this the wrong way—I appreciate the heads-up and all—but you're rolling over on your own people for *Tom*?"

"For Tom," she said, laying one hand to her bosom (and perhaps over her heart). "And for America! I will not see my new country be overrun by the kudzu of yet another franchise. Have you *seen* the way some of them treat their workers? If we kappas are to become a part of this great nation, we must not come as an attack force, but in peace. Surely we will be welcome."

"Mmmmmaybe. As long as you can find some dietary workarounds. And stay out of a few states I could mention. It'd be easier if you could get behind the Omizu Cup empire plan after all, because once people taste your coffee, they'll like you; even *Facebook* Like you!"

"All the more reason to put an end to Douglas's plan," Renri said grimly. "Will you help?"

Unhindered by a sloshing skull-bowl, Nicky was free to nod vigorously. "I think I've got the way to do this. I read the tradition that you kappas are super-polite, right? Okay, so let's go to the shop and I'll bow to your buddies. Doug and Irv and Trent will have to bow back, the water will spill out of their heads, and I'll make them swear to back off before I give them a refill. It'll be a cinch." He snapped his fingers.

Renri was not sanguine. "Yes, if we were still in Japan. But they have been in this country too long already. A bow from you will get a ''Sup?' from them at best."

Undaunted, Nicky moved to Plan B: "I could just knock their heads back." He wondered why Renri herself hadn't come up with such a simple and evident solution.

"With as much success as when you tried to do that to me?" she replied gently. "Male kappas are faster and stronger than female. Why else do you imagine I allow Douglas to boss me around?"

"Ummmm, bribing you with cucumbers is supposed to work."

"We have a standing order at Trader Joe's."

He frowned. "You're not making this easy. I wasn't thinking of *ordinary* cucumbers. I was thinking of those extra-long English ones."

"They would have to be *very* long and *very* big to get Douglas's attention. I told you what a pig he is; a picky, *gourmet* pig."

"Well, where am I supposed to get a cucumber spectacular enough to—?" And then Enlightenment hit him in a rush so glorious that he gasped. "Eu-motherloving-*reka*!"

"What? What?" Renri cried.

Nicky's answer was to pluck her discarded wig from the floor, cram it back into her hands, and say, "Omizu Cup. Ninety minutes. And when I get there, I want you to have the biggest damn pot of that mind-slaving mocha ready and waiting, okay?"

"Why? Tell me *something*. If I don't know, I can't back you up, and if you fail, Douglas will kill you!"

But Nicky was already past her, out the door, and running down the hill.

One and a half hours later, as a dull-eyed Tom sat among his fellow cappuccino captives, Nicky sauntered into Omizu Cup. A heavily laden hemp tote bag hung on his shoulder and what looked like an old Kodak Duaflex II camera dangled from a strap around his neck as he took a stance in front of the bar and cheerfully demanded, "Whose backside do I have to bite to get a cup of coffee in this dump?"

None of the clientele reacted to his loud intrusion, proof that all were in thrall to the kappa potion. As for the four kappas, Renri looked up sharply from her seat beside Tom, her face pinched with tension. Nicky caught her eye with an inquiring look. She bit her lip and bobbed her head ever so slightly. She followed this gesture with an expressive roll of her eyes in the direction of the Omizu Cup kitchen door. His smile grew a bit wider.

So you've got the stuff brewed and ready. Good girl. Now it's up to me.

He aimed his grin at the three kappas behind the counter. He didn't know Irving from Trent, but he recognized Douglas right away. The burliest of Renri's associates bared his sharp teeth in a sham smile.

"How may we serve you?"

Nicky patted the camera. "Well, you could show off those pearly whites a little more. It's not every day you get profiled in the dead trees daily. When I write you up, everyone in Seattle's going to know all about why Omizu Cup is spreading through this city like mildew."

Douglas's grimace became a tight, lipless line. "That won't be necessary. We find cheap publicity to be distasteful. We'd rather have our business grow and prosper through word of mouth. But before you leave, allow me to offer you a cup of our best brew, on the house. Renri? Renri!"

Renri was no longer in sight. While Nicky engaged Douglas's attention, the female kappa had slipped discreetly into the kitchen. Douglas glowered. "Irving, find her."

"No need for that, Irving my man!" Nicky's level of backslapping *bonhomie* was one degree below that of a hungry time-share salesman. He took the hemp bag off his shoulder and set it on the counter. "Okay, joke's over. You don't want P.R., I don't want a drink, but there's something we both want."

Douglas's almost invisible eyebrows rose beneath the brim of his peculiar cap. "And what would that be?"

"Him." Nicky waved one hand casually at Tom, who was demonstrating all the animation of a pile of laundry. "Except I want him more than you do. I know what you did to him and what you're planning. I'll bet a guy in your line of work doesn't want anyone spilling the beans—" He snickered at his own wit, which was just as well since Douglas didn't look in the mood for levity. "—so let's make a deal. You give my friend whatever the antidote is for your 'best brew' and I don't do *this*!" His hand flashed into the bag and came out holding a mandarin orange. "Think fast!" he shouted, flinging it in Douglas' face.

The chief kappa grabbed the golden fruit with unbelievably speed and without moving anything but his hand. There was a muted, moist sound as he crushed the orange into a wad of pulp and peel. "I see you know who we are," he said evenly. "A nice feint. Were you hoping I would duck *too* sharply to stay safe?" He smirked. "I'm surprised you didn't try getting me to bow."

Nicky's shoulders rose and fell. "I figured you wouldn't fall for that old trick, but I had to try *something* before I got down to bribery."

Douglas's eyes grew larger, rounder, and incandescent. "Bribery?"

"Sure! I came prepared. Like you said, I know you, so I'm hoping you're willing to swap old Tom there for—" His hand was back in the bag. "—tah-*daaah*!" The shiny, waxed skin of a common (or garden) American slicing cucumber caught the light.

Irving and Trent laughed. It sounded like frogs croaking. Douglas gave Nicky the stink-eye. "You call that a bribe? It's an insult!"

"So I lowballed you, okay? That's just good business practice, seeing what the other dude'll settle for. Look, I'll sweeten the deal—" His hand was back in the bag. "—with these!" He brandished a bunch of long, elegant, English cucumbers tied together with curly red ribbons.

"Ooooooh," said Trent, licking his lips. Irving dabbed the corners of his mouth. Douglas quelled his underlings' greed with a single withering look, and then turned a furious face to Nicky. Anger did something to the chief kappa: It blurred his human features, making them waver like a pool disturbed by a tossed pebble. Nicky glimpsed a turtle-like beak beneath the illusion of Douglas's nose, a subtle swelling at the back of his shirt that hinted of a curved shell beneath, and the same dappled, verdant complexion as Renri's when she'd been similarly stressed.

"I'm already willing to kill you," the kappa said. "I don't need any more provocation."

"But wait! There's more!" Nicky now plunged both hands into the still-bulging tote and pulled out a wicker basket heaped with *cucumis sativus* of every size, shape, and kinship that Susie's combat-level shopping skills could find in under ninety minutes. There were slicing and pickling cukes, gherkins, Lebanese, Persian and "apple" cucumbers, even a few round, yellow Dosakai from India. Nicky heard the gratifying sound of ravenous, almost amorous groans from the kappas. Even Douglas was not immune to so much crunchy temptation.

"Have we got a deal?" Nicky asked. "This for Tom?"

"We—we—" Douglas wiped saliva from his chin, webbed hands stretching out to clasp the object of his desire.

"*And* for you swearing to back off on your invasion plans!" Nicky snatched the basket out of Douglas's reach.

The kappa roared with rage. "I will destroy you! I will drown you in the iced coffee dispenser and drink your blood and then I will feast upon your so-called bribe!"

"Uh, Doug?" Irving tugged at his superior's sleeve. "We can't do that. You know the rules: Blood or cucumbers, not both."

"Right," Trent chimed in. "Remember what happened to Wade." A group moment of silence ensued.

"Fine," Douglas spat. "I'll settle for killing him. Take the top off the iced coffee—"

"Are you sure you don't want to hear my *final* offer?" Nicky was shaking inside, but he managed to speak is a husky, enticing voice worthy of the late Marilyn Monroe. He set down the basket so that it shielded the flat tote bag from the three kappas' view.

Douglas shot him a scornful look. "Whug—?" He swabbed away more drool and averted his eyes from the pile of cucumber-y goodness now taunting him. "I mean, *what* could you possibly have that would make us betray our holy cause, our sacred mission, our—?"

A stealthy tap to the smartphone in his pocket made the coffee shop resound with the opening chords of *Also Sprach Zarathustra*. A similarly sneaky manipulation of the supposed Kodak on his neck and Nicky called forth a holographic projection so imposing, so epic, so perfect in shape and color and detail that when he raised his hands it looked as if he were slowly, reverently elevating the awe-inspiring bulk of a cucumber the size of kayak. The dramatic music, the overwhelming presence of the illusory cucurbit, and the kappas' already heightened appetites conspired to rob them of all rational thought. Even Douglas was so entranced that he was incapable of uttering one skeptical word to question how a cucumber that big had come out of a bag that small. As with the placebo effect or the purchase of an ersatz "holy" relic, the burning desire to *believe* took logic to the mat for the count of three.

And as the cuke of cukes and gourd of gourds floated out of Nicky's hands and rose of its own accord toward the high ceiling of Omizu Cup, not one of the captivated kappas could tear his eyes away until their heads tilted all the way back, their hats fell unheeded to the floor, and the vital water in their skull-dips cascaded after. It was the trickle-down effect with a vengeance.

"Renri! *Now!*"

The kitchen door burst open and Renri ran in carrying a three liter airpot. As Nicky propped up each of the male kappas in turn, she poured its steaming contents into the depressions on top of their heads. They winced, they whimpered, tears came to their eyes, but one severe reprimand from Nicky and they fell into the same *Yes, Massssster* trance holding the rest of the Omizu Cup customers.

A few terse questions posed to his new half-shell helots and Nicky was privy to the hiding place of some very special scones. One taste released Tom from his mental captivity with only fuzzy memories of how he'd spent the past week (and part of his trust fund).

Once Renri and Nicky brought him up to speed, he asked: "What about them?" He indicated the still-rapt human victims of the kappas' insidious brew.

"We'll get them out of here before we fix them," Nicky replied. He jerked a thumb at the male staff of Omizu Cup. "I don't want them stomping Larry, Moe, and Curly there into mulch over what happened."

"But they took their money!" Tom protested. "And they drank their blood! And took their money! And drank their blood *that* way! And—!"

"All of which will be repaid in the profit-sharing arrangement we'll have my dad's lawyer draw up for everyone involved." He grinned at the slack-jawed trio of kappas. "They'll be more than happy to sign it and turn Omizu Cup into a cooperative venture."

"But the blood—"

"You want blood, *you* go to law school." Nicky folded his arms across his chest. "Now if you'll excuse me, I've got to return this compact little beauty—" He opened the sham camera, letting Tom glimpse the miniature holographic projector within. "—to my friend Morgana over at Ignatz Fatuus Productions. And by the way, you now owe her twelve of your jazz LPs, her choice."

"Not my vinyl!" Tom wailed, refusing all comfort until Renri calmly made him see that escaping life as a walking beverage dispenser was worth a stack of records.

Yes, even if Morgana *did* want his original pressing of *Mood Indigo*.

Two years later, Nicky, Tom, and Renri found themselves at the apex of a burgeoning coffee shop empire. The profit-sharing plan to reimburse the victims of Douglas's invasion scheme took on its own momentum. Once the documents were signed, Nicky and Tom realized that their bottom line would bleed money if they cut loose the bought-and-paid-for sites for new Omizu Cups. They had to expand or perish. Even Renri dropped her beef with franchises once Tom explained he couldn't marry her until he repaired the damage her kappa colleagues had done to his personal finances. She even offered to help.

She proved to be a keen businesswoman. Drinking blood was in her blood. Under her careful guidance, more of her fellow kappas were brought over two and three at a time, welcomed as part of the "invasion," and quickly tricked into the same coffee-for-water spill-'n'-swap maneuver that had overcome Douglas, Trent, and Irving.

Gratifying to see how quickly a business can grow when you've only got to pay your workers a daily cup of corpuscles (plus Dental). Omizu Cup, Inc. was Fortune's darling (the concept and the magazine both). Outlets proliferated throughout Seattle and began sending delicate tendrils into other cities. Other states took note and expressed interest.

Only one challenge to domestic security and world peace remained.

Tom's mother sat opposite Nicky at the dining table in her suite at the Four Seasons as they shared a late breakfast.

"Of course I'm always happy to see you, Nicky dear," she said, filling his cup with the hotel's excellent coffee. "But why isn't Tom here with you?"

Nicky straightened his tie. Ever since Omizu Cup, Inc. hit the big time, he'd made the change from hipster to Hugo Boss. "He'll be along later, Mrs. Stubbs. The official reason he's delayed is that he's got to put out some fires at our latest outlet, but I can't lie to the lady who served me my first g-and-t." His coffee vanished in a single gulp. "The real reason he's *delaying* is that he's bringing his fiancée to meet you and he wants me to give you a little advance prep first."

"Why do I need to be *prepared* to meet this girl? What's wrong with her? Is she after his money? Is she one of those awful mail-order brides?" Mrs. Stubbs's eyes narrowed. "Is she a *Methodist*?"

"No, ma'am," said Nicky. "She's a kappa."

"Oh." Tom's mother relaxed and smiled. "Well, that's all right, then. I'm a Delta myself. More coffee?"

In an Albuquerque waterhole, a soon-to-be-famous burglar spins a tale beyond belief . . . or is it? Offered, for your consideration, with a tip of the hat to Damon Runyon.

—BTS

Little Green Guys

by K.C. Ball

It is like this. I wait out the last six months of the war at Kirtland Field in Albuquerque. Peeling potatoes. Shoveling latrines. Not the sort of work a guy enjoys, but Uncle Sugar asked me nice. V-J Day, I have the points, so the Army cuts me loose right then and there.

This is before the business out at Roswell, a sorry spot in southeast New Mexico you would never want to look at once, let alone a second time.

But Albuquerque is not so bad.

Having an easy disposition, and a pocketful of greenbacks Uncle Sugar gave me when he said goodbye, I see no reason to depart New Mexico with haste in favor of New York City and the familiar lights of Broadway and Times Square.

I ask myself, what will it hurt to look around a bit and see what I can see? For the next two years, give or take one week or two, some of what I see are the faces of guys and dolls who frequent Cactus Bar & Grill, a joint where I am paid to mix and pour libations. On my own dime, I offer an ear to anyone who cares to tell a tale.

I get a lot of takers, too. What can I say? I got that sort of face. Besides, the drinks are free if I truly am impressed by the telling.

It is at Cactus Bar & Grill where I make the acquaintance of one In-And-Out Wachowski. He is called In-And-Out, or so I hear, because he is active duty with the dolls and never passes up an opportunity to dip his wick.

This time in 1940, after he is with a doll, she rattles to her many friends about the deed. "He was in-and-out so fast," she says, "I never knew he was even at it."

213

Not the most flattering sobriquet. Even so, it sticks because In-And-Out is also a second-story guy. What some might call a burglar. In-And-Out is not so blunt; he claims he is not opposed to being able to pay the bills, and second-story work is how he manages. I believe what he does is what he does. My old man taught me not to stick my beak in other people's lives, as long as they do not stick their beaks in mine.

So one afternoon, a week after the Roswell business, In-And-Out sidles into Cactus Bar & Grill even earlier than usual.

Keep in mind, this is before he comes to be known as the greatest second-story man in the American Southwest; maybe the entire country. Who knows? Even now, he may be working on the world.

It is plain from the look upon his mug the guy has something on his mind. The afternoon is slow, so when I set his usual before him—a gin and tonic with an extra twist of lime and five ice cubes, no more, no less—I bring along a seltzer water for myself.

Listening is thirsty work.

"What is buzzin', cousin?" I ask, to get things started.

He jumps right in. "I am clean and tight and living right. And you?"

"Fine as the proverbial frog hair," I reply.

We both smile at the exchange. His smile is nice enough, nothing special, for In-And-Out is a regular-looking guy. Not tall. Not short. Not thin or fat. Not the sort to look at twice, even if he is a crowd of one. He always wears the same brown suit, but there is something different that day. I give him a good once-over to figure out what I am missing and spot a small silver pin on his lapel. It is new.

"You join a lodge?" I ask.

He cups his hand over the pin. "That is not a matter I should speak on at any length," he says.

I offer him a little half-shrug. "Of course," I say. "It is none of my concern."

He sips his drink and returns to the conversation. "You read about that business out at Roswell?"

"You mean the flying saucers?" I ask.

He corrects me. "Flying saucer. There is only one."

I don't ask him how he knows. I figure he will tell me when and if he gets around to it. "I have read about that business," I say. "Why do you ask?"

"I have seen them."

"Who?"

In-And-Out takes a long pull on his gin and tonic before he adds, "Little green guys. I pulled a job for them."

In-And-Out Wachowski likes to work early afternoons, Monday through Thursday. No nights; no weekends. He has plied the trade a dozen years and is settled in his ways—just like his marks—because his ways have never failed him.

He works alone; no eager-beavers need apply. He only deals in cash and shiny things that fit into the deep pockets of his tailored jackets.

He is particular about whom he touches, too. Only older guys who live alone, are not doll dizzy, and do not trust the banks.

"That sort lives by a schedule," In-And-Out will tell you, if he trusts you. "I know when and where the guy is every second, day and night. I know without a doll, he has surplus dough. And since he will not use a bank, he keeps his loot at home in special hidey holes."

In-And-Out is very good at finding hidey holes.

So this day, he is standing in the doorway of a hardware store a few blocks south of downtown. He is waiting for his latest mark to finish an early breakfast at a night-hawk diner that is just across the street.

In-And-Out has risen early because he has hopes this job will be a large score—he feels the need to take some time away from work—so he is willing to give the guy some wiggle room. In-And-Out is settled in for the long haul, coffee and a sandwich—corned beef on rye with brown mustard—and a piece of apple pie with a little wooden fork.

He spews coffee through his nose when this voice whispers in his ear. "We know who you are and what you do."

Not being the religious sort, In-And-Out does not believe it is the big guy or His angels, taking a shot at getting In-And-Out to change his wicked ways. He looks around, even though the doorway is not big enough for someone to hide behind him.

There is no one there, of course. He doesn't see a radio or intercom, either. He is puzzled to be sure.

"Down here," the voice says. "On your shoulder."

In-And-Out turns his head. "The other shoulder," the voice sighs. "Please don't be an idiot."

There are two little guys perching on In-And-Out's right shoulder.

They are chrome-domes no more than three inches tall, dressed in silver threads. And their skin is the same pale green as the Hupmobile on the back of a ten-spot.

In-And-Out smiles. He has a soft spot for anyone or anything the same shade of green as money. His smile fades, though, when he notices both green guys hold tiny silver guns, both pointed at his nose. Cherry-red lights blink on both guns. In-And-Out reads *Amazing Stories* every month. He knows a ray gun when he sees one.

"I am curious," he asks, not being the sort to give in to panic quickly. "How is it you speak English?"

"We are very quick studies," the taller green guy says. The second green guy snickers.

In-And-Out nods; he is familiar with that little sarcastic laugh and he knows shit from Shinola when he hears it. Even so, In-And-Out also is the sort who knows which way is up and how to wait for things to change. He decides not to raise a fuss.

"Fair enough," he says. "Why are you aiming guns at me?"

The taller green guy twists his little face into a sneer. "So you will do our bidding," he says, doing a very respectable impression of Charles Middleton, who plays Ming the Merciless in the Flash Gordon serials.

In-And-Out should know; he is a front-seat regular at the movie matinees every Saturday.

"Then I have no choice, I expect," he says, in his most righteous Buster Crabb.

The little green guy's sneer disappears. His words have an eager edge to them when he replies. "The human you are watching has done us grave injury," he says. "He has stolen something from us."

The shorter green guy snaps. "*Grave injury*? Without what he stole we cannot go home."

"So you want me to steal this thing back for you?"

"Yes," they both say. It is as if they are speaking in a single voice.

"We can pay you," the taller green guy says. "We have gold aboard the ship."

"Not a lot," the shorter green guy quickly adds. "Just a *reasonable* amount."

One voice or not, no matter the color of their skin, they are speaking In-And-Out's language now. "What did this mook steal from you?" he asks.

"He took our . . . " they both begin and then clam up.

"What did he take?" In-And-Out asks again.

The green guys face him; draw their little shoulders back. Neither seems eager to be the one to speak.

Finally, the taller green guy blurts, "He took our ship!"

"Yes," the shorter green guy says. "He met us, where we landed, in the desert. He lied and told us he could take us to his leader. My colleague trusted him, until he took our ship, put it in his truck, and drove away!"

"Imagine that," In-And-Out says.

"You wanted to talk to him," the taller green guy blurts. "I wanted to draw our weapons right away."

"Of course," the shorter green guy says. "Blame it all on me. It is *always* my fault."

"It is no one's fault," the taller green guy says. He does not sound sincere.

"Can you call home and hitch a ride?" In-And-Out asks.

"No," the taller green guy says. "Our long-range communication gear is on the ship."

The shorter green guy curls his lip. "And of course, even if *we* could call, *we* would rather die here, lightyears from home, than ask for help."

In-And-Out notices the sarcasm. The shorter green guy truly has mastered that part of the language. In-And-Out also notices the taller green guy's face turn vivid apple green. In-And-Out might be rough-and-tumble, still he understands that blush.

He has been caught with his suspenders at his ankles once or twice; perhaps more often. And so he does his perfect Buster Crabb again, even to the arch of the actor's eyebrow.

"The bastard!" he growls. "We will have to take it back!"

Employing his usual techniques, In-And-Out is soon inside the mook's apartment. All the while, the green guys remain upon his shoulder. They are very good at hanging on.

The blinds are down; the lights are out, so the place is very dim. Even so, it is not difficult to see there is nothing out of the ordinary in the living room. Flying saucers are not that difficult to spot. The kitchen and bedroom are absent of such strange machines as well.

There is a fourth room, though, the biggest of the lot. Some might call it a den; without light—bare of furnishings the way it is—In-And-Out does not consider it to be much more than a plastered cave.

Even so, here they strike the jackpot.

"There it is!" the little green guys shout in that joint voice they use.

Of course, it does not matter what they say. In-And-Out knows what it is. He reads *Amazing Stories,* after all.

The disk is eight feet across; four or five times thicker at its center than its edges. A six-inch-high inset metal band separates the edges. It is balanced on four wooden pillars that have a rough-cut look to them. In-And-Out has knocked together such temporary pieces for his own work from time to time.

He cuts straight to business. "Can you fly it out?"

"Oh, sure," the shorter green guy says. "Let's all jump aboard."

"No," the taller green guy says. "That's why we needed you. To get us in and get us out."

"So I will have to . . ." In-And-Out begins.

"You will have to carry it; then we can give the reactor time to collect a charge."

"And how am I to do that?" In-And-Out asks. "Your ship must weigh a ton. I cannot just pick it up and walk out through the door."

"It weighs three thousand, five hundred of your pounds," the taller green guy says.

"Give or take a few hundred pounds," the shorter green guy adds. "But it will fit through the door—at an angle."

"I can't lift that alone," In-And-Out says.

"We don't expect that. We have something to help you."

In-And-Out shakes his head, truly perplexed. "Even so, once I have it outside, everyone will see it."

"We have something for that as well."

Each little green guy holds up a silver button just smaller than a dime. In-And-Out is not certain where they hide them—next to the little guys, the buttons look big as combat shields.

The taller green guy says, "Put this on your right lapel."

In-And-Out takes the button and does as told.

The shorter green guy hands over his button. "Put this over your heart. It will give you temporary strength to lift the ship and carry it outside."

"I wish I would have had that," a man's voice says. "Almost broke my back when I brought the damned thing in. Had to roll it up the stairs."

There is a man standing in the doorway and like the little green guys when In-And-Out first met them, the fellow has a gun aimed at In-And-Out.

In-And-Out sighs. This is becoming a bad habit.

It is the mook, of course. The man holds out his hand. "Give it to me."

"Give him the button," the shorter green guy says.

"Listen to the little man," the mook says.

In-And-Out feels a tiny bit of panic. "If he gets the button, he will take the ship again."

"Give him the button, you idiot!" the shorter green guy says.

"Yes," the taller green guy adds. "And do *exactly* what we say."

He hears the extra weight on that *exactly*, so In-And-Out steps forward and hands over the pin. The mook's attention wavers, and when it does the green guys both shout, "Push the other button!"

Without thinking, In-And-Out touches the other button . . . and the world around him freezes. Traffic sounds from outside cease. The mook stands at the door, as stiff and motionless as a wax statue. The second silver button hangs in the air, just an inch above the mook's palm. In-And-Out feels as if he is walking underwater, but he can still move.

And the little green guys can still talk.

"Take the button from him," one of them says. In-And-Out is not sure which one just now.

"What do the buttons do?" he asks.

"No time for that!"

"Tell me what the buttons do, damn it!"

"The first one multiplies your strength," the shorter green guy says. "The one on your lapel speeds up subjective time for those who are within its field. The world is functioning as it always has."

"But we are moving so much faster," the taller green guy says. "To them it seems as if we have disappeared."

In-And-Out is not sure he understands a word of that. "Uh huh," he says.

"Now get the button, damn it!" the shorter green guy says.

In-And-Out pushes through the soupy air and snatches the first button. It is warm against his skin and pulls at him when he moves his arm, but it comes along.

"Put it on," the shorter green guy says. "Over your heart, on your lapel."

In-And-Out does as told. It takes effort, but after a time he gets the button into place. Warmth creeps through his body, as if he has swallowed a good, stiff drink. He can move without any hindrance, as if nothing special has occurred.

"Hit him," the taller green guy says. "Hit him on the chin as hard as you are able."

In-And-Out delivers a whopping right hook. The mook drops the pistol, staggers back, and tumbles slowly across the living room. He hits the sofa square. In slow motion, it flips onto its back and the mook rolls out of sight. In-And-Out waits a breath or two, but the apartment remains silent.

"All right," the shorter green guy says. "Grab our ship and get us out of here."

In-And-Out finishes his fifth gin and tonic just as he finishes his tale. There is nothing left but pieces of the ice cubes. "So the little green guys are on their way home and I am here, alive to tell the tale," he says.

"And that is it?" I ask.

"It is."

"What about the buttons?"

"The one that makes me strong did not work after I put the ship down in a vacant lot. The little green guys took that button; they say it will not ever work again, even if it is recharged."

"Do you want another drink?" I ask.

He shakes his head and offers up a smile. "No. Five is more than plenty. What is the damage, or do I get my drinks free?"

I smile back. "Five drinks will be five dollars. I will accept the tale as tip."

"Not good enough?" he asks.

I shrug. "It is a good enough tale, but no cigar. Just a little too slick, you following the man who took the saucer. And that business with the buttons was complicated. I believe close to the bone always works the best when you tell a tale."

"Uh huh," he says.

"Two things puzzle me," I say. "First, did you bring that tale in with you, or did it come to you over your first drink?"

In-And-Out shrugs. "And the second thing?" he asks.

"You have not said what happened to the second button."

He sets his glass on the bar and stands to leave the joint. "I seem to be a little short," he says. "Put it on my tab?"

I shake my head. "There are no tabs at Cactus Bar & Grill. Like you, cash is all we accept."

"Maybe; maybe not." He grins and reaches to straighten his lapel.

"What does a lady have to do to get another drink?" a doll asks from down the bar.

I give her my attention for a second. Just a second, mind you. "Be right there," I say.

When I look back, a two-inch-square stack of gleaming little gold bricks is nested on the bar next to an empty gin and tonic glass.

And In-And-Out Wachowski is nowhere to be seen.

Actual diminuitive, stark naked little green men arrive to wreak havoc on Earth in Grandmaster James E. Gunn's amusing tale . . . —BTS

The March Of
The Little Green Men

by James E. Gunn

They were little green men. There was no doubt about that. They were little—no more than four-foot eight to four-foot eleven, with an occasional LGM measured at five feet even, though with footgear that might have included elevator inserts. They were green, with shades ranging from frog green to olive green, with no apparent status differences because of color. And they were male. That was obvious from the general absence of clothing that exposed their genitals to public evaluation. They were not mammalian-type genitals and would be clearly incompatible with anything available on Earth, but that was understandable; they were, after all, alien.

After that the similarity with traditional scenarios came to a jarring stop. Their spaceship materialized in Earth orbit causing bulletins on news services, headlines in the few remaining newspapers, consternation in official reactions, angry cables from foreign leaders, and mixed messages of welcome and dismay in social media. But reaction soon settled down when the spaceship announced its presence to space controllers by standard radio transmission, and requested permission to land—not at Kennedy in Florida or Edwards in California, or even at the new spaceport in New Mexico, but at Reagan National Airport in Washington, D.C. Permission was denied, of course, but the LGM ship landed anyway, courteously inserting itself, without disruption, into the landing traffic and descending vertically to a stop outside the main terminal, in a parking space that had been closed for repair. They were, on the whole, very considerate aliens.

Their ship was no flying saucer and not even clearly a ship. It was a shiny black cube, with no aerodynamic qualities. Apparently it needed none, since it seemed able to slow its orbital velocity without resort to retro-rockets or atmospheric friction. Jets scrambled to intercept its descent were unable to locate it until it was already descending on Reagan, and then it was too late to shoot it down, if that was even possible or politic.

Instead, the little green men emerged from a doorway that appeared in the lower section of the cube. They looked around at the airplanes, the runways, the terminal, the startled disembarked passengers staring from the terminal windows, and the not-too-distant buildings of Washington itself, just like any tourists. At the same time their ship broadcast the message: "We come as visitors to your great world to see its wonders and gaze upon its splendors. We want you to know that our vessel has been sterilized inside and out and that we ourselves have prepared ourselves for this visit by eliminating from our bodies any alien viruses or bacteria to which you wonderful people would not be immune, sheltered as you have been from the alien biota native to various worlds throughout the galaxy. And we have learned all your languages that you have broadcast to us over the years, so that we can converse with you and benefit from your unique experience."

In other words, they came as tourists, and most considerate tourists at that. They never said "Take me to your leader!" In fact, though they landed their ship where leaders were easy to be found, they never displayed any interest in meeting them. Instead they met me.

I was an intern at the State Department, assigned to the protocol office because I spoke French, Spanish, and Italian and was learning German, in addition to my native English. The State Department was chosen to deal with the little green men because—well, because nobody else wanted the responsibility and, anyway, the State Department was used to dealing with aliens, though not green ones. And I was chosen because—well, because I was the newest and lowest member of the Protocol Department and the easiest to offer up as a sacrificial lamb if something went wrong. As everybody assumed it would.

So that's how I found myself talking to a group of little green men just inside the Reagan National Airport.

★   ★   ★

"Welcome to Earth," I said. It was not inspired, nor would it go down in history as a classic message to our first visitors from outer space, but no doubt the people who write accounts for posterity would improve it. And when none of the LGM interrupted their gawking at the rather barren and uninspiring airport waiting room and the crowd of curious people to respond in kind, I added, "And welcome to Washington, D.C., the capital of the United States."

At that point one of the little green men—not the tallest, the greenest, or differentiated in any way that I could perceive—stepped forward. "Thank you for your gracious reception," he said in good American English, which only seemed odd because it came from thin green lips. "We bring greetings from the civilized worlds of the galaxy."

I waited for something more, some welcome to whatever galactic federation existed out there and for which these LGM were emissaries, but there was nothing like that. Perhaps I had read too many first contact stories in between my language lessons. "Are you the leader of this group?" I asked.

"The notion of leadership has been discredited and discontinued in the civilized galaxy," the LGM said. "These duties of representation fall upon the least senior among us, and I am that one."

"Just like me," I blurted out and then felt stupid. Surely these aliens who had traveled so far for heaven knows how long would expect something grander than a State Department intern.

But the LGM didn't seem to care. "You can call me 'George,'" he said. "That is, of course, not my real name, but my real name would be unpronounceable anyway."

"Well, George," I said, "what would you folks like to do first? Meet with my boss, the Secretary of State, or the President, or perhaps one of our citizen legislators—"

"As I said, we do not believe in leadership."

"Perhaps you would like food or drink," I said. "Or maybe hotel accommodations to rest up after your long trip."

"Our long trip has been nothing but rest," George said. "What we want to do is to meet the people of your world and to sample the art for which your world is deservedly famous." And as if to illustrate that preference, the LGM scattered to walk among the human spectators and engage them in conversation. It was a disturbing turn of events, and nothing for which the established protocols or my reading had prepared me.

Finally I called out, "George! George!" A green figure detached itself from the rest, who were engaged in serious conversation with the people who were willing to talk to them. Some of the others were edging away or moving toward the waiting room exit. The LGM who came toward me may well have been the same LGM who had spoken earlier, but it was difficult to be certain.

"Yes?" he said.

"We need to get organized," I said, fearing that everything was getting out of control and some incident would occur that would ruin my career before it even got started, and might even create an interstellar event that would result in Earth's annihilation.

"Organization has been—" George started to say, and I interrupted, again a breach of protocol, but one that seem warranted, as control was slipping away. "Discredited. I know But we've got to get things moving along."

"Moving along has not been discredited," George (if it was indeed George) said, and he uttered some indescribable sounds that brought the group back together in front of me.

"We're going to get into a bus that is waiting for us outside the doorway you entered, next to your—ship, or whatever you call it. We're going to take you to a guest house where you can decide what you want to do next."

And, to my surprise and relief, that is how it worked out.

The next morning the little green men dispersed. That was not in my playbook, or anybody's playbook, but the LGM were playing by different rules. They apparently needed no sleep and they'd brought their own concentrated food pellets in the pouches they wore around their middles, which, along with their shoes, were their only adornments. By the time I got back to the guest house in the morning, they were all gone except George. The guards who had been stationed to keep them contained, but ostensibly to protect them from curious or outraged intruders, were unable to say where they had gone or how.

"My companions have set off to explore your world," George said, "as is our mission."

"But—" I said. "But—" I could see my career, not even well started, disappearing in an explosion of headlines.

"You need not worry," George said. "They are experienced travelers. And now we ourselves must begin our own exploration."

"We?" I said weakly.

"Ah yes," George said. "As the least senior, it is my responsibility to maintain contact and answer the questions that newly contacted species always ask."

"How 'least senior' are you?" I asked.

He offered what might have been a shrug if he had human shoulders instead of extension of the lower part of his head into a swelling of his body and said, "Only a few thousand of what you call years."

"That means—" I said. "That means you have immortality."

"The proper term is 'longevity,'" George said. "Nothing is immortal. Even the stars die."

"But you can give us 'longevity,'" I said. "That is what aliens do when they arrive on Earth. They give us the benefit of their longer experience and greater wisdom."

"That has been—"

"'Discredited,': I said. "I know. But humans have short lives, not thousands of years, a hundred at most. Just think what we could do with a thousand more, or even a hundred!"

"That has been tried," George said. "And it has not worked out. First you must solve your other problems. Like excess reproduction."

"So," I said, "you have come to our world to reform us?"

"No," George said, "we have come to your world to enjoy its special qualities. And now we must be about it."

We toured the Smithsonian, not the Capitol, and the Metropolitan in New York, not Wall Street. In London, before we entered the British Museum, in the brief moment when even the staid British had parted their crowd of curious onlookers to allow us to enter, I said, "At least maybe you could give us a cure for disease. That wouldn't be a problem."

"Why do you insist on gifts?" George asked.

"That seems only right, you know," I said. "And, anyway, that is what always happens in first contact stories."

"Ah, stories," George said. "They are a peculiarly human product, and one the civilized galaxy treasures. But they are not real, you know."

"You know our stories?" I asked.

"You broadcast them to the galaxy. They are a source of great interest and enlightenment."

"Then you won't give us a cure for disease?"

"Even if that were possible," George said, "it would not be wise. We would have to eliminate all bacteria and viruses, you see, and many of these are essential to your wellbeing as well as the source of your illnesses, and then we would have to change your DNA to compensate, and then we would have to . . . You see? That has been tried and—"

"Discredited," I said. I was not going to get any points from my supervisor for completing my assignment with a major coup—or win any life-changing benefits for the human species, either.

We toured the Louvre in Paris, the Vatican Museum in Rome— where George commented on the special ability of the human species to invent religions—viewed the Parthenon in Athens—where George marveled at the fragility of human architecture— sat through a performance of a Rossinni opera at La Scala in Milan and a ballet at the Bolshoi in Moscow, toured the Hermitage in St. Petersburg, and inspected, observed, and absorbed so many examples of art, architecture, and performance that the trip became a great blur like the outcome of a tourism ad: see the world's great works in one week. I felt as if the entire world had been turned into a single great museum, as if George was demonstrating to me how much of humanity's efforts over the millennia had gone into these massive stone edifices and the ephemeral dabbings of colored oils on old cloth, on shouting or squealing strange sounds into the air, on contortions of the body into shapes they were never intended to achieve.

"You could, at least, give us a source of energy that would be cheap, plentiful, and non-polluting," I said. "Surely the civilized galaxy has solved that problem."

'Indeed it has," George said, "to its sorrow. I cannot tell you how many times such a gift has produced destruction rather than peace and plenty."

By now I had begun to think that the little green men were here to judge us rather than provide us with the keys to a happy future.

Finally, at the end of our trip, after we had visited the treasures of

China, Japan, and India, and departed from the view of treasures and the magnificent houses we humans have built to house them, we reached Nepal and gazed up at the peaks of the Himalayas. George was less impressed by the mountains than by his talks with the villagers.

"People climb those, you know," I said.

"Why?"

I thought about that for a moment, wondering what kind of answer would make a good impression. And then I gave up. "The first man who climbed the tallest mountain said, 'Because it's there.'"

"Ah," George said, "it's like your stories." He seemed pleased with the comparison.

As we were on the State Department jet back to Washington, D.C., and I could see my life fading into disgrace and ignominy, I said, "At least you could tell us how the worlds of the civilized galaxy have avoided destroying themselves. How did you outlaw war?"

"There's nothing that works better than having a common enemy," George said.

"But—" I said. "But—"

He would say no more until we stood on the concrete apron of the Reagan National Airport just outside the black cube. The other little green men had reassembled from their excursions. The entrance to the cube had magically appeared again, and they had disappeared inside. Only George remained in the entranceway.

There were so many questions I wanted to ask, so many things I wanted to know, and these creatures from the stars were going to leave without telling us anything. "At least tell us how we can get into interstellar space and apply for membership in what you call the civilized galaxy!" I pleaded.

George turned and looked at me from his little red eyes. "We have our own prime directive," he said. "We cannot interfere in the success or failure of any sentient species. In any case, we would not want to. You do not know it yet, but the way in which you turn your frustrations into things of the imagination is special, and the civilized galaxy treasures it."

"Special?" I said.

"The civilized galaxy is a very pragmatic place," George said. "It has to be in order to survive. So it gave up dreams. But it misses them."

"So," I said, "we will have to find our own path?"

"As all species do," he said, and turned to leave. He stopped. "We gave you this," he said. "You know we're there. The civilized galaxy is like the tallest peak of the Himalayas."

I had a sudden vision of this black cube appearing in strange worlds all over the galaxy, inspecting them, answering no questions, and I thought that it must be a lonely way of life. "But you," I said, "what do you make of all this? What are you little green men searching for?"

"Little green women," he said.

What might happen if first contact with an alien species involved, well, personal contact? Would you embrace the newcomers? How far would you be willing to go for interstellar understanding? In this story, co-editor Bryan Thomas Schmidt and collaborator Alex Shvartsman probe the possibilities!

—RWB

First Million Contacts

by Bryan Thomas Schmidt & Alex Shvartsman

Laura Estrada, director of the FBI's Kansas City field office, was out shopping for a new barbecue grill when she first saw the alien. It stood four feet tall, avocado green, and its eye stalks undulated like a pair of six-inch inflatable wind men. It waddled unhurriedly down the aisle separating outdoor cooking supplies from home appliances.

Shoppers gawked at the critter, pulling out their cell phones and snapping pictures, their carts forgotten for the moment. Estrada abandoned the gas grill she'd been checking out and stepped forward for a closer look.

The alien looked incredibly lifelike and it moved with a fluid gait dissimilar from that of a mechanical toy. This must've been a marketing stunt of some sort. The thing was there to promote some latest movie or video game. Estrada was sure she'd read something about this sort of viral marketing being all the rage in Japan these days. Whatever it was, she was certain it wasn't the strangest thing she'd ever seen in Walmart.

Until the alien walked up to a pimply teenage stock boy, stretched its neck upward like some sort of a rubber giraffe, and French kissed him.

Her phone went off in the store, just as she watched that poor kid scramble away from the amorous alien menace. "Code 416" flashed on the screen, and Estrada forgot all about the stunt happening in front of her. Code four-sixteen meant trouble with a capital T, and required all agents to report in with all possible haste. The last time it had been used was on 9/11/2001 and, thankfully, never since.

She breathed heavily after having run up several flights of stairs and observed the chaos at her office. The FBI occupied a long, two-story gray building downtown with a bright blue guard shack out front. Normally rows of desks were inhabited by agents quietly tapping on their keyboards, but today everything was in motion: agents and analysts shouted into their phones, secretaries rushed scribbled notes to and fro desks and offices of senior agents in the back, and seemingly every unattended phone was ringing. The office resembled the floor of the New York Stock Exchange rather than a dignified law enforcement facility.

Assistant Director Mitch Wellsley looked up from his desktop. "I can't believe I'm saying these words, especially before I had even a single shot of Scotch today, but we may be dealing with an alien invasion."

Estrada blinked. She'd seen it with her own eyes, but she still hadn't been prepared to hear it out loud. "You mean, like, *alien* aliens, or..?"

"Extraterrestrials. Little Green Men. Martians. You know, aliens. Not the illegal kind."

"What are we—living a Spielberg film?"

"Maybe they're just looking to phone home," Wellsely teased, and then turned serious. "According to the reports, they seem to be everywhere."

Before Estrada could formulate a response, Wellsley swiveled his monitor so she could share it. On it was the video of Times Square. A pair of little green aliens that could have been twins of the one Estrada saw in Walmart milled around, seemingly oblivious to a crowd of gawkers who surrounded them. The humans snapped pictures relentlessly, some of the more adventurous ones sidling up to the aliens in order to take selfies.

One of the aliens walked up to a group of several street performers dressed as various cartoon characters. They appeared surly and sullen as there were no tips to be had with the aliens stealing all the attention. The alien raised its hand and poked Elmo in the shoulder with its long, green finger.

The man in the Elmo costume slid farther away from the alien on the bench, other costumed performers giving them a wide berth. The alien stepped forward and poked him again. Elmo swatted away its hand, but the alien kept poking, undeterred. He got up and shoved at the alien, but the little green guy stood its ground and continued to poke.

Then the actor took off the Elmo head, revealing a sweaty balding face underneath and started shouting at the alien. Although there was no sound, Estrada was certain he was saying some very un-Elmo-like things.

The alien looked at the man, then at the Elmo head he was holding under his arm, then at the man again. After several seconds it seemed to have lost interest and zeroed in on a Mickey Mouse, who turned and ran as soon as the alien began making its way toward him.

"So much for Mickey Mouse being a hero," Estrada joked. "I saw one of these things in person, just before the four-sixteen came in. Are we sure this is an invasion? They don't seem particularly menacing."

"We don't know what this is, but Washington is freaked out," said Wellsley. "As are Moscow, Beijing, London . . . Reports keep pouring in. These things are everywhere. There are tens of thousands of them, if not more, and they appeared out of the blue, all over the planet."

The screen filled with an alien accosting a frightened woman on the sidewalk, and Estrada could swear she heard it say something that sounded like "ohhhhhh babeeeee" over the audio.

Wellsley reached for a decanter on his shelf. "I think I'm going to need that Scotch."

"Not as much as she does," Estrada motioned toward the frightened woman on the screen.

Wellsley chuckled as he pulled the top off the decanter and grabbed two glasses. "It's five o'clock somewhere, and I bet there are weird aliens wobbling around in that time zone, too." Although drinking on the job was technically against regulations, the occasion certainly called for it.

"You know, most people see little aliens *after* they drink," Estrada commented.

Wellsley chuckled and took a sip as he offered her the other glass. "We have to figure out what it is they want and where they come from."

Estrada got on the phone. She had access to the official reports, but had hoped to glean some insight from what her colleagues were experiencing firsthand.

"They're everywhere," Colin Maberry, an agent at the MI6's London office told her. "Snarling bloody traffic, harassing tourists at the changing of the guard, the Tower of London, two of the bastards even kissed a priest during Mass at Westminster Abbey last Sunday."

Estrada chuckled. "I'll bet that surprised the priest."

"The vicar hasn't had it so good since he took the oath," Colin agreed, laughing.

Her next call was to Rodrigo Cadeira down in Rio, the Brazil office. Cadeira offered similar reports and added a couple cases of probings.

"Probing? What kind of probing?"

"Exactly the kind you think of. You know, like in movies," Rodrigo said.

"With some kind of instruments?" Estrada asked.

"No, chefe," Rodrigo replied. "That's the odd part. Witnesses said the aliens used their tongues, or at least what looked like tongues."

"Tongues?" Estrada scowled and shuddered at the thought.

Rodrigo chuckled. "Hell, one homeless guy asked for more."

Similar reports were coming in from around the globe. All the victims appeared to have been chosen at random, and there was no pattern emerging in the encounters that seemed to reveal anything about what the aliens wanted. The aliens would not communicate: they had answered waves and greetings by parroting what was being said to them as best they could, but never said anything further, although they did make weird moaning sounds sometimes during probing.

After several more calls, Estrada was no closer to figuring out what was happening, and then Clarence Chester arrived. He was an informant she had used on a number of investigations back before she was promoted. The man was eccentric to say the least, but he had been useful in the past and she was willing to spare a few minutes and hear him out.

"When their tongue's in your mouth, that's when they suck out your brains," the informant was saying in the slow, drawn out accent common to the Deep South as Estrada fought the urge to laugh in his face. So far the man's testimony consisted of one clichéd paranoia theory after another. Only this time, some of the elements lined up with what Estrada herself had actually seen—such as the French kissing.

"Slow down, Clarence," Estrada said, leaning forward on her elbows to feign interest. "You actually saw someone get their brains sucked out?"

Diminutive and skinny, Clarence Chester wore a dirty red baseball cap smashed down tight as if it were part of his skull, his oil stained jumpsuit with his embroidered name barely showing on the pocket, face shadowed in several days' stubble. The mechanic scoffed, shaking his head. "You don't see them, Agent! They're all deceptive about it. That's what's so insidious. You don't even know they done it 'til everyone's a buncha zombies."

"So far everyone they've interacted with has been alert and shown no negative effects," Estrada replied.

Chester laughed. "No negative effects?! They sucked face with an alien and you call that no negative effects? That's what's wrong with you government types. Bad things happen to people and it takes extreme consequences 'fore you give a damn."

Estrada raised a palm, attempting to reassure him and deliberately relaxed her posture a bit. The banter she and Wellsley shared wouldn't be wise with him. "I care, Clarence. That's why we're here talking."

Chester leaned back in the brown metal chair and crossed his arms across his chest. "Yeah, you types always say *that*."

Estrada choked back the snark and kept her eyes from rolling. *The man oughta know. He spends enough time feeding any authority who will listen this bullshit.* Instead, she said, "We have doctors thoroughly examining each one of them, and I'll be talking to some of them just like I'm talking to you."

"Uh huh, you types always say *that*, too," Chester snapped, his face crinkled to insist he wasn't buying it. The man actually looked annoyed, as if he was the one whose time was being wasted.

"Have you ever encountered personally or heard of anyone you know being French kissed by an alien?" Estrada asked, with sincerity despite already knowing the answer.

Chester's forehead creased as he thought a moment. "Well, no."

Estrada nodded, encouragingly she hoped. "What about aliens who look like these?"

"Not exactly, no," Chester confirmed. "But I know my aliens, ma'am. I'm a real expert on 'em."

Estrada smiled again, doing her best to sound sincere. "Of course. That's why I'm talking to you."

"But you don't believe me," Chester said, leaning forward now, his eyes locked on Estrada's.

Estrada looked away, doing her best to hide her own thoughts and feelings from the informant.

He went on, "I'm an expert on this. Just like I am on all them auto theft cases you keep me around for. This is my area of *real* experience. You know I'm reliable."

Estrada nodded, but her shoulders sank a bit. "Yes, you have given me good information several times." She didn't add that this was a lot different.

"You people never take this seriously," he sounded disgusted. The chair legs screeched on the shiny worn tile floor as he scooted back and stood, heading for the door.

"We don't have a choice this time."

The mechanic stopped and turned back, his face quizzical.

"I'm just putting together all the pieces," Estrada continued. "There're clearly aliens here. Maybe you can help me."

Chester's shoulder slid back and he raised his head, his eyes confident again. "I can. If you trust me."

Estrada sighed and forced the sincerest smile she could muster. She didn't have much choice. "I'm doing my best, Clarence. I really am." And she actually meant it.

Estrada pulled her Escalade to the side of the dirt road off Missouri State Highway 7 near Pleasantville Township. Neat rows of green maize plants grew on both sides of the road. The plants were about four feet tall; she knew they would rise to at least twice that height once fully grown. She climbed out of the SUV and headed toward the farmhouse.

It had been two days since the aliens arrived, and the FBI—or anyone else for that matter—was no closer to solving the mystery than they had been on day one. The aliens continued to make a nuisance of themselves. Also, they seemed to be indestructible. Various agencies had tried everything from diamond saws to lasers to cut one open and had nothing to show for it. The Mossad managed to make a three-inch shallow cut in one, using a blade sharpened by some sort of a top secret ion milling technique, but found no flesh or blood, just the same rubbery substance that passed for their skin.

Restless and frustrated, Estrada took to handling some of the low-level reports herself. She'd always been at her best when working in the field, and she had hoped that first-hand experience would offer some kind of insight she'd missed while reading reports.

An old man in a checkered shirt and a Royals baseball cap stood in front of the farmhouse, his right hand leaning on a shotgun. He watched impassively as Estrada approached.

"Mr. Clyde Nelson?"

The old man pushed the peak of his cap up a little. "Who wants to know?"

"I'm Agent Estrada." She flashed her badge. "You called about a disturbance?"

Nelson squinted at the badge. "I didn't call no feds."

"You called pest control," said Estrada. "They contacted the local police, and they, in turn, contacted us. Alien related incidents fall under our jurisdiction."

"You got a taser?" the farmer snapped. Then he scowled again and yelled toward the cornfields beyond the house, "Keep it up, buster, gov'nment's here to barbecue you!"

Estrada shook her head. "That's not helping."

"Damn space critters are ruining my crops worse than a barrel of gophers, and I ain't even allowed to shoot 'em. This is America and them green midgets are trespassing!"

"Could you show me the damage please, Mr. Nelson?" said Estrada.

Nelson nodded for Estrada to follow him. When they rounded the farmhouse, there were more cornfields. One of them had several ten-foot-wide crop circles etched into it. A little green alien was busy creating yet another circle by laboriously flattening one corn stalk at a time.

"You see?" Nelson squeezed the barrel of his shotgun. "What are you gonna do about this?"

Estrada had read reports of the aliens making crop circles. She sometimes wondered if the aliens were playing some sort of a needlessly long practical joke on everyone.

"I'm sure we can get your insurance company to reimburse you for the damage," said Estrada.

Nelson marched toward the alien, who was busy destroying the field, Estrada in tow. He waved the shotgun at it. "Shoo, varmint!"

The alien turned and faced off against the farmer. Then, just like the one Estrada had seen in Walmart, it stretched its neck high and smooched Nelson on the lips.

Nelson stumbled backward and landed on his posterior. He growled, spat, and wiped at his mouth furiously with his sleeve. Meanwhile, the alien went back to bending corn stalks.

"That does it!" Nelson shouted, and before Estrada could react, he raised the shotgun to his shoulder and unloaded the barrel at the alien at nearly point-blank range.

The alien ignored him. The force of the blast didn't even knock it off its feet. It continued making the crop circle. A few of the pellets stuck to his side fell off harmlessly as the alien worked.

Nelson looked at the alien then at Estrada, dumbfounded.

Estrada shrugged. "As I was saying, I can help you with that insurance paperwork."

Another week went by, and Estrada had little to show for it. She was already frustrated by the time Clarence Chester showed up in her office again. She didn't have time or inclination to deal with the informant's paranoia. Estrada didn't even bother hiding her annoyance.

"Believe me now?" he said with a smug smirk as he flopped into the chair beside Estrada's desk.

She raised an eyebrow but continued reading through reports on her screen.

"Probing, poking, kissing, weird instruments, crop circles," he said. "Anyone turn up with no brain yet?"

The aliens continued acting as they had all long, their actions never crossing the line into dangerous. Estrada sighed, leaning back in her chair to look at him. "Okay, there have been some familiar incidents."

Chester harrumphed. "Just like I said." He nodded for emphasis.

Estrada stared at him a moment, waiting for more. When nothing came, she asked, "If you're such an expert then tell me: why are they doing this? What do they want? And why is it they're only repeating words back at us but never attempt to say anything else?"

Chester's face crinkled as he thought, then he scoffed. "You'd have to ask them, I guess, Agent. I mean, they're aliens. Everything they do is odd to us. How're we supposed to know?"

"You can't believe they came possibly millions of miles just to be a nuisance?"

Chester snorted. "I said I'm familiar with them, not that I know how they think." Then his face crinkled as he thought. "If you ask me, they just tryin' to greet us but they don't know how."

Estrada stared at the mechanic. "Explain."

"It's like you said, they're doing all these familiar things, right? Suppose they flew over here and they want to meet us. First, they gotta learn the language and the culture, so they watch TV broadcast signals to learn all about how a fella is supposed to behave here. And they learn about stuff, like shaking hands, bowing, kissing."

Estrada scratched her chin. Surprisingly, the conspiracy nut was making some sense. She leaned forward. "So you're saying the aliens are trying to follow the first contact protocols they think we want them to follow?" Suddenly, it all made sense. "Except we're not responding properly, because in real life people don't act the way they do on TV! Clarence, you magnificent bastard," she clapped the mechanic on the shoulder.

Chester smiled, and then turned serious again. "I'd still keep a watch for them brain suckers. Just because they's tryin' to be polite, don't make them friendly-like."

Estrada rubbed her hands in glee. Chester had given her a new idea to try, something they hadn't done before. "Thank you. I know just what to do next."

"What's that?" asked Chester.

"We're going to get past 'hello.'"

Estrada and Chester drove to the riverfront at Richard L. Berkley Park where aliens had frequently been reported to interact with humans. There, they witnessed several encounters taking place: a mother with a stroller running screaming from an alien trying to examine her and the baby, business suited salesmen actually attempting to sell products to the aliens, panhandlers looking for alien handouts, and even three preteen girls arguing over whose turn it was next for kissing practice.

"Just when you thought things couldn't get any weirder," Estrada mumbled as she parked her Escalade beside the curb. "Let's go," she said, motioning to Chester, and they both climbed out. "Any suggestion how to get started?"

No sooner had she said it than an alien stepped forward, eye stalks undulating, and grabbed Estrada by the cheeks, attempting to French kissing her.

Estrada scowled, and pulled away quickly, spitting, as Chester chuckled.

"Do they have bad breath?" the mechanic teased.

Estrada frowned and faced the alien, shaking her head. Instead, she raised a hand in greeting. "Hello."

The alien just stared, uttering a few unintelligible phrases, presumably in its own alien tongue.

Estrada tried again, raising her hand. "Hello," she said.

The alien looked confused, as best Estrada could tell, and turned to chatter with one of the others. Estrada repeated her gesture and words one more time.

The other alien's eye stalks froze as its face took on what he guessed was a look of recognition. It rushed forward, chattering with its companions and taking the kisser's place facing the agent. The alien stopped and raised its hand in imitation of Estrada. "Hewwo," it imitated.

"Hello. Welcome to Earth," Estrada said and extended her hand.

The alien extended its hand. "Hewwo, welcome tuh Eart."

Chester grinned. "Holy shit."

Estrada shot Chester a silencing look and clasped the alien's outstretched hand, shaking it slowly. "How may I help you?"

"Hewp?" the alien repeated the question, imitating the silencing look.

Estrada nodded, encouragingly. "What do you want from us?" she said slowly, articulating every word.

The alien's face took on sudden recognition. Its eye stalks undulated with excitement as its face took on what Estrada assumed was the alien equivalent of a smile. "Wat du yu wannnt . . ."

The aliens began chattering excitedly with each other for a moment, the alien turning away to interact with his fellows before turning back to face Estrada again. It leaned in to give her a hug.

Estrada frowned but hugged it back, although keeping as much of her body from touching it as she could manage.

"His hug was more sincere," Chester commented as the two separated again.

Estrada turned and glared. "Shut up."

"Shet up," the alien repeated.

Estrada laughed, nodding. "I think they're understanding things a lot better now." She turned back to the alien and noticed that other aliens and humans had stopped engaging and turned to watch. "Nothing like the pressure of an audience," she mumbled. "What do you want from us?" she repeated.

The alien said it back, but made no effort to react otherwise.

"Let me try," Chester said, stepping forward.

Estrada raised her hands in surrender and stepped aside as Chester took his place, facing the alien. He raised a hand in a greeting wave. "Hello."

"Hewwo," the alien replied, raising its hand likewise.

Chester stepped forward and hugged the alien. "How are you?" he said as they separated again.

"I fine, howwa yu?" the alien replied.

Chester smiled, nodding at Estrada, who watched with amazement.

"I'm fine, thanks," Chester replied. "Welcome to Earth." He extended his hand for a handshake.

The alien shook it, gripping it firmly. "Hewwo, welcome tuh Eart."

As they released hands, Chester nodded. "How was your day?"

"Fwine, tanks," the alien replied, looking pleased.

"Good," Chester said, and then leaned forward.

The alien leaned forward too and they French kissed, Chester actually moving his tongue in a way that made Estrada groan and scowl.

The two separated again and the alien, nodded. "Mmmm, tat was nice."

Chester smiled too. "Yes, thank you."

The alien then pulled Chester to it and began caressing and feeling him a bit like an overexcited teenager on a first date. Estrada made a face, but Chester just accepted it, returning a few caresses in kind. Behind them, the gathered aliens chattered excitedly. "Ohhhhh babee," the alien said at one point.

"Get on with it, Chester," Estrada ordered. "You're not here to pick up a date."

"You have to do it the way they learned it," Chester said, as he glanced at her over the alien's shoulder.

"You don't have to enjoy it," she snapped.

Next, Chester and the alien separated and slapped hands, like giving high-five. Finally, the alien pointed to a miniature crop circle someone had made nearby in a flower patch. "Take me to your leader," it said in almost perfect English.

"What was that?" Estrada said, amazed, stepping forward.

"Take me to your leader," the alien repeated.

"I think they've been practicing that one more," Chester said and smiled at the alien. "Okay," he replied and nodded then pushed Estrada forward. "You're on."

"What?"

The aliens broke into loud jitters and chatter, moving in to surround Estrada, Chester, and their fellow alien now, poking, prodding, excited.

"Well, I just imitated all the steps in the ritual as best I gathered," Chester said as a couple aliens poked and prodded him. A couple of times he grimaced when their prodding was particularly uncomfortable, but he went on. "I just did what they been doing until they got to the phrase they expected."

"Ritual? How'd you know the order?"

"Don't think it mattered none. They just needed someone to complete all the steps, I guess. But I gather they want to see our leader now."

"Who's that?" Estrada asked.

Chester chuckled. "Why the President, I suppose. Who else could it be?"

"They could be dangerous," Estrada said and shook her head.

"Yeah, President don't seem the kissing kind," Chester chuckled. "I suppose it doesn't matter if it's actually the President," he continued. "Just someone they think is in charge."

The aliens stopped probing him and backed away, waiting for some response.

"You're the closest thing we got to a leader here," Chester said, pushing her forward again. He locked eyes with the aliens and pointed to Estrada. "Leader. Leader."

The aliens' eyes widened and their eye stalks swayed enthusiastically as a taller, older-looking one in the back came slowly forward. Unlike the others, it wore a long robe and had some sort of odd electronic black necklace hanging from his neck. It approached

Estrada and stopped facing her, then raised its hand in a wave. "Hewwo."

Estrada repeated the gesture. "Hello."

After that, she just followed all the various steps, from shaking, to exchanging pleasantries, to pointing at the crop circle and hugging. She put off the kissing, hoping she could somehow get around it, but just as she thought she'd succeeded, the older alien rushed forward and French kissed her. Its breath had the distinct taste of spicy soil. She resisted the urge to spit again.

"Don't look displeased!" Chester warned.

Estrada forced an awkward smile as the older alien pulled away and said, "Mmmmm, tat was nice."

Suddenly, Estrada remembered what came next. The alien rushed forward, fondling, caressing, probing. Estrada wiggled, making it as difficult for the amorous extraterrestrial as she could.

"Ohhhhhhh babee," the alien said.

Then, as suddenly as it began, it was over. "We come in peace," the alien said as they faced each other, and it bowed its whole upper body forward slightly.

Chester motioned for Estrada to reciprocate.

Estrada sighed and bowed, too. "We welcome you."

The older alien looked pleased, and then turned, motioning and chattering at those behind it.

One rushed forward carrying another electronic necklace that appeared identical to the one the older alien was wearing. It walked straight up to Estrada and chattered at her, reaching for her neck. Estrada shot Chester a puzzled look.

"I think he wants you to put it on," Chester suggested.

Estrada stiffened, fearing the worst—shocks of some kind, radiation, something painful or damaging that she'd never recover from. She fought the urge to draw her sidearm. "What if it fries my brain? Shocks me? Kills me?"

"Then I'll be very glad it's you, not me," Chester said.

Estrada glared again, not amused, and cursed internally. Then she winced and bowed again. The alien reached up and slid the necklace over her head and down so it hung across her chest, then flipped a couple dials and buttons on it and hurried away, grunting at the older alien as it passed.

This time, as their eyes met again, the older alien spoke in his own singsong chattering, but the black box on Estrada's necklace lit up and she heard in English, "You are the leader?" It was somewhere between a childlike voice and a growl but it was clear as day.

"It's a translator!" Chester exclaimed, excited.

"No shit, Chester. Thanks for clearing that up. They have translators and they just now decided to use them?!" Estrada let her tension out all at once, frustrated.

"Careful. Don't make them mad," Chester warned softly again.

The alien chattered again. "We did not use the boxes because they are only for the masters to use, not the servants. Until you identified yourself, we did not know who you were."

Chester shot Estrada a knowing look as if to say: *See? Just go with it.*

Estrada glared at him then smiled to the leader. "Our apologies. We did not understand your purpose."

"We wondered why no one would complete the ritual," the older alien said. "Were we doing it incorrectly?"

"It wasn't a ritual to us," Estrada explained. "You seemed to be imitating things from our broadcasts, television we call it. But this is not how we usually greet one another."

The alien looked puzzled. "Hmmmm. But we thought everyone did this. We saw your shows. Perhaps you would say we are dumbass."

Estrada laughed. "I suppose you might have thought all Earthlings were dumbasses from the way we were responding."

The older alien's shoulders lifted as it cackled in imitation of Estrada's laugh. At least that's how the translator interpreted it. Then it turned serious again. "I am Th'lee Kohl, the leader of this group. I have come as ambassador to seek trade and friendship with your people."

"I can offer you friendship," Estrada said. "But I only speak for myself."

"Who speaks for Earth?" The alien said, the chittering ending with the recognizable 'Eart' from the previous attempts at conversing and then being translated by the box around Estrada's neck.

Word of Estrada's successful contact spread even as she and the older alien arranged proper meetings. Estrada coordinated with other law enforcement agencies to monitor things because some were trying to pass themselves off as leaders in efforts to gain favor, scam, or manipulate. But some world leaders, hearing the news, engaged the aliens directly. At times, Estrada wished the President of the United States would make things so easy.

When Chester showed up in Estrada's office a few days later, the agent was all smiles. "I've got great news, Clarence," she said. "The aliens are scheduled to meet the President at the White House tomorrow, and I'm invited to the ceremony. What's more, I described your invaluable contribution to solving this mystery in my report, and you're invited, too." She eyed Chester's dirty coveralls. "I hope you own a nice suit."

Chester shifted from foot to foot and chewed his lip. "I'm glad to help, Agent Estrada, I really am. But there ain't no way I'm coming with you to the White House."

Estrada stared at the mechanic in surprise. "Why not? You've already been French kissed and probed. How much worse could it get?"

"These aliens learned everything they know about how to behave proper-like from the teevee," said Chester. "So I can't help but wonder if they seen *Independence Day*."

Leave it to SF Grandmaster Robert Silverberg to bring us one of our stranger tales, this one of truly incomprehensible aliens and an invasion that may not be an invasion at all. But whatever it is, New York's Central Park is ground zero!

—RWB

Hannibal's Elephants

by Robert Silverberg

The day the aliens landed in New York was, of course, the 5th of May, 2003. That's one of those historical dates nobody can ever forget, like July 4, 1776 and October 12, 1492 and—maybe more to the point—December 7, 1941. At the time of the invasion I was working for MGM-CBS as a beam calibrator in the tightware division and married to Elaine and living over on East 36th Street in one of the first of the fold-up condos, one room by day and three by night, a terrific deal at $3750 a month. Our partner in the time/space-sharing contract was a show-biz programmer named Bobby Christie who worked midnight to dawn, very convenient for all concerned. Every morning before Elaine and I left for our offices I'd push the button and the walls would shift and 500 square feet of our apartment would swing around and become Bobby's for the next twelve hours. Elaine hated that. "I can't stand having all the goddamn furniture on tracks!" she would say. "That isn't how I was brought up to live." We veered perilously close to divorce every morning at wall-shift time. But, then, it wasn't really what you'd call a stable relationship in most other respects, and I guess having an unstable condo too was more instability than she could handle.

I spent the morning of the day the aliens came setting up a ricochet data transfer between Akron, Ohio and Colombo, Sri Lanka, involving, as I remember, *Gone With the Wind*, *Cleopatra*, and the Johnny Carson retrospective. Then I walked up to the park to meet Maranta for our Monday picnic. Maranta and I had been lovers for

247

about six months then. She was Elaine's roommate at Bennington and had married my best friend Tim, so you might say we had been fated all along to become lovers; there are never any surprises in these things. At that time we lunched together very romantically in the park, weather permitting, every Monday and Friday, and every Wednesday we had 90 minutes' breathless use of my cousin Nicholas's hot-pillow cubicle over on the far West Side at 39th and Koch Plaza. I had been married three and a half years and this was my first affair. For me what was going on between Maranta and me just then was the most important event taking place anywhere in the known universe.

It was one of those glorious gold-and-blue dance-and-sing days that New York will give you in May, when that little window opens between the season of cold-and-nasty and the season of hot-and-sticky. I was legging up Seventh Avenue toward the park with a song in my heart and a cold bottle of Chardonnay in my hand, thinking pleasant thoughts of Maranta's small round breasts. And gradually I became aware of some ruckus taking place up ahead.

I could hear sirens. Horns were honking, too: not the ordinary routine everyday exasperated when-do-things-start-to-move honks, but the special rhythmic New York City oh-for-Christ's-sake-what*now* kind of honk that arouses terror in your heart. People with berserk expressions on their faces were running wildly down Seventh as though King Kong had just emerged from the monkey house at the Central Park Zoo and was personally coming after them. And other people were running just as hard in the opposite direction, *toward* the park, as though they absolutely had to see what was happening. You know: New Yorkers.

Maranta would be waiting for me near the pond, as usual. That seemed to be right where the disturbance was. I had a flash of myself clambering up the side of the Empire State Building—or at the very least Temple Emanu-el—to pry her free of the big ape's clutches. The great beast pausing, delicately setting her down on some precarious ledge, glaring at me, furiously pounding his chest—*Kong! Kong! Kong!*—

I stepped into the path of one of the southbound runners and said, "Hey, what the hell's going on?" He was a suit-and-tie man, popeyed and puffy-faced. He slowed but he didn't stop. I thought he would run me down. "It's an invasion!" he yelled. "Space creatures! In the park!"

Another passing business type loping breathlessly by with a briefcase in each hand was shouting, "The police are there! They're sealing everything off!"

"No shit," I murmured.

But all I could think was Maranta, picnic, sunshine, Chardonnay, disappointment. What a goddamned nuisance, is what I thought. Why the fuck couldn't they come on a Tuesday, is what I thought.

When I got to the top of Seventh Avenue the police had a sealfield across the park entrance and buzz-blinkers were set up along Central Park South from the Plaza to Columbus Circle, with horrendous consequences for traffic. "But I have to find my girlfriend," I blurted. "She was waiting for me in the park." The cop stared at me. His cold gray eyes said, *I am a decent Catholic and I am not going to facilitate your extramarital activities, you decadent overpaid bastard.* What he said out loud was, "No way can you cross that sealfield, and anyhow you absolutely don't want to go in the park right now, mister. Believe me." And he also said, "You don't have to worry about your girlfriend. The park's been cleared of all human beings." That's what he said, *cleared of all human beings.* For a while I wandered around in some sort of daze. Finally I went back to my office and found a message from Maranta, who had left the park the moment the trouble began. Good, quick Maranta. She hadn't had any idea of what was occurring, though she had found out by the time she reached her office. She had simply sensed trouble and scrammed. We agreed to meet for drinks at the Ras Tafari at half past five. The Ras was one of our regular places, Twelfth and 53rd.

There were seventeen witnesses to the onset of the invasion. There were more than seventeen people on the meadow when the aliens arrived, of course, but most of them didn't seem to have been paying attention. It had started, so said the seventeen, with a strange pale blue shimmering about 30 feet off the ground. The shimmering rapidly became a churning, like water going down a drain. Then a light breeze began to blow and very quickly turned into a brisk gale. It lifted people's hats and whirled them in a startling corkscrew spiral around the churning shimmering blue place. At the same time you had a sense of rising tension, a something's-got-to-give feeling. All this lasted perhaps 45 seconds.

Then came a pop and a whoosh and a ping and a thunk—everybody agreed on the sequence of the sound effects—and the instantly famous not-quite-egg-shaped spaceship of the invaders was there, hovering, as it would do for the next 23 days, about half an inch above the spring-green grass of Central Park. An absolutely unforgettable sight: the sleek silvery skin of it, the disturbing angle of the slope from its wide top to its narrow bottom, the odd and troublesome hieroglyphics on its flanks that tended to slide out of your field of vision if you stared at them for more than a moment.

A hatch opened and a dozen of the invaders stepped out. *Floated* out, rather. Like their ship, they never came in contact with the ground.

They looked strange. They looked exceedingly strange. Where we have feet they had a single oval pedestal, maybe five inches thick and a yard in diameter, that drifted an inch or so above ground level. From this fleshy base their wraithlike bodies sprouted like tethered balloons. They had no arms, no legs, not even discernible heads: just a broad dome-shaped summit, dwindling away to a rope-like termination that was attached to the pedestal. Their lavender skins were glossy, with a metallic sheen. Dark eye-like spots sometimes formed on them but didn't last long. We saw no mouths. As they moved about they seemed to exercise great care never to touch one another.

The first thing they did was to seize half a dozen squirrels, three stray dogs, a softball, and a baby carriage, unoccupied. We will never know what the second thing was that they did, because no one stayed around to watch. The park emptied with impressive rapidity, the police moved swiftly in with their sealfield, and for the next three hours the aliens had the meadow to themselves. Later in the day the networks sent up spy-eyes that recorded the scene for the evening news until the aliens figured out what they were and shot them down. Briefly we saw ghostly gleaming aliens wandering around within a radius of perhaps 500 yards of their ship, collecting newspapers, soft-drink dispensers, discarded items of clothing, and something that was generally agreed to be a set of dentures. Whatever they picked up they wrapped in a sort of pillow made of a glowing fabric with the same shining texture as their own bodies, which immediately began floating off with its contents toward the hatch of the ship.

People were lined up six deep at the bar when I arrived at the Ras, and everyone was drinking like mad and staring at the screen. They were showing the clips of the aliens over and over. Maranta was already there. Her eyes were glowing. She pressed herself up against me like a wild woman. "My God," she said, "isn't it wonderful! The men from Mars are here! Or wherever they're from. Let's hoist a few to the men from Mars."

We hoisted more than a few. Somehow I got home at a respectable seven o'clock anyway. The apartment was still in its one-room configuration, though our contract with Bobby Christie specified wall-shift at half past six. Elaine refused to have anything to do with activating the shift. She was afraid, I think, of timing the sequence wrong and being crushed by the walls, or something.

"You heard?" Elaine said. "The aliens?"

"I wasn't far from the park at lunchtime," I told her. "That was when it happened, at lunchtime, while I was up by the park."

Her eyes went wide. "Then you actually saw them land?"

"I wish. By the time I got to the park entrance the cops had everything sealed off."

I pressed the button and the walls began to move. Our living room and kitchen returned from Bobby Christie's domain. In the moment of shift I caught sight of Bobby on the far side, getting dressed to go out. He waved and grinned. "Space monsters in the park," he said. "My my my. It's a real jungle out there, don't you know?" And then the walls closed away on him.

Elaine switched on the news and once again I watched the aliens drifting around the mall picking up people's jackets and candy bar wrappers.

"Hey," I said, "the mayor ought to put them on the city payroll."

"What were you doing up by the park at lunchtime?" Elaine asked, after a bit.

The next day was when the second ship landed and the *real* space monsters appeared. To me the first aliens didn't qualify as monsters at all. Monsters ought to be monstrous, bottom line. Those first aliens were no bigger than you or me.

The second batch, they were something else, though. The behemoths. The space elephants. Of course they weren't anything like elephants, except that they were big. Big? *Immense.* It put me in mind of Hannibal's invasion of Rome, seeing those gargantuan things disembarking from the new spaceship. It seemed like the Second Punic War all over again, Hannibal and the elephants.

You remember how that was. When Hannibal set out from Carthage to conquer Rome, he took with him a phalanx of elephants, 37 huge gray attack-trained monsters. Elephants were useful in battle in those days—a kind of early-model tank—but they were handy also for terrifying the civilian populace: bizarre colossal smelly critters trampling invincibly through the suburbs, flapping their vast ears and trumpeting awesome cries of doom and burying your rose bushes under mountainous turds. And now we had the same deal. With one difference, though: the Roman archers picked off Hannibal's elephants long before they got within honking distance of the walls of Rome. But these aliens had materialized without warning right in the middle of Central Park, in that big grassy meadow between the 72nd Street transverse and Central Park South, which is another deal altogether. I wonder how well things would have gone for the Romans if they had awakened one morning to find Hannibal and his army camping out in the Forum, and his 37 hairy shambling flap-eared elephants snuffling and snorting and farting about on the marble steps of the Temple of Jupiter.

The new spaceship arrived the way the first one had, pop whoosh ping thunk, and the behemoths came tumbling out of it like rabbits out of a hat. We saw it on the evening news: the networks had a new bunch of spy-eyes up, half a mile or so overhead. The ship made a kind of belching sound and this *thing* suddenly was standing on the mall gawking and gaping. Then another belch, another *thing*. And on and on until there were two or three dozen of them. Nobody has ever been able to figure out how that little ship could have held as many as one of them. It was no bigger than a schoolbus standing on end.

The monsters looked like double-humped blue medium-size mountains with legs. The legs were their most elephantine feature—thick and rough-skinned, like tree-trunks—but they worked on some sort of telescoping principle and could be collapsed swiftly back up into the bodies of their owners. Eight was the normal number of legs, but you never saw eight at once on any of them: as they moved about they always kept at least one pair withdrawn, though from time to time they'd let that pair descend and pull up another one, in what seemed like a completely random way. Now and then they might withdraw two pairs at once, which would cause them to sink down to ground level at one end like a camel kneeling.

They were enormous. *Enormous.* Getting exact measurements of one presented certain technical problems, as I think you can appreciate. The most reliable estimate was that they were 25 to 30 feet high and 40 to 50 feet long. That is not only substantially larger than any elephant past or present, it is rather larger than most of the two-family houses still to be found in the outer boroughs of the city. Furthermore a two-family house of the kind found in Queens or Brooklyn, though it may offend your esthetic sense, will not move around at all, it will not emit bad smells and frightening sounds, it will never sit down on a bison and swallow it, nor, for that matter, will it swallow you. African elephants, they tell me, run 10 or 11 feet high at the shoulder, and the biggest extinct mammoths were three or four feet taller than that. There once was a mammal called the baluchitherium that stood about 16 feet high. That was the largest land mammal that ever lived. The space creatures were nearly twice as high. We are talking large here. We are talking dinosaur-plus dimensions.

Central Park is several miles long but quite modest in width. It runs just from Fifth Avenue to Eighth. Its designers did not expect that anyone would allow two or three dozen animals bigger than two-family houses to wander around freely in an urban park three city blocks wide. No doubt the small size of their pasture was very awkward for them. Certainly it was for us.

"I think they have to be an exploration party," Maranta said. "Don't you?" We had shifted the scene of our Monday and Friday lunches from Central Park to Rockefeller Center, but otherwise we were trying to behave as though nothing unusual was going on. "They can't have come as invaders. One little spaceship-load of aliens couldn't possibly conquer an entire planet."

Maranta is unfailingly jaunty and optimistic. She is a small, energetic woman with close-cropped red hair and green eyes, one of those boyish-looking women who never seem to age. I love her for her optimism. I wish I could catch it from her, like measles.

I said, "There are *two* spaceship-loads of aliens, Maranta."

She made a face. "Oh. The jumbos. They're just dumb shaggy monsters. I don't see them as much of a menace, really."

"Probably not. But the little ones—they have to be a superior species. We know that because they're the ones who came to us. We didn't go to them."

She laughed. "It all sounds so absurd. That Central Park should be full of *creatures*—"

"But what if they do want to conquer Earth?" I asked.

"Oh," Maranta said. "I don't think that would necessarily be so awful."

The smaller aliens spent the first few days installing a good deal of mysterious equipment on the mall in the vicinity of their ship: odd intricate shimmering constructions that looked as though they belonged in the sculpture garden of the Museum of Modern Art. They made no attempt to enter into communication with us. They showed no interest in us at all. The only time they took notice of us was when we sent spy-eyes overhead. They would tolerate them for an hour or two and then would shoot them down, casually, like swatting flies, with spurts of pink light. The networks—and then the government surveillance agencies, when they moved in—put the eyes higher and higher each day, but the aliens never failed to find them. After a week or so we were forced to rely for our information on government spy satellites monitoring the park from space, and on whatever observers equipped with binoculars could glimpse from the taller apartment houses and hotels bordering the park. Neither of these arrangements was entirely satisfactory.

The behemoths, during those days, were content to roam aimlessly through the park southward from 72nd Street, knocking over trees, squatting down to eat them. Each one gobbled two or three trees a day, leaves, branches, trunk, and all. There weren't all that many trees to begin with down there, so it seemed likely that before long they'd have to start ranging farther afield.

The usual civic groups spoke up about the trees. They wanted the mayor to do something to protect the park. The monsters, they said, would have to be made to go elsewhere—to Canada, perhaps, where there were plenty of expendable trees. The mayor said that he was studying the problem but that it was too early to know what the best plan of action would be.

His chief goal, in the beginning, was simply to keep a lid on the situation. We still didn't even know, after all, whether we were being invaded or just visited. To play it safe the police were ordered to set up and maintain round-the-clock sealfields completely encircling the park in the impacted zone south of 72nd Street. The power costs of this were staggering and Con Edison found it necessary to impose a 10% voltage cutback in the rest of the city, which caused a lot of grumbling, especially now that it was getting to be air-conditioner weather.

The police didn't like any of this: out there day and night standing guard in front of an intangible electronic barrier with ungodly monsters just a sneeze away. Now and then one of the blue goliaths would wander near the sealfield and peer over the edge. A sealfield maybe a dozen feet high doesn't give you much of a sense of security when there's an animal two or three times that height looming over its top.

So the cops asked for time and a half. Combat pay, essentially. There wasn't room in the city budget for that, especially since no one knew how long the aliens were going to continue to occupy the park. There was talk of a strike. The mayor appealed to Washington, which had studiously been staying remote from the whole event as if the arrival of an extraterrestrial task force in the middle of Manhattan was purely a municipal problem.

The president rummaged around in the Constitution and decided to activate the National Guard. That surprised a lot of basically sedentary men who enjoy dressing up occasionally in uniforms. The Guard hadn't been called out since the Bulgarian business in '94 and its current members weren't very sharp on procedures, so some hasty on-the-job training became necessary. As it happened, Maranta's husband Tim was an officer in the 107th Infantry, which was the regiment that was handed the chief responsibility for protecting New York City against the creatures from space. So his life suddenly was changed a great deal, and so was Maranta's; and so was mine.

Like everybody else, I found myself going over to the park again and again to try and get a glimpse of the aliens. But the barricades kept you fifty feet away from the park perimeter on all sides, and the taller buildings flanking the park had put themselves on a residents-only admission basis, with armed guards enforcing it, so they wouldn't be overwhelmed by hordes of curiosity-seekers.

I did see Tim, though. He was in charge of an improvised-looking command post at Fifth and 59th, near the horse-and-buggy stand. Youngish stockbrokery-looking men kept running up to him with reports to sign, and he signed each one with terrific dash and vigor, without reading any of them. In his crisp tan uniform and shiny boots, he must have seen himself as some doomed and gallant officer in an ancient movie, Gary Cooper, Cary Grant, John Wayne, bracing himself for the climactic cavalry charge or the onslaught of the maddened Sepoys. The poor bastard.

"Hey, old man," he said, grinning at me in a doomed and gallant way. "Came to see the circus, did you?"

We weren't really best friends any more. I don't know what we were to each other. We rarely lunched any more. (How could we? I was busy three days a week with Maranta.) We didn't meet at the gym. It wasn't to Tim I turned for advice on personal problems or second opinions on investments. There was some sort of bond but I think it was mostly nostalgia. But officially I guess I did still think of him as my best friend, in a kind of automatic unquestioning way.

I said, "Are you free to go over to the Plaza for a drink?"

"I wish. I don't get relieved until 2100 hours."

"Nine o'clock, is that it?"

"Nine, yes. You fucking civilian."

It was only half past one. The poor bastard.

"What'll happen to you if you leave your post?"

"I could get shot for desertion," he said.

"Seriously?"

"Seriously. Especially if the monsters pick that moment to bust out of the park. This is war, old buddy."

"Is it, do you think? Maranta doesn't think so." I wondered if I should be talking about what Maranta thought. "She says they're just out exploring the galaxy."

Tim shrugged. "She always likes to see the sunny side. That's an alien military force over there inside the park. One of these days they're going to blow a bugle and come out with blazing rayguns. You'd better believe it."

"Through the sealfield?"

"They could walk right over it," Tim said. "Or float, for all I know. There's going to be a war. The first intergalactic war in human history."

Again the dazzling Cary Grant grin. Her Majesty's Bengal lancers, ready for action. "Something to tell my grandchildren," said Tim. "Do you know what the game plan is? First we attempt to make contact. That's going on right now, but they don't seem to be paying attention to us. If we ever establish communication, we invite them to sign a peace treaty. Then we offer them some chunk of Nevada or Kansas as a diplomatic enclave and get them the hell out of New York. But I don't think any of that's going to happen. I think they're busy scoping things out in there, and as soon as they finish that they're going to launch some kind of attack, using weapons we don't even begin to understand."

"And if they do?"

"We nuke them," Tim said. "Tactical devices, just the right size for Central Park Mall."

"No," I said, staring. "That isn't so. You're kidding me."

He looked pleased, a *gotcha* look. "Matter of fact, I am. The truth is that nobody has the goddamndest idea of what to do about any of this. But don't think the nuke strategy hasn't been suggested. And some even crazier things."

"Don't tell me about them," I said. "Look, Tim, is there any way I can get a peek over those barricades?"

"Not a chance. Not even you. I'm not even supposed to be *talking* with civilians."

"Since when am I civilian?"

"Since the invasion began," Tim said.

He was dead serious. Maybe this was all just a goofy movie to me, but it wasn't to him.

More junior officers came to him with more papers to sign. He excused himself and took care of them. Then he was on the field telephone for five minutes or so. His expression grew progressively more bleak. Finally he looked up at me and said, "You see? It's starting."

"What is?"

"They've crossed 72nd Street for the first time. There must have been a gap in the sealfield. Or maybe they jumped it, as I was saying just now. Three of the big ones are up by 74th, noodling around the eastern end of the lake. The Metropolitan Museum people are scared shitless and have asked for gun emplacements on the roof, and they're thinking of evacuating the most important works of art." The field phone lit up again. "Excuse me," he said. Always the soul of courtesy, Tim. After a time he said, "Oh, Jesus. It sounds pretty bad. I've got to go up there right now. Do you mind?" His jaw was set, his gaze was frosty with determination. This is it, Major. There's ten thousand Comanches coming through the pass with blood in their eyes, but we're ready for them, right? Right. He went striding away up Fifth Avenue.

When I got back to the office there was a message from Maranta, suggesting that I stop off at her place for drinks that evening on my way home. Tim would be busy playing soldier, she said, until nine. Until 2100 hours, I silently corrected.

Another few days and we got used to it all. We began to accept the presence of aliens in the park as a normal part of New York life, like snow in February or laser duels in the subway.

But they remained at the center of everybody's consciousness. In a subtle pervasive way they were working great changes in our souls as they moved about mysteriously behind the sealfield barriers in the park. The strangeness of their being here made us buoyant. Their arrival had broken, in some way, the depressing rhythm that life in our brave new century had seemed to be settling into. I know that for some time I had been thinking, as I suppose people have thought since Cro-Magnon days, that lately the flavor of modern life had been changing for the worse, that it was becoming sour and nasty, that the era I happened to live in was a dim, shabby, dismal sort of time, small-souled, mean-minded. You know the feeling. Somehow the aliens had caused that feeling to lift. By invading us in this weird hands-off way, they had given us something to be interestingly mystified by: a sort of redemption, a sort of rebirth. Yes, truly.

Some of us changed quite a lot. Consider Tim, the latter-day Bengal lancer, the staunchly disciplined officer. He lasted about a week in that particular mind-set. Then one night he called me and said, "Hey, fellow, how would you like to go into the park and play with the critters?"

"What are you talking about?"

"I know a way to get in. I've got the code for the 64th Street sealfield. I can turn it off and we can slip through. It's risky, but how can you resist?"

So much for Gary Cooper. So much for John Wayne.

"Have you gone nuts?" I said. "The other day you wouldn't even let me go up to the barricades."

"That was the other day."

"You wouldn't walk across the street with me for a drink. You said you'd get shot for desertion."

"That was the other day."

"You called me a civilian."

"You still are a civilian. But you're my old buddy, and I want to go in there and look those aliens in the eye, and I'm not quite up to doing it all by myself. You want to go with me, or don't you?"

"Like the time we stole the beer keg from Sigma Frap. Like the time we put the scorpions in the girls' shower room."

"You got it, old pal."

"Tim, we aren't college kids any more. There's a fucking intergalactic war going on. That was your very phrase. Central Park is under surveillance by NASA spy-eyes that can see a cat's whiskers from fifty miles up. You are part of the military force that is supposed to be protecting us against these alien invaders. And now you propose to violate your trust and go sneaking into the midst of the invading force, as a mere prank?"

"I guess I do," he said.

"This is an extremely cockeyed idea, isn't it?" I said.

"Absolutely. Are you with me?"

"Sure," I said. "You know I am."

I told Elaine that Tim and I were going to meet for a late dinner to discuss a business deal and I didn't expect to be home until two or three in the morning. No problem there. Tim was waiting at our old table at Perugino's with a bottle of Amarone already working. The wine was so good that we ordered another midway through the veal pizzaiola, and then a third. I won't say we drank ourselves blind, but we certainly got seriously myopic. And about midnight we walked over to the park.

Everything was quiet. I saw sleepy-looking guardsman patrolling here and there along Fifth. We went right up to the command post at 59th and Tim saluted very crisply, which I don't think was quite kosher, he being not then in uniform. He introduced me to someone as Dr.

Pritchett, Bureau of External Affairs. That sounded really cool and glib, Bureau of External Affairs.

Then off we went up Fifth, Tim and I, and he gave me a guided tour. "You see, Dr. Pritchett, the first line of the isolation zone is the barricade that runs down the middle of the avenue." Virile, forceful voice, loud enough to be heard for half a block. "That keeps the gawkers away. Behind that, Doctor, we maintain a further level of security through a series of augmented-beam sealfield emplacements, the new General Dynamics 1100 series model, and let me show you right here how we've integrated that with advanced personnel-interface intercept scan by means of a triple line of Hewlett-Packard optical doppler-couplers—"

And so on, a steady stream of booming confident-sounding gibberish as we headed north. He pulled out a flashlight and led me hither and thither to show me amplifiers and sensors and whatnot, and it was Dr. Pritchett this and Dr. Pritchett that and I realized that we were now somehow on the inner side of the barricade. His glibness, his poise, were awesome. *Notice this, Dr. Pritchett, and Let me call your attention to this, Dr. Pritchett*, and suddenly there was a tiny digital keyboard in his hand, like a little calculator, and he was tapping out numbers. "Okay," he said, "the field's down between here and the 65th Street entrance to the park, but I've put a kill on the beam-interruption signal. So far as anyone can tell there's still an unbroken field. Let's go in."

And we entered the park just north of the zoo.

For five generations the first thing New York kids have been taught, ahead of tying shoelaces and flushing after you go, is that you don't set foot in Central Park at night. Now here we were, defying the most primordial of no-nos. But what was to fear? What they taught us to worry about in the park was muggers. Not creatures from the Ninth Glorch Galaxy.

The park was eerily quiet. Maybe a snore or two from the direction of the zoo, otherwise not a sound. We walked west and north into the silence, into the darkness. After a while a strange smell reached my nostrils. It was dank and musky and harsh and sour, but those are only approximations: it wasn't like anything I had ever smelled before. One whiff of it and I saw purple skies and a great green sun blazing in the heavens. A second whiff and all the stars were in the wrong places. A third whiff and I was staring into a gnarled twisted landscape where the trees were like giant spears and the mountains were like crooked teeth.

Tim nudged me.

"Yeah," I said. "I smell it too."

"To your left," he said. "Look to your left."

I looked to my left and saw three huge yellow eyes looking back at me from twenty feet overhead, like searchlights mounted in a tree. They weren't mounted in a tree, though. They were mounted in something shaggy and massive, somewhat larger than your basic two-family Queens residential dwelling, that was standing maybe fifty feet away, completely blocking both lanes of the park's East Drive from shoulder to shoulder.

It was then that I realized that three bottles of wine hadn't been nearly enough.

"What's the matter?" Tim said. "This is what we came for, isn't it, old pal?"

"What do we do now? Climb on its back and go for a ride?"

"You know that no human being in all of history has ever been as close to that thing as we are now?"

"Yes," I said. "I do know that, Tim."

It began making a sound. It was the kind of sound that a piece of chalk twelve feet thick would make if it was dragged across a blackboard the wrong way. When I heard that sound I felt as if I was being dragged across whole galaxies by my hair. A weird vertigo attacked me. Then the creature folded up all its legs and came down to ground level; and then it unfolded the two front pairs of legs, and then the other two; and then it started to amble slowly and ominously toward us.

I saw another one, looking even bigger, just beyond it. And perhaps a third one a little farther back. They were heading our way too.

"Shit," I said. "This was a very dumb idea, wasn't it?"

"Come on. We're never going to forget this night."

"I'd like to live to remember it."

"Let's get up real close. They don't move very fast."

"No," I said. "Let's just get out of the park right now, okay?"

"We just got here."

"Fine," I said. "We did it. Now let's go."

"Hey, look," Tim said. "Over there to the west."

I followed his pointing arm and saw two gleaming wraiths hovering just above the ground, maybe 300 yards away. The other aliens, the little floating ones. Drifting toward us, graceful as balloons. I imagined myself being wrapped in a shining pillow and being floated off into their ship.

"Oh, shit," I said. "Come *on*, Tim."

Staggering, stumbling, I ran for the park gate, not even thinking about how I was going to get through the sealfield without Tim's gizmo. But then there was Tim, right behind me. We reached the sealfield together and he tapped out the numbers on the little keyboard and the field opened for us, and out we went, and the field closed behind us. And we collapsed just outside the park, panting, gasping, laughing like lunatics, slapping the sidewalk hysterically. "Dr. Pritchett," he chortled. "Bureau of External Affairs. God damn, what a smell that critter had! God damn!"

I laughed all the way home. I was still laughing when I got into bed. Elaine squinted at me. She wasn't amused. "That Tim," I said. "That wild man Tim." She could tell I'd been drinking some and she nodded somberly—boys will be boys, etc.—and went back to sleep.

The next morning I learned what had happened in the park after we had cleared out.

It seemed a few of the big aliens had gone looking for us. They had followed our spoor all the way to the park gate, and when they lost it they somehow turned to the right and went blundering into the zoo. The Central Park Zoo is a small cramped place and as they rambled around in it they managed to knock down most of the fences. In no time whatever there were tigers, elephants, chimps, rhinos, and hyenas all over the park.

The animals, of course, were befuddled and bemused at finding themselves free. They took off in a hundred different directions, looking for places to hide.

The lions and coyotes simply curled up under bushes and went to sleep. The monkeys and some of the apes went into the trees. The aquatic things headed for the lake. One of the rhinos ambled out into the mall and pushed over a fragile-looking alien machine with his nose. The machine shattered and the rhino went up in a flash of yellow light and a puff of green smoke. As for the elephants, they stood poignantly in a huddled circle, glaring in utter amazement and dismay at the gigantic aliens. How humiliating it must have been for them to feel *tiny*.

Then there was the bison event. There was this little herd, a dozen or so mangy-looking guys with ragged, threadbare fur. They started moving single file toward Columbus Circle, probably figuring that if they just kept their heads down and didn't attract attention they could keep going all the way back to Wyoming. For some reason one of the behemoths decided to see what bison taste like. It came hulking over and sat down on the last one in the line, which vanished underneath it like a mouse beneath a hippopotamus. Chomp, gulp, gone. In the next few minutes five more behemoths came over and disappeared five more of the bison. The survivors made it safely to the edge of the park and huddled up against the sealfield, mooing forlornly. One of the little tragedies of interstellar war.

I found Tim on duty at the 59th Street command post. He looked at me as though I were an emissary of Satan. "I can't talk to you while I'm on duty," he said.

"You heard about the zoo?" I asked.

"Of course I heard." He was speaking through clenched teeth. His eyes had the scarlet look of zero sleep. "What a filthy irresponsible thing we did!"

"Look, we had no way of knowing—"

"Inexcusable. An incredible lapse. The aliens feel threatened now that humans have trespassed on their territory, and the whole situation has changed in there. We upset them and now they're getting out of control. I'm thinking of reporting myself for court-martial."

"Don't be silly, Tim. We trespassed for three minutes. The aliens didn't give a crap about it. They might have blundered into the zoo even if we hadn't—"

"Go away," he muttered. "I can't talk to you while I'm on duty."

Jesus! As if I was the one who had lured *him* into doing it.

Well, he was back in his movie part again, the distinguished military figure who now had unaccountably committed an unpardonable lapse and was going to have to live in the cold glare of his own disapproval for the rest of his life. The poor bastard. I tried to tell him not to take things so much to heart, but he turned away from me, so I shrugged and went back to my office.

That afternoon some tender-hearted citizens demanded that the sealfields be switched off until the zoo animals could escape from the park. The sealfields, of course, kept them trapped in there with the aliens.

Another tough one for the mayor. He'd lose points tremendously if the evening news kept showing our beloved polar bears and raccoons and kangaroos and whatnot getting gobbled like gumdrops by the aliens. But switching off the sealfields would send a horde of leopards and gorillas and wolverines scampering out into the streets of Manhattan, to say nothing of the aliens who might follow them. The mayor appointed a study group, naturally.

The small aliens stayed close to their spaceship and remained uncommunicative. They went on tinkering with their machines, which emitted odd plinking noises and curious colored lights. But the huge ones roamed freely about the park, and now they were doing considerable damage in their amiable mindless way. They smashed up the backstops of the baseball fields, tossed the Bethesda Fountain into the lake, rearranged Tavern-on-the-Green's seating plan, and trashed the place in various other ways, but nobody seemed to object except the usual Friends of the Park civic types. I think we were all so bemused by the presence of genuine galactic beings that we didn't mind. We were flattered that they had chosen New York as the site of first contact. (But where *else*?)

No one could explain how the behemoths had penetrated the 72nd Street sealfield line, but a new barrier was set up at 79th, and that seemed to keep them contained. Poor Tim spent twelve hours a day patrolling the perimeter of the occupied zone. Inevitably I began spending more time with Maranta than just lunchtimes. Elaine noticed. But I didn't notice her noticing.

One Sunday at dawn a behemoth turned up by the Metropolitan, peering in the window of the Egyptian courtyard. The authorities thought at first that there must be a gap in the 79th Street sealfield, as there had at 72nd. Then came a report of another alien out near Riverside Drive and a third one at Lincoln Center and it became clear that the sealfields just didn't hold them back at all. They had simply never bothered to go beyond them before.

Making contact with a sealfield is said to be extremely unpleasant for any organism with a nervous system more complex than a squid's. Every neuron screams in anguish. You jump back, involuntarily, a reflex impossible to overcome. On the morning we came to call Crazy Sunday the behemoths began walking through the fields as if they weren't there. The main thing about aliens is that they are alien. They feel no responsibility for fulfilling any of your expectations.

That weekend it was Bobby Christie's turn to have the full apartment. On those Sundays when Elaine and I had the one-room configuration we liked to get up very early and spend the day out, since it was a little depressing to stay home with three rooms of furniture jammed all around us. As we were walking up Park Avenue South toward 42nd, Elaine said suddenly, "Do you hear anything strange?"

"Strange?"

"Like a riot."

"It's nine o'clock Sunday morning. Nobody goes out rioting at nine o'clock Sunday morning."

"Just listen," she said.

There is no mistaking the characteristic sounds of a large excited crowd of human beings, for those of us who spent our formative years living in the late twentieth century. Our ears were tuned at an early age to the music of riots, mobs, demonstrations, and their kin. We know what it means, when individual exclamations of anger, indignation, or anxiety blend to create a symphonic hubbub in which all extremes of pitch and timbre are submerged into a single surging roar, as deep as the booming of the surf. That was what I heard now. There was no mistaking it.

"It isn't a riot," I said. "It's a mob. There's a subtle difference."

"What?"

"Come on," I said, breaking into a jog. "I'll bet you that the aliens have come out of the park."

A mob, yes. In a moment we saw thousands upon thousands of people, filling 42nd Street from curb to curb and more coming from all directions. What they were looking at—pointing, gaping, screaming—was a shaggy blue creature the size of a small mountain that was moving about uncertainly on the automobile viaduct that runs around the side of Grand Central Terminal. It looked unhappy. It was obviously trying to get down from the viaduct, which was sagging noticeably under its weight. People were jammed right up against it and a dozen or so were clinging to its sides and back like rock climbers. There were people underneath it, too, milling around between its colossal legs. "Oh, look," Elaine said, shuddering, digging her fingers into my biceps. "Isn't it eating some of them? Like they did the bison?" Once she had pointed it out I saw, yes, the behemoth now and then was dipping quickly and rising again, a familiar one-two, the old squat-and-gobble. "What an awful thing!" Elaine murmured. "Why don't they get out of its way?"

"I don't think they can," I said. "I think they're being pushed forward by the people behind them."

"Right into the jaws of that hideous monster. Or whatever it has, if they aren't jaws."

"I don't think it means to hurt anyone," I said. How did I know that? "I think it's just eating them because they're dithering around down there in its mouth area. A kind of automatic response. It looks awfully dumb, Elaine."

"Why are you defending it?"

"Hey, look, Elaine—"

"It's eating people. You sound almost sorry for it!"

"Well, why not? It's far from home and surrounded by ten thousand screaming morons. You think it wants to be out there?"

"It's a disgusting obnoxious animal." She was getting furious. Her eyes were bright and wild, her jaw was thrust forward. "I hope the army gets here fast," she said fiercely. "I hope they blow it to smithereens!"

Her ferocity frightened me. I saw an Elaine I scarcely knew at all. When I tried one more time to make excuses for that miserable hounded beast on the viaduct she glared at me with unmistakable loathing. Then she turned away and went rushing forward, shaking her fist, shouting curses and threats at the alien.

Suddenly I realized how it would have been if Hannibal actually had been able to keep his elephants alive long enough to enter Rome with them. The respectable Roman matrons, screaming and raging from the housetops with the fury of banshees. And the baffled elephants sooner or later rounded up and thrust into the Coliseum to be tormented by little men with spears, while the crowd howled its delight. Well, I can howl too. "Come on, Behemoth!" I yelled into the roar of the mob. "You can do it, Goliath!" A traitor to the human race is what I was, I guess.

Eventually a detachment of Guardsmen came shouldering through the streets. They had mortars and rifles, and for all I know they had tactical nukes too. But of course there was no way they could attack the animal in the midst of such a mob. Instead they used electronic blooglehorns to disperse the crowd by the power of sheer ugly noise, and whipped up a bunch of buzz-blinkers and a little sealfield to cut 42nd Street in half. The last I saw of the monster it was slouching off in the direction of the old United Nations Buildings with the Guardsmen warily creeping along behind it. The crowd scattered, and I was left standing in front of Grand Central with a trembling, sobbing Elaine.

That was how it was all over the city on Crazy Sunday, and on Monday and Tuesday too. The behemoths were outside the park, roaming at large from Harlem to Wall Street. Wherever they went they drew tremendous crazy crowds that swarmed all over them without any regard for the danger. Some famous news photos came out of those days: the three grinning black boys at Seventh and 125th hanging from the three purple rod-like things, the acrobats forming a human pyramid atop the Times Square beast, the little old Italian man standing in front of his house in Greenwich Village trying to hold a space monster at bay with his garden hose.

There was never any accurate casualty count. Maybe 5000 people died, mainly trampled underfoot by the aliens or crushed in the crowd. Somewhere between 350 and 400 human beings were gobbled by the aliens. Apparently that stoop-and-swallow thing is something they do when they're nervous. If there's anything edible within reach, they'll gulp it in. This soothes them. We made them very nervous; they did a lot of gulping.

Among the casualties was Tim, the second day of the violence. He went down valiantly in the defense of the Guggenheim Museum, which came under attack by five of the biggies. Its spiral shape held some ineffable appeal for them. We couldn't tell whether they wanted to worship it or mate with it or just knock it to pieces, but they kept on charging and charging, rushing up to it and slamming against it. Tim was trying to hold them off with nothing more than tear-gas and blooglehorns when he was swallowed. Never flinched, just stood there and let it happen. The president had ordered the guardsmen not to use lethal weapons. Maranta was bitter about that. "If only they had let them use grenades," she said. I tried to imagine what it was like, gulped down and digested, nifty tan uniform and all. A credit to his regiment. It was his atonement, I guess. He was back there in the Gary Cooper movie again, gladly paying the price for dereliction of duty.

Tuesday afternoon the rampage came to an unexpected end. The behemoths suddenly started keeling over, and within a few hours they were all dead. Some said it was the heat—it was up in the 90s all day Monday and Tuesday—and some said it was the excitement. A Rockefeller University biologist thought it was both those factors plus severe indigestion: the aliens had eaten an average of ten humans apiece, which might have overloaded their systems.

There was no chance for autopsies. Some enzyme in the huge bodies set to work immediately on death, dissolving flesh and bone and skin and all into a sticky yellow mess. By nightfall nothing was left of them but some stains on the pavement, uptown and down. A sad business, I thought. Not even a skeleton for the museum, memento of this momentous time. The poor monsters. Was I the only one who felt sorry for them? Quite possibly I was. I make no apologies for that. I feel what I feel.

All this time the other aliens, the little shimmery spooky ones, had stayed holed up in Central Park, preoccupied with their incomprehensible research. They didn't even seem to notice that their behemoths had strayed.

But now they became agitated. For two or three days they bustled about like worried penguins, dismantling their instruments and packing them aboard their ship; and then they took apart the other ship, the one that had carried the behemoths, and loaded that aboard. Perhaps they felt demoralized. As the Carthaginians who had invaded Rome did, after their elephants died.

On a sizzling June afternoon the alien ship took off. Not for its home world, not right away. It swooped into the sky and came down on Fire Island: at Cherry Grove, to be precise. The aliens took possession of the beach, set up their instruments around their ship, and even ventured into the water, skimming and bobbing just above the surface of the waves like demented surfers. After five or six days they moved on to one of the Hamptons and did the same thing, and then to Martha's Vineyard. Maybe they just wanted a vacation, after three weeks in New York. And then they went away altogether.

"You've been having an affair with Maranta, haven't you?" Elaine asked me, the day the aliens left.

"I won't deny it."

"That night you came in so late, with wine on your breath. You were with her, weren't you?"

"No," I said. "I was with Tim. He and I sneaked into the park and looked at the aliens."

"Sure you did," Elaine said. She filed for divorce and a year later I married Maranta. Very likely that would have happened sooner or later even if the Earth hadn't been invaded by beings from space and Tim hadn't been devoured. But no question that the invasion speeded things up a bit for us all.

And now, of course, the invaders are back. Four years to the day from the first landing and there they were, pop whoosh ping thunk, Central Park again. Three ships this time, one of spooks, one of behemoths, and the third one carrying the prisoners of war.

Who could ever forget that scene, when the hatch opened and some 350 to 400 human beings came out, marching like zombies? Along with the bison herd, half a dozen squirrels, and three dogs. They hadn't been eaten and digested at all, just *collected* inside the behemoths and instantaneously transmitted somehow to the home world, where they were studied. Now they were being returned. "That's Tim, isn't it?" Maranta said, pointing to the screen. I nodded. Unmistakably Tim, yes. With the stunned look of a man who has beheld marvels beyond comprehension.

It's a month now and the government is still holding all the returnees for debriefing. No one is allowed to see them. The word is that a special law will be passed dealing with the problem of spouses of returnees who have entered into new marriages. Maranta says she'll stay with me no matter what; and I'm pretty sure that Tim will do the stiff-upper-lip thing, no hard feelings, if they ever get word to him in the debriefing camp about Maranta and me. As for the aliens, they're sitting tight in Central Park, occupying the whole place from 96th to 110th and not telling us a thing. Now and then the behemoths wander down to the reservoir for a lively bit of wallowing, but they haven't gone beyond the park this time.

I think a lot about Hannibal, and about Carthage versus Rome, and how the Second Punic War might have come out if Hannibal had had a chance to go back home and get a new batch of elephants. Most likely Rome would have won the war anyway, I guess. But we aren't Romans, and they aren't Carthaginians, and those aren't elephants splashing around in the Central Park reservoir. "This is such an interesting time to be alive," Maranta likes to say. "I'm certain they don't mean us any harm, aren't you?"

"I love you for your optimism," I tell her. And then we turn on the tube and watch the evening news.

In co-editor Robin Wayne Bailey's story, little green men launch the Greens Party to enter American politics and the country will never be the same . . . Those of you without dogs just might want to get one, too.

—BTS

The Fine Art Of Politics

by Robin Wayne Bailey

The Fermi ships dropped out of space utterly undetected by any Earth instrument or observatory until they began screeching through the upper reaches of the atmosphere. For three days, the pair of gleaming saucers circled the planet, leaving glowing white-hot counterclockwise contrails as they braked to slower and slower speeds.

At sunset on the third day, the first Fermi vessel settled into a stable position just above the cold rolling waves of the North Atlantic Ocean. The second ship took up a position over the Indian Ocean. For two more days, nothing happened. The ships hovered, rotating, silent, and mysteriously splendid. The world watched in awe, but also in suspicion.

The military jets of a dozen countries scrambled in the skies above each of the invaders, all weapons locked on and ready. Battleships and aircraft carriers raced to the sites. The most powerful submarines of four nations charged forward beneath the waves in secret. Press corps and television crews hired, commandeered or stole anything that could float and did their very best to interfere and get completely in the way. Yet, with all that technology in the water, it was a lowly operator on an insignificant, conservative radio station, CWTF, operating on the coast of Newfoundland, who first noticed that the Fermi ships were not silent at all. He broadcast a warning immediately to his small base of listeners. "Don't let them fluoridate your water!"

An American fighter pilot, intercepting the broadcast signal, mistook it for a lock-on. His itchy finger squeezed, an air-to-surface missile launched, and CWTF went permanently off the air. Fortunately, the embarrassed pilot thought, it was Newfoundland, so nobody would learn of his mistake for two years at least. Meanwhile, the waters beneath the Fermi saucers began to churn as hundreds and thousands of whales arrived in answer to a sub-sonic signal that only the former radio station had noticed. Sperm whales and Killer whales, Humpback and Blue whales, short-finned and long-finned Pilot whales, newborn pups and sandy-backed monsters, it made no difference. From all corners of the world, cetacean species raced, drawn by the strange summons, and when the seas roiled and frothed with the creatures, the Fermi ships unexpectedly shuddered and rose to a new stationary position one thousand feet higher.

Across millions of television screens, red banners rolled, interrupting culturally important soap operas to proclaim *Breaking News!* National Emergency Broadcast systems commandeered the radio waves, while every tornado and storm siren in the western world simultaneously sounded a hysterical warning, in turn setting off the incessant barking of dogs and the equally annoying declarations of street preachers certain that the end was near.

On satellite feeds, cable networks, and internet news services, a breathless world watched with hands over ears. Then, white-hot beams of energy erupted from the bellies of the alien vessels. At both sites, monstrous clouds of smoke and steam shot into the sky. The trade winds seized up the stench. Greenland swore they could smell the burning for days afterward; France announced they would conduct a poll to determine if they could, also. Fox News Worldwide, meanwhile, with their usual aplomb, pronounced it all one whale of a fish-fry and no proof at all of global warming.

For five more days, the Fermi ships held position. Fighter jets lobbed rockets only to see them explode harmlessly off electronic defensive screens. Russian and British submarines and battleships had no better luck with volleys of surface-to-air missiles. For all the effectiveness of such weapons, Earth might as well have fought back with spud guns and spit-balls.

Then, on the sixth day, a message interrupted every form of media. *We are the Greens Party.* The voice spoke in accented English, heavily auto-tuned with Theremin overtones. *And we are saving the planet!* A significant pause followed, as if the speaker expected applause or cheers, before it continued. *For ourselves!* For three days and nights, the message continued. Nothing could shut it off or silence it.

The Fermi vessels finally began to move. On a slow course, they glided straight for Washington, D.C. The president summoned his cabinet; the Pentagon marshaled the military; the National Gun Rights Lobby declared that only good aliens with guns could stop bad aliens with guns and urged that immigrants be drafted to the front lines of any battle of Earth versus the flying saucers.

One ship positioned itself over the National Mall. The second ship hovered over Georgetown. In older times, the locals might have met the monsters with torches and pitchforks. Now they turned out with handguns and assault rifles. Thousands of humans filled the parks and streets. "Remember the dolphins!" someone shouted. "Whales!" someone corrected. It didn't matter. Here was a perfect excuse to blow stuff away. Guns trained skyward and lead filled the air, and of course, what goes up must come down. Clouds of gun smoke obscured the city like fog from the Chesapeake Bay until nobody could clearly see who or what they were shooting at. With tranquil precision, the Fermi vessels slowly rotated, indifferent to the chaos as the human body-count climbed.

The next morning, the Fermi broadcast a second message. *We will appear to your Congress when your sun is directly overhead. We will appear to your Congress when your sun is directly overhead.* A long break in the broadcast followed before the alien voice resumed. *Meanwhile, people of Earth, come on down to our shop at 1415 Wisconsin Drive! Let us share the wonders of Fermi technology with you! You won't be disappointed! Hundreds of items at prices you can afford!*

Congress immediately declared a golfing holiday and adjourned. In their stead, they chose a single liaison to greet the aliens.

Air Force Major Thomas Kincaid waited with his feet up on the Speaker's desk, in the hallowed halls of the House of Representatives. To outward appearances he was alone, but security men were stationed behind every curtain and trashcan in the building and behind every camera and listening device. In his right hand, he held his grandfather's gold pocket watch. The ancient hands slowly ticked off the minutes as they circumnavigated the smiling face of Mickey Mouse.

Precisely at noon, the chamber doors swung open. Silhouetted in sunlight, two figures stepped across the threshold and paused. The Major rose to stand, glad for the 9 mm. Glock secretly holstered in the small of his back and for the .38 holstered on his right ankle and for the small Sig Saur holstered on his left ankle. He hoped the visitors couldn't make out the heavy outline of the brass knuckles in his jacket pocket.

He couldn't really tell much about the aliens. They wore bulky uniforms not unlike NASA spacesuits, and helmets concealed their features. They stood no smaller than an average man, but no taller. Major Tom frowned and sighed, then as Congress's appointed liaison, he extended the traditional greeting. "All right, aliens," he snarled. "What the fuck do you want?"

The two creatures walked slowly down the aisle that divided the Republican side from the Democratic side until they stood right before the Major. "I am Doctor Poh," one of the aliens said, looking up. He gestured to his companion. "This is Doctor Ree."

Major Tom's frown deepened. "A pair of Fermi docs," he said.

"We seek citizenship among your people," Doctor Poh continued. "Acceptance and tolerance and, eventually, the right to marry. In exchange, we offer the benefits of Fermi knowledge and technology."

Major Tom folded his arms across his chest. "My agents have already checked out your so-called store in Georgetown," he said. "Your free replicators intrigued us, but it turns out that all they replicate are junk food and sex toys."

Doctor Ree nodded and shrugged. "Give the people what they want," he answered. "By doing so, we win hearts and minds. That is a fundamental tenet of Earth politics."

"Along with its corollary," Doctor Poh added, "Tell the people what they want and by hyperbole, lies, and subterfuge, make them believe it."

Major Tom had to acknowledge the wisdom of that. Earlier in the morning, he had experimented with one of the replicators, and he had to admit that the anal vibrator had been amazing. But leave it to aliens to produce the best anal probes. However, he brushed those thoughts aside. "So why did you kill the whales?" he demanded. "What was the point?

Doctor Poh turned his gloved palms upward. "We make it a policy when we conquer a new world to exterminate its most intelligent species. It makes the other species so much more malleable."

"Ah hah!" Major Tom moved a hand closer to the gun at his back. "So this is a conquest!"

Doctor Ree shrugged again. "In a manner of speaking," he answered. "But nothing as violent as the weapon you're reaching for on your belt or the weapon on your right ankle or the weapon on your left ankle."

Major Tom breathed a secret sigh of relief. They didn't know about the brass knuckles.

"No, nothing like that," Doctor Poh agreed. "Your people will surrender themselves to us without violence, lured not just by junk food and sex toys, but by all the wonders we Fermi have to offer."

"Cures for cancer?" Major Tom pressed. "For the common cold?"

"Better," Doctor Ree said. "A cure for the common mother-in-law. Observe." He drew a slender wand from a pocket on his sleeve and pointed it at a congressman's desk. With a bright flash, the desk disappeared, leaving no trace at all. "It works as well for ex-wives and old boyfriends," he added. "Just stand your ground the next time one of them, as you humans say, gets in your face. We sent a few of these weapons to your gun lobbyists, who are at this moment preparing legislation supporting the rights of all citizens to own superior Fermi weaponry."

Doctor Poh took up the narrative. "You see, we have studied your laws and your political systems. We will easily use them to rise to positions of power and dominance first in America and then around the planet. Humans, in their desire for security and free stuff, will become complicit in their own subjugation."

"And if free stuff is insufficient," Doctor Ree added, "we have an undefeatable secret weapon." He nodded to his companion, and they both removed their helmets.

Major Tom gasped, and his heart sank. The Fermi looked like cats. More precisely, they looked like kittens—adorable kittens with large eyes and green-tinged fur. What human would be able to resist such cuteness?

Still, for the sake of the world, he had tried. "Shoo!" he ordered, waving a hand toward the chamber doors. With his other hand, he drew the gun on his belt. It was a signal to all the other men hidden behind the cameras and throughout the building. Armed agents, both military and civilian, rushed forward.

They might not have bothered—the Fermi were gone.

Major Tom slammed his fist on his office desk as he addressed his agents. "Do everything you have to, but keep them out of the press! No images and no photographs. The last thing we need is a cute cat-alien on the twenty-four hour news channels! We have to get rid of them!"

One of his agents looked up from the notebook he held. "The news channels or the cute cat-aliens?"

"Why choose?" another agent answered.

All his men wore worried expressions. "How?" one said from the back of the room. "We can't touch their ships, and we all saw what that wand-thing did on the security cameras!

"I don't know!" Major Tom shot back. "Get down to that shop of theirs and grab them! Tie them in a sack and drop them in the river!"

"Sir!" The toughest and best trained hard-asses in the service all looked shocked.

"Don't look at me like that!" Major Tom shouted. "They're not really cats—get that through your heads!" He dropped his voice as he leaned back and stared toward a corner of the ceiling. "I've got a cat, myself," he confessed. "A little tuxedo that sleeps with me every night . . ."

A collective *awwww!* went around the room.

A petite blond woman pushed through all the men surrounding his desk. With squared shoulder, jutting chin, and a stern demeanor, she cut an impressive figure in her captain's uniform. "Maybe that's your problem, Major," she said, raising her voice a level as she cast a haughty gaze over her colleagues. "You all love your pussies too much!"

Major Tom shot to his feet in outrage. "I assure you, Captain Piper, I do not love . . ." He stopped himself before he made any damaging admission. Then, he narrowed his brow and collected himself. "Do you have a suggestion?"

Captain Piper folded her arms across her chest and tried to look taller than she was. "I'm suggesting," she said slowly, "that if you want to chase cats, you need a dog. So put a dog-lover in charge." A tight smile turned up the corners of her mouth. "I, myself, have two German Shepherds with teeth as big as the vibrator you have in your pocket."

He felt his jacket pocket. "That's not a vibrator," he said defensively. "It's a brass knuckles."

Captain Piper smirked. "My suggestion is a good one," she

persisted. "A dog-lover won't be susceptible to the crass sentimentality these Fermi evoke in cat-lovers. Give me a squadron, Major, and let me pick the pilots. I promise you that I'll chase their furry tails across the yard and back into the galaxy they came from." She looked back over her shoulder. "No cracks about chasing tail."

Major Tom picked up his grandfather's watch and tapped it on his palm. "Let me think about it," he said. "You may be onto something, but I still don't know how we penetrate their defensive screens. There may be a PR problem, as well. In less than a day, those junk food replicators have become very popular. The line around their store stretches for blocks, and it's easy to see why. Have you tried them?" He looked around the room and then hung his head. "They make incredible fries."

His agents filed out with their assignments. Patty Piper, the last to go, shot a look back over her shoulder. Her blue eyes gleamed with confidence and self-certainty, but Thomas Kincaid harbored lingering doubts about, well, everything. If, in the eyes of the Fermi docs, the whales were the most intelligent species on Earth, what did that make humans? *Ants*, he realized. Ants lived in large colonies, built cities, and used rudimentary tools, just like humans.

Just like humans, ants regularly made vicious and inexplicable war on other ants.

The human race, which had so for so long thought itself the pinnacle of creation, had just been downgraded. He opened his grandfather's pocket watch, stared at the antique hands. He couldn't help feeling that the grinning mouse trapped inside the mechanism was laughing at him.

After a time, he put the pocket watch away and stabbed a button on his desk intercom. He hoped that his aide, Corporal Stephens, was still on duty. "Any word yet from our men in the field, Stephens?" he called into the intercom. "Have they shut down that damned alien store yet?"

"Yes, sir," Stephens answered, his voice crisp over the machine. "But there was a problem. Estimates put the crowd outside the shop at over a thousand, and none of them were happy about the closing. They felt obligated to express their displeasure."

"In the usual way?" Major Tom asked. "Bottles, rocks, random handgun shootings?"

"It's plain why you're a major, sir," Stephens responded with barely concealed sarcasm. "But it gets worse, I'm afraid. Before our men could close the shop on Wisconsin Avenue, another shop opened in DuPont Circle. Then, a third opened at the end of Capitol Avenue."

Major Tom roared. "How long does this go on?" he said. "Is there a fourth shop?

Corporal Stephens sighed. "I'm afraid so, sir, although not a store exactly. It's a kiosk on the steps of the Air and Space Museum. It's a bit different, though. Instead of junk food, the replicators produce packets of Tang—the drink of astronauts—and freeze-dried space rations in little silver pouches like you could only find in the gift shops at outrageous prices before."

Major Tom looked thoughtful. "What about the sex toys?" he said quietly.

Corporal Stephens fell silent, but then loudly gulped. "We have a more immediate problem, sir," he said. "Some of our right-leaning agents took it upon themselves to redefine *alien shop*. They busted a couple of *tiendas* in the Mount Pleasant neighborhood, and one of the shops caught fire. The neighbors aren't too happy, and news crews are all over it. They're predicting riots by night fall. It's Ferguson, Missouri all over again."

Major Tom scowled. "Get Captain Piper back in here at once." He stabbed his finger down on the intercom button and pushed his chair back. He needed a plan of action, and so far, the captain was the only one on his staff with an idea. He paced back and forth across his carpeted office with his hands behind his back until a knock sounded at his door. "Come in!" he barked. "And close the door!"

Captain Piper looked smug as she stared at the wall behind his head, but she gave a smart salute and stood at attention. "If I may say so, sir," she said, "you're sounding more like a dog-lover already."

Major Tom glared and began barking orders. "Assemble your team," he said. "Choose whatever pilots you need. Hand pick them yourself. Then chase those bastards back to wherever they came from!"

The captain showed no emotion. "Sir, does this mean that diplomacy has failed?"

Major Tom frowned, and then inclined his head. "Diplomacy?" He sat down at his desk and put his head in his hands. After a moment, he looked up again. "Well, I suppose I should have tried that, of course. Why do you ask now?"

"The United Nations, sir," she answered. "It's all over the news. They're involved now. The Fermi pair of docs paid an unexpected visit to today's session of the General Assembly. They formally requested refugee status. The International Planetary Society is supporting them."

"That's just great." Major Tom resumed his pacing. "Tomorrow, Mike Brown and less than five percent of the members of the International Astronomical Union will declare Fermi a dwarf planet, and all our problems will be solved when our pair of docs takes off in a fit of pique."

"Science always has an answer, sir," Piper said. "So, do you still want me to start shooting at them?"

A long silence followed as Major Tom weighed his options. There were one hundred and ninety-three members in the United Nations. That meant at least that many opinions on the Fermi problem, and probably more. But the saucers were over United States territory at the moment, and that made the United States' opinion the only one that counted—same as always. So, he reasoned, unilateral action.

He turned to Captain Piper. "Where's the president?"

"At an undisclosed location," she reported, "playing golf with the rest of congress, all of whom deny they're in hiding."

"And the vice-president?"

"The same," she answered. "You want to know his handicap?"

"He's the fucking vice-president," Major Tom shot back. "That's his handicap." He went to the window and stared across the National Mall. He could just make out the Washington Monument thrusting skyward like a giant finger to the alien invaders. He drew courage from that. Congress had put him in power, but he was just a lowly major. That meant everybody else higher above him had hiked up their skirts and run for the outhouses. It really was all up to him.

He went back to his desk and pressed the intercom button. "First things first," he said to Captain Piper. "Stephens," he barked into the machine. "Put me in for a raise. A big one! And while you're at it, put yourself in for one, too. And Captain Piper!"

Stephens's voice came back across the speaker. "Justification, sir? Payroll always wants one."

The major waved a hand in irritation. "Make something up, Corporal! Everybody else does. Give us some awards or medals or bonuses or something. Earn your pay, man!" He shut the intercom off, settled back in his chair again and turned to Captain Piper. "At ease, Patty," he continued, having kept her at attention long enough. "Now tell me about this plan of yours. I hope it's grandiose."

A mere one hour later, Major Thomas Kincaid stood on the tarmac of Andrews Air Force Base watching as the twelve hand-picked members of the hastily named *Pussies No More Flying Circus*, all women and all crackerjack fighter pilots, climbed into the cockpits of twelve F-16 Fighting Falcon fighter jets, each carrying eighteen thousand pounds of laser-guided weaponry. It wasn't exactly the usual military code name for an attack squadron, but Captain Piper had chosen it, herself, with her squad's approval. "Give them a gold finger for me, Captain," Major Tom muttered as the aircraft taxied out onto the runway.

"Beautiful sight, isn't it?" Doctor Poh said. He held a bag of replicated French fries and offered one to the major. Without thinking, Major Tom accepted one, put it to his mouth, and then did a double-take.

"Too hot?" Doctor Poh asked innocently. "Too much salt?"

Major Tom threw down the French fry. "This is a restricted area! You can't be here!"

"You mean I can't stand idly by as you launch an all-out assault on my ship?" He extended the package of fries again. "By the way, we call them *friends fries* now. Much, well, friendlier, don't you think?" With his other hand, he held out a white envelope. "And by the way, this is for you. It's a temporary injunction. I'm afraid you'll have to call off your dogs."

"You went to court?" Major Tom shrieked.

"With cameras," Doctor Poh nodded. "We're all over the press at this very moment. In fact, if you look back toward the gates, you'll see hundreds of reporters with very big camera lenses all trained on us. A dozen snap-polls show us with high favorability ratings, and we're trending in social media. My colleague, Doctor Ree, says we'll own your planet even sooner than anticipated." He held out the fries once more. "Sure you won't have one?"

"Get out! Get off my base!" Major Tom shook his fists, barely able to control himself as he stared at the alien's damnably cute feline face.

"I can't stop the attack now even if I wanted to. We're at Def-con thirteen!"

Doctor Poh purred. *Actually purred*! "You're making that up, Major."

One by one, in quick succession, the twelve F-16 Fighting Falcons thundered down the runway and climbed at steep angles into the blue sky. The heat of their engines rolled in a powerful wave across the tarmac. Major Tom's cap blew off and rolled away. Doctor Poh's fur stood straight back. The Falcons fanned out in sharp arcs to attack their first target from all directions. "Chesapeake Bay, here they come!" he said through gritted teeth. He turned to Doctor Poh, but the alien was no longer there. The press still pressed up against the gates, however.

Corporal Stephens, all shiny in his dress uniform, came running toward him. "I just heard on the news about an injunction!" he said breathlessly.

"What injunction?" Major Tom raised an eyebrow and then tore the unopened envelope into pieces that blew away like confetti across the airfield. "Now get ready. I'm betting that if we attack the Chesapeake Bay ship, the ship over the National Mall will go to its aid, and we'll be spared from dropping bombs on Lincoln, Jefferson, and Washington."

"Not to mention, our own people, Major," Stephens added.

Major Tom shrugged. "Collateral damage must be expected." He pulled his grandfather's gold watch from a pocket, opened it and noted the time, and then he gazed skyward again. "It's about time for Black Sheep Squadron," he said. He pointed upward. "Here they come!"

From the west, north and south, thousands of drones flew up from the horizons—black drones, silver drones, even red and blue drones, some with single rotors and some with eight and more. Cheap drones and expensive drones, remote-controlled and sophisticated, programmable vehicles. And all privately owned. "Get an injunction against that!"

The drones hummed as they violated Andrews' air-space, as they violated White House air-space. "How did you organize them?" Stephens shouted as he covered his ears.

"Organized, hell!" the Major answered. "I called up some favors with the National Drone Pilots Association. They put out the call across their networks. Now, let's go—I've got a copter waiting out of sight in Hangar B!"

As they ran across the field, a shadow fell over them—Doctor Poh's ship leaving its position above the mall to join Doctor Ree's. The drones gave chase, and the Fermi ship wobbled.

A pilot waited in the copter. Major Tom and Corporal Stephens leaped aboard, buckled up, and clapped on headsets. In no time, the copter swept out of the hangar and into the air, climbing high enough to allow a complete view of the coming conflict. Corporal Stephens whipped a small camera out of his trousers pocket. "A go-cam!" he explained as he affixed it to the brim of his cap. "I'll be famous on the internet!" He reached into his other pocket and pulled out a package of French fries. "Have a *friends fry*?" he offered.

"We're not at the movies, Corporal!" Major Tom shouted, forgetting the headset's microphone. The pilot cringed from the feedback and ripped off his earphones. His knee slammed against the cyclic stick; his foot slipped off the anti-torque pedals. The copter pitched downward. French fries flew about the cockpit, sticking to the Plexiglas canopy, to the corporal's eyeglasses, to Major Tom's left cheek.

"We're gonna die!" the corporal screamed.

"From grease and cholesterol," Major Tom muttered angrily. He slapped the pilot in the back of the head. "Snap out of it and get us back on course before we miss the good stuff!"

The pilot righted the copter and, dodging drones, they raced toward the bay. Both Fermi vessels hovered over the water side-by-side, spinning erratically as the F-16s strafed them. The alien force fields flared occasionally, but suddenly a drone got through and destroyed itself spectacularly against the Fermi's hull.

The copter pilot gave a triumphant yell. Both officers in the back seats cringed and ripped off their headsets. "Bastard!" Major Tom shouted. He nudged Stephens as they both put on their headsets again. "Watch what happens next."

The wobbling of the Fermi ships increased. One pitched toward the water as one angled toward the sky. Another drone penetrated the force field, but this time, an F-16 immediately fired a sidewinder missile through the window the drone had created. Drone and missile exploded, and the Fermi ship shook.

"What the hell?" Stephens said, careful to keep his voice under control. "How did that happen?"

"It's Captain Piper's idea," he said. "The Fermi are cats. Cats can't resist shiny play-toys. Well, we've filled the air with shiny play-toys. It's driving the Fermi crazy!"

Stephens turned pale. "That's your plan to save the Earth?" he said. "That's insane!"

"That's politics!" Major Tom answered. "If it's not insane, it won't work, and if it's not extreme, it won't resonate!" He nodded toward the pair of ships, barely stable as they fought off a hail of Vulcan gattling fire from Captain's Piper's Flying Circus. The force fields flared.

More drones pushed through, followed by more missiles. "The Fermi are resonating now."

"They were so cute," the Corporal whispered into his microphone. "Guess I'd better put in for some civilian medals of honor, and by the way, Major, I doubled both our salaries. Major Patty's, too, but with a twenty-percent reduction for being female."

"It's not our job to break through the glass ceiling, Stephens," the major answered, "just the defenses of these aliens." He leaned outward for a better at the battle. "Looks like we're doing just that."

One of the Fermi ships lurched forward suddenly. Seemingly out of control, it flew inland and cut like a knife through the Washington Monument. Hundreds gathered on the mall died, crushed beneath the falling stone. "Collateral damage," the major reminded his aide.

The second Fermi ship fired its heat-weapon from its belly. The waters of the Chesapeake frothed and boiled. A score of sailboaters and windsurfers were instantly flash-fried, as was the crew of Donald Trump's yacht at anchor there with a full complement of reporters, fashionistas and hairstylists.

The drones taunted the Fermi relentlessly. It seemed for every drone destroyed two more took its place, and Major Tom envisioned the shelves of every Walmart and Hobby Lobby completely emptied of the aerial devices. But the drones stayed away from the belly of the ships.

The belly was for Captain Patti Piper and her hand-picked crew of dog-lovers. With the drones challenging the force fields from above, six Falcons suddenly dived, then angled upward. All six unleashed hell on the ships' underbellies.

No cat could ever stand that.

The heat-rays sputtered, flared and sparkled out. The first Fermi vessel knocked away the flag and the upper half of the White House dome. Then, over the headsets came a tumultuous barking and howling and general canine ruckus as the No Pussies Flying Circus, sensing their victory, mocked the Fermi.

Finally, at an astounding rate, both alien ships climbed skyward. Even the Falcons could not follow, but the ladies angled their jets and fired every remaining piece of ordnance after the saucers. The Fermi shot higher and higher and took off for the depths of outer space and, perhaps, for easier mice.

"You know Congress is going to take credit for this," Stephens said as he rubbed a smear of grease from his eyeglasses.

Major Thomas Kincaid leaned back in his seat and sighed. His aide was only half-right. Congress would try to claim credit, of course, but the individual members would be so busy scrapping among themselves about who deserved the most credit and who deserved the most blame, that nobody would ever really get either. And that was probably as it should be. Meanwhile, Earth was left with a few interesting pieces of alien technology. He scraped a French fry off the canopy and flicked it out of the copter.

The drones were fewer now as their pilots called them home, and the F-16s continued to hot-dog over the city. Let them have their moment. There would be paperwork and red tape soon enough. Finally, though, he called an end. The battle was won. The war? Who really knew?

He touched his microphone control and spoke to Captain Patty Piper. "Lassie," he said, "come home."

Editor Bios

Robin Wayne Bailey ("The Fine Art Of Politics") is the author of numerous novels, including the ongoing *Frost* series, the *Brothers Of The Dragon* trilogy, the young adult fantasy trilogy, *Dragonkin*, as well as *Shadowdance, Nightwatch*, the Fritz Lieber-inspired *Swords Against The Shadowland*, and still others. He's authored over one hundred and fifty shorter works, many of which have been collected in *Turn Left To Tomorrow* and its companion volume, *The Fantastikon: Tales Of Wonder*. His novelette, "The Children's Crusade," was a 2008 Nebula Award nominee. He is a two-term president of the Science Fiction and Fantasy Writers of America, and one of the founders, along with James Gunn, of the Science Fiction Hall of Fame, which now resides in Seattle as part of Paul Allen's Science Fiction Museum and Hall of Fame.

Bryan Thomas Schmidt ("First Million Contacts") is an author and Hugo-nominated editor of adult and children's science fiction and fantasy novels and anthologies. His debut novel, *The Worker Prince*, received Honorable Mention on Barnes & Noble's Year's Best Science Fiction Releases of 2011, and was followed by two sequels. As editor, his anthologies include *Galactic Games* (Baen, 2016), *Shattered Shields* (Baen, 2014), *Beyond The Sun* (Fairwood, 2013), *Raygun Chronicles* (Every Day Publishing, 2013) and *Space Battles* (Flying Pen Press, 2012) with *Little Green Men—Attack!* co-edited by Robin Wayne Bailey and *The Monster Hunter Files* co-edited by Larry Correia forthcoming from Baen in 2017 as well as *Joe Ledger: Unstoppable*, co-edited with Jonathan Maberry for St. Martin's Griffin, *Infinite Stars*, and *Predator: If It Bleeds* forthcoming from Titan Books. In novels, he was first editor on books by Todd McCaffrey, Tracy Hickman, Alan Dean Foster, and more, and is noted as the first editor of *The Martian* by Andy Weir. He is a frequent guest and panelist at World Cons and other conventions. His website is *www.bryanthomasschmidt.net* and his Twitter handle is @BryanThomasS.

Authors Bios

Mike Resnick ("The Little Green Men Take Their Hideous Vengeance, Sort Of") is, according to *Locus*, the all-time leading award winner, living or dead, for short science fiction. He is the winner of five Hugos from a record 37 nominations, a Nebula, and other major awards in the United States, France, Spain, Japan, Croatia, Catalonia and Poland. and has been short-listed for major awards in England, Italy and Australia. He is the author of 76 novels, over 250 stories, and 3 screenplays, and is the Hugo-nominated editor of 42 anthologies. His work has been translated into 26 languages. He was the Guest of Honor at the 2012 Worldcon and can be found online as @ResnickMike on Twitter or at www. mikeresnick.com.

Kristine Kathryn Rusch ("Little (Green) Women") writes in every genre she reads, which happens to be most of them. As Kristine Grayson, she writes goofy paranormal romances. As Kris Nelscott, she writes noir mysteries. As Kristine Kathryn Rusch, she writes whatever she pleases. Mostly, though, she's known for her science fiction and fantasy. Nominated for every award in sf (and many in the other genres as well), she's also won a lot of awards, including several readers choice awards from various magazines, a World Fantasy Award, and two Hugo awards (one for editing, and one for her short fiction). Her short work has been in over 20 years best collections, including four in 2016. Her novels have hit bestseller lists worldwide. Recently, she published the 8-volume Anniversary Day Saga, set in her Retrieval Artist universe, as well as the Interim Fates trilogy as Kristine Grayson. She's series editor for *Fiction River*, with her husband Dean Wesley Smith, and she edits some of the volumes including November's *Hidden in Crime*. She and John Helfers edited the *Best Mysteries of the Year* for Kobo Books. Kris just edited the *Women of Futures Past* project for Baen Books. She works and occasionally sleeps on the Oregon Coast.

By day, **Dantzel Cherry** ("Good Neighbor Policy") teaches Pilates and raises her daughter, and by night/naptime she writes. Her baking hours follow no rhyme or reason. She is prone to dance as the need arises, and it often does. Her stories have appeared in such markets as *Fireside, Galaxy's Edge,* and *InterGalactic Medicine Show.* She lives in Fort Worth, Texas with her husband, daughter, and requisite cat.

Ken Scholes ("Stuck in Buenos Aires With Bob Dylan On My Mind") is the award-winning, critically-acclaimed author of four novels and over fifty short stories. His work has appeared in print for over fifteen years, including the critically acclaimed epic fantasy series *The Psalms of Isaak* from TOR Books. Ken's eclectic background includes time spent as a label gun repairman, a sailor who never sailed, a soldier who commanded a desk, a preacher (he got better), a nonprofit executive, a musician and a government procurement analyst. He has a degree in History from Western Washington University. Ken is a native of the Pacific Northwest and makes his home in Saint Helens, Oregon, where he lives with his twin daughters. You can learn more about Ken by visiting *www.kenscholes.com.*

Jody Lynn Nye ("Rule The World") lists her main career activity as "spoiling cats." She lives northwest of Chicago with one of the above and her husband, author and packager Bill Fawcett. She has written over forty books, including *The Ship Who Won* with Anne McCaffrey, eight books with Robert Asprin, a humorous anthology about mothers, *Don't Forget Your Spacesuit, Dear!,* and over 140 short stories. Her latest books are *Rhythm of the Imperium* (Baen Books), and *Wishing On a Star* (Arc Manor Publishing).

Seanan McGuire ("School Colors") is the *New York Times* bestselling author of more than a dozen books, all published within the last five years, which may explain why some people believe that she does not actually sleep. Her work has been translated into several languages, and resulted in her receiving a record five Hugo Award nominations on the 2013 ballot. When not writing, Seanan spends her time reading, watching terrible horror movies and too much television, visiting Disney Parks, and rating haunted corn mazes. You can keep up with her at *www.seananmcguire.com.*

Martin L. Shoemaker ("Meet The Landlord") is a programmer who writes on the side . . . or maybe it's the other way around. Programming pays the bills, but a second place story in the Jim Baen Memorial Writing Contest earned him lunch with Buzz Aldrin. Programming never did that! His work has appeared in *Analog*, *Clarkesworld*, *Galaxy's Edge*, *Digital Science Fiction*, *Forever Magazine*, and *Writers of the Future Volume 31*. His novella "Murder on the Aldrin Express" was reprinted in *Year's Best Science Fiction Thirty-First Annual Collection* and in *Year's Top Short SF Novels 4*. His short story "Today I Am Paul" was reprinted in *Year's Best Science Fiction: Thirty-third Annual Edition*, *The Best Science Fiction of the Year: Volume One*, *The Year's Best Science Fiction and Fantasy*, and *The Year's Top Ten Tales of Science Fiction 8*, and appeared in French translation in *Galaxies* magazine.

Steven H. Silver ("Big White Men—Attack") has worked as a writer, reviewer, editor, and publisher. His stories have appeared in *Black Gate*, *Helix*, and various anthologies. He was the founder and original editor and publisher of ISFiC Press and has also edited books for DAW Books and NESFA Press. Steven also serves as SFWA's Events Manager. He has been nominated for the Hugo Award 15 times without a win.

Selina Rosen ("The Green, Green Men of Home") is the author of over twenty-five novels including *Sword Masters* and *Strange Robby*, and she has had dozens of short stories published in professional venues including *Thieves World* and *Impossible Monsters*. As editor-in-chief of Yard Dog Press she has edited *ten* anthologies including *Bubbas of the Apocalypse*. She is married, owns a small farm, and has kids and grandkids. She is a carpenter, a rock mason, a sword fighter and an all-around swell gal.

Beth L. Cato ("A Fine Night For Tea and Bludgeoning") Cato hails from Hanford, California, but currently writes and bakes cookies in a lair west of Phoenix, Arizona. She shares the household with a hockey-loving husband, a numbers-obsessed son, and a cat the size of a canned ham. She's the author of The Clockwork Dagger (a 2015 Locus Award finalist for First Novel) and The Clockwork Crown (an RT Reviewers' Choice Finalist) from Harper Voyager. Her novella Wings of Sorrow and Bone was a 2016 Nebula nominee. Her novel Breath of Earth begins a new steampunk series set in an alternate history 1906 San Francisco. Follow her at BethCato.com and on Twitter at @BethCato.

Peter J. Wacks ("The Game-a-holic's Guide") is a bestselling cross-genre writer and formerly managing editor WordFire Press. He has worked across the creative fields in gaming, television, film, comics, and most recently, when not busy being controlled by little green men from outer space, he spends his time writing novels.

Peter started his writing career in the gaming industry when he created and wrote the storyline for the international bestselling game *Cyberpunk CCG*. He moved on from there to work on ABC's *Alias* as a game consultant, and has since also written tie-ins for *Veronica Mars, G.I. Joe,* and *Heroes Reborn*. To date he has over 100 stories published and has been nominated and balloted for multiple awards. His hobbies include scotch tasting, IPA drinking, and sword fighting. He can be found online at *www.peterjwacks.net*

Author and editor **Josh Vogt's** ("The Game-a-holic's Guide") work covers fantasy, science fiction, horror, humor, pulp, and more. His debut fantasy novel is *Pathfinder Tales: Forge of Ashes*, alongside the launch of his urban fantasy series, The Cleaners, with *Enter the Janitor* and *The Maids of Wrath*. He's an editor at Paizo, a Scribe Award finalist, and a member of both SFWA and the International Association of Media Tie-In Writers. Find him at JRVogt.com or on Twitter as @JRVogt.

Before becoming a science fiction author, **Allen M. Steele** ("Day of The Bookworm") was a journalist who'd worked for newspapers and magazines in Massachusetts, New Hampshire, Missouri, and his home state of Tennessee. After ditching journalism to focus on his first love, science fiction, Steele has published twenty novels and nearly a hundred short stories. His work has received numerous awards, including three Hugos, and has been translated worldwide, mainly in languages he can't read. He formerly served on the Board of Advisors for the Space Frontier Foundation and the Science Fiction and Fantasy Writers of America. He also belongs to Sigma, a group of SF writers who frequently serve as unpaid consultants on matters regarding technology and security. Steele lives in western Massachusetts with his wife Linda and a continual procession of adopted dogs. He collects vintage science fiction books and magazines, spacecraft model kits, and dreams. His latest novel is *Avengers Of The Moon* from TOR Books.

Elizabeth Moon ("A Greener Future") has published twenty-six novels including Nebula Award winner *The Speed of Dark*, over thirty short-fiction pieces in anthologies and magazines, and three short fiction collections, most recently *Moon Flights* (2007). Her most recent novel is *Crown of Renewal* (Del Rey, May 2014) and she is at work on new books in her *Vatta's War* series of space operas. When not writing, she may be found knitting socks, photographing wildlife and native plants, poking her friends with (blunted) swords, or singing in the choir. She likes horses, dark chocolate, topographic maps, and traveling by train.

Nebula Award winner **Esther Friesner** ("A Cuppa, Cuppa Burnin' Love") is the author of over 40 novels and almost 200 short stories. Educated at Vassar College and Yale University, where she received a Ph.D., she is also a poet, a playwright, and the editor of several anthologies. The best known of these is the Chicks in Chainmail series that she created and edits for Baen Books. The sixth book, *Chicks and Balances*, appeared in July 2015. *Deception's Pawn*, the latest title in her popular Princesses of Myth series of Young Adult novels from Random House, was published in April 2015. Esther is married, a mother of two, grandmother of one, harbors cats, and lives in Connecticut.

K.C. Ball ("Little Green Guys") lives in Seattle. Her short fiction has appeared in various print and online magazines, such as *Analog, Beneath Ceaseless Skies, Daily Science Fiction* and *Lightspeed*, as well as her first collection, *Snapshots From A Black Hole & Other Oddities*. K.C. won the Hubbard Writers of the Future award in 2009 and is a 2010 graduate of the Clarion West Writers Workshop.

James E. Gunn ("The March Of The Little Green Men") has had a career divided between writing and teaching, typified by his service as president of the Science Fiction and Fantasy Writers of America and as president of the Science Fiction Research Association, as well as having been presented the Grand Master Award of SFWA and the Pilgrim Award of SFRA. He now is Emeritus Professor of English at the University of Kansas and continues to write. He has published more than 100 short stories and has written or edited 42 books, including *The Immortals*, *The Listeners*, *The Dreamers*, *Alternate Worlds: The Illustrated History of Science Ficton*, *The Road to Science Fiction*, and, most recently, *Transcendental* and its sequel, *Transgalactic* from TOR Books.

Alex Shvartsman ("First Million Contacts") is a writer, editor, translator and game designer from Brooklyn, NY. Over 80 of his short stories have appeared in *Nature*, *Galaxy's Edge*, *InterGalactic Medicine Show*, and many other magazines and anthologies. He won the 2014 WSFA Small Press Award for Short Fiction and was a finalist for the 2015 Canopus Award for Excellence in Interstellar Fiction. He is the editor of the *Unidentified Funny Objects* annual anthology series of humorous SF/F. His collection, *Explaining Cthulhu to Grandma and Other Stories* and his steampunk humor novella *H. G. Wells, Secret Agent* were both published in 2015. His website is *www.alexshvartsman.com*.

Robert Silverberg ("Hannibal's Elephants") is rightly considered by many as one of the greatest living Science Fiction writers. His career stretches back to the pulps and his output is amazing by any standards. He's authored numerous novels, short stories and nonfiction books in various genres and categories. He's also a frequent guest at Cons and a regularly columnist for *Asimov's*. His major works include *Dying Inside*, *The Book of Skulls*, *The Alien Years*, *The World Inside*, *Nightfall* with Isaac Asimov, *Son of Man*, *A Time of Changes* and the 7 *Majipoor Cycle* books. (A major bibliography can be found at here.) His first *Majipoor* trilogy, *Lord Valentine's Castle*, *Majipoor Chronicles* and *Valentine Pontifex*, was reissued by ROC Books in May 2012, September 2012 and January 2013. *Tales Of Majipoor*, a new collection bringing together all the short *Majipoor* tales, followed in May 2013.

Robin Wayne Bailey ("The Fine Art Of Politics") co-edited this volume with **Bryan Thomas Schmidt** ("First Million Contacts"), and their bios together can be found on the Editor Bios page.